the Potluck Club
Trouble's Brewing

the Potluck Club
Trouble's Brewing

A NOVEL

Linda Evans Shepherd
and Eva Marie Everson

Revell
Grand Rapids, Michigan

© 2006 by Linda Evans Shepherd and Eva Marie Everson

Published by Fleming H. Revell
a division of Baker Publishing Group
P.O. Box 6287, Grand Rapids, MI 49516-6287
www.revellbooks.com

Printed in the United States of America

Library of Congress Cataloging-in-Publication Data
Shepherd, Linda E., 1957–
    Trouble's brewing : a novel / Linda Evans Shepherd and Eva Marie Everson.
       p.   cm. — (The Potluck Club)
   ISBN 10: 0-8007-3065-8 (pbk.)
   ISBN 978-0-8007-3065-9 (pbk.)
    1. Women—Societies and clubs—Fiction. 2. Female friendship—Fiction.
 3. Prayer groups—Fiction. 4. Women cooks—Fiction. 5. Colorado—Fiction.
 6. Cookery—Fiction. I. Everson, Eva Marie. II. Title.
PS3619.H456T76 2006
813´.6—dc22   2006002690

To the women in my life who have formed a prayer circle around me. (You know who you are.) I could not have survived this year without you.

—Eva Marie Everson

To my dear friends Sharon Williams, a caregiver; Pam Hyink, a therapist; and Betty Murch, a teacher. You three women are God's earth angels who have blessed and enriched not only my life, but the life of my beautiful, disabled daughter, Laura. Thank you for all you've done to teach her to be, to love, and to live a joyful life. You were the ones who first believed in Laura when no one else could. Thank you for sharing your lives with one of God's little ones who can never say thank-you. This is my way of saying it for her.

Also, a special thank-you to the many who have cared and ministered to my precious child. I can't name you all here, but know that I love and cherish you too.

—Linda Evans Shepherd

Contents

1

Good to the Last Drop

Clay Whitefield burrowed under the musky blankets, eking out an attempt at a few minutes more sleep before heaving himself out of bed. The weight from the quilt his grandmother had handmade upon his arrival into the world lay over him like the history of her people, the Cheyenne. But his grandmother and her people were the last thing on his mind.

Outside the window of his second-story flat, the town of Summit View, Colorado, was coming to life. With or without him. His boss, the editor and publisher of the *Gold Rush News*, was most likely sitting at his desk by now, wondering what time Clay would amble in. Shifts were changing at the hospital and down at the sheriff's department. Children were preparing for school. Sally Madison, owner of Higher Grounds Café, had already unlocked the doors to her establishment. Larry, her cook, had slapped a heap of lard onto the flat grill, readying it for the morning specials. One of Sally's girls had started the coffee. The very thought of it brewing interrupted Clay's dreams, and his nose twitched.

He opened one eye. Across the room on a scarred table, his gerbils, Woodward and Bernstein, lay wrapped around each other as though they were one. Nearby, his laptop sat at attention, the screen saver banner sliding across its face, teasing him.

CLAY WHITEFIELD, it said. ACE REPORTER.

He'd worked last night until the early hours of the morning; thus his attempt at sleeping in. The big story of his career had kept him up, driving him toward a completion he feared would never come. This story—this single story—had tickled his imagination when he was a child, encouraged him to do well when he'd gone off to the University of Northern Colorado to study journalism, and had propelled him back to his hometown upon graduation.

It was the story of a group of women who called themselves the Potluck Club. But it was more than their monthly gatherings that kept his fingers to the keyboard and his pen and notebook in an ever-ready position. It was their past secrets and current escapades.

It was, most particularly, their youngest member.

Because Clay Whitefield believed, with everything his journalistic heart had in it, that Donna Vesey was carrying the deepest secret of them all.

Donna

EASY MEATBALLS IN A CROCK POT

½ LB HAMBURGER
½ CUP RICE
½ CUP FINELY CHOPPED ONIONS   1 EGG
½ CUP FINELY CHOPPED GRN PEPPERS   1 tsp SALT
                                     ¼ tsp PEPPER
KNEAD TOGETHER ALL INGREDIENTS EXCEPT   1 CAN TOMATO-
TOMATO SOUP AND TOMATOES. SHAPE HAMBURGER   SOUP
MIXTURE INTO ROUGHLY 20-24 MEATBALLS ABOUT
1-½ INCHES AROUND. PLACE MEATBALLS -

2

Grilling Interrogation

It was a bad night to be driving in the mountains. I pulled into one of my favorite retreats, a quiet wooded area, to wait out the storm. I took a sip of my hot coffee and watched the wipers slap at the rain that had altered my view of once stick-straight pines into twisting shadows. As if to add to my concern, the voice of dispatch crackled out of my radio. "Unit three, we have a report of a vehicle in trouble at mile marker eight on River Canyon Road."

"Roger that. Unit three en route."

I hit my siren and raced my white Bronco down the canyon as the dark sky exploded in brilliant flashes and the rock walls throbbed in time to the rotating lights.

At mile marker eight, my headlights illuminated a frantic man who darted from behind his parked jeep, waving his arms. I reached for my radio to call dispatch. "Unit three arrived at destination."

"Roger. Be advised the National Weather Service has just issued a flash flood warning."

"Roger." I powered down my window as rain pelted my face. "What seems to be the trouble?" I asked the drenched man who appeared to be in his midforties. He shivered before me in his T-shirt and jeans, his only defense against the storm's chill.

He leaned down, his eyes wide. "Hurry! You may be able to save her."

"Who?"

"The lady in the car that slid into the river."

He pointed, and I turned my attention to the raging mountain river only a few yards from the road. Normally the river would be nothing more than the peaceful gurgle of melted snow, but tonight it roared as if demons coursed down its winding path. I blinked as I observed the glowing taillights of a sedan just beneath the river's surface.

My heart sunk as I surmised what must have happened. Canyon River Road was awash in a thick cushion of water. When the driver had tried to negotiate the curve, her car had hydroplaned off the road and into the river.

I picked up the radio. "Dispatch, car with occupant submerged at Canyon River Road, mile marker eight. Additional rescue units requested."

I hung up the radio, reached for a length of rope I kept beneath my seat, and stepped into the downpour. A flooded canyon road was not a good place to be without backup.

The man followed me to the river's edge.

"Did you see anyone besides the woman in the car?" I asked.

The man's Rockies baseball cap shielded his eyes from the deluge that rolled off his gray brim. His voice rose to compete with the angry river. "Only the driver."

I looked back at the river. The current was already tugging the submerged car farther downstream.

At this point, I knew an attempt to rescue the occupant would result in certain death, either from drowning or from prolonged exposure to the ice-cold water. Even if I stood taller than five-foot-two, and even if I weighed two hundred pounds with rippling muscles as did some of my male counterparts, that current would knock me off my feet and carry any recoverable parts to a closed pine box to be displayed down at the local funeral home.

13

The man turned to me. "What are you going to do?"

I simply stared, scanning the black waters for signs of life. Suddenly, a head bobbed to the surface. It was the woman! She tried to call to us but gagged and choked against the raging current.

With the woman out of the car, I saw a chance for rescue that couldn't wait. Quickly, I knotted one end of the rope around a nearby pine and tied the other to my waist.

"I'm going in," I told the man before plunging into the frigid swirl of bone-chilling darkness.

The current caught me like a limp rag doll, and the force of the water made me feel as if I were tied to the tail of a kite. When I caught my breath, I called to the woman, who clung to the hood of her car, which had bobbed above the river's surface.

"Let go and I'll catch you!"

Brave words for a young deputy who knew she'd taken on the impossible. Even if I could snag the woman as she swept past me, I would never be able to tow her back to the bank.

I couldn't tell if the woman obeyed my command or if the river itself pried her from the side of her car. Suddenly, she hurled toward me. I reached out as far as my tethered line would allow, my fingers just catching the hood of her jacket. I had her.

"Grab on," I called. And grab she did, climbing me as if I were a ladder. Her frenzy pushed my head beneath the surface, where foam, feet, knees, and elbows jabbed into my body and head.

Inhaling a mouthful of water, I fought my attacker, spinning her around and grabbing her by the neck in a rescuer's hold. I called back to the man on the shore. "Can you pull us in?"

"I'll try!"

With slow progress, the three of us were finally united in a wet, exhausted heap on the river's bank.

The young woman, who had been silent against the overpowering waves, finally caught her breath and cried, "My baby! My baby's still in the car!"

I sat up and turned to look at the car, which had spiraled upside down, scraping its hood on the rocky river bottom as it slowly made its way downstream. Occasionally, the car's headlights would penetrate the dark waters as if to illuminate its journey toward destruction.

The woman continued to weep as she pushed strands of wet, brown hair from her face. Still sprawled on the bank, she rolled toward me and grabbed my sleeve. Her eyes wide with terror, she pleaded, "Please, save my baby!"

Trembling, I stood to my feet, still gasping for breath. In an instant, I realized the car was moving into position. If I went back into the floodwaters, my length of rope might be able to reach it.

I looked down at the woman. "Is your baby in the back-seat?"

"Yes! She's strapped in her car seat."

I scoured the dark road for signs of headlights. Where was my backup?

To my dismay, I was still the only rescuer at the scene. Not only was I alone, but the river was rising in a great yawn. That was a bad sign. A flash flood could be imminent and would result in a great wall of water and rock funneling down the canyon, wiping out everyone and everything in its path. I couldn't predict if the wall of water would bear down on us or not, but I could predict a baby would die unless I tried to save her.

When I looked back at the submerged car, I knew what I had to do. With no time to spare, I leaped back into the frigid waters.

I felt disoriented as the river spun me downstream. When the rope jerked taut, it took me a second to get my bearings. That's when I saw the car was upon me. I dove down, the light from the headlights creating a strange luminance in the churning waters. My feet had just touched the bottom when the car lifted then settled back against my foot. To my horror, I was pinned beneath the water. I fought to free myself, but it was of no use. I was caught fast. Just as my lungs felt as if they would explode, the current shifted the car, and I broke for the surface. Filling my lungs with air, I dove back down, grabbing a rear door handle. I used the handle as a handhold to pull myself to peer into the car. I was amazed to see a crying baby inside a pocket of air. She was alive!

With numbed fingers, I managed to open the rear door, releasing the floodwaters upon the infant. I had only seconds to unbuckle her, knowing her lungs would quickly fill with water. When I finally yanked the buckle free, I pulled her limp body into my arms and swam for the surface.

When my head broke above the flow, the ghost of my breath swirled above the water. My next gasp was met by an icy wave. My ears filled with water, and I could only hear the fizzy shush of the roar above me. I opened my eyes in the eerie underwater light. Before me were the wide eyes of the child staring back. I could see she was only barely alive. That realization quickened my efforts. As I fought to get her to the bank, a pine log careened into my shoulder. For a moment I was stunned. But before I could recover, the wild current ripped the child from my arms. In one terrible second, the baby was gone.

The screams of a heartbroken mother woke me as I fought my tangled bedsheets, once again drowning in the old memory.

I sat up and squinted against the morning light that peeked through the cracks of my heavy drapes. I sucked in a deep breath of cool morning air as I waited for my heart to stop pounding. It was only a dream. It wasn't real. It wasn't. Real. It was . . .

Pain gripped me by the heart, and I put my face in my hands and began to berate myself once again.

What in God's name is wrong with me? It had been three years since the accident.

I mean, what does it take to put one's life back together? I had grieved, I had practically spent my life's savings on a shrink, and I had finally moved from Boulder back home to good old Summit View, Colorado.

It was a good move. With my dad's influence as the local sheriff, I became one of his deputies. Not only did I have a "low stress" job, spending most of my time writing up reports about tourists with lost wallets, but also I gained respect. The townsfolk knew

I never backed down when awarding traffic tickets to deserving offenders, including the mayor and most of the Grace Church deacon board. My ticket-writing trademark, "It's such a pleasure to write you up," had raised more than a few eyebrows, not to mention a slew of letters to the editor of the local *Gold Rush News*. Hah. That kind of publicity only enhanced my tough-broad reputation. And that image comes hard-earned when you resemble a pixie.

I rubbed my eyes and then forced my sleep-deprived body to the coffeepot and started a fresh brew. If I didn't get a grip, I'd start to look as haunted as Wade Gage, my old high school sweetheart.

Minutes later, I peered out my tiny kitchen window at Mount Paul shining bright in the morning sun. The mountain towered just behind my neighborhood of log bungalows. With the price of real estate in the Colorado high country, this tiny cabin was all I could afford. My landlord certainly appreciated my million-dollar view. He saw to it that I always coughed up the rent with his monthly threat, "I'd hate to sell this charmer out from under you, Donna, but as long as I get my rent on time, I'm happy."

Good ol' Bob Burnett, Grace deacon, landlord, and RV park owner.

I pictured his eyebrows arching up his bald head whenever I'd remark, "Careful, Bob, a couple of deserved speeding tickets could ruin your tidy profit."

After I'd drained the last of the coffeepot into my favorite mug, I contemplated a trip to Higher Grounds Café for some pancakes smothered in maple syrup. If I was lucky, I'd find Clay White-field, our local newspaper reporter, sitting in his favorite spot, poring over the Denver papers. I'd hate to admit this, especially as I'm still ticked at him for a couple of his recent news reports (one about Vonnie's long-lost son and the other about how I ran from a bear), but he's the closest thing I have to a friend. That is, unless you count the members of the Potluck Club, Grace Church's prayer group. But who could say where I really stand with them? I've always suspected it was Vonnie who made the girls "play nice" whenever I walked into the room. Well, at least they know me well enough to obey the traffic laws.

I set my mug of coffee on my bedroom dresser as I slipped into my favorite jeans and white T-shirt, complete with the word *Dangerous* emblazoned in red. Then, with coffee mug in hand, I sat down at my desk and logged onto the World Wide Web for a quick email check.

I scanned through the usual mortgage and "find anyone" ads along with my membership-only news digest from the *Deputy Daily* for "the country's finest deputy sheriffs."

An email from MedicDH, a one David Harris, popped out at me. It was about time he emailed me after what I'd been through helping him locate his birth mother.

> Hi, Donna,
> My mother, Vonnie . . . Wow. That sounds so weird I have to say it again. My mother, Vonnie, was such a pleasure to finally meet. I'd always figured my birth mom to have been both unwed and desperate. But the truth is fascinating. To think what she must have gone through when my father was killed in Vietnam, not to mention how she must have felt when she was told I had died at birth. Now that my adopted mom has passed, it's time to get to know Vonnie. I've decided to move to Summit View. I'm going to get my paramedic's license from the State of Colorado. Who do you know at the Colorado Health Department I can call to see what's involved?

I stared at the screen, narrowed my eyes, and blinked. *Give me an everlasting break! Harris in Summit View?* I didn't like the sound of this. Did he have a clue as to the havoc he had created when Fred Westbrook found out his wife of thirty-five years had been married before? And if Clay Whitefield pegged Vonnie as Harris's long-lost mother, even God himself couldn't keep it from becoming front-page news.

I clicked off the screen without hitting "reply" or checking the rest of my mail. This was one email I needed to think about. I didn't think I could ever willingly share Vonnie with a long-lost son. After my mom had walked out on Dad and me, Vonnie was the only mother I had.

I sat on the edge of my bed and laced my tennies.

Beside Hurricane Harris, I had an even more threatening situation to contain. It seemed my fellow Potlucker and formidable opponent, Miss Evangeline Benson—Evil Evie, as I liked to call her—was making sudden progress on her lifelong goal of marrying my father.

That wrinkly old spinster had been on a slow boil ever since my dad married my mom instead of her.

Humph. Something told me I shouldn't waste time in putting that relationship to an end. It was the only way to save my father from certain doom.

I looked in the mirror and finger-combed my crop of short blond hair. It was growing out, long enough now to ripple into soft curls. From the looks of the new growth, I'd have to duck into the barbershop for a trim. If one more fat tourist called me "cutie," it could mean life in prison for either one or both of us.

I grabbed the truck keys off the kitchen table and opened my front door. The sleepy town of Summit View was like a cat curled in its favorite window. *Which of its nine lives will spring up today?* I wondered, then inhaled the morning air. *Pines and coffee. That's a good combination.* I hopped into my Bronco for a quick drive to the café, pulling up into one of the prime parking spots right in front next to Clay Whitefield's old blue and white jeep.

The café itself was in a remodeled white clapboard one-room schoolhouse that had been standing on Main Street for more than a century. The old schoolhouse bell hung from a small rooftop loft crowned with a green-shingled steeple. The bell regularly chimed during all scheduled parades, which duly marched down Main Street every Saint Paddy's Day, Veterans Day, Fourth of July, Labor Day, and Halloween.

This morning the bell hung silent while the sun shone on the gold letters that spelled "Higher Grounds Café" on a large plate glass window. The sun's glare made it hard to see which of the gang had arrived before me, though I could guess. I pushed open the glass door, and a tiny bell above jingled my entrance.

Just as I'd thought. Wade Gage was hunkered on a stool at the counter, and Sally Madison was refilling his cup. Wade had probably just risen from a late night at the Gold Rush Tavern, where he was prone to put away a few brews. He was getting his usual late-morning start with a cup of black joe. Of course, the local handymen set their own hours, making sure work didn't interfere with their hangovers or ski season.

Wade looked up, his dirty denim baseball cap pulled low over his eyes. Despite his haggard appearance, he was still a hottie, with his tall, muscled frame and sun-bleached hair, though I'd never let him know I still thought so. He gave me one of his haunted looks. "Morning, Deputy."

"Morning, Wade."

Dee Dee McGurk, the old barmaid from Gold Rush Tavern, sat alone at a corner table facing the door. She smoked a cigarette as she sipped her coffee and ate her usual toast and scrambled eggs. Her tired blue eyes snapped to mine.

"Donna," she said with a slight nod. I nodded back, for an instant trying to imagine her former beauty lost decades ago to . . . what? Deep sadness? Hard living? Bad choices? All of the above?

No one around here seemed to know, because Dee Dee is a newcomer to town. She'd lived next to Sal in the trailer park behind the café for the past six months and pretty much kept to herself.

A cheerful voice interrupted my musings. "How's it going, Deputy Donna?" Dora Watkins, the owner and operator of the Sew and Stitch, had called out as she reached for her purse. "I'd love to pull up a chair for a visit, but we're having a floss sale down at the shop this morning so I've got to scoot."

I nodded, relieved. Dora would have only tried to reminisce over Jan's funeral—the beloved wife of our pastor had just died—and I wasn't in the mood.

As she paid her bill, I saw Clay Whitefield in his usual spot in front of the window, ready to catch any hint of a news story that might roll through town. He was studying the Boulder *Daily Camera* with his ever-present reporter's pad plopped next to what was left of a biscuit and sausage special.

He looked up from his reading as I slid into the chair across from him. "Donna, my favorite informant."

"Is that all I am to you?"

He glowered beneath his Rockies baseball cap. "Don't play coy with me, Deputy. You owe me some information. Our game of cloak-and-dagger, fun as it was, is over." He tapped his pen on the table and studied me before leaning back in his chair with folded arms. "So, care to tell me who David Harris's mother is?"

His Irish Indian heritage shone through a splash of orange freckles flung across his olive cheeks and nose. He pushed his baseball cap a bit higher with the edge of his pen, revealing auburn hair. The humor in his brown eyes beckoned me to confess the juicy secret he knew I kept. Somehow I couldn't help but feel sorry for him. Poor man. Didn't he know I'd never reveal what I knew?

"Dream on," I said, signaling Sally for a cup of coffee by pointing at Clay's cup.

Clay looked a bit too smug as he reached for his reporter's pad. "If I know you, I'd say it's got to be one of your Potluck friends. Someone like, say, Lizzie? Perhaps her gig as the high school librarian is simply a cover for her shady past."

I could only shake my head.

Clay wrote the name "Lizzie Prattle" on his notepad then scratched it out. "That's two off my list of suspects."

"Two?"

"Well, it can't be you, now can it? You're only old enough to be his sibling. Hey, is that it? You're Harris's evil twin sister?"

"Ha-ha. Clay, promise me you'll never try to write fiction."

Clay wrote my name under Lizzie's and scratched through it. "This investigation is progressing nicely. I have only a few more suspects."

Sal arrived with my coffee. Her graying blond hair was pulled back into a hairnet. The apron of her crisp red uniform was tied tight around her too-thin waist, revealing the fact that she spent too much time on her feet. "Pancakes?" she asked.

I nodded. "Don't forget the syrup."

Sally laughed. "And risk jail time?"

"Aw, Sal, Donna's not as bad as that," Clay said.

Sally jerked her head toward the kitchen. "That's not what my cook says. He's still steamed about that ticket she gave him last month—it cost him a big fine," she called as she whirled herself back into the kitchen.

Clay looked amused then asked, "How could you ticket poor Larry? You went to high school with him."

"And that makes him family? Larry, like everyone else around here, lied to me. He deserved it."

"So it's truth you want. Maybe you'll enjoy knowing that I've already figured out this little secret of yours."

I flinched, and my voice rose a bit louder than I intended. "Look, Clay. I'm not going to help you."

"Okay, suit yourself, but I already know Harris's mother is Evie."

When I barked a laugh, he wrote down Evangeline Benson's name then scratched it out too.

I held up my hands. "Okay, enough's enough. I came for the town scoop. I didn't come to play gossip. Now, you tell me, who's doing what to whom?"

"I'm the one desperate for news. Not much happening around here except for Jan Moore's funeral last week."

I reached for my napkin and tried to center it in my lap, carefully smoothing out its creases. I didn't want to engage in this conversation so I kept my eyes on the napkin. "She was a fine lady," I said quietly.

Clay studied me. "That's why I've never suspected her to be Harris's mother," he said finally. "She was too much of an angel to have had such a secret." Clay wrote down Jan's name then scratched it out.

"Clay!"

"Sorry. I couldn't resist. But, say, I am writing a story about Jan. Would you mind telling me your fondest memory of her?"

"Well, off the record."

He poised his pen above the pad. "Go on."

"I mean it, Clay. Drop that pen."

Clay put the pen behind his ear then leaned back.

I said, "Okay, it's just that I don't want anyone to think I'm a softie."

"You?" Clay smirked. "Just tell me what happened."

I took a sip of coffee, then said, "Once, when I'd stopped her for tearing down the mountain at eighty-five miles an hour, she pleaded, 'Guilty as charged, Donna. Give me a ticket.' I was so taken by her honesty that I told her, 'Never mind, Jan. Seeing that it's you and knowing you're probably on some heavenly mission, I'll give you a little grace. But watch your speed, will ya? I'd hate to see you run that Taurus off a cliff.'"

I paused a moment, caught in memory. "Jan looked so cute—those big brown eyes framed by her brown curls. Remember? I even remember what she was wearing that day: a denim skirt with a red-scooped tee. She may have had the look of Texas about her, but I never held it against her . . .

"She said, 'Donna, what a dear you are. And yes, I am on a mission. Jeanie Thompson just got word that her mother's had a heart attack. Jeanie needs me to watch her kids so she can run to the hospital. I'm afraid she's a bit hysterical, and I'd hoped to spend some time in prayer with her before she faced the doctors.'"

I looked up at Clay, who nodded his approval. "That was Jan," he said, "always on a mission from God."

"That's what's so hard to understand," I admitted. "If she served a loving God, why would he allow this sudden cancer to take her away from us?"

"Questions are my department." Clay tapped the paper. "If God ever grants me an interview, I'll ask him."

"Mmm." I tapped page one too and crooked my head. "Clay's interview with God explains all mysteries."

23

Clay leaned back in his chair. "It would make a great front page. Speaking of mysteries, I was at the funeral luncheon following the service. The potluck was hosted by your little club, right? Did you contribute?"

"Only the meatballs."

"No kidding? I'd like to have that recipe."

I shrugged. "Just a little recipe I picked up off the Internet—RecipeCoach.com. Check it out. Nah. I'll print you a copy. In truth, I avoid the kitchen at all costs."

"Like you try to avoid Lisa Leann Lambert?" Clay was writing her name in that notebook of his, only to scratch it off as he said, "Who, by the way, is off my list simply because she's new to town."

"That makes her the perfect suspect."

"But she's not one you'd try to protect. I heard what she said to you."

"Pastor Kevin's wife hadn't been in the grave more than half an hour when she'd started up." I exaggerated her Texas drawl. "'Darlin', you know, marrying off Pastor Kevin could be the biggest social event of the year. Donna, you're single, aren't you? I think you'd make a lovely bride. The age difference between you and Pastor Kevin isn't so much. You're early thirties, right? And Pastor Kevin is probably late fifties. My, that could work.'"

Clay chuckled. "So, Donna, are you going to take her up on her offer?"

"Yeah, right. If I hadn't choked on my Kool-Aid, the deacons would have thrown me out of the church for swearing. Good thing Lizzie came to my aid. She said, 'Lisa Leann, this is Jan's funeral. Have you no respect?'" I laughed, then caught Clay writing another name on his list. I tried to look. "What are you doing?"

"I'm officially scratching Lisa Leann's name. Which brings us to my two main suspects: Goldie Dippel and Vonnie Westbrook."

I felt the color rise in my cheeks as I stood to my feet, almost knocking my pancakes out of Sal's hands.

I turned to her. "Uh, Sally, I've gotta run. Could you box those up for me?"

Clay pulled his pudgy frame from his chair. "Well, Donna, looks like I'm getting warm. I'd even say that I'm getting pretty hot."

I turned and looked him up and down. "Hot? Who? You and Sponge Bob Square Pants? You wouldn't be hot even if you were covered in Larry's five-alarm chili."

3

Half Reporter, Half Detective, 100 Percent Curious

Clay watched Donna walk out of the café, then stared back down to his notepad. *Man, she's good*, he thought, then smiled at the two remaining names.

Goldie Dippel and Vonnie Westbrook.

Goldie was a transplant, having moved from some sleepy little town in Georgia right after she married Coach Jack Dippel; she was one of his favorite people, the kind of woman who would never do anyone any harm, in spite of the fact she was married to the world's biggest jerk.

However, he mused, she and Coach had recently separated. Could it be over the Harris man? Could his unexpected arrival in Summit View have been the catalyst that caused the breakup? Or had Mrs. Dippel finally had her fill of Coach's roaming ways?

This, of course, brought him to Vonnie Westbrook. Vonnie had lived her whole life in Summit View, as far as he knew. He'd already gone down to the local high school, checked out an old yearbook, and discovered that her goal in life was to be a nurse. From all indications, she'd gone to college, returned home with her degree, married Fred Westbrook, and worked for Doc Billings until retirement.

A thought struck him. She'd attended college back in the sixties, and he'd heard some wild stories about that free love era.

Clay looked back up to the door where Donna had exited, thinking for a moment about who his favorite deputy would be more likely to protect. Surely, Vonnie. The woman was like a mother to Donna . . .

Clay shook his head. For the life of him, he couldn't imagine Vonnie Westbrook—no matter what era she'd grown up in—carrying a STOP THE WAR sign in an antiwar march or dancing around half dressed at a rock fest like Woodstock.

The slow steps of Dee Dee McGurk leaving the café interrupted his imaginings. She sniffed, and he looked up at her weathered and deeply tanned face. Was she crying, he wondered, or did she have a cold?

Considering the change in weather of late, probably a cold, he concluded, then watched her walk out of the same door Donna had gone through moments before.

Donna . . . all thoughts seemed to come back to her. He felt himself blush, and he swore under his breath. How could a little thing like her have such an effect on a man?

No sooner had he asked himself that question than Wade Gage walked up to his table. "You're so gone over her," he said.

"Who? Dee Dee?"

Wade chuckled. "Yeah. Dee Dee." He shook his head as he took two steps toward the door. "See everyone later," he called out.

Clay could still smell the lingering stench of beer from the night before on his old friend. He narrowed his eyes. Wade Gage had been Donna's sweetheart back in high school. He knew what it felt like to make her laugh or blush, to hold her and kiss her . . .

Clay slammed his notebook shut. *Enough of this*, he thought. He had better things to do than wonder about Wade Gage and Donna Vesey. He had some investigations to continue and articles to write. The ladies of the Potluck were sure to serve up something . . .

Lizzie

Grilled Hamburgers

Ingredients:
- 1 lb. burger (Angus)
- 1 lb. B. sausage
- 1½ c. mushrooms, finely chopped
- ½ c. onion, finely chopped
- ¼ c. Barbeque Sauce
- ¼ c. Ketchup/Mustard Mix
- Salt & Pepper

4

Marriage Waffles

The phone at my desk rang, and I scurried from the American History Reference section of the high school library where I've worked longer than I care to admit to the small glass-encased office at the back of the room. "Library. Mrs. Prattle," I answered, a tad breathless.

"Yes, I'd like to place an order please."

"I'm sorry," I said, looking down at the phone. The call had come in from an outside line. "You must have the wrong number."

"No, I think I have the correct number," the male voice said, a hint of humor in his tone.

I pulled my reading glasses from my face and laid them gently on my desk. This was just what I needed today, and I mean that with all the sarcasm I can muster. "Okay," I said, deciding to play along. After all, years of dealing with high schoolers had taught me to be just as obnoxious as they were when pushed. "Since I'm quite certain you are one of our students who has decided to give me a difficult time, I'll take a stab at this. What would you like to order? Prince Albert in a can? A pizza? What?"

"Hmm . . . I was thinking more along the lines of one of your great hamburgers right off the grill."

"What?"

"Hi, Mom."

"Tim!" I sat in my swivel chair, pulling it closer to the desk with a scootch of my feet. "What are you doing trying to fool your mother this way? You sounded just like one of the kids around here." Even as I said the words, a couple of giggly female students entered the library, arms wrapped around their notebooks. I watched as they moved slowly toward the YA fiction section, then looked back down to my desk, where a scattering of papers and a few stacks of books had managed to take up residency since lunchtime.

He chuckled. "Ah, I've still got a few tricks up my sleeve. Nice to know all those drama classes at college were for a good cause."

"You're a stinker." I noticed that a book in one stack belonged in another and made the transfer. When I did so, I saw the *Gold Rush News* clipping of Donna's great escape from the bear during one of our Potluck gatherings. I giggled in spite of myself.

"I haven't been called that in a few years," Tim said after a pause. "I can think of a few other names I've been called lately, but not stinker."

I rested against the back of the chair. "To what do I owe the pleasure of this phone call? The kids okay? Samantha?"

"Always the mother, aren't you? The kids are great. They're always great."

I narrowed my eyes, waiting for a report on my daughter-in-law. "And Samantha?"

"Ah, my dear sweet wife Samantha." The dramatic tone was back in his voice, placing emphasis on the "man" in her name.

"Tim . . ." I sat up straight but dropped my head so as to keep my preferred quiet in the library, even behind the glass wall.

"You never answered me," he said.

"Answered you?" I heard the library door open again, and I looked up to see three more students entering. "I don't remember there being a question, but I'm keenly aware that you are avoiding mine. Son . . ."

"Mom, what would it take for me to get one of your grilled hamburgers?"

I turned my chair to face the back of my office. "What's going on?"

Again he chuckled. "I'm just hungry, that's all. And I've got a craving for one of your hamburgers."

Once again I heard the library door open, only this time I didn't bother to turn to look. A sense of dread ran down my spine, then leaped into my stomach, settling there like a heavy rock. For some time I'd been worried about my son's marriage to his college sweetheart. I'd hoped I was wrong, of course. A mother always knows when her children are in some sort of trouble, but we always pray for the best. But just recently Tim had called his sister Michelle—our deaf daughter who works at a resort in Breckenridge—telling her he was building a bigger home for himself and his family, something I thought a great waste of money . . . and also a "tale-tell." Something was rotten in Denmark!

When I'd pressed my husband, Samuel, about it, he pooh-poohed my concern away, telling me if I wanted to know if anything was going on, call Tim and ask. But then . . . Jan . . . and I simply let it slide.

Now, with this phone call, I knew there was trouble.

"Tim, I've been meaning to ask you . . . wait . . ." I swiveled back around. "I want to close my door—" My words faltered. There, standing on the other side of the glass wall, was my handsome son, cell phone pressed to his ear.

"Hi, Mom." He smiled a forced smile. His thinning light brown hair was tousled—probably from being windblown—but he still managed to look sharp in a pair of dark slacks, gray oxford, and multicolored sweater. His brow moved up and down in an imitation of Charlie Chaplin, an attempt to make me laugh—or at the very least, smile—but I couldn't. I just couldn't.

From the looks of things, my youngest boy had come home. And, the good Lord willing, not to stay.

I decided to take the rest of the afternoon off. Tim had flown into Denver and rented a car, so I suggested that he follow me home. "Don't say anything," I admonished him as I gathered up my keys and purse. "Just follow me home and we'll . . . talk there." I told him I needed to advise the assistant librarian and he should meet me in the employee parking lot. "Go," I whispered, then made a hasty retreat to the American Lit section, where Ellie Brestin was filing away returned books. I made a quick excuse (Ellie is a dear, but she doesn't need to know my family business) and then rushed out past the stacks, into the hallway, and out a side door.

Naturally I called Samuel on my cell phone during the drive. Samuel is the president of the Gold Mine Bank and Loan, and I knew he'd be busy, but I also knew he'd not want to come home to any surprises, such as a married son complete with suitcase but without wife and kids.

While I waited for his secretary to patch me through, I passed by Lisa Leann's new bridal shop on Main Street. A wild thought ran through my mind, namely, *Oh, dear Lord, what will Lisa Leann have to say about this?* It seemed to me that Lisa Leann Lambert had something to say about everything, and most of it was none of her business.

Samuel answered his extension with a "What's up, Liz?" and I jumped right in with both feet.

"I told you, Samuel. I told you something was up." I pressed my foot harder on the accelerator, then released it as soon as I realized what I was doing.

"Back up, Lizzie. Are you in the car?"

"I am. And our son is in a rental car directly behind me." I glanced in the rearview mirror just to make sure. I don't really know why I had to make sure. Where did I think Tim would go?

"Sam?" he asked, meaning Samuel Jr. "Why would Sam be following you?"

"Not Sam. Tim."

"Tim?"

"And I told you something was up a few weeks ago when he called Michy and said he was building Samantha a bigger house."

"Did he say what he's doing home?"

I braked for a red light, then looked back in my rearview mirror again. Tim was behind me, cell phone also pressed to his ear. I could tell by the expression on his face the conversation was serious. Was he talking with Samantha? One of the kids? "No. And I told him to just wait until we get home. But he said Samantha's name as if it were a curse word. Oh, Samuel!" Tears began to well up in my eyes. "What if they get a divorce?"

Samuel paused before answering. The light before me turned green, and I pressed the accelerator. "I'm sure it's just a spat."

"A spat? Samuel, for a spat you don't fly from Louisiana to Colorado. For a spat, you take a walk around the block . . . or go to the club and play racquetball or something. For a spat you get a cup of coffee at the local diner and mull things over."

"All right then, Lizzie. You're on your way home?"

I sniffled. "Yes."

"I'll leave in a few minutes to join you. But you listen to me, now. If you fall apart, you won't get anywhere with him. Just take some time and listen. Or, better yet, try not to get into anything before I get home. Hear?"

I nodded, silent.

"Did you hear me, honey?" I knew he threw the "honey" in as a comforter.

"I hear you. And I'll see you shortly."

Even as I said the words I pulled into our driveway, and Tim's rental, a silvery gray Altima, bounded in behind me. When I met him at the driver's door, he was flipping the top of his cell phone down, ending his call. His face seemed flushed, and in spite of the chill in the air, I could see rivulets of sweat escaping from his hairline and trailing down the jut of his jaw.

He opened his door and looked up at me. A sigh escaped my lips. He no longer looked like a grown man or a husband or a father. He looked like a little boy.

More specifically, my little boy.

"Samantha?" I asked Tim, my brows raised in an empathetic arch.

He nodded. "Yeah." He swung his legs out of the car, and I stepped back. "I wanted to let her know I'd made it back home."

Tim cut a sharp glance from me to the brick split-level perched before us. "For a while, okay, Mom? This is home . . . but I promise it won't be for long. Just until I can get on my feet . . . feel things out . . ." He looked up at the sky, blinked a few times, then slammed the car door shut.

I stammered. "Oh . . . sure. Of course this is home. It always has been, you know that." I followed my son to the back of the car, where he opened the trunk and pulled out several pieces of matching luggage. It looked brand-new. And expensive. "Nice luggage," I said, like some ninny trying to make casual conversation with my own son.

Tim shrugged. "Wilson's," he said. "I bought it yesterday . . . maybe it was the day before." He shrugged again. "Doesn't matter, though, does it. Luggage is luggage."

"Apparently not." I reached for the rolling duffle bag. "I'll get this one," I said.

We strolled to the rust-colored front door in silence, Tim alone with his thoughts and me alone with mine. I gripped the roller handle in a tight fist, thinking about the new house Tim and Samantha were supposedly building, the expense of the leather luggage, even the cost of the clothes my son wore.

Tim could easily afford it, and I knew this, but I'd always warned my children against becoming too materialistic. Just because their father and I earned good salaries didn't mean we spoiled them. They hadn't necessarily wanted for anything, but sometimes their wants were just that. Wants.

"No one ever died from a disease called Wanting," Samuel used to tell them.

I recalled that on more than one occasion Tim lashed back, "Yeah, well . . . when I'm grown and making my own money I'll buy whatever I want. I don't care what it costs."

Samuel, wise and consistent, would reply, "When you're grown and on your own, you can certainly do with your money whatever you'd like. But this money belongs to Mother and me."

Tim had stayed true to his word—or, in those days, threats. He'd graduated with a double degree in business and finance, then taken a job as a reimbursement analyst for one of the top hospital chains in Louisiana, making more money his first year than his father and me combined at this stage in our careers. New homes and pricy leather luggage he could afford, but I worried. Had my son become too . . . uppity? Was this the cause of his marital problems?

As soon as we entered the foyer of the house Tim said, "Mom, just drop that bag here. I'll take all this down to my old room and then grab a quick shower if that works for you."

I smiled a weak smile. "Of course, son. Your father will be home soon, so when you're done, come back up, okay?"

Tim leaned over and kissed my cheek. "Will do." He hoisted several of the bags and made his way toward the staircase leading to the first floor, where he and his brother, Sam, had shared a room during their growing-up years.

Sam . . . I'd need to make a few calls to the other siblings—Sam, Sis, and Michelle—as soon as I had more information; certainly something more than "Your brother has come home."

I raised my chin and sighed. If my son wanted grilled burgers, I'd better get started with the preparations. I headed for the kitchen.

While Samuel and Tim sat at the old farm kitchen table talking more like two grown men than father and son, I stood at the double sinks, peeling potatoes. "Potato salad too, okay, Mom?" Tim had asked after he'd come back up the stairs and found me mixing the ingredients for the burgers. "What're burgers without your potato salad?" He turned to see his father sitting at the table. "Hey, Dad," he said, then crossed the room and shook his father's hand.

Samuel drew him close in a hug. "Son," he said, slapping his back.

I gave a slight roll of my eyes, catching a glimpse of the overhead shelf lined with my collection of antique teapots covered in a light layer of dust. *The dust will have to wait,* I thought. *My married and successful son has come home.*

I listened to them speaking to each other about the way of things in Louisiana and somehow managed to keep my mouth shut. *Get on with it . . . find out what's going on in his marriage, not his state,*

I thought, but said nothing. The more you listen, the more you learn, I always say.

"I don't know, Dad." Tim's words brought me out of my thoughts. "It's like the more I buy her, the more she wants from me. If I get her a one-carat diamond ring, she wants a two-carat cluster."

I narrowed my eyes and focused on dicing the potatoes. I knew my son, of course, but I'd known Samantha for a lot of years, and somehow I couldn't imagine my daughter-in-law being that materialistic.

"Is that why you were talking about building a bigger house?" Samuel asked.

"Yeah. She's always complaining about this thing or that thing in the house on Myrtle. I thought, well, build her one she won't have anything to complain about. You know, give her a good year's worth of projects, and maybe she'll get off my case about stupid stuff like the faucets in the bathroom not being modern enough . . . about Mary Kate's new wallpaper and Joan's solid oak crown molding."

"Who?" I couldn't help myself; I had to ask.

Tim shook his head as though dismissing the women. "Friends of hers. Wives of the very well-to-do. My salary can't hold a candle to what they're bringing in."

Samuel nodded. "Had you bought property yet?" he asked, getting back on track. I returned my attention to the cooking.

"No. Only looking. Though I had to do the majority of it. I mean, here I am, Dad, working ten hours a day, sometimes twelve, and then having to squeeze in property shopping before going home for dinner. My gosh, by the time I got to bed every night—what with having personal things to do, to boot—I just collapsed." He guffawed. "And sex? Forget about it."

I twisted my neck so fast bones cracked. "Timothy!"

He threw his hands up in the air and gave me a wide-eyed stare. "What? Mom, you do know we have sex, right? And I say that lightly. I can't remember the last time—"

"Mother," Samuel warned. "We've always had an open door policy in this house. Our children can talk to us about anything."

I pressed my hand to my breast and swallowed. "You're right, of course." I looked back at my son. "Sex—or the lack thereof—within a marriage is critical, Tim. Continue." I turned back to the diced potatoes lying in a mound in my favorite light blue Tupperware bowl. I began to rinse them, watching the starch mix with the cool water, then looked out the window at the near-naked trees of my backyard. The sky was gray, a sign that it was turning bitter cold out.

Tim shifted before continuing. "Like I said . . . I can't remember when. She hardly kisses me anymore. It's like we're strangers living in the same house, parenting the same children, even sitting in the same pew at church. But strangers nonetheless."

"What about counseling?" Samuel asked.

"I dunno, Dad."

"It's worth a shot, though, right?"

"She mentioned it once, but . . . I hate airing my dirty laundry. For crying out loud, I'm a man from the Colorado high country. We don't go around telling everyone our personal business. Even if we pay them to listen."

I dumped the water in the bowl and added fresh for a second rinse. "What about your pastor?" I asked, looking sideways at him.

Tim shrugged again. "Maybe. I dunno. For now," he said, slapping the palms of his hands against the top of his thighs, "I'm going to take my two weeks' vacation and just think. Here. At home."

As soon as the potatoes were set for a slow boil on the stove, I made a beeline for the upstairs bedroom I shared with my husband and called my friend Vonnie Westbrook. I needed someone to talk this over with, someone who was logical and levelheaded in a dramatic setting. Someone like me . . . when the scene didn't involve my family.

I didn't even bother to close the bedroom door; I just planted myself in the middle of the high-backed antique bed, crossed my legs, and pulled the phone from the edge of the nightstand to where I was sitting.

"Two weeks?" Vonnie Westbrook asked after I gave her the rundown. "He's taking his two weeks' vacation to come home and think?"

"That's what he said, Von."

Vonnie paused before continuing. "Where are he and Samuel now? Still talking?"

"No. Samuel's firing up the grill, and Tim's downstairs in his old room. I imagine he's resting . . . probably tired from his trip."

"Sons and vacations," she said with a sad sort of laugh.

I nodded. Her son, who had been adopted out at birth, had taken vacation days not too terribly long ago and traveled from California to Colorado in search of Von. Not that it was public knowledge as of yet, but we Potluckers knew as much as anyone could, and that wasn't much. "True."

"Have you told the other kids?"

"Only Michelle, right after we got home." I'd called Michelle at her job in Breckenridge, using the TTY operator in order to communicate with her. In spite of her disability, Michelle has become quite successful and adept in life. "I barely got the words out when I heard Samuel's voice downstairs, so she's the only one I've told. I'll have to call the others later."

"Well, you're calling me before calling them, obviously, so what can I do for you?"

"Pray, of course."

"Of course."

Music drifted from downstairs, pushing its way past the plush, rose-colored bedroom carpet. I'd left Tim's old stereo system in his room along with his collection of albums and other musical memorabilia, thinking it all might be worth something someday. Apparently, my son—given more to books and music than sports—had decided the value was worth a trip down memory lane. I turned my left ear upward, attempting to place the name of the song.

"What's wrong?" Vonnie asked. "Why are you being so quiet?"

I chuckled. "Oh," I said, smoothing the floral comforter with the back of my fingertips. "Tim's playing an old record in his room. Chicago, I think it is."

"Chicago is unmistakable, Lizzie."

"It's Chicago."

"What's the song? Do you know?"

I listened a bit more intently, then frowned. "'Will You Still Love Me,'" I answered her.

"Hmmm," she said. "I'll pray." And then we ended our call.

I slipped off the bed, crossed the room, and then closed my bedroom door, attempting in the process not to make too much noise. I returned to the bed, sitting as I had before, and dialed another number. This one with a 225 area code.

"Hello," my daughter-in-law answered.

"Samantha?"

There was a deep sigh from the other end. "Hi, Mom."

Well, at least she was still calling me Mom. For a moment I pictured her standing at the kitchen counter—where she always seemed to be, cooking up this recipe or baking that recipe—wearing tall-girl jeans with a basic T-shirt, her long, dark hair scooped up in a ponytail. My daughter-in-law had looked like a Barbie doll in her youth, and she continued to do so even now. "Are you okay?" I asked her.

She began to cry, something I hadn't expected, though I'm not sure what I thought I was going to get. Seemed to me that a woman who wasn't happy in her marriage would be glad for the break.

"Oh, Samantha . . ." I let my voice trail off as my shoulders slumped. "Oh, dear. I'm so sorry. I didn't mean to upset you."

"You haven't. I just . . . thank you for thinking enough of me to call."

I sat ramrod straight. "Of course I think a lot of you. Samantha, you're my daughter-in-law . . . the mother of my precious grandchildren."

"I know," she whispered through her sobs.

"What can I do, Samantha? Tell me, other than pray, what can I do?"

"Just pray."

I heard a door open and close from downstairs. Most likely it was Samuel coming in from the patio. "You know I will." I paused.

"Samantha, is there any chance . . . I mean . . . I have to ask . . . you don't think this is going to end in divorce, do you?"

"What did Tim tell you?" she asked.

I didn't want to betray my son, but if it would help in any way . . . "Nothing much, really." I certainly wasn't going to get into the part about their sex life, at least not yet. "Dad asked him about counseling but . . ."

"Tim said no, right? Yeah, I know." A certain sarcasm filled her voice. "I've been saying counseling for months now, and I've gotten nowhere. Be sure to let me know if you do."

"You've suggested counseling?"

"Yeah. Wait a minute. What did he tell you?"

"Only that he didn't want to air his dirty laundry."

She scoffed at my words. "Oh, is that what he said? Mom, what else did he tell you?"

"That he was home for two weeks to think."

"Mom, he's quit his job already, okay? He's home for more than you're thinking. He's—"

Samantha was interrupted when from the background I heard my grandson, six-year-old Brent, saying something to his mother. "No, baby. It's not Daddy. It's MeMa. Want to talk with her for a second?"

My heart tore in two and fell to my stomach. Those precious children.

"Hey, MeMa!"

"Well, hello! Did you go to school today?"

"Yes, ma'am. I did some math problems, and guess what?"

"What?"

"I have a wiggly tooth."

"You do?" I asked, wide-eyed.

"Yeah. And my best friend is Trey, and I gotta go now, okay, MeMa? Bye," he said in one breath.

"Mom?" Samantha was back on the line. "Look, I've got to go now too. I can't talk in front of the kids, but . . . well, I have a feeling things aren't being portrayed to you and Dad as they really are. So, you pray . . . and I'll call you back soon, okay?"

"Of course." From beyond the closed door I could hear Samuel's steady footsteps ascending the stairs.

"And, Mom?"

"Yes, dear?"

I heard her choke a bit before she continued. "Don't say anything about him quitting his job, okay? Just tell Tim I do still love him, okay?"

I slumped again. "But, if you love him—"

"Just tell him, Mom. Good-bye."

I returned the phone just as Samuel opened our bedroom door then leaned against the door frame. "Who was that?" he asked, frowning.

I gave him a wry smile. Samuel hated it when I talked to others about our personal lives. "Samantha," I answered quickly. "And from the sound of things, I think you and I need to talk."

5

Clay's "One Thing"

Clay suspected most people thought he spent too much time at Higher Grounds Café. But, the truth of the matter was, it was the hotbed of Summit View. Located at the center of Main Street, it offered him plenty of viewing privileges. Not a whole lot went on without Main Street being involved, and he had the best seat in the house.

There was, of course, an unwritten rule about anyone sitting in his chair . . . at his table. This gave him both the inner and outer observation he needed as an ace reporter. But it also meant he had to keep his eyes opened, his ears alert, and his attention peeled to the things that really mattered.

Being so keenly trained at his job came in handy, especially when he saw Lizzie Prattle driving past the café too early in the day for her to be going home from her job at the high school. But, when he saw what appeared to be her son driving right behind her, he was a little more than intrigued.

What was Tim Prattle doing in Summit View?

He took out his pad and began to jot down a few notes. "Thanksgiving?"

That was more than a week away.

"Samantha?"

Now there was a hot potato if there ever was one. He remembered the hushed gossip when those two "had" to get married after they'd gone off to college.

Not that he didn't like Lizzie and her husband, Samuel. They were good people. But sometimes churched people, they could get a little uppity. Like they could do no wrong and no wrong could be done to them. Tim and Samantha's marriage had put a real kink in that theory . . . though it was certainly a long time ago. Being a man, Clay didn't hold anything against Tim.

But, he wondered . . . maybe Tim had come home because . . . because he and Samantha were having some problems? Clay sighed. That would mean one more single man back in Summit View. One more contender for Donna's heart.

"Donna," he wrote.

Yeah, all things came back to her.

Vonnie

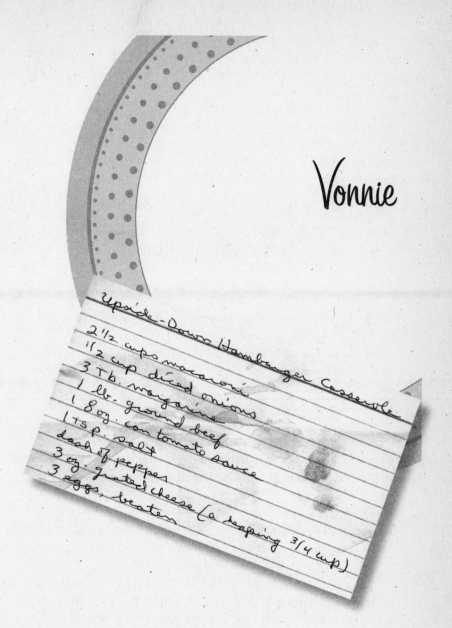

Upside-Down Hamburger Casserole
2 1/2 cups macaroni
1 1/2 cup diced onions
3 Tb. margarine
1 lb. ground beef
1 8 oz. can tomato sauce
1 tsp. salt
dash of pepper
3 oz. grated cheese (a heaping 3/4 cup)
3 eggs, beaten

6

Juicy Love Letters

It was the first time I'd allowed myself to hope that things would get back to normal.

The news that I'd been married before had come as quite a shock to my chubby Swede husband of thirty-five years. But when the son I thought had died at birth arrived in Summit View, the door to my secret past flew open. Stunned by the revelations, Fred had spent the last several weeks brooding in silence.

The atmosphere was tense. After each wordless meal, Fred would slink into the recliner to watch monster truck reruns on cable before retiring to his side of the bed. Then last night, over one of his favorite dishes, upside-down hamburger casserole, he'd said, "Vonnie, this hasn't been easy for me."

I suspended my fork in midair, bracing myself for the rebuke he'd surely been rehearsing. Instead, he asked, "Why, Vonnie?"

I put down my fork. "I was young and . . ."

Fred's platinum eyebrows arched into his wrinkled brow. Portly and bald or not, he still looked like the handsome man I married. He continued, "No, what I want to know is why didn't you tell me?"

I twisted the paper napkin in my lap. "I don't know. Mom said you'd think less of me because Joe was half Mexican. She said that if you thought I'd been with what she called trash, you'd leave me." I managed to look up. "Was Mom right about you?"

His bright blue eyes were intense. "Joe's heritage has nothing to do with this. The way I see it, you buried a man you loved. Now he's gone."

I nodded and replied quietly. "Yes, Joe's gone."

He hesitated. "But I'm here, and you love me. Right?"

I leaped from my chair and threw my arms around his neck. "Oh, Fred. Of course I love you. I'm sorry I never told you about Joe and the baby, but Mom said—"

He interrupted. "Are you two speaking again?"

"I'm afraid I haven't had much to say to her lately," I admitted, sitting back down in my chair. "I need time."

Fred reached over and patted my hand. "Be patient, Von. We all do."

That conversation had been a good start to rebuilding what was left of our broken relationship. That night, for the first time since he'd learned of my past, Fred had pulled me to him to spoon into our favorite sleep position. As I had cuddled in his arms, a feeling of warmth enveloped me. Yes, there was hope.

The morning was getting past me. After my call from Lizzie yesterday afternoon, I'd spent a little more time this morning praying about that son of hers who'd apparently come home to relive his boyhood. My extended prayers had gotten me a bit behind on my morning chores.

As I rose from the dark blue padded chair perched by the side of the bed, an old Sunday school song, "I've Got Peace Like a River," hummed through me. I stopped and pulled up the light yellow bedspread covered in blue roses and tucked it around the pillows. With the nights turning colder, it was time to pull out the pink flannel blanket I kept in the chest at the end of the bed. The chest was topped with one of my many baby dolls, Joe-Joe, who looked so adorable dressed in blue pj's as he curled into sleep with his hands tucked under his cheeks. "Sorry to disturb you, little one," I said as I carefully lifted him and moved him to the edge of the bed.

I turned to dig into the wooden chest; the scent of cedar tickled my nose. My hand touched a box buried deep inside. I pulled out the blankets and set them next to the doll, then reached back for the box. Carefully, I pulled it out and stared. Thirty-five years earlier I had scrawled the words *feminine napkins* across the lid and tucked it into the bottom of my old hope chest. The label had been my only defense from Fred's prying eyes. It was a ruse that so far had worked well. Even I hadn't cracked open the box in decades.

My hands trembled. Dare I disturb the past?

I looked at my dog, a king kong bichon, who shadowed my every step. "What do you think, Chucky?" I asked.

Chucky simply wagged his tail and followed me to the living room, where I nestled into my recliner, still caressing the box. I reached up and clicked on the floor lamp that hovered above my chair while Chucky stretched and curled onto his dog blanket.

With trembling fingers, I carefully untied the twine, then lifted the yellowed lid.

My past swam before my watering eyes.

I reached into the box and pulled out two white crocheted baby booties. These were the shoes I had crocheted for baby David. The ones he never wore.

Gently, I placed them on my lap and reached for a large sealed manila envelope simply labeled "J J," my personal code for "Joseph Jewel."

I tore it open, and the contents spilled onto my lap. Our gold wedding bands hit the floor and rolled toward Chucky. He raised his sleepy head and blinked.

"Good dog," I said, reaching to give him a pat as I scooped up my past. The process caused the letters on my lap to slide to the floor. I pulled at the recliner's side lever and kicked down the leg stand and stood up. Gathering my lost treasures, I took them to the kitchen table, where I carefully arranged the letters into two piles: Joseph's letters to me and my letters to Joseph, which had somehow been returned to me by the United States Army following Joe's death before I left L.A.

I pulled out a piece of plain white stationery from an envelope addressed to Mrs. Vonnie Jewel.

Dear Vonnie,

What I would give to be back on our honeymoon at the Boulderado Hotel. I often picture you as you slept entwined in my arms. It's as if I can still feel your silky, golden hair. I remember how I gently stroked it as I kissed you awake. Your smile invited me to continue the ecstasy of our lovemaking.

I wonder, of the passionate moments we shared, which was the moment that saw the creation of new life, the life of our now hidden child?

I wish I could see you as our baby grows in your womb.

Though I can imagine it.

It is that picture of you, of the two of you, that I carry in my heart as I turn my face to this terrible war.

My love, you are in my every waking thought. Someday Vietnam will be behind us. How I long for the moment where once again we will lie entwined in passion—

The ring of the phone shrilled from the wall. I stood up abruptly, almost knocking down my chair. I reached for the receiver, breathless.

"Hello?"

"Vonnie, is that you?"

"Yes."

"Are you okay?"

I tried to steady my voice. "Donna? Yes, dear. I was just . . . just carrying a load of laundry up those basement stairs."

"It sounds as if you've been crying."

My hand reached up to wipe the dampness from my cheeks. "No, dear, just winded is all."

I looked up at the gold and white clock on my pale yellow kitchen wall. Was it noon already? Fred had promised to come home on his lunch break. I heard an engine and looked past the tumbling stained glass babies that hung in my kitchen window. "It's Fred!"

"Home for lunch?"

"Yes." I turned on the oven, then opened the refrigerator and pulled out my leftover upside-down hamburger casserole. When I set the dish next to the oven, I saw Joe's letters still on the kitchen table. "Oh dear."

"Sounds like this is a bad time. Let me call you later. I mainly just wanted to confirm that the potluck is next Saturday."

I stuffed the booties and gold rings into my apron pocket, then swooped up a handful of love letters and stuffed them into the box.

I interrupted. "Yes, dear. Can I call you back?"

"Yes and—"

"Bye now." I hung up as Fred walked up the front steps and stopped to check the mail in the box outside the front door. I ran to the bedroom and dumped my past into the cedar chest. I slammed the lid shut just as Fred stepped into the bedroom.

"There you are!" He gave me a peck on the cheek. "What's for lunch?"

I turned and gave him a hug. Out of the corner of my eye, I saw a fallen letter lying on the rug in front of the bed. In my mad dash, it must have fluttered from the box.

While still locked in my hug, I slid the letter beneath the bed with my foot.

"Frisky today, are we?" Fred said as he gave me a more serious kiss.

"Not now, dear, I've got to put our lunch in the oven."

He followed me out of the bedroom. I scurried to the kitchen while he walked over to the recliner. "I think I'll stretch out for a moment and watch the news."

"Sounds good," I said as I set the casserole in the oven. "Lunch will be ready in ten minutes."

"Have you seen the remote?" he asked.

"Try my chair." I turned to see him stretched out in my recliner, reaching down beneath the cushions. "What's this?" he asked as he pulled out one of my old letters to Joe.

"Oh, I . . ." I ran to his side to retrieve the envelope before he could open it.

I was too late. "This is your handwriting, Von." He began to read aloud, "To my dearest Joe."

He stopped and looked up at me. I froze but managed to stammer, "Dear, let me take that." He continued to read.

I felt the baby move today, and I was so filled with joy that I wept. How I love carrying your child.

Life with your family in L.A. has been rich and wonderful. Did you know your mother taught me how to make tamales with little Nina's help? Oh how that sister of yours misses you. But we all miss you, me especially, and especially when I crawl into my bed at night. Sometimes, I bunch up the pillows and pretend you're next to me, holding me tight.

Oh Joe, I've never felt so passionate and alive until you. To remember the sweetness of your touch makes me long to lie with you, to feel the warmth of your strong body, to feel your kisses along my neck, to—

Fred stopped reading. His face registered shock.

"Fred," I pleaded, "give me the letter."

As he was too stunned to protest, I easily pulled it from his fingertips.

He looked up at me, his eyes glistening. "How can this be? Vonnie, I was there for you. I was always there. You and I were high school sweethearts, remember? When you went to college, I was at home, waiting for you. I never dreamed you'd found passion in the arms of another man, much less carried his baby."

"Fred, I . . . I'm so sorry. I . . ."

"Suddenly, this seems so real. You were in love with another man."

I knelt down and reached for Fred's hand. He pulled it away.

"Vonnie, I thought I knew you. You were the love of my life; I thought I was the love of yours. But now I see, compared to your memories of Joe, I'm only a distant second."

I stood up and walked back to the kitchen and looked out the window. I turned. "Fred, I'm sorry. I'm sorry you saw that. Yes, I loved Joe. Yes, he was my husband, for three whole days before he left for Vietnam. But as you say, that was the past. Joe is gone. You've been my husband for thirty-five years. How can that compare?"

Fred leveled the recliner down and stood up. "After reading those words you wrote, I can see Joe is not gone."

"But Fred—"

"Joe is still alive and living in your heart. You are in love with another man."

With that, Fred grabbed the keys to the truck and left. I felt my shoulders quake as I stood at the window, watching his Ford pickup pull out of the driveway. The hope I felt completely vanished, and I gave in to anguish for both my marriage and the husband I had lost.

The phone rang again.

"Hello?" I said as I wiped the tears from my eyes.

"Vonnie, now I know something's wrong. You are crying."

"Fred and I had a fight."

"Over David Harris? Then Fred knows?"

"Knows what, dear?"

"That David's coming to live in Summit View. He told you, right?"

I sat down hard and shook my head no. But I said, "Yes. When did he tell you?"

"In an email yesterday morning."

"Okay."

"Vonnie? You don't sound good. I'll be there in a minute."

"I'll be waiting, dear."

I didn't hear Donna's knock. When she found me, I was sitting on the floor next to my cedar chest, holding baby Joe-Joe tight.

"Vonnie! Don't you have a smoke alarm? Smoke was pouring from your oven. I'm afraid your lunch is—" She knelt down beside me. "Aw, Vonnie, here, give me the doll." She gently tugged it from my grasp and laid the baby on the foot of the bed.

That's when I finally looked at her. She was wearing her favorite black sweats instead of her deputy's uniform. "You must be off today," I murmured.

She looked worried. "Do you want me to call Fred?"

I shook my head no as she stood up and got a couple of tissues from the dresser and handed them to me. She sat back on the floor next to me just as if we always sat on the floor of my bedroom. "What happened?"

At first I couldn't speak. I managed to whisper, "Fred saw my letter to Joe."

Donna looked around. "What letter?"

I pulled it from my apron pocket. As Donna read it, her face blanched. "Oh my" was all she said before looking back at me. "I take it Fred didn't handle it well."

I squeezed my eyes tight against the memory of the expression of betrayal on his face. "How could he? I hurt him."

Donna placed her arm around me, and I leaned into her, dabbing my eyes with a tissue.

"I loved Joe."

"I know."

"I love Fred too."

"Of course." Donna turned to face me. "But Vonnie, why did you keep the letter?"

At last I said, "I've kept them all. How could I throw them away? They don't just represent an old fling, Donna. They represent a man's life."

"There are others?"

"In the chest."

Donna lifted the chest's lid. The old box sat on top of the blankets, betraying its contents as letters jutted at odd angles from the closed lid. She opened it and stared. "Did Fred see these too?"

"No, thank God."

"May I?"

I nodded as Donna opened an envelope and read one of Joe's letters to me. Her eyes wide, she looked up, wanting to ask a question she couldn't voice.

I twisted my wedding band once around my finger. "I know what you're thinking, Donna. But Joe and I were husband and wife. We were in love."

She nodded and put the letters back into the box before placing my time capsule into the chest. She turned to me. "I guess I just never . . . I mean, I know you had a son together, but it's difficult to . . . Here, let me help you up."

I leaned over to push off on the chest, and I saw the fallen letter under the bed. As I reached to retrieve it I noticed it felt thinner than the others. When I got to my feet, I saw that the handwritten scrawl on the envelope addressed to "My daughter Vonnie" was nothing like my mother's neat penmanship.

I carefully unfolded the note . . .

My Daughter,

My heart is broken. Your mother called and tell me Joe's baby is dead. I call the nurse, and she say, "The baby is lost."

Such terrible news.

I come to your bedside, but your mother told me to go home. How could I leave you? I wait till your mother found me outside your room. She so very angry. She say I not wanted. She say you go back to Colorado and that I not to write or call you. She say for me to bring your suitcase to hospital. She say you leave tonight on the airplane and that I not say good-bye.

My heart is heavy. Joe is gone. The baby is gone. Soon you too are gone. Today, I pack your suitcase. I send your letters and Joe's letters in the pockets of your coat. Maybe your mother never find them.

Vonnie, please come home. I miss you with my whole heart.

Love,

Your Maria

Beneath the closing, I read, "Vonnie, please come home to us. We miss you. Your sister, Nina."

I covered my eyes with my hand. I was suddenly transported to another place and time, to Maria's tiny white clapboard home in L.A. Though my own mother had sent me packing at the news that I not only married a Mexican American but also that I carried his child, Joe's mother, Maria Jewel, had swung wide her doors.

"You are my Joe's wife. Now you are my daughter," she'd said.

Joe's little sister, Nina, who was all of ten, became a special friend to me, helping me learn to cook the Mexican dishes. I helped her with her spelling words, and she joined me on long walks in the nearby park.

One sunny Saturday morning, as we perched on the swing set, enjoying the breeze we made as we rocked to and fro, she asked me, "Vonnie, why did you fall in love with Joe?"

I kicked up my feet and glided for a moment. When I stopped I turned to her. "He fell in love with me first. When I saw the love in his eyes, how could I help but fall in love with him? I mean, who could resist those big brown eyes of his?"

Nina giggled and pushed off in her swing, long black braids soaring behind her. She called back over her shoulder, "Did you know about our family?"

I stopped and watched her sail through the air. When she returned to earth, she dragged her well-worn Keds on the ground so that she came to a full stop. I turned to her. "Not at first, Nina, but when he told me, I fell in love all over again—with all of you."

Nina pushed her too-long bangs from her eyes. "And we are in love with you, especially Mama."

It was true. Maria and I had instantly bonded. Our deepening friendship somehow connected us to Joe. She spent hours telling me about his childhood and the happier times before Joe's father was killed in a terrible car crash with a drunk driver.

I, in turn, described how Joe and I had met in the school cafeteria, our long walks at sunset overlooking the mountains, and our Boulder wedding. I told her of the happiness of my childhood growing up in the Colorado Rockies.

I can picture her now, tiny and plump, sitting at her kitchen table as she stuffed her chilies with cheese. She was dressed in a purple housedress with her soft black curls pulled into a ponytail. "You are such a brave girl to ski down a mountain. No wonder my Joe married you. You will be a good mama to the children."

I laughed. "I should teach you, Maria! Then we could ski down the mountain together with sticks tied to our feet."

"What ideas you have!" Maria said, waving her hand as if to brush away the mental image I'd created.

"Hey, don't forget me! I'll tie sticks to my feet too!" Nina said.

We laughed at the thought of the three of us tumbling down a snowy mountain. But our laughter turned to sad smiles when I added, "Of course, Nina. We'll bring you, the baby, and Joe too."

Our eyes met in silence as we thought of our dear Joe, so far away from home.

I'd tried to be brave. I said, "The time will pass quickly. Maybe we'll all spend next Christmas in Colorado."

One day, when we were dicing onions and peppers in Maria's yellow kitchen bright with geraniums, she said, "Vonnie, how glad I am you are Joe's wife. We miss him while he is in Vietnam, but he left us you." She patted my belly with her brown hand and smiled at me. "And soon the baby."

Had it really been over three and a half decades since that moment in time? I sat on the edge of the chest and covered my face with my hands. "Maria, Nina!" I sobbed, suddenly homesick for L.A.

Donna took the letter and read it. She looked at me. "From Joseph's mother and sister?"

I nodded.

"Did you ever call them?"

"No. I wanted to, and I think I would have if I had found this note. But Mother convinced me it would be too hard for them to hear my voice. It would make them miss Joe all that much more."

"Where is Maria now?" Donna asked.

"If she's still living, I suppose she's in L.A."

"Do you have her old number?"

I stood and walked out of the bedroom to the kitchen. I noticed that Donna had put my blackened hamburger casserole in the sink and opened a window. I reached into the desk drawer and pulled out my ancient address book stuffed with yellowed papers. I uncoiled the rubber bands that held it together and flipped to the *J*.

"Jayne . . . Jacob . . . Jerrod . . . Jewel. There it is."

Donna picked up the phone.

"What are you doing?" I asked.

"I'm calling the number. Unless they've moved, it should be the same as long as we dial the area code. Don't you think it's about time Maria knows her grandson is alive?"

"Surely, Maria is no longer there—".

Donna interrupted. "Hello? Maria Jewel, please . . . To whom am I speaking? . . . Nina Gonzales? . . . Maria's daughter?"

Donna put her hand over the receiver and looked at me and smiled. "We found her." She took her hand off the receiver. "Yes, well, actually, I'm calling for a friend. Vonnie . . . Yes, Joe's wife. Do you want to talk to her?"

As I shook my head no, Donna extended the phone toward me. "Vonnie, it's Nina. I'm afraid the past wants to speak to the present."

I pulled up a kitchen chair and put the phone to my ear. "Nina? Is that really you?"

She sounded as if she were in the next room. I could hear the sound of children in the background. "Vonnie? I can't believe it. Why didn't you call before today?"

"I wanted to, so many times. But after so much time had gone by, I figured I was forgotten."

"Forgotten? No, Vonnie, Mama talked about you often. She'd say, 'Nina, I pray especially hard today. Maybe today will be the day Vonnie calls.'"

A gasp escaped from my lips. "I . . . I don't know what to say."

"Say that you will come back, Vonnie."

"To L.A?"

"Mama is in the hospital. I just came home to get a few things before going back. She needs to see you."

"Nina, what happened?"

"It's her heart. After all these years, her broken heart has finally caught up with her. The doctors say she may not live through the week."

"Oh no!"

"Vonnie, please. It would mean so much to Mama . . . We need you."

"I . . . I won't come alone."

"Yes, bring your family. We'd like to meet your husband and the kids. Of course, I'm assuming you married again."

"Nina. The baby—"

"I know . . . If only Joe's baby could have lived. That would have been such a comfort."

"But . . ." I lowered my voice. "But he did live."

There was a long silence on the other end of the line. "What are you talking about, Vonnie?"

"Nina, that's the reason I called. I've only learned the truth myself. Joe's baby is alive." I started to weep. "Nina, did you hear? All this time. Joe's baby is alive!"

7

Young Girl, Get Outta My Mind

Clay had just finished a second cup of coffee with his High Country burger when Eleana Bertrill came in for her shift at the café. She was young—too young for Clay—but she smiled at him every afternoon as though she wasn't fully aware of their age difference.

Clay figured her to be no more than nineteen or twenty. She'd grown up in Summit View; he'd gone to school with her parents way back when. Though they were older than him, he remembered them well, and he wondered how they might feel if they knew how their little girl liked to flirt with the regulars at Higher Grounds.

As soon as she spotted him she winked, then reached for the green bib apron Sally had her employees wear. Each one had a white-stitched view of the Summit View mountains on the top left corner with the name of the café arched above them.

"Hi, Clay," she said, walking past the knotty pine tables and chairs already filled with customers. "Can I get you another cup of coffee?" She dipped her head into the hole of the apron, then pulled the waist strings behind her back and began tying them into a bow.

Clay shook his head. "Nah, I think I'm good to go."

"Have you tried the caramel lattes we just starting making?" She licked her lips. "They're out of this world dee-lish."

He shook his head. "I'm not really a latte kinda guy."

Eleana looked out the window where his perfect viewpoint of the town lay on the other side. "It sure is gray out there. Bet we'll see a lot of snow soon. Me, personally, I can't wait. Good skiing weather, right?"

"Well, I'm not a skiing kinda guy either," he said.

As best Clay could tell, she looked genuinely disappointed.

"Eleana," Sally called out. "That's not your station."

Eleana beamed a look of innocence, then winked at Clay once more. "I'll see you around," she said.

Clay nodded, then twisted his body a bit to watch her walk back toward the extensive glass counters filled with Sally's delectable goodies. When he returned to his usual position, he caught the tail end of Donna's Bronco as it passed by.

He jumped up so fast his chair toppled to the floor and landed with a crash. He reached for his black leather jacket—folded and tossed over the chair next to him—stepping over the fallen chair and skipping to keep from tripping. He knew he looked foolish, but he didn't care. If he hurried, he could catch her.

He cussed himself all the way out to his old blue jeep parked in a nearby parking lot. If he hadn't been checking out the view on Eleana, he would have easily been able to catch Donna.

It was her day off . . . which meant it was a good time to check up on her. He slid into his jeep and spun out of the parking lot, turning left to follow Donna's trail. It took him a few minutes—with the amount of pedestrians Summit View had, it didn't pay to speed—but he finally saw her as she made a left turn.

He flipped his signal, then slowed down. Wherever she was going, he didn't want her catching him in his chase.

Minutes later he saw her pulling into the Westbrook neighborhood. He rolled to a stop, waited an appropriate amount of time, then continued on, parking a few houses down.

He had a plan. When she came out, he'd ease out into the street, feign shock at seeing her, and ask her to join him for a cup of coffee or a slice of Sally's blueberry cheesecake. He'd tell her he had some things to talk over with her. She'd bite for that, and he knew it.

In spite of the cold in the air, he felt himself beginning to sweat. What gossip would he use for bait?

He jumped when his cell phone vibrated in his shirt pocket. He reached for it, saw that it was his editor, then flipped open its top. "Whitefield," he said.

"Clay . . . drop whatever you're doing and get to the office. I've got a story I want you to follow up on, and I need you to do it pronto."

Clay gazed through the windshield at the Bronco parked ahead of him. "Can't you get someone else?"

"Who would you suggest? You're it, Whitefield. I'll give you ten minutes to get here or you're fired."

Clay slammed his cell phone shut. Donna would have to wait till another time.

Goldie

Chicken Casserole

2 small chickens
2 cans cream of mushroom soup
½ can water
(1) 8-oz carton sour cream
1 stack of Ritz crackers
½ ts poppy seeds
1 stick melted margarine

(over)

8

Sticky Situation

"Good morning. Chris Lowe's office. This is Goldie, how may I help you?" I took a deep breath and repeated myself, this time putting the emphasis away from the word *good* and more on *help*. After all, this was a law office. For the caller it may not be a good day at all. "Good morning. Chris Lowe's office. This is Goldie, how may I help you?" And then once more for good measure, again changing emphasis. "Good morning. Chris Lowe's office. This is Goldie, how may I help you?"

After nearly a month of working for Chris Lowe, attorney at law, today was the day I'd be left alone to answer the phones without Chris's daughter's help. I had practiced all evening the night before. I even blurted out my little spiel during dinner.

"What'd you say?" my daughter, Olivia, asked from her end of the dining room table.

Her husband, Tony, looked up from his plate of baked chicken casserole. His eyes held merriment. "I think she just answered the phone at Mr. Lowe's office."

I frowned. "I'm sorry. Tomorrow I answer the phones for the first time alone." I raked my fingers through the curls of red hair that seemed to be graying by the minute.

"Mom, they're just phones. You've been answering phones since you were a child." She arched a brow. "I think you can handle this."

I shook my head at the very thought of finally being alone at the administrative desk of Chris's law practice. Jenna Lowe was going out of town with her mother, Carrie, as they prepared for Jenna's departure to college in a month and a half. "I may have been answering the phone since I was a child, but this is the first time in many a year that I've done so professionally." I reached for my mug of hot tea and took a sip. It had turned tepid in the time since I'd placed it on the table. "I just want to do a good job. Jenna answers 'Chris Lowe's office,' but I want to do something a little more . . . professional. After all, Jenna is his daughter. She could answer with peanut butter in her mouth, and he wouldn't complain. Me? I'm a charity case." I set the mug down and picked up my fork, mainly for something to do. I'd hardly touched a bite of food since we sat down for dinner.

"You are most certainly not a charity case, Mom."

I nodded my head as though I agreed with her, but truth be told, I am. A month ago I'd walked into his office hoping for advice concerning my recent separation from my husband, Jack. "Coach Dippel" to the students at the high school and "Dad" to my daughter . . . and even more importantly, "Grandpa Jack" to our grandson, Brook. My shoulders slumped at the thought of it all.

Chris Lowe, in his graciousness, had offered me a job on the spot.

I'd hoped to talk about alimony—fellow Potlucker Lisa Leann Lambert had insisted upon it—but I suppose a job, in the end, is better. It has certainly made me stronger. Being married to Jack nearly drained me dry of all the strength I'd ever possessed.

Jack Dippel is a runaround.

Of course, I've always known it. Well, not always. But since we'd been married about a year or so . . . and he began to shower me with expensive gifts, like his father had given his mother every time he'd had an affair. Like Father Dippel, Jack had managed to keep his extracurricular activities and interests away from Summit View. Until Charlene Hopefield, that is.

Charlene is both the high school Spanish teacher and a floozy. She's also minus one boyfriend. Since my unexpected departure from the home we'd shared for all these years, Jack has dropped Charlene like yesterday's garbage and has practically kissed the ground I walk on ever since.

Not that he's getting anywhere with me. I'm going to stand firm no matter what. Either Jack Dippel is getting help for his apparent addictions or I'm getting myself a divorce and moving on with my life.

I arrived at work fifteen minutes early, as is my habit, entering through the door leading out to the alley. I hung my coat on a chrome coat tree in the employee break room of Chris's law office, which is upstairs from the Alpine Card Shop, and began making coffee. While it brewed, I ran downstairs to the sidewalk running along the front of the building in order to retrieve the Denver newspaper Chris had delivered to the office.

Back inside, I moved past tables of gift items and the displayed stacks of Hallmark cards divided by category. Because the card shop doesn't open until 10:00, and Chris's office officially comes alive at 9:00, I was alone in the building. Not a single light on. It was, somehow, comforting. There is a peace in the early morning blues and grays that I enjoy spending in solitude.

Sadly, that time had to come to an end. As I made my way up the staircase leading to the office, I flipped on the light, then did the same as I entered the main room of our offices and welcomed a new workday.

The aroma of coffee greeted me. I laid the newspaper on my desk, walked into the break room, and poured two cups of coffee, preparing the first as Chris preferred his and the second as I preferred mine. I then took both cups to my desk, where I deposited mine, and picked up the paper and stepped into the large office at the end of the hall.

There, I turned on Chris's computer, laid his paper out neatly in the center of his desk, and placed the steaming cup of coffee next to it.

By the time I reached my office, I heard Chris coming in the back door.

"Morning, Goldie," he greeted me, sight unseen.

"Good morning. Your coffee and paper are on your desk."

Chris walked into the front office, his overcoat slung over his arm and a briefcase dangling from one hand. "Here, let me take your coat," I said, bustling toward him.

Chris smiled at me, handing his coat over. "Ready for your first day at the desk without Jenna?"

I took the coat and squared my shoulders. "I'm ready." My brow shot up. "Did Carrie and Jenna get off okay?"

Chris moved toward his office. "Bright and early this morning," he answered without looking back. "Give me about a half hour, and then we'll go over my schedule for the day."

"Yes, sir," I said, reverting to my Southern upbringing of referring to those in superior positions as "sir" and "ma'am."

I grew up in one of the most rural sections of Dixie: Alma, Georgia. I'd still be living there today had it not been for our high school's senior trip to Washington, D.C., where I met Jack Dippel. Met him, fell madly in love with him, and then married him a few years later after a long-distance relationship that sappy love novels are made of.

I shuddered, then took Chris's coat into the break room to hang on the coatrack. Moments later, I was back at my desk, switching on my computer and giving the phone set a "cautionary eye," wondering who the first caller would be.

"Good morning," I whispered to it. "Chris Lowe's office. This is Goldie, how may I help you?"

Okay, Lord. We can do this. Yes, sir, we can.

"Good morning, Chris Lowe's office. This is Goldie, how may I help you?" I answered my first call of the day at a little after 9:30. The emphasis was placed on none of the words but rather on keeping my tone professional and kind.

"Hi, Mom."

It was Olivia.

"Olivia? What's wrong?"

I could hear Olivia's sweet smile through the phone line. "Nothing. I just knew you were nervous about answering the phone, so I thought I'd call as soon as I had a minute and let you practice. How's it going?"

I smiled. "It's going. So far, everything that Jenna taught me is making me more competent by the minute. She's a smart girl. I wish I'd gone to college like she's doing. Maybe I wouldn't be in my fifties working for the first time in goodness knows how long, sweating over a silly telephone."

"You'll do just fine. You always do. I won't keep you. Just wanted you to know I was thinking about you."

"Thank you, my sweet thing. I'll see you after 5:00."

"Bye, Mom."

I returned the handset to the phone and turned back to a stack of invoices to be mailed. I stamped the signature space of each one with CHRIS LOWE, ATTORNEY AT LAW, then folded them and placed them in their corresponding envelopes. With each stamp-fold-stuff I felt more and more like a new woman. A liberated woman. A businesswoman. A woman in charge of her own destiny!

The phone rang, and I jumped. "Good morning—"

Before I could recite my greeting, Jack's voice interrupted. "Goldie."

I hunched over my desk. "Jack," I hissed. "I've asked you not to call me at work."

"Goldie, listen to me. Let's have lunch together today. Okay, baby? Just one hour of your time, that's all I'm asking for."

I pursed my lips. "I've already made lunch plans for today, thank you."

"With whom?" he stormed.

"Jack," I said, hunching even closer to the top of the desk. "I refuse to be intimidated."

"Now you listen to me, woman. This has gone on long enough. I've done what's right. I've ended the . . . uh . . . relationship with Charlene."

"Good-bye, Jack. I'm working and cannot be disturbed."

I returned the handset, my hand quivering, and nearly knocked the entire phone unit off the side of the desk. "Get a grip," I said to myself, teeth clenched. I pulled my right hand into my left and clasped it. It didn't help the pounding in my heart, though. I took in a deep breath, then let it out ever so slowly. I did it again and again until I felt myself returning to normal.

"Goldie?"

I jumped a near mile. "Chris!"

"You okay?"

"Yes. Yes." My bottom lip quivered, giving me away. "That was Jack on the phone. He wanted to have lunch."

Chris nodded, staring hard at me, waiting I suppose for me either to have a good old-fashioned hissy fit or to say something brave and strong. I did neither.

He discreetly cleared his throat. "I'm expecting an old friend of mine from law school today. Van Lauer. We're going to have an early lunch and then head over to Loveland Pass to try to get some early skiing in this afternoon." Chris pointed toward his office with his thumb. "He just called my private line. Said he's going to be in town for a few weeks for a much-needed vacation and a little private work." Chris seemed genuinely excited. "It'll be good to have my old friend in town. Could you do me a favor and cancel the two or three appointments I have this afternoon?"

"Certainly."

Chris smiled at me. "Tell you what. Why don't you take the rest of the day off? After Van gets here, I mean."

"I'm having lunch with Lizzie," I said, as though that complicated matters.

Chris placed his hands on his hips. "Lizzie? She's not working at the high school today?"

"She had a dentist appointment so she took the day off. We thought we'd have lunch. Get caught up."

"Ah," he said, then turned to go back to his office. My eyes scanned the room, darting about like a ping-pong ball. Why had I felt the need to tell Chris that I had a lunch date with Lizzie? Or that she had a dental appointment?

"Get a grip," I said again as I returned to my work.

At exactly 11:00 the front door swung open. I looked up from the keyboard of my computer, where I'd been typing the letters Chris had dictated into a tape recorder the afternoon before, and pulled the earphone from my ears. "Good morn—"

I stopped short. My eyes scaled upward, taking in what had to be all six feet, six inches of one of the most handsome men I've ever laid eyes on.

And that includes Jack Dippel, darn his hide.

I swallowed. "Excuse me. Good morning." I pressed my fingertips lightly against the hollow of my throat. "I must have swallowed wrong."

Tall, Dark, and Gorgeous was peeling away his overcoat as he spoke. "You must be Goldie. You'd have to be with such pretty red hair," he said, his crystal blue eyes twinkling against deeply tanned skin.

"I am. And you are Mr. Lauer?"

He extended his hand to me, and I took it. It was warm and soft, and, God as my witness, I noticed immediately that his nails were buffed to a shine.

"Van," he said, looking me straight in the eye. "Please call me Van."

I met Lizzie at Higher Grounds Café a few minutes after noon. The restaurant was nearly filled already, what with the downtown working crowd finding their way there for lunch.

Naturally, Clay Whitefield was sitting in his usual spot, front and center where he had a clear view of the people coming and going, both on the sidewalk in front of the café and on the street just beyond. He spoke his hellos before we had a chance to greet him.

"Mrs. Dippel, Mrs. Prattle."

"Clay," we both said in unison. I noticed he had a small notebook spread out next to his plate of tuna salad sandwich, chips, and pickle. On it, what appeared to be a list of items, crossed out.

Clay can be a strange one at times. He's a nice enough boy, but . . . strange.

"Don't mind my asking, Clay, but do you ever leave this place? I mean, other than to go home or to make a quick trip to the newspaper office?" I asked.

Clay chuckled good-naturedly. "I can't think of a better place to get the news for the newspaper, can you? There's not a thing that goes on in this town that doesn't somehow get talked about in here."

"Here and the Sew and Stitch," I said, speaking of Dora Watkins's craft shop. If you ever need craft supplies or just a good dose of gossip, the Sew and Stitch is the place to go.

"I have to admit you've got a point," Clay answered. "But for the life of me I'd have to say I'd stand out like a sore thumb in a ladies craft shop."

Lizzie and I laughed, Lizzie patted Clay on the shoulder, and then we sat at a table in the center of the room, a few feet behind Clay, with me sitting with a clear view of his back. Within minutes, one of Sally's new servers—Eleana, according to her name tag—was standing over us, asking what we'd like to drink. We both said, "Water with lemon."

As soon as Eleana, a pretty young woman with thick auburn hair that curled unabashedly in a ponytail, walked away, we opened the menus she'd left for us, though I daresay we both knew the menu at Higher Grounds as well as we knew the ingredients in our own pantries. "Know what you want?" I asked Lizzie.

"I'll probably get the same thing I always get," Lizzie answered, then looked up at me. "Do you think we're becoming creatures of habit, Goldie?"

I shook my head. "No. Not me, anyway. Goodness, my actions in the past month have proven that."

Lizzie frowned. "Are you doing okay?"

71

"I'm doing well. I really am . . . and I'm not just saying that." I glanced down at the menu. "So what do you say? Let's shake things up a bit and order something we don't usually order."

"Let's do it," Lizzie agreed.

And we did. We ordered chicken potpie and then got really crazy and said, "And apple pie for dessert. With ice cream."

While we waited, I grabbed the opportunity to ask her about the latest in her life. "So, what's new with you?"

Lizzie sighed. "Apparently, you haven't heard."

I leaned forward, and in doing so, immediately noted that Clay appeared to lean backward a bit. Almost like he was stretching . . . but not really. I cocked a brow and put my finger up to my pursed lips. "Shhh," I mimed.

Lizzie gave me a confused look.

"Clay," I mouthed, then crooked my finger in a "come closer to me" gesture, which she did.

Elbows on the table and shoulders hunched, she lowered her voice as she leaned closer to me. "Tim came home."

I drew back a few inches, then leaned back in. "What do you mean, 'came home'?"

"He and Samantha have separated."

My shoulders drooped. "Oh, Lizzie."

Lizzie took a sip of her water. "I know," she said, then reached for the lemon wedge and squeezed it into the icy water. "I could just cry." She shrugged a shoulder. "Well, I have cried. I've cried buckets."

"What happened? If you don't mind my asking."

"You'd hear about it at the next meeting, anyway," she said. "I've already called Vonnie."

"Vonnie?"

Lizzie pinked. "I would have called you too, but you have enough on your plate without worrying about me."

I have to admit I felt a bit jealous. After all, didn't Vonnie have a plateful too? "I always have room on my plate for you, Lizzie. My goodness. If it weren't for the advice Samuel gave me after my separation from Jack . . . well, I don't know what I would have done. He's been an absolute gem, your husband, helping me with the little things like opening my own account . . ."

"Samuel is a good man."

"Did you call anyone else? I mean, of the girls?"

"No. I'm not really ready to talk about it yet, though Tim's sure to be seen around town soon enough. He's quit his job and now says he'll be getting a job soon."

"A job? He's come home for good?" I looked over Lizzie's shoulder. Clay leaned forward again, I suppose having given up on eavesdropping into our conversation. I gave Lizzie a look that told her our conversation was, once again, safe. I watched her relax into her chair.

"I'm afraid so. I talked with Samantha night before last . . . the same day as Tim came home. From what Tim says, well, he can't make enough money to satisfy her. But Samantha . . . Samantha paints an entirely different picture."

I looked out the row of windows to my right, beyond the street and buildings on the other side to the mountains that rose behind our little place in the world. They rolled gracefully and were already snowcapped. It wouldn't be too long, I thought, before the out-of-state skiers dropped in like flies on honey. Thanksgiving was a week away . . . then it would be Christmas and then the new year. "Hmmm."

Lizzie looked over her shoulder. "What are you looking at?" she asked, turning back to me.

"Nothing. Just the mountains. Just thinking about the seasons in our lives and that life can change so quickly."

"That it can."

Eleana arrived with two plates of piping hot chicken potpie. "Here you go," she said, setting them on the table. "Anything else?"

"I don't think so," Lizzie answered for us. As soon as Eleana walked away, we bowed our heads for prayer, which Lizzie led. Then we picked up our forks and dug in. "So, do you have an hour before you have to get back to the office?" Lizzie asked.

"Actually, no. I have the rest of the afternoon."

Lizzie's eyes widened. "Really?"

"Chris had an old friend—a law school classmate, actually—who came into town. They're having lunch and going over to Loveland Pass."

Lizzie stopped and stared at me for a moment.

"What?" I asked. "Do I have food on my face?" I brushed at my cheeks.

"Nooo."

"Then what?"

"What was that look you just had, Goldie Dippel?"

"What look?"

"You blushed. When you spoke of Chris and his friend."

I speared at my pie; the steam rose from it, hitting me square in the face. "I did not." I looked back up at her. "Why would I blush?"

"You tell me."

I leaned over a bit. "I did not blush."

Lizzie took a sip of her water, swallowed, and then smiled a wicked smile. "Cute, huh?"

I rolled my eyes. "Like nothing you've ever seen."

"Goldie—"

I waved her away with my fork, which I had perched in midair. "Oh, don't worry so, Lizzie. I'm separated from Jack, but I'm still married to him." Then I smiled, in part so she really wouldn't worry. "But I'm not blind. So, yes. He was very cute. Very, very cute. Now, finish your lunch and tell me what you're planning to serve for Thanksgiving next week."

The last thing I really wanted to think about was Thanksgiving. I was sure that Jack hadn't yet figured out that the big day was just a little over a week away, in spite of the fact that it meant getting to eat my sweet potato soufflé and having a few days off from school. Every year the "Big Game" between Summit View and Rocky Point takes place on the Friday night after Thanksgiving. It is one of the biggest events of the school year, followed by a homecoming dance, and is something Jack and I attend together every year. We've never missed, not once, even the year he was carrying on something fierce with a woman in a nearby town who demanded his attention like none other ever had. During those months I saw Jack very little on weekend nights . . . but that one Friday night he was mine.

That was also the year I got the pretty diamond brooch shaped like a crown. "You're a real queen," he'd said to me as he presented it, to which I thought, *And you're the king of all hypocrites.*

After lunch with Lizzie, I decided to just walk around town for a while, to feel the cool air on my face, to stare into storefront windows at all the things I could now scarcely afford, and to take the time to think . . . and pray. But I found myself praying very little. Rather, I vacillated between thinking about Thanksgiving and the big game and wondering how long Van Lauer would be in town.

Then I'd scold myself for allowing my mind to go there.

Still, something inside me felt . . . tingly . . . remembering the look of him, the sound of his voice—smooth and baritone—the feel of his hand as it took mine in greeting. And his left hand, well, that was even better. His left hand had been devoid of a wedding ring or even the tan line left by one.

I stopped in front of my favorite corner gift shop and peered through the glass at the display of handcrafted jewelry, then looked up to see if Greta, the owner, might be nearby. I didn't see her, but caught my own reflection in the window.

Reaching up, I touched my hair. I wore it in the exact same way I'd worn it for years—cut around my jawline and permed for soft curls. It was so familiar it made me sick.

I frowned at the rest of my reflection. Like most women in the Colorado high country I saw little use for makeup, but now . . . I thought I looked so pale. So . . . old. Or, at the very least, so much older than I was.

What must Van have thought when he met me?

I shook my head, as if to cast the very thought aside, then glanced around the corner and down the avenue. A shingle for Marisa's Hair Salon swung over a doorway. Marisa trimmed my hair every six weeks or so, and I wondered what she'd say to a walk-in. For a shampoo and cut and coloring and a whole new style.

For the works.

As soon as I paid for my new hairdo with money I'd been saving for a new place to live, I walked as fast as my legs could carry me to the old Victorian on Main Street where Lisa Leann Lambert was setting up shop for her new bridal boutique. I opened the door to the sound of wind chimes that tingled as beautifully as anything I'd heard in a long time.

"I'll be right there," Lisa Leann called from the back.

I took a quick look around. Lisa Leann had certainly done a lot with this old fixer-upper, no doubt about that. The front room had been refurbished completely. The floors had been stripped and then polished to a shine. An antique Victorian settee with matching chairs flanked a marble-top coffee table where bridal magazines were fanned out invitingly. Massive prints were framed in gold leaf, prints of Romance-period lovers and Renaissance cherubs. The walls were wallpapered in ivory satin. The old fireplace bricks had been painted in ivory as well, and the mantel was drenched in a Victorian silk arrangement. Rose-scented candles burned at either end.

"Sorry to keep you," I heard Lisa Leann say from behind me. I spun around and watched the surprise register on her face. "My goodness! Goldie! Look at your hair." She immediately came up and began to run her fingers through the new, shorter style. "This is fabulous, girlfriend." She placed her hands on her hips. "You look ten years younger," she declared, then cocked an eyebrow. "Wanna know what would make you look even younger than that?"

"Makeup?"

She crossed her arms. "How'd you know I was going to say that?" she asked, teasing me with her eyes.

"Will you help me?" I asked, nearly choking on the words. *Lord, if Evie hears about this, I may as well drop out of the Potluck before she boots me out . . . asking Lisa Leann for anything such as this.*

"Will I help you? Will I help you? Well, darling, you just come on back to my office." She turned and was halfway out the door of the old parlor. "I'll have you fixed up so fast and with that new hairdo, well, honey, Jack Dippel won't know what hit him!"

Jack, I thought following close behind her. *Jack*.

I groaned inwardly. Jack had been the last thing on my mind.

9

Puttin' On the Ritz

Clay did a double take when he saw Goldie Dippel entering Lisa Leann's new bridal boutique. Her hair—what was it about her hair that looked so . . . different?

He pulled out his notepad and jotted a few words next to her name, which was scrawled alongside Vonnie Westbrook's. What would make a woman her age do something so . . . so . . . radical?

Women in the high country just weren't ones for putting on airs. He shook his head even as he had the thought. That is, he corrected himself, until Lisa Leann Lambert had swooped into town. He craned his neck to see what vantage point he might have through the tall windows of the boutique. Though they were hardly picture-perfect clear, it appeared that Lisa Leann was making a great to-do about Goldie's new hairstyle.

Goldie's new hairstyle . . . Clay didn't know women very well, but what he did know was that women didn't just go around doing something to beautify themselves for no apparent reason. This could mean only one thing: Goldie was on the make. Someone new had caught her attention, and she was going for it.

Well, way to go, Mrs. Dippel, he thought. *Make ole Coach sweat for once. Give him a dose of his own medicine. Make him suffer and wonder . . .*

Clay's shoulders slumped. "Like you have for Donna," he muttered, then rose from his chair and reached for his coat.

Lisa Leann

Chocolate Meringue Kisses

Ingredients:

3 large egg whites (room temperature)
1/4 Tbs. Cream of Tartar
Pinch Salt
1 Tbs. sugar
1/2 cup cocoa
1/2 Tbs. vanilla
2 Tbs. vanilla
1 cup chopped walnuts or Rice Krispies

10

Buttering Up Reporters

Imagine my surprise at the sight of Goldie standing in my new bridal boutique, her splendid red hair cut and colored. There she was, looking gloriously like a potential bride.

It's not that I was desperate or anything—my bridal shop wasn't even a month old, and we'd barely just opened.

For goodness sakes, my Henry and I were just finishing with the painting and resurfacing of this old Victorian charmer. Now I was busy ordering inventory and unpacking boxes.

But I needed to start on my marketing campaign sometime. And today looked like the day.

I could see it all, Goldie and Jack Dippel renewing their wedding vows, perched at the front of Grace Church. Goldie wearing an exquisite candlelight dress, picked out by me, of course. Her bridesmaids, the sisters of the Potluck Club, would be by her side in gold satin designer gowns.

How lovely her flowers—a huge bouquet of blushing ivory roses clasped in her manicured hands. The whole of the church would be splashed in roses tied in golden bows, all ordered and arranged by me.

This was my opportunity to do what I do best: shine. And this opportunity was hand delivered to me by Goldie's sudden new look, which of course had to be all about a man. Though, come to think of it, she never said which man, now did she? I assumed the fresh look was for Jack. But since their separation, it was possible that Goldie was on the rebound. Hmmm. That could represent a small kink, but one I would definitely work out, one way or another.

Still, the thought of it . . . a wedding in the Potluck sisterhood. My, the sound of that made my heart skip a beat. It would give me a chance to give those poor wrinkling faces some soothing creams and beauty tips, not to mention a splash of personalized color fashioned to put sparkle in their eyes.

The possibilities were just too exciting to think about. In the process of serving as Goldie's wedding consultant, I could achieve my ultimate goal, the presidency of the Potluck Club. Move over, Evangeline Benson. I'll be wielding your gavel yet.

I surveyed my beautiful new parlor. My colors were exquisite, ivory and gold with touches of pinks and sage from my lovely arrangements of silk roses and framed cherubs. Then, there was the antique oak counter Henry had just refinished and put into place the night before. It glowed in leaded beveled glass, revealing a display space already a swirl of ivory satin. Soon I'd have a few baubles to nestle there—bridal necklaces of pearls and crystal, sparkling tiaras, and silk bouquets.

The massive cabinet had been fitted with a lovely marble top that held not only my antique cash register but also a lovely silver tray covered with a batch of my fresh chocolate meringue kisses and my silver decanter filled with freshly brewed vanilla coffee. The coffee was ready to pour into my lovely collection of ivory and gold Royal Doulton teacups.

It was step one of my marketing plan.

With my shop right on Main Street, across the street from the Higher Grounds Café, I planned to become the information center of town. With my fresh-baked goods and hot coffee, I would woo those who either had access to the latest in the romance gossip or who needed my help in finding a mate. I already had my college son, Nelson, on the job, looking to set up my new matchmaking software that would help my shop become the area's dating service hot spot.

Yes, making matches is definitely one of my spiritual gifts, one I would employ on the dear citizens of Summit View, whether they knew they needed it or not.

In fact, as I looked out my front window, I spied one of my prime wedding candidates, a Mr. Clay Whitefield, Summit View's newspaper reporter, leaving the café and climbing into his rattletrap jeep. I opened the door of my shop and waved to him as he backed into the street.

Clay looked both surprised and pleased to see me in the doorway. With a quick U-turn, he was parked right in front of my store.

"Clay Whitefield," I said. "Just the man I wanted to see."

Clay climbed out of his jeep. "Lisa Leann, it looks like you're making a lot of progress with this old place."

"That's what I wanted to talk to you about," I said as I latched on to his elbow and tugged him through the beveled glass door. "I want to show you around and ask you to run a front page feature about what I've done here."

Clay let out a low whistle. "Lisa Leann, from the looks of this, I'd say you've given this town a touch of class. This is beautiful."

"Thank you, Clay. Of course, I'm not done yet. A lot of inventory has yet to arrive. But you can see that the space on the south end of the shop is set up to display a lovely selection of bridal gowns. We've got the dressing rooms set up, and I found this beautiful antique full-length mirror. Of course, you'll notice this area is filled with natural lighting, giving our brides-to-be a natural blush. Plus a natural blush is what each of my brides will receive with her complimentary makeover."

"A makeover."

"Yes, see my makeup vanity in the corner? As I am a makeup expert, I will show the brides the best way to do their makeup for their wedding day."

"Looks to me like you've already had your first client."

"My, Clay, you are one observant fellow," I said as I straightened my makeup brushes while I topped a tube of lipstick. "Yes, I just made over one of the members of the Potluck Club."

"Pray tell me, Lisa Leann, who was it?"

"You'll see my handiwork soon enough, because I'm telling you, Goldie Dippel absolutely glows."

"Goldie? Interesting. Why would she have a makeover, just after leaving Jack?"

I gave Clay a sideways look. "Clay Whitefield, just how do you know about that?"

"I'm the local news guy. I make it my business to know these kinds of things."

I gave him one of my most charming smiles. "Is that so?" I reached for my silver platter of chocolate meringue kisses. "Try one."

Clay's eyes lit up. "I've heard you're a fine cook." He took a bite of my melt-in-your-mouth meringue, an old family recipe handed down by my great-grandmother Louise Annabelle Appleton. With his mouth still full, he chuckled. "Now I've got proof."

"Have a seat and let me pour you a cup of my fresh French vanilla coffee."

"Don't mind if I do."

"And help yourself to another meringue or two or three."

Clay sat down on my fabulous gold chenille settee, and I placed the kisses and his china cup of vanilla coffee on the marble coffee table in front of him. I settled in the matching winged Victoria.

I waited till Clay had taken a sip of coffee and popped another meringue into his mouth. "So tell me about yourself. Are you seeing anyone?"

My, was that a bit of color rising in his cheeks? Clay swallowed, blinked, then smiled wryly. "I'm the one who gives the interviews around here."

I batted my eyes and smiled. "Oh, and you do a marvelous job at that. But being the proprietor of this lovely new bridal boutique, and seeing that you are one of our town's most eligible young bachelors, well, I can't help but be a bit curious."

Clay shifted uncomfortably then stared me down.

"My love life is something I absolutely do not talk about," he said with a grin. "Especially with wedding consultants."

"Oh, then, you're a man with a past. Tell me, anyone I know?"

Clay stood up and glanced at his watch. "Look at the time, and me with those deadlines."

I rose and faced him, blocking his exit. "Now, Clay, I didn't mean to scare you off. If you don't want to talk about it, I understand. Just know that I am your friend, a safe friend. I'll only bring up the subject again when you're ready to try out my new dating service."

Clay stopped looking toward the door and turned his full attention on me. "A dating service?"

"Certainly. A computerized dating service. My son is going to install it for me when he visits me from college—he goes to University of Texas, you know. He's coming in for Thanksgiving this week."

"Really."

"And I'm going to need a few volunteers to beta test it for me. Imagine, you can sign up, complimentary of course, because you are the press. A little investigative reporting about the benefits of my dating service will provide another fabulous front page story, I think."

I couldn't tell if Clay was shell-shocked or just terribly impressed with the enormity of my proffered gift.

"Why, that is one incredible idea. As a matter of fact, I'm looking for someone to write a local gossip column, or, should I say, advice for the lovelorn. You seem to have a way with words, and I think you would be perfect for the job. You could draw in your wedding advice so it would be a form of advertisement. Understand, you would pay for the privilege of seeing your name in print. Still, I think such a column could have a lot of benefits, for both you as well as for my paper."

My, the thought of it all was enough to make the blood rush to my head. "Clay. Did anyone ever tell you that you, you are a genius?"

Clay smiled in a very satisfied way. "Not nearly enough."

"Listen, I plan to have fresh-baked treats every morning here at the shop. Now, I'm not an official bakery. But to tell you the truth, my baked goods will be complimentary for people like you, people who can keep me informed, if you know what I mean."

"I know exactly what you mean. And as I too am in the information business, it would be my pleasure to stop in and see you."

The phone rang. When I picked it up, I heard the impatient voice of Deputy Donna on the other end of the line.

"Lisa Leann? I was wondering if you have some luggage I could borrow."

"Donna! Are you going on a trip?"

With my keen peripheral vision, I noticed that when Clay heard Donna's name, he took a step closer. The look in his intense brown eyes told me his secret. *Donna! Clay's got the hots for Donna!* I smiled.

Donna answered, "I'm thinking about taking off for Los Angeles with Vonnie. It seems she has some unfinished business there."

"No kidding? Los Angeles. Imagine the two of you there."

"Lisa Leann, I'm just driving past your shop."

I looked up, and sure enough, there she was in her sheriff's Bronco. I waved. Clay turned around and watched her pass.

"Don't tell me that you've got Clay Whitefield in there."

"I do. Clay just made me a little business offer."

"Oh boy. Listen, you can't say anything to him about my trip with Vonnie."

"Why not?"

"He's got his pad of paper out, right? He's writing something down about our conversation right now. Right?"

I looked up, then turned my back on Clay. "Well, Donna, yes, as a matter of fact. What's all this about?"

"Clay's been nosing around about the David Harris situation. I can't let him expose Vonnie, not yet, anyway. She's much too fragile for that."

"I see." I turned and looked back at Clay. He was a nosey one. "Don't worry, Donna, I'll take care of it. And yes, you can borrow my luggage. However, with my daughter's due date coming up, I'll need it back within a few months as I'll be heading for Texas to help her care for the new baby. But the two of you won't be gone that long, will you?"

"No, no, just a few days. Hey, appreciate it. Well, look at that. A tourist just ran the town's stoplight. Gotta run."

I hung up but could still hear Donna's siren whoop as she pulled her speeder over. I turned back to Clay. "Now, where were we?"

Clay stood with his arms folded, a smirk on his face. "Oh, was that Donna? She and I were talking earlier today. Told me she was going to see David Harris in Los Angeles with . . ." He paused for good measure and grinned all the more. "Goldie, I believe she said."

Why, that sly dog, I thought as I looked at Clay with admiration. My new friend here was on a fishing expedition and thought he was clever enough to outwit me. So help me if I didn't giggle.

Clay was immediately suspicious. "What's so funny?"

"Just that you seem to know more about the Potluck sisterhood than me."

"Well, this is a small town, and I do share a history with each of those ladies."

Now, that comment raised both my suspicions and my eyebrows. "A history? What sort of history? Like in romantic?"

Clay shook his head. "Those ladies are old enough to be my mother."

"Not Deputy Donna."

Clay turned his attention to the door, looking to make a quick exit. "No, no, no. She's like a sister. Uh, I really do have to get on that deadline. And I'm looking forward to getting your first column."

I smiled. "And my deadline is?"

"How about tonight by 5:00." Clay fished in his pocket for his business card and handed it to me. "You can email it to me. Say, about five hundred words?"

"And my cost?"

"The first one's free. Let's take this one step at a time."

I shook his hand. "Deal."

As I watched Clay pull into traffic, my phone rang again. "Lisa Leann's Weddings."

It was Donna. "You say that like you have a rotating marriage policy and several ex-husbands."

I had to laugh. "Good point. I'm still trying to find the perfect name, but that obviously isn't it. What's up?"

"I'm down the street in my Bronco, just finishing up this ticket, and I saw Clay drive off. What does he know?"

"Only that you and Goldie are about to leave for L.A. to see David Harris."

"Goldie?"

"That was his conclusion. I just didn't correct it."

She sighed. "For Pete's sake."

"Okay, Donna, I did my part, now spill the beans. What's going on with Vonnie? I thought she and Fred had worked through all the theatrics of this delicate discovery."

"Well, they had . . ."

"What happened?"

I could hear the hesitation in Donna's voice. "Don't say anything to the girls, but Fred found one of Joseph Jewel's old love letters."

"Okay, I can see why that would present a problem. But why is Vonnie heading for L.A.?"

"It's her former mother-in-law. She's on her deathbed, and no one has told her that her grandson is alive. Vonnie and I are going to give her the news and introduce her to David. We'll give a full report at our December meeting, I'm sure. But you're one of the sisters now, so I'm trusting you not to talk."

"Honey, they couldn't pry that bit out of me, even if wild Texas horses were tied to my tongue."

"Can't say that's a comforting thought," Donna said. "Just keep this quiet."

"I'm giving you my Potluck Club word of honor," I said. "And don't worry. I, Lisa Leann, will fix Clay's wagon but good."

After we hung up, I had a great idea. I walked over to my computer and turned it on and opened a Word document. I stared at the screen. Perhaps what I needed was a pseudonym for my new column. *Let's say I call it "Aunt Ellen Explains Everything"?*

Hey, I like that. My clandestine column could run with a nearby ad for the shop. My strategy would be to give my advice, anonymously, and hope that it would lead my readers to the altar, and thus, my wedding services. I typed:

AUNT ELLEN EXPLAINS EVERYTHING

Dear Aunt Ellen,

Recently when my husband was cleaning out the garage, he came across a shoe box filled with some old college love letters from my dearly departed boyfriend, who was killed in a motorcycle accident a couple of decades ago. I'd never told "Alex" about "Peter."

Now, my husband is hurt, and our marriage is crumbling.

What should I do? How can I get my marriage back together?

Signed,
Grave Letters

Now, that was a letter I knew at least two people would read with great interest. I had changed the details enough so that they would never suspect my reply was so personally directed at them. Yet this letter would pique not only their interest but the interest of the whole town.

Dear Grave Letters,

You are a woman with many secrets, which have been kept far too long. It may not seem like it, but it's good to get these things out in the open.

Remind Alex that Peter is not only dead and buried but that Peter predates your meeting and dating him.

Still, I'm guessing your old love's handwritten words are now seared into your husband's brain. There's only one way to undo the damage. Invite your husband to a letter-burning event. Hand off each of Peter's old love letters to your husband, then let your husband burn them (without reading them) to demonstrate that the past is history.

Then, it would be nice if the two of you thought about renewing your own wedding vows. Your local wedding consultant could lend a hand.

Sincerely,
Aunt Ellen

I reread my words and grinned. There, I was off to a good start. Now I had to come up with one more letter. This one I was secretly dedicating to Clay and Donna. I only hoped Clay would see himself without recognizing my intentions.

Dear Aunt Ellen,

I've secretly been in love with a woman I'll call "Mona," though I've never been able to tell her so. Any ideas on how I can let the cat out of the bag? I mean, what if I tell her I think she's the cat's meow, but she tells me to scram? Just because I think she's purr-fect for me doesn't mean she'll think I'm purr-fect for her.

What should I do?

Signed,
Fraidy Cat

Dear Fraidy Cat,

If you are going to let fear block you from finding out if the girl of your dreams could be attracted to you, you have rejected her before you even gave her a chance to embrace you. Yes, that's playing it safe, but it's lonely play. So, be a man. Take a chance. Ask "Mona" out for a date. If she says no because she's not interested, then that will be your signal to move on. Heal, then find somebody else who will love and cherish you.

Otherwise, I'm afraid you will never know the joy of walking the love of your life down the aisle of matrimony. You will live a lonely life, thinking of the possibilities instead of enjoying a wife.

Aunt Ellen

Girl, you have outdone yourself.

91

I pulled out Clay's business card and logged on to AOL, glad my hubby had already set up my computer in the back room, which was soon to be my dating agency.

I typed Clay a quick e-note.

Dear Clay,

Hope you like my Aunt Ellen pseudonym. It's probably the best way to address the real lonely heart issues of Summit View. This and a lovely print ad should suffice at this stage of my marketing plan. We'll talk soon.

Sincerely,
Lisa Leann

After I attached my document and hit send, I pulled out my list of things to do. I had more boxes to unpack, more orders to make, and I probably should wave a few more locals over to try out my chocolate meringue kisses. I pulled out the pen I had tucked behind my ear and tapped my desk. *And tomorrow's treat would be, let's see. How about my grandmother's pecan pie cookies?* With the holiday season starting next week, that recipe would be the perfect delight.

11

Can He Get a Witness?

Clay practically danced to his jeep, and he would have too, if he hadn't thought he'd look so ridiculous. As soon as his plump fanny slid across the faded leather upholstery of the driver's seat, he flipped open his pad and in bold letters wrote: Goldie Dippel—Harris's mother.

He traced the letters several times, trying to imagine the scenario. Harris was half Mexican. Mexican field hands, he'd once read somewhere or another, were quite common in Georgia, where Goldie hailed from.

Maybe she'd gotten involved with one of her father's field hands . . . if her father even had any field hands. Maybe she'd married Coach just to get away from the scandal. The possibilities were endless.

He flipped open his cell phone and dialed his editor. As soon as his editor answered, Clay said, "I've got an idea for an article about migrant workers being used and abused in the South. If you need me, I'll be at the library doing some research."

With his thumb he pressed "end," then revved up the old engine of the jeep. A quick glance out the dust- and dirt-caked windshield before he pulled out in traffic revealed that the Who-What-

When-Where-and-How of his existence was stepping back into her Bronco.

He didn't have time for that right now, though. He had bigger fish to fry. But, despite himself, he smiled. Wouldn't Donna get a kick out of knowing he'd cracked the case? She'd be mad enough to rant and rave a good ten minutes, flailing her arms about like a girl gone mad.

He couldn't wait, he just couldn't wait.

Evangeline

Mama's German Chocolate Cake

Ingredients:

1 pkg. (4 oz each) BAKER's
GERMAN's Sweet Chocolate
½ cup water
2 cups plain flour
1 tsp. soda
¼ tsp. salt
1 cup butter softened

12

Sweet and Sour Romance

I made a quick phone call to my friend Lizzie, who'd been having a tough time of late, while I thumbed through my mother's recipe book for what felt like the millionth time in three days. As soon as Lizzie answered, I leaned my narrow hip against the kitchen countertop and jumped right in to a conversation that had nothing to do with anything. The important thing for me to do was to help Lizzie take her mind off her troubles.

"Lizzie? Evie, here. Can you believe it? The week before Thanksgiving, and they're playing Christmas music in the stores and on the radio and . . . do you know what I saw on television the other evening?"

"Hello, Evie," Lizzie said with what sounded to me like a hint of humor in her voice. Lizzie is one strong lady in any storm, and this tsunami apparently was no exception.

"Hello, my friend." I stopped thumbing through Mama's recipe box.

"What did you see on television the other night?"

"Do you remember that Folgers commercial? The one they only play during the Christmas holidays?"

"Remind me."

"You know. The one where Peter comes home from wherever he's been, and the cute little girl with the blond braids is coming down the stairs—"

"Oh, yeah. That one always makes me a little weepy."

I took a deep breath, then exhaled. That was my cue. "How's Tim, Lizzie?"

"Tim is Tim. Michelle took him to work with her the other day, and he landed a job."

"At the resort?"

"Mmm."

"What's he doing there?"

"He'll be in their financial department, of course." Lizzie paused, and I stayed quiet. "He starts after Thanksgiving. I was . . . I was hoping that he wouldn't be here that long, that he would . . . you know . . . work things out with Samantha. But . . ."

"But?"

"They've only spoken once or twice, and both times it ended badly." She paused again. "Both times."

"Oh, Lizzie. I'm so sorry. Seems like it's always something, doesn't it?"

I heard a sniffle, then another sigh. So much for my "strong in any storm" theory. "What's new with you, Evie? Have you talked with Leigh?"

"I talk with Leigh every single night." Leigh, my beloved niece, had lived with me until just a few weeks ago. She'd come cross-country from her home in West Virginia for refuge and a little Aunt Evie TLC, I suppose. She'd been seven months pregnant at the time. Unmarried. And completely confused.

When she left, she was the mother of our precious Baby Faith . . . and the wife of Faith's daddy, Gary, who flew into town just in time to witness the birth and to propose marriage.

This time it was I who sighed. "No one seems to be doing things like they used to," I remarked. "But at least they're married, and she sure sounds happy."

"She's doing well then."

"Wonderful. In fact, I'm calling her right after I get off the phone with you."

"So, what are you doing for Thanksgiving? Do you want to come over here? We'll have plenty to eat. The entire clan will be here, with the exception of Samantha and the kids, of course. We'll have a houseful if you think you can stand it, and I know I couldn't enjoy myself if I thought you were alone."

I smiled so wide I'm surprised my cheeks didn't split open. "No, but thank you for the kind offer. I have plans."

"Oh?"

I blushed appropriately, in spite of the fact that not a soul was in the room—or the entire house—with me. "Vernon and I will spend the holiday together."

"Oooooh."

"Oh, stop."

"You love it, and you know you do."

I looked around my kitchen as though I were some character in a Broadway play, stalling for the sake of delivering the perfect line. "Yes. Yes, I most assuredly do." I giggled, which is just absurd. A woman my age, giggling over the attentions of a man.

But not just any man. Vernon Vesey. The love of my life. The man I'd been waiting for since I was twelve years old and he'd kissed me full on the lips at Ruth Ann McDonald's birthday party. Everything from then on would have been so perfect too, had Doreen Roberts not come along and thrown herself at him like some seventh grade floozy.

Years later Vernon and Doreen married, had Donna, and then Doreen ran off with the choir director at Grace Church, the church I've been attending since the day I was born.

For a long time, I figured Vernon deserved what he got when he married Doreen, and goodness knows Donna and I have merely tolerated each other, but the truth of the matter is, I've loved Vernon since we were pups, and Donna . . . well, I could love Donna like my own, if she'd just let me.

"Has he said the *L* word yet?" Lizzie asked.

"Oh, sure. We don't say it a lot . . . it's all so new, and our relationship is still a bit fragile, what with Donna not exactly approving and all . . ."

"She'll come around, Evie."

"We'll see, won't we?" I said. "I'd better hang up, Lizzie. I promised Vernon I'd make him one of Mama's German chocolate cakes."

"Is he coming over tonight? Taking you out?"

"No. He says it's dangerous to see each other every night . . . whatever that means."

I heard Lizzie giggle again. "You two are just too cute. Think you'll get a ring for Christmas?"

A blush began at my toes and ran up the entire length of my body before settling in my cheeks. "Lizzie," I whispered. "Wouldn't that just be something? At my age?"

The following morning, cake on a flat cake plate and cake plate in hand, I braved the freezing weather and made my way to the sheriff's office downtown, where I hoped I'd see Vernon. Of course, he could be out on one of his many important calls, and if Donna wasn't there, that pretty much meant the place would be empty except for one of the dispatchers. My shoulders slumped as I set the cake plate on the floorboard of my car's front passenger side. The dispatchers there still looked at me funny, in spite of the fact that Vernon and I had been seeing each other for the past few weeks.

I straightened. Had it been only a few weeks? In my heart it felt as though we'd been together forever.

I drove my car down my driveway and then eased the wheels toward town. The scenery around my beloved Summit View, where my daddy had been mayor before the tragic accident that claimed his and Mama's lives, was certainly changing quickly. The snows had already started, and before long we'd be seeing nothing but a blanket of white lying over our little corner of the world. Personally, I couldn't wait. It was my favorite time of year.

Minutes later I was pulling into an empty space in front of Vernon's office. As I cut the car off, I looked around to see if his car was anywhere in sight, but I didn't see it. I frowned but got out of

99

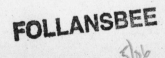

the car anyway, walked around to the passenger's side, retrieved the cake, and headed toward the front door, aware only of the crunching of snow and ice below my feet.

"Well, Evie! What do you have there?"

I spun around so quickly I almost lost my footing on the ice. The cake wobbled on the plate, and I stared in horror as it began to slip forward. I was then aware of two hands—two very masculine hands—reaching for the plate, righting it, and then holding it steady.

When I looked up, Bob Burnett was standing before me, grinning like a cat.

"Hello, Bob Burnett," I said. "Thank you for your help. I most certainly would have dropped the cake."

Bob patted my arm. "Well, now. Had it not been for me calling out to you like I did, you wouldn't have teetered there."

I could smell Bob's aftershave. It was a bit too strong, but I have to admit, it wasn't altogether offensive. Bob smiled at me again, and I noted a little twinkle in his eye.

My eyes narrowed, and I cocked a brow. Was this man coming on to me? "Well, don't worry about it."

I heard the approach of tires on the street, then a loud honking followed by a shrill, "Evie! You need to call me, girl. We need to talk!"

I turned in horror. There went Lisa Leann in her Lincoln Town Car, driver's window down and her leaning out of it, red hair blowing and her arm waving about like a porpoise in water. "Oh, good heavens," I muttered.

Beside me, Bob chuckled.

"It's not funny," I said, staring after her. "That woman may as well have been raised in a barn, the way she acts sometimes. You'd think this was a parade, and she was the grande dame."

Bob chuckled again. I suppose I should be glad to know he hasn't lost his sense of humor over the years. I turned back to him. "So, what brings you out on a Friday morning?"

"Banking day,"

I nodded, waiting for him to say something else, anything else. But Bob Burnett is a man of few words—a lot like Vernon, I suppose. "I see," I said finally.

"Speaking of banking," he said, "you know, without a wife or kids to drain my account dry, I've done pretty well for myself."

"Come again?" What was this? First Lisa Leann hanging out a window, and now Bob Burnett telling me his financial accomplishments? Had the entire world gone nuts while I was sleeping last night? I got the sinking feeling that Bob Burnett was about to ask me out on a date. Call it woman's intuition, if you will, but it was pretty strong.

"I said that I've done pretty well for myself. And, to be honest with you—"

Footsteps from behind us interrupted. I turned, happy to see whoever it was. I mean, it could have been Jack the Ripper, and I would have leaped into his arms, singing "Glory, hallelujah!" at the top of my lungs. But when I turned, I saw Donna approaching.

"Hey, Burnett," she called out. "Banking day, eh?"

"Deputy," Bob returned. "Looks like you're heading out somewhere."

It was then I noticed that she wasn't in uniform and had a tote bag in her hand. "Where are you going?"

She gave me one of her "eat dirt and die" looks. "Not that it's any of your concern, Evangeline, but what I have here is my workout clothes."

"Oh," I said.

"You look all dressed up. Where are you going?"

I had taken some extra time this morning with my choice of outfit before seeing Vernon, pulling on a new denim patchwork jacket with appliquéd autumn leaves in celebration of the upcoming holiday.

I ignored the question. Donna knew good and well where I was going. Sensing my determination not to answer, she then peered at my covered cake plate. "Looks like you've got something sweet there."

I smiled. "It's for your father."

Donna smirked. "I figured. Apparently you're unaware of his high cholesterol."

Bob chuckled again. Good heavens, that man must have one fine-tuned sense of humor. "Oh, so that's for Vernon, is it?" Bob asked. For a moment I could have sworn there was a hint of disappointment in his voice.

"Yes." I turned my gaze toward the building but kept my feet planted firmly in place. If Donna and Bob were going to keep talking, I wanted to make sure I didn't become the subject matter of their conversation.

"Hey, Donna," Bob said, turning his attention back to Donna. "I've got a question for you. Have you met the new gal down at the tavern?"

"I haven't met her exactly, but I know who you're talking about. In fact, I see her just about every day over at the café."

I broke in. "There's someone new in town?" My next thought was of Lisa Leann and how she'd swooped into town and tried to butt in on my position as president of the Potluck.

Donna nodded. "Name's Dee Dee."

"McGurk," Bob supplied the last name. "Not a bad little number."

Donna screwed up her face. "If you don't mind the washed-up type. That woman's got more lines on her face than a map," she said. "She might have been pretty once, but who can tell? Keeps her head down most of the time. I suspect she's been abused, the way she acts. Burnett, don't tell me you're interested."

Bob straightened his belt, readjusting it to his hips. "Maybe I am, maybe I'm not," he answered, winking at me. A wink that unfortunately didn't escape Donna's eagle eyes.

I decided I'd had enough of this banter. "Er, is he . . . your father . . . is he inside?"

"He is," she said, then patted her bag. "I'd best be going. Good to see you again, Burnett." She looked at me and forced a smile. "You be careful around that old lady Dee Dee. You never know what trouble she might stir up."

I hurried into the county building and headed straight for the sheriff's office, which is really just a square room with a lot of desks, filing cabinets, and a smaller office jutting off the back wall just for Vernon. Not that it's top-notch on privacy. The door is half glass, and the walls on either side are glassed from about the waistline of a normal adult on up. In a way, this is nice because it allows anyone who comes in to see straight through to the walls behind Vernon's desk, where a real man's man exhibit is displayed. Awards, plaques, framed newspaper articles, a gun rack stacked with rifles, and—Vernon's prize—a personally autographed, framed glossy photo of himself and President George W. Bush.

"W" is Vernon's hero.

As soon as I slipped into the main office, I had a clear view of Vernon sitting at his desk, looking intently at something he held in his hands. I couldn't tell what; Vernon has such stacks of papers and files on his desk, it's hard to sort one thing from another. I offered to organize it for him once, and he said if I touched a thing he'd shoot me with one of the guns off the rack. I don't think he was serious, but with a man like Vernon you can never be sure. He did, however, allow me to dust the plaques and awards . . . and the old framed photo of him and Donna, taken when she was about four or five years old. About the time Doreen took off.

But enough about her. I set the cake plate on the nearest desk to the door, then crept up, ready to surprise him with my presence.

"Hello, Mr. Law Enforcement," I called out as I reached the opened door.

Vernon looked up as if he'd been shot, then dropped what he'd had in his hand, which by now I could make out was an old brass frame. Probably the one around the picture of him and Donna, I figured. "Evie," he said a bit too gruffly. "You scared me." He stood so quickly his chair rolled backward, stopping only when it hit the wall behind him.

I looked toward the desk and the piles of papers and stacks of files to where Vernon had dropped the frame. My mouth fell open and formed a silent *O*.

"Evie—it's not what you think."

"It's exactly what I think! Why are you looking at an old picture of Doreen Roberts?" I asked. But before he could answer I turned on my heel and headed for the door. "No, never mind. I don't think I want to know." I stopped at the desk, where my cake sat on top, and whirled back to face Vernon. He hadn't moved from behind his desk. "Here's the cake you wanted. I hope you choke on it!"

I turned again and headed out the door.

"Evie, wait!" he called out, but I kept walking, slamming the door on my way to the parking lot, where once again I saw Bob Burnett. This time, though, he was headed away from the bank.

"Evie, you all right?" he asked.

"I'm just fine, thank you very much," I said, not so much as stopping. Mainly for fear that Vernon would come out the door and make a scene in the middle of town. A quick look over my shoulder, however, told me that he had made no such move.

"Trouble in paradise?" Bob asked.

I stopped and glared at him. "Paradise, Bob Burnett, is a fairy tale made up by people too silly to grow up and face the realities of life."

Bob laughed loudly. "I don't have a clue as to what you're talking about, but if you and Vernon are having a little tiff—and I suspect you are—then this is my lucky day. I wanted to ask you earlier if you'd like to go to a movie or to dinner or something . . . but then Donna interrupted me and—"

"Do you mean like on a date?"

Bob shrugged. "If you want to call it that. If you don't, we can just say we're two old friends having dinner . . . or going to a movie . . ."

"But we're not old friends. We've hardly been friends at all."

"We've known each other our whole entire lives, Evangeline. Sure we're friends."

"Why me, Bob Burnett? I'd have thought you'd be calling . . . what was her name? Dee Dee?"

Bob grinned at me. "Jealous?"

From the corner of my eye I saw the front door of the county building opening and then Vernon stepping out. "Evangeline!" he called, but I ignored him.

Bob chuckled again. "If this were paradise," he said, reverting to the old subject at hand, "I'd say the snake has just crawled in, and Eve's got a decision to make. You gonna eat from the tree or not, milady?"

I looked from Bob to Vernon (who had come to a stop between us and the building, I suppose trying to figure out what was going on) and back to Bob again.

Bob Burnett. He'd always been a weasely man in my opinion, but I guess not altogether distasteful. At least he didn't have Doreen Roberts in his background, clouding up what could have been and should have been the bright spot of my entire lifetime.

I turned toward my car, took a few steps, then turned back and said, "Tonight. Pick me up at 7:00, and we'll go get something to eat." I was just loud enough for Vernon to hear me, and I glanced his way to make double sure he had. From the look on his face, my fiery dart had hit the mark. I looked back to Bob. "And don't be late."

13

Between a Rock and a Hard Place

If he hadn't been hot on the trail of another story, Clay would have missed what was surely something he needed to look into a bit further. Evangeline Benson, frozen between Bob Burnett and Sheriff Vesey.

He rolled his jeep to a slow stop near the side entrance of the county building, then leaned over and rolled the passenger's side window down just enough to hear the confrontation.

Evie Benson and Bob Burnett? Going out on a date?

Well, this should make Donna happy, if nothing else. He pondered whether or not to call her. She'd be getting ready to head to L.A. Maybe, if he caught her off guard, he could find out who she was going with and if she were meeting Harris there for a . . . fling.

He closed his eyes against the thought, then jerked straight when Sheriff Vesey spoke from the opened window. "Get what you came for, Clay?"

Clay stared into the steely eyes of the sheriff. "Ah . . ." he stammered, then flushed. "Just dropping by to check the arrest sheet."

"Arrest sheet, my eye," Vernon retorted. "Go on, now. Get off government property before I make you a permanent resident."

Flustered, Clay forgot about his reporting assignment and headed back toward his one comfort in life: Higher Grounds Café.

Donna

REUBEN SANDWICHES

1/8 CUP MAYO
1/4 T CHILI SAUCE
4 PIECES OF RYE BREAD (2 SANDWICHES)
1/8 POUND SLICED SWISS CHEESE
1/8 POUND SLICED COOK CORN BEEF
1/4 CAN (4 OZ) SAUERKRAUT, DRAINED

MIX MAYO & CHILI SAUCE THEN SPREAD ONTO FOUR SLICES OF BREAD. THEN —

14

Rye Getaway

I had spent a busy morning running errands around town. Now, I walked down to the bus stop, located only a few hundred yards down the mountain from my bungalow, pulling a piece of Lisa Leann's red designer luggage behind me. The suitcase left a trail of grooves in the layer of fresh snow.

The noontime sun warmed my face as the frigid air frosted my breath. As I walked, I reviewed my and Vonnie's bold escape plan to slip out of Summit View for a mad-dash weekend trip to Los Angeles. I felt a shiver of excitement as I sat down on the bench and swung my large canvas bag beside me.

"Besides the suitcases you'll need a tote bag," Lisa Leann had informed me. "For the personal things you want to take on the plane, including your purse, a water bottle, a good book or magazine, and food. That is, unless you want to pay ten bucks for a greasy, oversized hamburger at the gate."

As an inexperienced traveler, I had taken Lisa Leann's advice, borrowing a tote bag from my dad before packing it with a couple of Reuben sandwiches for Vonnie and me.

Beneath the startling blue sky, I inhaled the cold air into my lungs and looked down the mountain into the town spread before me in miniature. From my vantage point, I could watch the progress of the town's shuttle creeping up the grade toward me and belching puffs of bus exhaust.

As I surveyed the town, I could see the "Potluck Players" were moving into place.

Fred's truck was pulling out of his neighborhood toward town. And Goldie's car was already in front of the Higher Grounds Café, parked next to a blue jeep. Lucky for us, Goldie had the afternoon off because her boss was entertaining an old friend. I had called her at her daughter's home the night before. She'd been rather enthusiastic. "You got it, girlfriend! I'd love to help Vonnie by playing a decoy and driving the two of you to DIA. Sign me up!"

Even now, she was probably sitting in the café, watching Clay watch her. I could just imagine him sipping his coffee and jotting notes on the fact that Goldie's car displayed a bit of luggage protruding out of the backseat (my own, but he would never guess that).

My bus pulled up to the stop, and the double doors opened. I nodded at the driver and took my seat. The bus turned around at the end of the cul-de-sac across from my log bungalow, then headed back toward town.

It was a beautiful day. The pines were iced with snow while the aspens lifted their now sleeveless arms into the clear, cold sky. A warm feeling of satisfaction engulfed me. All was ready. This would be a good day to outwit Clay Whitefield. Let the games begin.

It was, in fact, Clay who opened the door to the café for me as I struggled to roll my luggage through. It was just my carry-on, but he had no way of knowing that. In fact, my whole rendezvous with Goldie at the café was a ruse to point suspicion in Goldie's direction, without having to lie.

"Here, let me help you."

Clay's eyes were shining bright with anticipation. "Looks like you're heading out for a trip."

I shrugged. "Looks that way."

He followed me to Goldie's table. She looked radiant with her new haircut, but the glow on her face, well, even Lisa Leann's high-powered blush couldn't have painted that. It had to be from the anticipation of our "great escape," I decided. I sat down across from her. "Looks like I have time for the ham quiche special and a cup of coffee," I said. Even as I spoke, Sal was on the job, pouring a cup.

"The quiche," she said, having overheard me.

I nodded, and she disappeared.

I looked up at Clay, who still stood at our table. "You're staring, Clay."

"Well, I'm curious. Where are the two of you going?"

Wade Gage undraped himself off a nearby stool at the counter and joined Clay.

"Morning, Wade." I turned back to Clay. "The two of us?"

Clay indicated Goldie's car with a nod of his head. "You're not the only one with luggage I see."

Goldie beamed. "I'm not going anywhere but to drop Donna off at DIA. That's her luggage I picked up earlier."

Wade folded his arms, a look of suspicion etched on his face. He turned to Clay. "I can tell you where Donna's going," he said. "Wasn't it just a month ago when she took up with her new Hollywood boyfriend, David-what's-his-name?" He frowned. "She's going to see him."

Wade's twist to my carefully created intrigue was one I hadn't thought of, but it only added to my ruse. I gave the boys the protest they expected, careful not to deny or confirm their conclusion about my destination. "David Harris is not my boyfriend."

Clay turned and looked at me, contemplating this new idea. "Wade, that's something to consider."

Again, I repeated myself, this time with irritated emphasis. "David Harris is not my boyfriend."

Wade turned back to Clay, who said, "The lady doth protest too much."

Wade followed with, "Definitely a cover-up."

I rolled my eyes. "Wade, even if Dave Harris and I were, ah, close, it'd be none of your business." I turned my attention back to Clay. "Or yours."

Clay asked, "But you are going to L.A., right?"

"If you must know, an old friend is in the hospital. Goldie's dropping me off at DIA." I finished my coffee and stood up, walking to the counter, where Sally was waiting. "Give me the quiche to go," I said. "I'm out of time, and I've still gotta swing by the bank."

Moments later, as Goldie and I put my suitcase in the backseat of her car, Clay and Wade stepped out onto the sidewalk to watch our departure.

"Have a nice trip, ladies," Clay said. "I want a full report on how David Harris is doing when you get back."

Wade pulled his denim baseball cap lower over his eyes. "Well, now, that makes two of us."

Before Clay could get in his jeep to follow us out of town, Lisa Leann called to him from her shop, right on cue. "Clay!"

She darted across the street. "You're just the man I wanted to see." She turned to Goldie and me as we climbed into the car. "Pardon me, ladies, Clay and I have some unfinished business." She winked at me, then put her arm through Clay's and led him back to the restaurant door. She said, "Now, the next edition of the paper comes out on, what day did you say, this Monday—or is it Wednesday?"

Clay looked back over his shoulder, and I waved to him. For a moment he looked confused, but before he could react, Lisa had pulled him through the door, leaving only Wade to stare at our departure.

Goldie giggled. "That was the most fun I've had in ages," she said, pulling into the bank parking lot. "Honey, I had no idea you had so many beaus."

"Those two knuckleheads?" I asked. "No thanks to either one of them."

She pulled to the back of the bank, next to Fred and Vonnie's pickup truck. Even if Clay had his nose pressed to the Higher Grounds window, he would never be able to see our little gathering.

As I was getting out of Goldie's Crown Victoria, Evie popped her head out of the bank and glared. Oh boy. She must have somehow found out about our secret mission to L.A. If so, she'd be especially steamed because she would know I had rather intentionally neglected to mention it when I saw her down at the county building earlier.

"Donna Vesey, what kind of stunt do you think you're pulling? Did you think I wouldn't find out about these shenanigans?"

"Good afternoon to you too, Evie. What stunt are you referring to?"

"Now, I'm not saying that what you're doing isn't right. I mean, we've got to get Vonnie to L.A, and behind Clay Whitefield's back too."

I studied her. Evie was once again wearing new clothes, a cute denim appliquéd jacket, new jeans, and kicky black boots with heels. What a difference from the Evie of a month ago who looked like she'd been stored in mothballs in the back of her closet. I blinked. Why, she even appeared to have a dash of Lisa Leann's lipstick splashed across her prim mouth. Hopefully she wasn't planning on kissing my dad with those painted lips.

I took a deep breath. *Be nice,* I told myself. *Don't show her a spark of your outrage.* I kept my voice even, though my hands were perched on my hips. "So, Evie, what's the problem?"

"The problem is you've tried to leave me out of one of the biggest coups the Potluck's ever pulled."

"You mean you didn't know?"

"How could I? I only found out because of Lisa Leann's insistence that I call her."

"Imagine, Evie, you not staying in touch with the girls enough to know when their lives have been turned upside down. Something, or should I say someone, else captured your attention lately?"

Evie stood staring at me with her mouth open, wanting to defend herself but not wanting to give me a report concerning the status of her relationship with my father.

She unfolded her arms, then refolded them. "I am keeping up," she finally said. "That's why I'm here."

"Good, then you'll help us get this show on the road."

Goldie and I exchanged glances as we followed Evie into the bank. I wasn't prepared for what I found there.

Vonnie and Fred sat in the brown padded leather chairs in the bank's lobby. Fred was staring into space while Vonnie dabbed at her eyes with a crumpled tissue.

"All set?" I asked.

Fred stood. "I'll get your luggage," he said to Vonnie, Goldie following him so she could open her trunk. I turned back to Vonnie, who rose slowly as Evie gathered her into her arms. "Vonnie, you poor dear. You're a mess."

"If only Fred would go with me," she said, watching him load the car. "But he's barely speaking to me as it is."

"It's that bad, is it?" Evie said.

Vonnie nodded and blew her nose.

Evie hugged her again. "Then I'll pray. I'll pray for your trip, you, and of course, Fred."

"I appreciate that, Evie, I really do."

The two women walked through the door. I followed them, then walked around to the car and started to pull the suitcase out of the backseat. It had served its purpose as a prop at the Higher Grounds Café but now needed to go into the trunk so I would have a place to sit.

Just as I bent over to plop the suitcase onto the pavement, two cowboy boots stepped into my line of vision. "Here, let me get that."

I looked up. Wade was standing before me. "That goes in the trunk," I said.

He stared down at me, then turned to watch Vonnie climb into the front passenger seat. "Donna, what's going on here?"

"Well, the girls and I are trying not to alert the local press."

"Clay? He's on alert, all right. He'd be here himself if that Lisa Leann woman hadn't shanghaied him. Is something going on between you two?"

"Me and Clay? No. It's just that he's following a particular story a little too closely, if you know what I mean."

Wade stared at Vonnie, then at me. "Then you are going to California, but with Vonnie?"

I nodded. "That's right. And that's a little fact I'd like you to keep to yourself."

Wade popped my luggage in the trunk and shut the lid.

"All right, but only if you promise me something."

I climbed into the backseat, and Wade leaned over the door. "What's that?"

"You and I have some unfinished business. When you get home, we need to talk."

I nodded reluctantly as he shut the door.

After our good-byes, Goldie giggled as she pulled out of the parking space and toward the exit. When she turned onto Main Street, she headed away from the café and on toward Highway 9.

"Darlin'," she said, "you are full of surprises. You'd better not let Lisa Leann find out about how many men are wild for you, or she'll be planning your weddings. But what I want to know is which of these bachelors will be waiting behind the door of the church?"

I sank into the seat and covered my eyes with my hands. "Neither."

Vonnie leaned over the seat and patted my leg. "This thing with you and Wade, it's bothering you, I can tell. Do you want to talk about it?"

"No."

"Why not, dear? You and Wade almost got married when you graduated from high school. Whatever happened between you two?"

"That was a bazillion years ago, and nothing happened that I'd care to discuss."

Goldie made eye contact with me through the rearview mirror. "Well, when you're ready, the Potluck girls will be there for you."

Ready? I mused to myself. That would never happen. There were some parts of my dark past I'd never be ready to reveal. Ever.

15

Texas Lassoed

Clay couldn't believe his luck—or lack thereof. If he were a betting man, he'd have laid money on Lisa Leann having deliberately swooped out of her new bridal shop in order to waylay him.

Women, he thought. *They always stick together no matter what. They can stab each other in the back one day, and pray for one another the next. They can fight like cats over a single man on a Friday night, then one helps the other snag him on Saturday.*

Still . . .

He drove back to his apartment, a one-room overlooking Main Street. He could afford better, but living alone—with the exception of his boys Woodward and Bernstein—why bother? If he'd ever married, it might be different. But he hadn't . . . and it wasn't.

He threw his jacket over the chair shoved under his desk, then plopped down on his bed. The box springs creaked under his weight, a not-so-gentle reminder that he could stand to lose a few pounds.

Clay sighed and closed his eyes, squeezing them so tight a kaleidoscope of colors formed behind his lids, which were dissipated by pictures of Donna with David Harris. *Well, why not?* he asked himself. Harris was a good-looking man by anyone's standards, while Clay was . . . well, he was the Opie Taylor of Summit View. His face was splattered with "little boy" freckles, and his hair was too red. Plus, he was overweight by anyone's standards.

He reckoned he couldn't do anything about the freckles and the hair, short of having it dyed like some girl, which he wouldn't even begin to consider. But he could lose a few pounds, couldn't he? What was the name of that new diet everyone was going nuts over?

He hoisted himself off the bed, booted up the laptop on his desk, and began to research, something he knew well how to do. An hour later, he had a full plan . . . a plan for life.

Evangeline

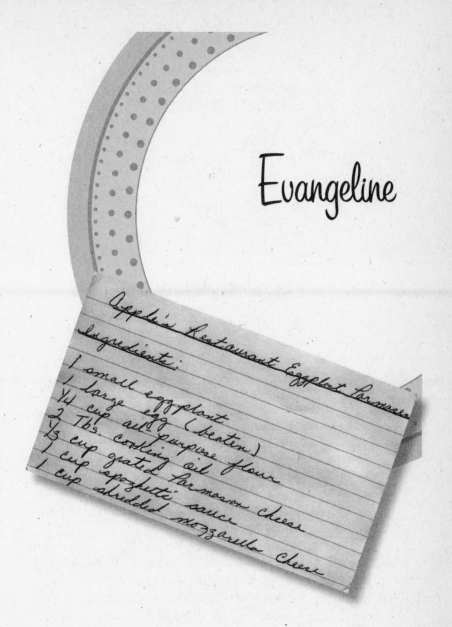

Applie's Restaurant Eggplant Parmesan

Ingredients:

1 small eggplant
1 large egg (beaten)
1/4 cup all-purpose flour
2 Tbs. cooking oil
1/3 cup grated Parmesan cheese
1 cup spaghetti sauce
1 cup shredded mozzarella cheese

16

Spoiled Alliance

I knew the whole . . . episode with Vernon had upset me because by noon I had done three uncharacteristic things.

Make that four.

One, I had created a scene in public. I couldn't remember the last time I had made a scene for the world to see. Oh, yes I could. Not too long ago I'd embarrassed myself immensely by verbally attacking Donna when I thought she had betrayed Vonnie to Clay Whitefield. Turns out she hadn't, but boy, what a fuss we had right there on Main Street. I feared this morning might have been an even more mortifying moment for me, because, of course, this time it involved my personal life.

Two, I had accepted a date with Bob Burnett. What was I thinking? Not that Bob was the worst man in the world. He was, after all, a deacon at Grace, but he's hardly the kind of man I ever thought I'd date. In the middle of what Goldie would call a hissy fit I had thrown to hurt Vernon, I had unintentionally made a complete donkey's behind out of myself. Now, I had to go out with Bob Burnett. Out to dinner.

Dinner . . . at Apple's restaurant, a quaint little Italian place (known for their eggplant parmesan) owned by David and Mica Apple, who were Grace members and all-around nice people.

So how bad could dining at Apple's be? I silently asked myself, then quickly said out loud, "Don't answer that, Evangeline." A lot of Grace people were sure to be there . . . would see me . . . talk about me . . . call me all day long tomorrow for the scoop.

Three, I had gone home and actually phoned Lisa Leann to see what in the world she'd been harping about earlier. When she told me about the little escapade Donna had planned for her and Vonnie (and involving poor Goldie, of all things!), I marched right back to my car and drove straight to town to confront the little sneak. First her father, now her. I'd had enough of the Vesey trickery for one day.

Four, I made another horse's patoot out of myself in front of Donna. The one person I was hoping to somehow bridge a gap with. Of course, as soon as she heard about the breakup of her father and me, she might love me to death.

The breakup of her father and me . . .

Now, back at the house, I sank into my favorite chair (the one near my bed; it had been Mama's favorite chair too, and always brought me comfort) and cried. First I cried out of anger, then I cried out of heartache, and then I cried out of anger again. Somewhere in between all that, I cried about every rotten thing that had happened in my life since the age of twelve when Vernon first kissed me and then Doreen Roberts stole him away from me. Now, she was doing it again.

"Lord," I said to the ceiling, internally hoping God couldn't hear me, "how I hate that woman."

Of course, I didn't mean it. Not really.

Oh, who was I kidding? Of course I did. I reached for the nearby phone atop a small pedestal table and dialed Lizzie's home number. Tim answered.

"Oh, hello, Tim. This is Evangeline Benson."

"Hello, Miz Benson," he said. I thought for a moment how much his accent sounded like Goldie's, then remembered he'd been living in Louisiana for a good number of years, so it only went to reason.

"Is your mother there?" I asked.

"Ah, no. Mom's at work."

I looked at my watch. It was only a little after 1:00. "Of course. I'm sorry, Tim. It feels like it ought to be midnight."

There was a pause between us before he said, "Miz Benson, are you all right?"

I coughed out a laugh. "You know, Tim, you and I have a lot in common. We're both in the middle of a breakup." Then I laughed like a complete fool. "Isn't that funny?"

"Uh . . . okay. Sure. I guess so. You're in the middle of a breakup or a crack-up, Miz Benson?" Then he chuckled a bit before adding, "That was rude. I'm sorry."

"No, no. You may be closer to the truth than you know. Either way, love can be pretty stinky, can't it?"

"Love hurts," he answered. "If you don't mind my borrowing from a song."

It wasn't familiar, but if he said so . . . "Have you ever hated anyone, Tim?" I asked.

"Mmm . . . yeah, I think so. I guess we all have at one time or another . . . you know, felt hate."

"It's not of God."

"No. No, you're right there. I mean, God says we are to hate sin. At least I think he said that. But we wouldn't be human if we didn't, at some point, hate something or someone." He cleared his throat a bit. "I take it you're struggling with that."

I crossed one leg over the other and stared down at my jeans. Jeans. Who was I trying to impress, suddenly getting all dressed up in things like jeans and stylish sweaters? "I'm an old maid, Tim," I told him, shaking my head. "I know it's silly, me telling you this. I'm a friend of your mother's—and your father's, I suppose—so I don't know why I'm rattling on."

"It's okay. I've got nothing but time here."

I smiled a wry smile. "You are your mother's son. She's got such a listening ear. That's why I call her and talk to her so much when I'm struggling."

"Like with hate issues?"

"Yes."

"Wanna tell me who you hate? Or is that unimportant?"

For the life of me, I have no idea why, but the next thing I knew I was spilling my soul out to this young man who was on the brink of his own crisis. Somehow I felt we were bonded. I didn't picture the young boy I remembered running up and down the aisles at Grace after services, giving his mother a fit. I didn't think about the young man who "had" to get married to his girlfriend in the middle of college. I pictured a grown man with troubles of his own and a tender, compassionate heart. A half hour later, when we hung up the phone, I felt somehow better. Tim had even made me laugh, talking about the two of us sneaking into the sheriff's office, stealing the picture of Doreen, and then putting it up in my garden to scare off the birds.

Not that I have a garden, but it was a funny thought.

Tim ended the phone call on a strange note, though. "Well, I would say I'd pray for you, Miz Benson, but I'm hardly in a talking position with God right now. But I would suggest that you pray."

I said I would most certainly do that, and then we hung up.

"That poor man," I said aloud as I pushed myself out of the chair. I should have told him we're never in a position where we can't talk to God.

Vernon called about a half dozen times before the afternoon was over, but I hung up on him every time.

Call me juvenile.

Naturally, he came over, pounding on the front door, ringing the doorbell ad nauseam. "Evie!" he called out, over and over. "You answer this door, do you hear me? I'm not moving from this front porch until you do."

Oh, yeah. That ought to do it. Order me around, you big brute, and see what happens. I planted myself in one of the living room chairs—the one facing the front picture window—and crossed my arms over my chest and one leg over the other. My jaw was set so tight, I wondered if I might get lockjaw or something. I was determined to get through this, one way or the other.

When Vernon's face suddenly appeared at the window—with a clear shot of me sitting there like the ninny I am—I bounded up so fast, my hip popped. I limped over to the front door, muttering "Ow, ow, ow" the whole way, then jerked the door open to see Vernon standing there. "Now look what you did," I accused. "My hip is out of joint, I'll probably have to have surgery and walk with a cane the rest of my life . . ."

Vernon pushed past me. "Evie, what in the world are you raving about? Would you just give me five seconds to explain something to you?"

"No," I said, but I shut the door anyway. "No, not if it has anything to do with Doreen Roberts. No, sir."

Vernon pointed his finger at my nose. "You are one stubborn woman, Evangeline Benson."

"Don't you point your finger at me, Vernon Vesey," I said, pointing my finger right back at him. "There's no possible explanation for you pining away over that woman. Look at what she did to you. To your daughter. Don't you have any sense of pride? Any sense of loyalty, even?"

"Loyalty?" he asked. He dropped his finger, and I did the same. "Loyalty?" he repeated, then rested his hands on his gun belt.

I had half a mind to take that gun and . . .

"Yes, loyalty. To me . . . to Donna."

Vernon looked down at his shoes and shook his head. "Evie-girl, you don't know what you're talking about. You don't have a clue."

"I don't have a clue?" I strode to the chair I'd earlier leaped out of, turned, and sat in one fluid motion. Again, I crossed my arms and legs. The pain in my hip seemed to have lifted. "You think I don't have a clue? Oh, I have a clue all right. The clue was in your hands not a few hours ago. I saw it myself."

Vernon took short, calculated steps over to the sofa, then leaned his rump on the arm, looking down at me. He crossed his arms and shook his head again. I heard the crunching of the leather gun belt, the tick-tocking of my grandfather clock, and the pounding of my own heartbeat pulsating in my ears. I glanced over to the window. Outside, the snow had begun to fall again.

"Evie," he finally said, bringing my eyes back to him. His voice was soft and low. "I love you, girl. You know I do. And I wish I could explain everything to you—"

"What do you mean?" My voice had lowered a few notches too. Funny how when one person yells, the other does, and when one person lowers his voice, the other will too.

"What I mean is, I can't talk about the picture right now. But I want you to trust me, Evie. It's not what you think." Vernon's cool eyes looked right at mine.

I just looked at him. Looked at him for what felt like a hundred years—or at least the years between my twelfth year and now. Part of me saw the boy from years gone by; part of me saw the man he'd become. He still had dark blond hair, but it now receded handsomely. His eyes were still vibrant and blue. His skin, naturally tanned, was only mildly creased with age. This was the man I had loved for so long.

I wanted to trust him. I did. But . . . all that had happened . . . Doreen's taunts when we were in school. It seems I remembered every one of them. I remembered the way she went on and on every Monday morning in homeroom about their weekend dates when we were in high school, the flaunting of their prom pictures when we were seniors. She talked about his kisses and how things "almost got out of control," just loud enough for me to hear during lunchroom breaks. She'd played me from day one. Played Vernon too. Goodness knows she'd even played Donna. There was no possible explanation, no way I could even begin to trust Vernon when it came to her.

I set my jaw again, stood, walked over to the door, and opened it. "I don't think I can, Vernon. I'm sorry. I really am. There's just been so much hurt."

Vernon walked over to me. "Evangeline," he said. I could hear the pain in his voice, but it didn't quite meet the pain in my heart. He touched my arm with his fingertips. I felt my flesh go wild with goose bumps, but I moved my arm away from his hand.

"Don't," I whispered, choking on the words. "Please, Vernon. Don't make this difficult." I looked down to the floor. There was a small puddle there, left behind by the snow on Vernon's shoes. A fleeting thought occurred to me that when he was gone, I'd lie down on the floor and allow my tears to join that puddle. I took in a shaky breath and then exhaled.

Vernon stood quiet for a moment. "All right, then. Let me know if you change your mind, Evangeline. Call me an old fool, but I've waited this long for you to love me . . . I can wait a little longer for you to learn to trust me again too." He made a snorting sound. "Call me an old fool."

17

If Oprah Can Do It . . .

Clay read and reread the details of the diet. He was starving. But according to the list of "can haves," chicken marinara was near the top. The best place he knew for the dish was Apple's.

He picked up the handset of his phone resting in its cradle on top of his desk, and pulled the restaurant's menu from the top right-hand desk drawer.

"Apple's," the voice said on the other end.

"Hey, this is Clay Whitefield."

"Yes, sir."

"Ah . . . yeah. I'd like to place a take-out order if I may."

"Yes, sir."

"Chicken marinara," he said, scanning the menu.

"Anything else with that?"

He dropped the menu and picked up the paper containing the list of foods he could eat, which he'd made from the Internet. "Do you have steamed green beans?"

"We can steam them, yes, sir."

"I'd like a side order of those too."

"Anything else?"

Yeah, he thought. *A large slice of your New York–style cheesecake.* A picture of Donna flashed across his mind, and he let the dessert idea drop. "That's it," he said. "That's it for now."

"It'll be ready for you in about forty-five minutes, Mr. White-field."

"I'll be there," he said, then wet his lips in anticipation of what was to come.

Goldie

Stuffed Peppers

2 large green peppers
1/4 ts salt (for sprinkling)
3/4 pound ground beef
1/3 cup chopped onion
1 - 7½ ounce can of cut up tomatoes
   (undrained)
1/3 cup long grain rice (uncooked)
1 TB worcestershire sauce
                    (over)

18

Tossed Together

For the second time in no more than a few days, Chris had given me the afternoon off. But once I took Donna and Vonnie to the airport, there was little for me to do. The most important thing, of course, was for me to lie low. If Clay Whitefield saw me, he'd know what was up, and Vonnie's cover might be blown. I could go back home, but I already felt I was more in the way than a help these days and, well, I just didn't want to spend the rest of my Friday sitting at home with Olivia, no matter how much I might love her.

So, I did what any self-respecting workingwoman who'd been given the day off would do . . . I went back to the office to get "caught up" on a few things.

I walked through the card shop leading to the upstairs office door and noticed a display of Christmas figurines. One in particular caught my eye, so I stopped and picked it up.

"That's the kneeling Santa," I heard a voice behind me say.

I turned to see one of the young sales associates standing there, dressed in jeans and a long-sleeved turtleneck, all of which was covered by her big red bib apron with the store's logo stitched at one top corner. "It's fascinating," I commented, looking back at the figurine in my hand. "I don't believe I've ever seen anything like this."

"They came out . . . oh, goodness, maybe twenty years ago? I dunno. I remember my mother buying one, though, at least that long ago. Anyway, as you can see, Santa has taken off his cap and has kneeled before the baby Jesus lying in the manger. Says a lot without saying a word, don't you think?" She smiled a perfect dimpled smile. "My name is Britney, and I'm new in town," she said, extending her hand for a shake.

I obliged by taking it. "I didn't think I recognized you," I said. "Around here, you pretty much know everyone."

Britney smiled again. I guesstimated her to be in her midtwenties, maybe a tad older. She was one of these "right off the cover of a magazine" girls. Perfect little figure, lightly applied makeup, wavy blond hair that seemed to dance on her shoulders as she spoke. "We moved here about two weeks ago. I just started working here yesterday." She crossed her arms and raised her shoulders momentarily in one of the cutest motions.

Youth, I thought as my eyes wandered ever so briefly to her left hand. It was ringless, so apparently she wasn't speaking of her husband and herself. "We?" I asked.

"My parents and me. Oh, and my brother. He's working at one of those resorts in Breckenridge."

I nodded. "I have a friend whose daughter works over that way. At Ridge Pointe."

"Hey! That's where Adam works too." She smiled at me again. "Maybe they know each other."

"Small world," I said, then smiled. "And how nice that you and your brother moved with your parents. Most young adults your age would have stayed behind, I'd think."

Britney shook her head. "My mom and I are very close, and my brother wanted the opportunity of working at one of the resorts."

"I see." I took a deep breath, looked back at the figurine, and tilted it so I could check out the price. It wasn't too bad. In fact, I thought it might look right nice on my desk upstairs. "You know, I think I'll get this." I extended it to her.

129

Britney took the figurine from my hand. "Great. I'll ring it up for you." She turned toward the front of the store, and I followed on her heels. Before we reached the counter, she turned her head and spoke over her shoulder. "So, how long have you been here?"

"Since I was probably about your age," I answered. She stepped around the counter, which was loaded down with a computer cash register and every conceivable sales display, including a stack of cinnamon candles in the shape of a Christmas tree. "A long time ago . . . when I married my husband."

She began keying in the kneeling Santa as I began digging around in my purse, my fingertips blindly seeking my wallet. Finding it, I pulled it out, opened the flap, and reached for a twenty when my eye caught the silver glint of the credit card Jack had given me a couple of years ago in case of an emergency. I'd used it just once, not being one for relying on credit.

"Will that be cash or credit?" Britney asked.

I paused. Jack would really be miffed if I used a credit card to buy some novelty for my desk, which was in itself a clear representation of my newfound freedom. Well, then. All the more reason. "Credit," I answered, whipping out the card. "And I'll take one of those candles too," I added, nodding my head at them.

The kneeling Santa was settled in his new home atop my desk as I plugged away at some menial tasks I'd pushed to the side but that now demanded my attention. I had made a fresh pot of coffee, lit the cinnamon candle, and turned the overhead stereo system to a radio station already playing twenty-four-hour Christmas music. I was completely immersed in my work when the office door opened.

I jumped, startled to see Chris sauntering into the office. Van Lauer was directly behind him. They were both wearing ski gear.

"Goldie," Chris said, peeling off his gloves and opening his parka.

"Oh. Hello," I said, darting my eyes from Chris to Van and back to Chris again. Van was, like Chris, stripping out of his outer gear.

"What are you doing here? Didn't I give you the day off?"

"Loyalty," Van commented. "Now, why can't I ever find a loyal employee?" He handed Chris his parka, his eyes never leaving mine.

Chris took the coat, all the while giving his old friend a faux look of threat. "Don't even think about trying to steal her away from me," he said.

Van winked at me. I felt a chill run over my body as my armpits broke out in a sweat. It was bad enough my mind was at war with itself, now my body was at odds too. "Any woman who would come in to work on her day off couldn't possibly be persuaded to leave," he said. He tossed his gloves onto the nearby sofa.

I attempted to confirm his logic, but nothing would come out of my mouth. I could only focus on the cut of his body, made more apparent by the asphalt gray ski pants and the black tek tee. It seemed to me that the black and gray had been specially coordinated to the color of his hair and the steel gray of his eyes. I finally forced a smile and then looked back to Chris, who was hanging the coats on the brass coatrack.

"Do I smell coffee?" Van asked.

"Hmm?" I asked, returning my gaze to him.

"Coffee. Do I smell coffee?"

"Goldie, are you okay?" Chris asked.

"You want coffee?" I asked, standing so fast my thighs bumped against the middle drawer of my desk, causing a thunderous stir. I plopped back into my chair, which in turn slipped on the slick chair mat. The next thing I knew the chair was sailing toward the wall behind me, and my fanny was making a hard bounce on the floor below.

"Goldie!" Chris darted across the room, but not before Van was able to reach me, grabbing for my arms, which were still—somehow—dangling over the edge of my desk.

"I've got her," he said.

I wanted to die. If I could have, I would have. But I couldn't and I didn't. I could only manage to stutter and stammer, "I'm okay. Really. I'm okay."

Not that I truly was. My backside was throbbing, the intensity of which was second only to my throbbing pride.

"Are you sure?" Chris asked.

"Positive." I even giggled for good measure, looking directly at him. I didn't dare look at Van, who continued to stand over me, smelling deliciously of cologne and fresh air. "I was going to get you two a cup of coffee," I said and attempted to stand again.

Van's hand came down on my shoulder. Again, I felt the chills and a popping of sweat. "For heaven's sake," he said. "We can get our own coffee. You take it easy and make sure you're not hurt." He looked over at my employer and said, "I'll take mine with cream and sugar."

Chris turned toward the break room as Van came around to the nearby sofa and took a seat.

I scrambled for something to say . . . or do . . . anything to relieve the embarrassment of a few moments ago. "So, how was your day?"

"Good. We headed back up to Loveland Pass." He smiled.

"Oh. How nice."

Van shrugged. "This time of year . . . you know how it is."

I understood. Loveland Pass was a favorite place for the locals to get in some early skiing before the rest of the world swooped down after Thanksgiving. But Loveland oftentimes blended man-made snow with the real thing. You could ski, sure, but it wasn't like a nice long run of powder, at least not this early. I picked up a pen and began fiddling with it. "Are the two of you going out to dinner tonight?" I asked.

"No. Carrie and Jenna will be back."

I mouthed an "Oh" just as the phone rang. "Excuse me." I turned to the phone. "Chris Lowe's office," I answered. It was Carrie. "Hello; we were just talking about you."

"You and Chris?"

I looked over at Van. "No. Van Lauer is here. They just came back from Loveland Pass."

"Wonderful. So, then Chris is there? I'm calling from the road and wanted to let him know about what time we'd be home."

Even as she asked, Chris stepped into the room, carrying two mugs of steaming coffee. "He's just walking back in. I'll let him know you're on the line." I placed the call on hold, looked over at Chris, and said, "Carrie."

"Ah. I'll take it in my office," he said. "Excuse me."

Once again, just Van and me in the room. Endless minutes to fill with conversation about . . . something. But what?

"So," Van began. "It's a Friday. Will you and your husband be dining out tonight?" He took a sip of his coffee and swallowed loudly.

"Oh, no. I'm not . . . I mean . . . we're not . . ." I sat straight in my chair. "We're separated. Jack and me. Jack's my husband. We're separated." *Oh, Lord! Do I sound as much like an idiot as I think I do?*

"Really? I'm sorry to hear that."

I waved a hand at him. "Don't be. Please. It was a long time coming. I mean, we may still work it out, but I don't think so. You never know what—"

"God will do," we both finished.

Another smile broke across his face. *He's a Christian!* My heart soared.

"Goldie?" he said, clutching the mug of coffee by lacing his fingers around it. "How about I take you to dinner tonight?"

My heart stopped beating as I took in a deep breath. "I don't think . . . I mean, I don't know . . ."

"As friends, I mean. I don't have anything going on . . . and I'm assuming you don't either."

"Well, I was going to make stuffed peppers for my daughter and son-in-law."

"I see." The look on his face was—I believe it was!—genuine disappointment.

"But," I began, watching his face for a hint of hope, and what do you know, there it was, "I suppose I can still prepare the peppers for them and go to dinner with you." I cleared my throat discreetly. "As friends."

Van stood. "Seven o'clock?"

I stood too, but don't ask me why. "Sounds good."

"How about we go to Apple's? Chris and I went there last night . . . excellent food."

"I love Apple's."

"Then Apple's it is." Again he reached for my hand, and I happily offered it to him. "Seven o'clock."

Oh, Lord. What have I done, what have I done, what have I done? And explain to me, if you will, how I will ever tell Olivia?

My warring mind sent up anxious and disjointed prayers to God as I headed home that afternoon, driving way below the speed limit. The sooner I arrived home, the sooner I'd have to face the glare and accusations of my daughter. Olivia would never understand why I'd accepted the invitation from Van. Heavens, I hardly understood it myself. *Yes, yes, the man is nice looking. Okay, let me be honest. I mean, if I can't be honest with God, who can I be honest with?*

Lord, you know the man is nothing short of gorgeous. You ought to know it; you created him. And I can't help but wonder what in the world he would see in a woman like me; if in fact he sees anything at all. Maybe he just felt sorry for me, having fallen and making such a show of myself in the office. Or maybe he's just lonely . . . or desperate.

That's it, isn't it, Lord? He's desperate. Desperate, and he feels sorry for me. He thinks I'm lonely. Well, I'll certainly straighten that misconception out first thing. Oh, Lord, help me tell Olivia. Help her to understand this isn't a date. No, it's not a date at all . . . it's just two friends having dinner.

What's wrong with two friends having dinner, Lord?

I could delay no longer. I pulled into the driveway of Olivia and Tony's small ranch-style home, shut off the car's engine, and made my way to the front door, all the while fiddling with the wide strap of my purse. The door swung open just as I reached the bottom step of the porch. I looked up to see Olivia framed by the doorway. "Oh, good, you're home. I've been worried."

I stopped with one foot on the first step and my hand on the wrought-iron railing. "Why were you worried?" I asked.

"I thought you were going somewhere with the girls of the Potluck and then coming straight home."

I shook my head no as I continued up the steps. "I ended up going to the office. Just for something to do, really."

Olivia nodded as she moved back into the house, holding the door open for me and stepping to one side. As I passed her I rubbed her tummy only slightly round with child. "How were you today?" I asked. "Feeling okay?"

"I'm fine, Mom." She closed the door behind us and headed into the kitchen. "Hey, listen. I know you said you were going to make stuffed peppers for dinner, but Tony called and was craving chicken parmesan, so I thought I'd indulge him. Oh, and Dad called."

"Jack?" I stopped briefly, then continued following her, stopping at the dining room side of the countertop separating the two rooms. I set my purse to the right of the half-opened mail.

Olivia opened a cabinet, reached for a jar of Italian sauce, then set it on the countertop in front of her, all the while talking. "Yeah. He called about Thanksgiving. He wants us to be together for the day, and I told him—"

"What did you tell him?" I asked, gripping the edge of the counter.

Olivia gave me one of her "looks." "Well, I told him I'd have to talk to you first, of course. But, I have to tell you, he seemed pretty sure you'd balk."

I opened my mouth in protest as Olivia raised a hand to stop me. "I told him," she continued, "that you are not unreasonable and you'd surely be happy to have Thanksgiving dinner as a family. Mom, please say you'll think about it. We're still a family, you know."

I reached for my purse and then turned to walk away, heading toward my bedroom. This was not going as I expected. How was I supposed to tell Olivia that I had a date—though not a real date, just dinner between two friends—when all she could do was babble on about next Thursday's holiday meal?

"Mom," Olivia called. I realized she was coming up behind me, so I turned.

"Olivia, we'll talk about it later, okay? I'll call your father and discuss this whole thing with him. I will, I promise."

My daughter crossed her arms over her middle and cocked out a hip as though she found my words very difficult to believe. "Fine," she said. "When? When will you call him?" Apparently our conversation wasn't going as she'd planned either.

"Olivia, I don't know . . ."

"Tonight? Will you call him tonight?"

"Not tonight, no."

She looked at me with wide eyes as her lips formed a circle of disbelief. "Why not? Why can't you call him tonight?"

I stood straight. "Because I have a . . . because I have other plans."

"What other plans?"

"I'm going out to dinner with a friend."

"Who? One of the Potluckers? How long will that take? You can't take five minutes out of your evening to call Dad?"

"Olivia, stop it!" I raised my hand to my forehead and attempted to rub away the tension forming there. "I'm going out to dinner with a gentleman—"

"Excuse me?"

"A gentleman, Olivia. And before you have a heart attack, just let me say this is not a date. He's just a friend."

Olivia began to flail about. "Ohmigosh. Oh . . . my . . . gosh. Mom, you can't be serious. You're a married woman." She ran her fingers through the short mop of red curls atop her head. "You cannot be serious." Her voice squealed on the last word.

I took a step toward her. "What does my being married have to do with this? Besides, I'm not married. Not really. I don't care what you say."

"Mom, you are not going to honestly look at me and tell me you're not married."

"Okay. All right. I'm married. Legally, yes, I am. But that shouldn't stop me from having dinner with a man who—"

"You're justifying!"

"A man who is no more than a friend. A business associate." Olivia opened her mouth to say something else, but I held up my hand to stop her. "Olivia, I want you to stop. I'm a grown woman, and I am, above all else, your mother. I'm not your sister or your best friend. I am your mother. Treat me thusly." My bravado not being all I'd like to pretend it is, I turned and hurried into my bedroom, closing the door firmly behind me.

I met Van at Apple's a few minutes after 7:00. He'd already been seated, but as soon as I entered the cozy, candlelit restaurant I saw him rise from his seat in the lower section of the room. He walked toward me with an air of confidence and familiarity, something I couldn't quite see "Coach" Jack Dippel doing. Unless he was down at the Gold Rush Tavern, of course.

I met Van halfway on the three small steps leading down, my eyes darting around the restaurant—which was divided by a polished wood half wall that separated the upper level from the lower—attempting to take in who was there, who might see me. *Lord, if I'm just having dinner with a friend, why should I care who sees me?*

An inner voice whispered, *You know the answer to that, Goldie.*

"I was a few minutes early," I heard Van say, "so I went ahead and got a table for us."

I looked to the small, square table draped in white linen and graced with a small candle and floral centerpiece. It appeared Van had already ordered himself a drink as well, something I wasn't remotely accustomed to. If Jack ever drank—when he did—it wasn't with me. "Of course," I answered, just as the overhead music changed from Doris Day's "Que Sera, Sera" to Dean Martin's version of "That's Amore."

"Shall we?" he asked, extending his arm toward the setting.

I nodded just as the hostess, who hadn't been at the front when I entered, came up beside me and said, "I'm so sorry I wasn't up front, Mrs. Dippel. May I take your coat?"

I blushed, grateful for the dim room so Van wouldn't see the giveaway of my emotions. *Mrs. Dippel. Oh, Lord. Maybe I really shouldn't be here.* "Yes, thank you," I answered her, slipping out of the heavy outerwear. She took my coat with one hand while reaching for my chair with the other, pulling it away from the table so I could take a seat. "Thank you," I said again. My voice quivered . . . another giveaway.

Van sat opposite me. "What would you like, Goldie?" he asked. He wrapped his fingers around his drink. His voice was smooth and easy, and I felt myself beginning to relax.

"I'll, um . . . I'll have . . ." I looked up at the hostess, a pretty young girl whose honey complexion accentuated the brightness of her smile. "Actually, a cup of hot tea would be nice," I said.

"Hot tea, it is," she said. "I'll bring a coat-check ticket to you in a minute."

I nodded at her and then watched her walk away.

"I hope you don't mind my indulgence," Van said, nodding his chin toward the small glass in his hand. He raised it, and I heard the clinking of ice against crystal, mixing beautifully with the hush-toned conversations, the overhead music, even the flickering of candlelight.

"No, of course not. I'm just not a drinker. Never have been."

He winked at me. "Good for you." He took a sip of his drink, then eyed me. "You look very nice this evening, Goldie. I have to say I'm quite taken with the simplicity with which the women of the high country dress."

I looked toward my lap and brushed away an imaginary piece of lint before looking back to him. I hadn't wanted to dress up, of course. Didn't want to give the wrong impression, not to Van, or to Olivia—or even to myself—so I'd chosen a pair of black wool slacks and an oversized sweater, under which I wore a complementary turtleneck. I'd kept my jewelry simple too. A strand of pearls and matching pearl stud earrings, both of which I'd purchased for myself. None of the fancy, expensive stuff Jack had given to me over the years for absolution.

The only thing I wore from Jack was the plain gold band on my left ring finger.

"It took some getting used to," I commented. "When I first moved here, I mean."

Van's eyes widened. "Oh? I assumed you were from here."

"Oh, no. I'm from Georgia. Small hometown. Good people." *People who would never understand why I'm dining out with a man other than my husband,* I reminded myself. *No matter what I'm calling it.*

"I do business in Georgia from time to time," Van said. "Atlanta, mostly. I don't guess you can call that a small town, though."

I shook my head and let out a nervous giggle.

"Sometimes I'm called in on cases over there." He waved his hand as though to brush away the topic. "But let's not talk about business."

"What should we talk about, then?" I asked. I placed my hands in my lap and squeezed them into tight fists.

"Let's talk about you."

"Me? Oh, there's really nothing interesting about me."

The hostess reappeared with a cup and saucer, a small teapot of hot water, and an ornate mahogany tea chest, which she opened to reveal neat little rows of gourmet teas. I stared at them for a moment as though I'd never seen a selection of teas before, then chose a fragrant chai spice. Before the hostess left, she laid my coat-check ticket on the table and slipped it toward me. I mouthed a thank-you and watched her walk away.

"How many children do you have?" Van asked.

I prepared my tea, keeping my attention on my hands as I answered. "One. Olivia. Married to a fine man—Tony. They have a little boy—my heart—named Brook. He's such a character." I could feel my face brighten. Any mention of Brook brought a surreal joy that washed over me like a fountain of springwater. "Olivia and Tony are expecting another baby in about seven months." I looked over at Van. "I'm living with them."

"I know."

"You know?"

"Chris told me . . . somewhere in the middle of his admonishments."

"I don't understand."

Van chuckled. "He's not overly happy with me taking you to dinner." He leaned over the table as though he were about to indulge a confidence. "He doesn't want me to take advantage of your situation."

I felt my face flush, and Van chuckled again just as another young woman approached our table. "Good evening, welcome to Apple's," she said, setting two small menus at our places. "My name is Summer, and I'll be your server this evening. I see you have your drinks. I'll give you a few minutes to look over the menu and be right back to take your order." She smiled at Van. "Sir, may I get another drink for you from the bar?"

Van shook his head. "No, I'm fine for now, thank you."

"Alrighty then. I'll be back in just a bit." She turned and walked away, her long ponytail swinging from side to side as she bounded up the step.

"Ever notice," I said, "how a person's name fits them? She's tanned, blond, and blue eyed. What better name than Summer?"

"Is that how you got the name Goldie?"

I reached up and with my fingertips touched the underside of my hair at the nape of my neck. "It's not a given name. But I certainly suppose it fits. Or at least used to more than it does now." I cocked my head a bit. "What did you mean when you said that Chris doesn't want you to take advantage of my situation? Didn't you tell him we're just friends?"

As I asked the question, I felt a shot of cold air from the opening of the front door hitting me squarely in the back. "Welcome to Apple's," I heard the hostess say. I looked over my left shoulder and over the half wall to see who might have entered. My eyes widened.

"Someone you know?" Van asked.

"That's Evangeline and . . . Bob Burnett?" My voice was barely above a whisper. "What in the world is she doing here with Bob Burnett?"

Van smiled broadly. "Maybe they're two friends having dinner?" He raised his glass to me in a mock salute.

I didn't answer him. I kept my eyes on Evangeline, wondering if she and Bob would be seated where they could see me . . . see me and Van having dinner.

Together.

I breathed a sigh of relief when they were shown a table within my view, but with me out of theirs.

"Who are Evangeline and Bob Burnett?" Van asked.

I looked back at him. "Evie—Evangeline Benson—is a friend of mine, and Bob Burnett is . . . well, he's a deacon from our church, but . . . I don't understand why the two of them are here together. Evie dates Vernon Vesey, for heaven's sake."

"Vernon Vesey?"

"Sheriff Vernon Vesey."

Van peered over his shoulder in amusement, then looked back to me. "Evangeline, the deacon, and the sheriff of Summit View. Sounds like a book title."

"Yeah, and it would begin with 'It was a dark and stormy night.'"

"You want to go over there? Say something to her?" he asked. I noted the twinkle in his eye.

"Goodness, no. If she saw me here with—"

"Me?"

I stopped short, then reached for my menu. "We'd better decide what we're going to order."

Van reached for his menu as well. "Good save," he said.

I sighed deeply as I smiled at him. "You know, I'm fairly nervous being here. I don't suppose that's any big surprise."

"No. Not really."

"I mean, I am married—legally. Chris isn't happy with you. Well, my daughter is not overly happy with me right now, either. One of my best friends is across the room, and I'm a nervous wreck she's going to see me. I'm sure half of the people in this room are watching us, wondering who you are and why I'm sitting at the table with you. Maybe even wondering where Jack is, though they surely know the answer to that. My leaving Jack, I'm quite certain, has made all the local gossips happy." I rolled my eyes. "All that to say, in spite of the fact that I'm a little nervous . . ."

Van arched a brow.

"Okay, a lot nervous . . . I'm finding you to be an easy man to be with. You make me want to laugh, and laughing is not something I've done in a long while."

"And how have I managed to do that, Goldie?"

"You seem to find humor in this whole episode. Well, thank you. I need a little humor in my life."

"Glad to oblige you." He looked to the menu he held between his hands, then closed it and set it on the edge of the table. "The lasagna here is good."

I closed my menu as well. "Make it two." I swallowed. "May I ask you a question or two now?"

He spread his arms to the width of the table. "I have no secrets. Ask away."

"Married?"

"I was. About a hundred years ago. My wife was killed in a car accident on the night of our fifth anniversary."

"Oh, Van."

He shook his head before I could give him my condolence. "That was a lot of years ago. And, no, I never married again. Never wanted to. I dedicated myself to my work and Dillon. Mercedes—my wife—and I had a son. Dillon was two and a half when Mercedes died. He's in law school now. Not married, so no grandchildren as of yet." The merriment had left his eyes and returned all within the same reply.

"I had no idea."

"Why should you?"

"Every life has a story, doesn't it?"

"It does at that."

Summer returned to our table. "Are we ready?" she asked. I turned my head to look at her, to give my order, but something caught my eye before I could do so.

142

Something . . . someone . . . standing at the doorway of the restaurant. Watching me.

I swallowed hard, pursed my lips, and then smiled ruefully.

Clay Whitefield.

Uh-oh.

19

Woodward and Bernstein and Shredding Machines

Clay gripped the Styrofoam take-out box in his left hand as he attempted to get the keys to his apartment out of his coat pocket with his right. Apple's being only a few blocks from his apartment, he'd chosen to walk there for his dinner. After all, he could use the exercise, right?

Seeing Goldie Dippel with . . . who was that man? . . . shot his "David's biological mother theory" to blue blazes and back.

When he was finally able to retrieve his keys, he took the inside stairs leading to his second-story flat two at a time. He shoved the key in the lock, turned it, and then pushed his way through the door.

He tossed the chicken marinara onto his desk, where a stack of papers—lined pages filled with research on migrant workers—lay nearby. He picked them up and ripped them into several sections, then—realizing what he'd done—attempted to put them back together again as though they were pieces to a puzzle. "I can still use this," he admonished himself out loud. Bernstein and Woodward watched him from their cage, apparently just as shocked by his actions as he.

For the second time that night he reached for his phone, this time dialing Donna's cell phone number. The call immediately went to voice mail.

He didn't bother to leave a message.

What would he say to her anyway? Before he could whistle "Dixie," Goldie Dippel would probably be making the exact same phone call, letting Donna know that she'd been busted and that he knew she was alone out there in L.A. with Harris.

He picked up the take-out box, said, "I'll feed you guys in a minute," to his gerbils, walked over to the recliner he kept parked in front of the television, and plopped down into it.

Oh, well, he thought. *I may as well enjoy my dinner.*

Vonnie

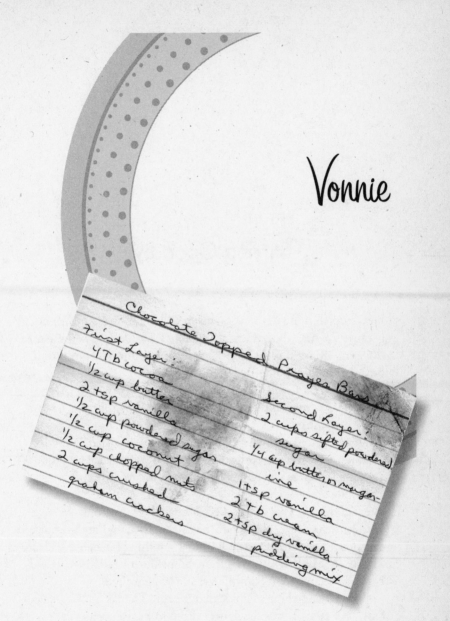

Chocolate Topped Prayer Bars

First Layer:
4 Tb cocoa
1/2 cup butter
2 tsp vanilla
1/2 cup powdered sugar
1/2 cup coconut
1/2 cup chopped nuts
2 cups crushed
graham crackers

Second Layer:
2 cups sifted powdered
sugar
1/4 cup butter or margarine
1 tsp vanilla
2 Tb cream
2 tsp dry vanilla
pudding mix

20

Stirring Good-Bye

Heavens. All those sleepless nights must have caught up with me, because the next thing I knew a blonde stewardess tapped me on the arm. "Ma'am, please put your seat in an upright position in preparation for landing."

That's when I realized my head had sunk deeply onto Donna's shoulder. I turned and looked at her, surprised. "Oh, my. I must have fallen asleep."

Donna patted my hand. "You're probably exhausted."

I pulled my seat forward, and the stewardess smiled at us. "It was a pleasure to serve you and your daughter today."

Donna and I exchanged glances. It wasn't the first time someone had mistaken us for mother and daughter. Not only were we both petite blondes, though my hair had grayed and my dress size expanded, Donna was, after all, the closest thing I had ever had to a child. At least that's what I'd thought, before my birth son, David Harris, had arrived in Summit View looking for me.

Donna handed me a Ziploc plastic bag. "Thanks for the prayer bars," she said. "It was the perfect finish to the Reuben."

I tucked the bag into my oversized purse to recycle later. "One of Fred's all-time favorites."

I keenly felt his absence. He hadn't wanted me to make this trip. But it was something I had to do. Something he'd have to understand.

The jet's landing gear suddenly dropped, and I grabbed Donna's hand.

"It's okay, Vonnie. We're almost there. Look out the window."

And there it was, the Los Angeles I'd left over thirty-five years ago, shining like a jewel in the late afternoon sun. As the plane soared in over the runway, I knew I was finally closing this unfinished chapter in my life. A chapter that made my heart pound with uncertainty. I was facing either a homecoming or the reckoning I justly deserved.

Half an hour later, Donna and I were standing by the luggage carousel in LAX when I sucked in my breath as the image of my dead husband, Joe, bounded toward me.

"Ladies, you made it," David Harris called.

Somehow, I couldn't resist allowing him to pull me into his strong arms. He even smelled like Joe. At least, he had the same taste in aftershave cologne, definitely Old Spice. His black hair was parted on the side, just like his dad's, and he flashed that famous Jewel smile with those beautiful pearly teeth.

Donna stood back. "You're late," she told him.

"Traffic," he said as he reached to hug her too. Despite herself, Donna seemed caught in his embrace before she pushed away. "I'm not your sister."

His brown eyes twinkled. "I know."

Donna frowned, ignoring the comment. "There's one of our bags now," she said, pointing.

"I'll get that for you," David said then, moving toward the rolling conveyer belt covered in suitcases.

We squeezed into David's black Mazda 3 and headed for the freeway. David asked, "I can't take the suspense much longer. What's the big mystery?"

Donna's voice practically squeaked from surprise. "You don't know?"

I turned around and looked into her round blue eyes. I reached back and patted her leg. "It's not his fault, dear," I interjected. "I didn't know how to tell him."

He glanced at me, amused. "Well?"

I flopped my head on the headrest and shut my eyes. "Take us to the hotel, and I'll explain everything."

"I wish you'd let me take you to the house."

"No, no. I don't want to impose. Besides, that was your mother's house."

David was quiet for a moment. "I'd love to share those memories with you."

I shook my head then looked at my grown child who was almost a stranger to me. "It's hard enough to imagine my only child was alive and raised by another woman, but to see her house, I suppose that would do me in."

David raised his eyebrows but kept his eyes on the road, shifting into higher gear. "But why?"

"She was a movie star. Me? I'm just a nurse and a mechanic's wife."

David chuckled. "You don't know just how good that sounds to me. But promise me that you and Donna won't leave until I serve you dinner there at least."

"You cook?" Donna asked from the backseat.

"I have a few specialties, and I'm a whiz at the grill."

"Make it steaks, medium rare," Donna said. "And we'll be there."

After we had arrived at the Holiday Inn and wheeled our luggage to the room, I patted the bed beside me. "Sit down, David."

David crossed the room and stood before me. I tried to make eye contact with him but couldn't.

"What's this all about?" David asked, sitting beside me on the bed.

How could I tell him? Why hadn't I already? I guess it was because my silence was a habit I didn't know how to break. Besides, I didn't know how David would react to the news. I took a deep breath. "Your grandmother, Maria Jewel, and her family are here in L.A."

"I have family here?" He stood. "Why didn't you tell me?"

"The Jewels and I, well, we've been estranged, I guess. I . . . I wasn't ready to face them."

He looked down at me. "What made you change your mind?"

"After you found me, I finally called the family, and when I did, I got some bad news."

He sat back on the bed and reached for my hand. "What's wrong?"

I looked into his earnest eyes. How could I deliver David such a blow? I took a deep breath before pressing on. "It's your grandmother, Maria. She's had a heart attack. The family has asked us to come to the hospital."

David walked to the window and looked out at the parking lot and the freeway beyond. He turned back, his features awash with worry. "How bad is it?"

I stood up. "I . . . I don't know. We'll find out when we get there. The family is expecting us."

David was silent as we drove through the evening rush-hour traffic. When we pulled into the hospital parking lot, he helped me with the door, then Donna climbed out of the backseat.

The sun had set, giving way to a horizon of gold gilding an inky blue sky that blotted into darkness. The crescent moon had risen, and scattered stars competed with the glare of the parking lot's overhead lights.

I took David by the hand. "I haven't seen Joe's family in over thirty years. I don't know how they'll feel when they see me or how they'll react when they see you."

We rode the elevator without speaking. When the door opened in the hall outside the lobby of the ICU, the three of us hesitated. Finally, Donna stepped out and reached for my hand. "Come on, Vonnie."

David followed like a lost puppy.

When we rounded the corner, I wasn't prepared for what I saw—a room filled with familiar faces. When they spotted us, a stunned silence interrupted their conversations. A woman who looked remarkably like the Maria I remembered stood up. "Vonnie, is that you?"

I hesitated. "Nina?"

The pause that followed terrified me. I was returning to a world I had betrayed with my absence. I couldn't expect grace, but I hoped for mercy.

Nina's eyes filled with tears. "Vonnie! Yes, it's me." She held out her arms, and I rushed into her embrace. "It's been over thirty years. I'm no longer that ten-year-old in braids," she said.

Donna stepped beside me. Nina turned to stare. "Who's this? Your daughter?"

Before I could answer, she saw David, and her hand went to her mouth. "Joe! Oh!" Her legs buckled, but David reached to steady her.

"I'm David Harris," he said. "Joe's son."

Nina gasped then buried her face in her hands and leaned into David's chest. At first, David looked bewildered; then he did what came naturally to him. He wrapped his aunt in his arms and held her while she wept. When she was able to catch her breath, she smiled up at him then turned to the family, including her husband and their three grown children, all older teens and young adults, one holding a sleeping toddler on her lap.

"This is Joe's son, everybody. David. He's home at last."

The crowd of relatives gathered around David, taking turns hugging him, welcoming him to the family. David's eyes at first registered shock, then filled with a warm pleasure. He seemed starved for the hugs they were desperate to give. I stood back with Donna and tried to take it all in. As I watched the fanfare, I couldn't help but wonder. What had David Harris's life been like with his movie star mother?

Nina finally turned to me, wiping her eyes. "Vonnie, I don't know whether to shake you for running away from us or to kiss you."

I hung my head. "I know, Nina. It was so unfair to you all."

Nina turned to stare back at David. "But you know, Vonnie, it's okay now. Joe's son is home. And it was you who brought him back to us."

I nodded. "I would have never known he was alive if he hadn't come looking for me."

Nina smiled, and I decided to brave the subject I was dreading. "How's Maria?" I asked.

"Let's sit over here away from the commotion," Nina said, pointing to a bank of gray padded chairs. Donna and I sat beside her.

She leaned toward us. "Mama's dying. She doesn't know yet about David, but she's been asking for you. Are you ready to see her?"

I nodded. Nina stood and took my hand. "Then come with me, Vonnie. It's time."

Together, Nina and I pushed through the double doors and into the corridor of the ICU to room four. The name on the door read "Maria Jewel."

Nina pushed me ahead. "Mama. It's Vonnie. She's come to see you."

I was shocked by what I saw. There before me lay one of the strongest women I'd ever known, now grayed and fragile. She was wired to a heart-rate monitor while one of her skinny, wrinkled arms was connected to an intravenous drip, and a pulse-ox clamp gripped her index finger, measuring her oxygenation, which to tell the truth, wasn't all that great. I noted that despite her nasal canella hooked to two liters of oxygen, Maria registered at only 40 percent saturation. Not so good.

Maria opened her eyes then beckoned me closer. Her voice was weak. "Vonnie."

I went to her side. "Maria, yes. It's me."

"Vonnie, I've been waiting for you. The angels are ready for me, but I knew you would come. I had to wait till you came."

I leaned over her and pressed my cheek next to hers. "Oh, Maria!" I sobbed. "How I've missed you."

As I pulled back, a lone tear trickled down her cheek. "And I you."

The talking seemed to tire her, but she continued. "Our world was ripped apart the day Joe died. But I wanted you to come home, I wanted to tell you . . ."

I stroked her gray curls, not realizing that Nina had slipped out of the room. She continued, "I wanted to tell you that I loved you like a daughter. I wanted to tell you that I go to see Joe and the baby now."

I swallowed hard. "But the baby . . ."

"Mama?" Nina stood at the doorway again, this time with David by her side. "Mama, here's someone I want you to meet."

Maria's eyes left my face and fastened on David. "Joe," she breathed. "Oh, Joe. Are the angels here?"

Nina said, "No, Mama. This isn't Joe. This is Joe's son, David."

Maria blinked. "David? But how?" Her eyes shifted back to mine. "This is my grandson?"

"Yes, Maria," I said. "I've only just met him myself. I never knew until a short time ago that he lived."

Maria stared at David then lifted her bony hand. "Come here, my son."

David approached, his eyes locked to hers. She touched his hand, and he leaned toward her.

"David, you look just like your father," she said, stroking his cheek.

"Yes, ma'am," David said.

"Call me *Abuelita*."

"It means 'little grandmother,'" Nina supplied.

"*Abuelita*," David said, smiling down at his grandmother.

She squeezed his hand. "My Joe was a fine man. To be like my Joe, you cannot only look like him, you have to be good like him."

"I'll try, *Abuelita*."

Maria placed David's hand on top of mine. "You have your mother now; she will help you be like your father."

Her eyes fluttered, and the green pulsating lines on her heart-rate monitor became erratic.

"Mama, you need to rest now," Nina said.

Maria smiled. "Yes. I can finally rest with God."

The heart-rate monitor hummed one long note and displayed a long green line across the screen as Maria turned her head toward the empty corner of the room. She cried out, "The angels are here now. Oh, they've come with Jesus and my dear husband, and Joe."

With those final words, Maria Jewel closed her eyes and was reunited with those she had lost so many years ago. The three of us who were left behind could only imagine the reunion.

The poor dear had been holding on for my arrival, I realized as I watched Maria Jewel slip into eternity. At her last words, my heart stirred as it had never stirred before.

Though I think I wouldn't have broken down so if David had not looked so absolutely shocked. To meet his grandmother and then to lose her, almost within the same breath, had to be overwhelming.

He still hovered over her, holding her hand. "*Abuelita?*"

The nurse entered the room and turned off the alarms. She smiled sadly. "It's over," she told him.

He tried to argue. "That can't be. I . . . I've only just met her."

I noticed the Do Not Resuscitate sign attached to Maria's bed and turned to Nina, managing to ask, "Why the DNR order?"

Nina shook her head as she swatted at a stray tear. "Her last heart attack caused too much irreparable damage. We knew it was only a matter of time. If we brought her back now, it would only be for a few more earthly moments. And forgive me, I wouldn't want to interrupt the reunion she's having with the Lord and Papa, not to mention Joe."

I could only nod.

"She was eighty-two," Nina continued. "She'd said her good-byes. She was only waiting for you."

The three of us stood there marveling at the expression of peace on Maria's face. She looked so beautiful, as if the pain of her death had been overcome by joy. So help me if the tormented face of my own mother didn't come to my mind. After all the heartache she'd caused by her deception when she gave away my son, it made me wonder. *Will Mother enter into a final peace? I'm not sure that's even possible.*

I put my arm around David, and he me. "Maria was a great lady, wasn't she?" he asked.

I caught my breath. "The greatest."

Nina patted my arm. "Come, let's go tell the family."

Together, we went into the waiting room where the family sat, their faces turned to us for news.

Nina spoke to them. "Mama got to say her good-byes to Vonnie and David. Now she's gone home. She's with Papa and Joe."

The sounds of soft weeping began to fill the room. Donna stood and wrapped me in her arms. That's when I totally broke down. Donna whispered, "Vonnie, I'm so, so sorry."

I'm not sure how long we stood like that, but David finally encircled us with his arms and said, "The family is going to Maria's house now. I've got the directions."

Numbly, I wiped my eyes with a tissue and followed him, holding Donna's hand as we made our way back to the parking lot.

The chill of evening nipped the breezy air, and I shivered. David opened the car door for me then handed me the sweater I'd left inside.

Donna helped me put it on before she climbed into the backseat. Silently, we got back on the freeway and drove to East L.A.

Donna asked David, "Do you know the way to the house?"

"Yeah," he replied. "I've driven those streets many times as a paramedic. Lots of knife and gunshot wounds in that old neighborhood."

"It wasn't like that three-plus decades ago," I said.

"Thirty-five years of gangs changes things," he replied.

When we pulled up to the house, I was surprised. Though its appearance was still neat and clean, the house was a lot smaller than I remembered. With the street already jammed with cars from Maria's relatives, we had to park a couple of blocks away. David hopped out to open my door, but I hesitated.

"What's wrong?" he asked.

How could I explain all the things that were wrong—starting with my own Fred. If only he were here to go through this with me, to hold me in his arms. I needed him not to pull away but to pull closer, to hold me tighter.

I sniffed, then looked up at David, his brown eyes glittering in the moonlight. His resemblance to my dead husband almost overpowered me. Swirling with so many complicated emotions, I somehow managed to stammer a reason he could grasp. "It's been so long, too long. I'm sure the family must hate me by now. I just don't know if I can face them on this already very difficult night."

I felt Donna pat my arm from behind. "Vonnie, David and I will be with you. If it gets too weird, we'll take you back to the hotel."

David reached for my hand. "We're in this together," he said.

Soon we were swept into the warmth of the house. The terracotta walls were painted in sherbet oranges and pineapple yellows. But even with these hues of cheerfulness, the house was darker and smaller than I remembered, though so familiar it made my heart hurt with longing. Nina, or her daughter, had lit the house with soft globes of candlelight that illuminated sudden memories of those happy days I'd waited, heavy with child, for my young husband to return from Vietnam. And the pictures in the hallway. So many of Maria and of Joe, I stopped, entranced. My eyes fastened on one of Joe, all of ten years old, opening a present beneath the Christmas tree while Maria, garbed in a housecoat, clapped her hands with joy; then there was Joe as a little tot, holding hands with Maria, who was a slim, dark-haired beauty. It must have been Easter, judging from the way the pair was dressed. My! Joe had been an adorable child with his big brown eyes and soft black curls. I stole a look at David, suddenly aware of all I had missed with him. I turned back, drawn to a photo of Joe in his uniform. David followed my gaze.

"Oh. That's a younger version of me," he said quietly.

I bit my lip and nodded, remembering the wonder of this man who had been my husband so many years ago.

We left the safety of the hallway and faced the family. I blinked against the memories I saw in their faces lined now with age, faces I remembered. The family was polite but distant, though very interested in David. I found myself introducing him and Donna repeatedly as I ate a slice of Nina's Mexican cake, one of Maria's heirloom recipes.

"Uncle Alberto, I'd like you to meet Joe's son, David."

Uncle Alberto looked up from his place on the couch. "Joe's son? I thought Joe's baby died."

David took Uncle Alberto's hand. "My death was greatly exaggerated, I'm afraid."

Uncle Alberto reached for his cane, struggling to stand. He patted David on the back. "Sure looks that way!" The older man pulled his black-rimmed glasses from the pocket of his plaid shirt and put them on. "You look just like Joe, did you know?"

His wife, Reya, wasn't as kind. She stood up from where she was sitting, livid. Her face pinched with both wrinkles and anger as her voice rose with indignation.

"Joe's son?"

Aunt Reya looked frail but tough. I figured she had to be pushing eighty herself. "You're Joe's wife, Vonnie? You mean you let poor Maria think her grandson was dead all these years? Do you know how his death broke her heart?"

I opened my mouth to speak, but no words came. Donna answered for me. "She didn't know her baby was alive. She's only just met David herself."

Aunt Reya put her hands on her hips. "Didn't know her son was alive?"

Nina rushed to intervene as the family encircled the confrontation. "Aunt Reya, Vonnie was unconscious at the time. She was tricked. We all were. We all thought the baby had died."

Reya's eyes were cold. "Tricked? How could that be?" She walked over to the coffee table, where a photo of our wedding sat. She picked it up then waved the photo in my face. Despite her rage, my eyes couldn't help but fasten on the framed couple so in love. There I was, my golden hair flowing as I held a bouquet of tiger lilies, with Joe in a polyester sky-blue suit, looking at me with so much love. Aunt Reya's voice jolted me back to the present. "I knew you were trouble as soon as I laid eyes on you. To think how you ripped the heart out of this family. You betrayed Joe, you betrayed Maria, and you betrayed all of us. *Por qué?*"

"I'm so sorry," I said, saying it more to the photo of Joe than to Aunt Reya. David jumped in, trying to redirect his aunt's wrath. "Aunt Reya, are you *Abuelita's* sister?"

She whirled back to him, then stopped her tirade, somehow melting under his resemblance to his father. Her tone took on a sudden spirit of graciousness as she pulled him away from me. "Yes, David, I'm your great-aunt." She gave me a withering look then led him to the sofa. "Come and tell me about yourself."

David looked back at me, and I tried to smile. "You go on. You've got a lot of catching up to do."

As the relatives turned back to their own conversations, I became aware of Donna hovering by my side. She crossed her arms and leaned toward me. "The nerve. Don't they realize what you've been through? What it took for you to get here?"

I put my hand on her shoulder. "No, they don't have a clue. But this isn't your fight, dear. Let it go."

"But you're crying."

I shrugged. "I'm old; I leak a bit," I said, drying my eyes with my tissue. "Besides, the greatest woman I've ever met is gone. I'm allowed to cry."

Nina gave me a hug. "Vonnie, if my mama forgave you for running away from us, then so do I."

Nina and I sat together for a while, quietly remembering the woman we loved. When a relative whisked her away, I went out back to get some fresh air. Donna joined me on the patio with a glass of ice water. "Thank you, Donna."

Donna gave me a consoling hug. "We'll be leaving soon. I just told David this is all too much for you."

"Dear, you didn't need to do that . . ."

Donna sat down next to me. "I know, but Vonnie, it's time to say your good-byes."

"Do they know when the funeral will be?"

"The family had already gathered tonight to grieve. The rosary will be Saturday night and a private burial will be later."

"Good, we'll be able to make the rosary. Our flight doesn't leave until Sunday morning."

Soon David stuck his head out the back door. "I hear you two ladies are ready to go."

Donna practically leaped from her aluminum chair. "Yes, we are."

Despite dear old Aunt Reya, I hated to once again walk out of the place that had been such a loving home to me, but I could see Donna thought it best. Though, if I could've had my way, I'd still be part of the family. I'd never have left this loving sanctuary in the first place. I would have raised my child here.

Donna helped me gather my purse, and soon we were saying our good-byes and walking back to David's car.

David put his arm across my shoulders as Donna tagged behind. I looked up at my handsome son and gave him a wistful smile. "I bet you never expected our visit would turn out like this."

"I couldn't have imagined. To think, I lost my grandmother tonight, a grandmother I never even knew I had."

"I'm sorry you didn't know, and I'm sorry I didn't tell you sooner."

David gave my shoulders a squeeze. "I understand. I do. But still, it's all hard to take in."

I simply nodded.

Just as Donna climbed into the back of the car, her cell phone rang and she answered. "Hello? Goldie? Yeah, we made it okay, but it's been a rough evening. Vonnie's mother-in-law died while she was with her in the ICU . . . I know. Here, let me hand her the phone."

She passed the phone to the front seat, and I placed it to my ear. "Goldie? It's so good to hear from you."

Goldie's voice sounded strained. "Oh, Vonnie, I'm so sorry to hear about Mrs. Jewel."

"The poor dear was holding on just for me. To think I almost didn't come."

"But you did. It sounds like you got to say good-bye."

"Yes. And David got to meet her."

"How's David holding up?"

I looked at my son as he pulled out of the parking spot. "He's good. It's been so nice to be with him tonight."

"That's wonderful, Vonnie."

Goldie paused, and I said, "Well, thanks for checking up on us."

"That's not the only reason I called. I'm afraid I have more bad news."

"What happened?"

"Clay. He saw me at Apple's."

"Oh no!"

"I feel like such an idiot for not staying home. Do you forgive me?"

"Of course."

"Vonnie, you are such a dear. I don't deserve your friendship." She sighed. "Nevertheless, I had to warn you. Your cover may have been blown. Clay's got to know Donna and I tricked him today. That means you may have just been elevated to his number-one suspect."

My mouth went dry. All I could think of was how mortified Fred would be to see the news that I was David's birth mom splashed on the front page of the *Gold Rush News*. "Missing Jewel Is None Other Than Fred Westbrook's Wife, Vonnie."

Not that I was ashamed, not anymore, anyway. It was that Fred wasn't ready to announce the news. We had a lot of healing to do before our marriage could be rocked by this kind of public scrutiny. I sighed. "Oh dear. Thanks for letting me know."

We said good-bye, and I handed Donna the phone.

"What is it?" she asked.

"Clay. He saw Goldie."

Donna sounded calm. "No worries, Vonnie. This calls for Plan B."

David looked puzzled. "Plan B? What's all this about?"

"We've had a press leak," Donna explained.

"What? You're still trying to cover up that you're my mother?"

161

"Oh, David, no. It's just Fred. He's not ready to go public yet. I've got to respect that."

David drove in silence for a while, then said, "I can't wait to meet Fred. I guess that will have to wait till I move to town."

"And what a time that will be," Donna said.

21

Stranger in Town

After dinner, Clay decided to implement an exercise plan. Each day, beginning that evening, he'd walk all the way to the end of Main Street, cross over, then come back up until he reached the café. It wasn't much, but it was a start.

He dressed appropriately, then headed down the stairs leading to his apartment. When he reached the street below, he turned right. Within no more than a few steps he eyed the café across the street. He stopped, breathing in and out frosty air, trying to decide whether or not to just cross over now or go with his original plan.

A mental picture of Donna and Harris helped him to decide, and he kept going.

His brow furrowed a bit. There was something she needed to know . . . something he had to tell her. A stranger had come knocking earlier in the day, asking about Donna.

Clay, like all good reporters, had felt his sense of "danger" pique. It wasn't, he surmised, his favorite way to feel.

Donna

BREAKFAST ENCHILADES (CALIFORNIA STYLE)
2 CUPS SHREDDED CHEDDAR
1/4 CUP CHOPPED HAM
1/3 CUP GR ONIONS
1/3 CUP CHOPPED RED BELL PEPPER
8 CORN TORTILLAS
4 EGGS
1 1/2 CUP MILK
1/4 C. SALSA   1 TABLESPOON FLOUR
                 SLICED RIPE OLIVES
— IN SM BOWL, COMBINE CHEESE, HAM, —

22

Lavish Breakfast

"What is Plan B, exactly?" David asked from the front seat.

I eyed the back of his head. How could I say it without giving him the wrong idea? I managed a coy, "Patience, David. All will soon be revealed."

David eyed me from his rearview mirror. I decided to distract him before he could protest. I pointed to a Burger King sign. "Let's do a quick run-through," I said. "I'm starving. I'll tell you about it later."

Just as I took a bite of my Double Whopper sandwich, my cell phone rang again. "Hello?"

A snide voice greeted me. "Donna, it's Clay Whitefield. How's your sick friend?"

I swallowed, then said, "She's not sick anymore."

"Oh really?"

"Yeah, she died."

There was a long silence. "What, you and David have a fight?"

Bingo. I acted all innocent. "David?"

David spoke from the front seat. "Donna, who's that?"

Clay sounded triumphant. "That's Harris's voice. You went to L.A. to be with David."

I tried not to chuckle. Clay was making this all too easy. I feigned irritation. "Is that why you called, to check up on me?"

"Yes and no," Clay admitted. "I wanted to warn you. Not that you deserve it, but I'm trying to do you a favor." He cleared his throat, then spoke in hushed tones, like he was with the CIA or something. "A stranger in a suit came around looking for you today, at the café. Looked official, like, I don't know, a detective or something."

That got my attention. "What did he want?"

"I'm not sure, but I got bad vibes. He gave a phony story. Said he was a consultant doing an evaluation for the sheriff's department; didn't even know your dad's the top guy. He asked a lot of people a lot of questions about you."

I felt my face grow hot. "What kind of questions?"

"Like the state of your mental health and how often you use your gun."

"You're kidding me."

"Afraid he got some pretty interesting answers, especially from Wade. But mainly he got an earful about your speeding ticket exploits. You got any high-powered enemies out there?"

I was silent. "I'm in law enforcement. Sometimes it seems like the public is my enemy."

Clay laughed. "No, Donna, that's who you're paid to protect. Anyway, I just wanted you to know." Sarcasm soured his voice. "My good deed is done. Good night, Donna. Enjoy your weekend with David."

He hung up, and I was left wondering if Clay was on the level. I leaned back in the seat and reviewed what I knew about him. Clay was smart, smart enough to try to weasel his way into my confidence. But he was honest. What he said about the stranger had to be true. I sighed and rewrapped my burger and put it and my cell phone into my tote bag. My appetite was ruined.

"What did Clay say?" Vonnie asked.

"Nothing. He thinks I'm with David."

David actually chuckled. "I love that idea. If that's Plan B, I heartily approve."

I bristled. "Whatever. Clay can think what he wants if it will buy us some time."

I could see Vonnie bob her head in agreement. "That's all we really need," she said. "A little more time."

When Vonnie and I finally slid the plastic card key into the lock of our hotel room, I was exhausted, but not as much as Vonnie.

"What a day," I said, collapsing into the padded chair by the desk.

Vonnie only nodded and headed for the bathroom to wash her face before smothering it with cold cream. She slipped into a faded blue gown and topped her hairdo with a pink silk nightcap. I was left wondering if she held the secret identity of a space alien. She noticed my stare and shrugged. "Keeps my look fresh."

"Is that what Fred says?"

She nodded and climbed into her side of the bed. "Mmm-hmm."

"Aren't you going to call him?"

She answered sleepily. "Already did, at Maria's. Just before I went to sit on the patio."

"What did he say?" I waited for the answer, but got none. "Hello? Vonnie?"

I turned to discover she had already drifted into dreamland. I watched her chest rise and fall before climbing into my old black sweats, which, come to think of it, weren't so different from my black tee and jeans I'd worn all day. When I finally crawled into bed, my mind was spinning. I'd never expected the day to be so emotional. What a list of troubles—first Clay, then Wade, then Vonnie, then David, then Maria's death, and now this . . . a stranger nosing into my business, asking my neighbors about my so-called mental health.

I laid my head on my pillow and squeezed my eyes shut, determined to sleep. Yet, every time I peeked at the clock, the red digital numbers had advanced only ten more minutes. Great.

Finally, dreams swirled into dark, yellowed images that made my heart pound. It was *the* dream, all so familiar—the rainstorm, the canyon, the man who flagged me down, the woman in the submerged car . . . the baby.

I was once again beneath the roaring river, trying to hold the baby tight. I opened my eyes in the eerie underwater light. Before me were the wide eyes of the child staring back. The baby's eyes held my own. This time, she spoke. "Mommy, please don't kill me. Mommy?"

My baby!

"Donna, dear, wake up. You're having a nightmare," Vonnie said as she gently shook me. "David will be here soon to take us to breakfast."

I blinked, then ran to the bathroom to wash the salty tracks from my face, hoping Vonnie hadn't noticed. No sooner had I slipped into my blue jeans and peach tee than there was a knock on the door.

Vonnie, all dressed in her khaki slacks and pale green sweater, opened the door. "David, right on time."

I was staring in the mirror, giving my blond curls a run-through with my fingers. "Where are you taking us for breakfast?"

I looked up, and David was grinning at me. "Donna, you're letting your hair grow out. It looks good."

So help me if I didn't blush. "Ah, thanks."

"To answer your question, we're heading for the Hills, to 21st Place."

"Sounds swanky," I said. "But you're in jeans, so it can't be too over the top. Right?"

David merely grinned.

After a forty-minute car ride, I began to understand what David meant by "Hills" as he drove us into the heart of some fine old mansions in Beverly Hills.

"David, where are you taking us?" Vonnie asked.

"I hope you don't mind, but we're going to my house. I've prepared quite the spread."

"So you do cook," I said.

"You can be the judge of that."

David parked his Mazda in the driveway of what could only be described as his glorious mansion, complete with lovely grounds blooming with flowers. The manor had beveled glass windows and marble columns at the front door. It reminded me of Jed Clampett's old place.

Vonnie sat stunned while I said, "Oo-la-la, David."

I believe the man blushed as he helped Vonnie out of the car. He said, "I know. It is over the top, but it's my inheritance from Harmony. In fact, I just moved out of my apartment downtown so I could take care of it. But it's such a hassle. That's one of the reasons I'm selling—I'm discovering I don't own this place, it owns me."

Vonnie nodded mutely as she followed him into the house.

When he pushed open the door, Vonnie and I entered a totally new dimension, at least new to a couple of high-country Colorado girls. The entryway came complete with a spiral staircase made of mahogany, brass, and marble.

But the thing that impressed me most and the very thing that made poor Vonnie mute was Harmony Harris's framed movie posters surrounding us on the main living room walls. Of course, since Harmony was the musical movie queen of the late fifties and early sixties, there she was, dressed as a slave girl in *Song of Solomon*, then again dressed as a gypsy in *Gypsy Wedding Dance*, then again as a Victorian princess in *The Runaway Courtship*. She was displayed in all her glory, with all that long, golden hair. Her great figure poured into her incredible and very sexy costumes. It was all terribly impressive.

After viewing the posters then walking through several luxurious rooms, David finally guided us to the patio overlooking the pool. There, on a beautifully set table, were three crystal goblets filled with layered fruit and yogurt parfaits topped with granola and raisins.

Vonnie sat down woodenly. As I saw she was almost catatonic, I spoke for us both. "These look great, David. Did you make them yourself?"

He grinned. "Nothing's too good for my ladies."

I decided to let the comment slide. Vonnie and I ate in silence as David talked about delightful meals served here at 21st Place, with the likes of leading men and women like Dick Van Dyke, Marlon Brando, and Julie Andrews. Finally, he said, "I've got breakfast enchiladas too. I'll slip into the kitchen and bring them out."

As soon as he turned his back, I turned to Vonnie. "You going to be okay?"

She looked up. "What? Oh. Yes, I think."

"Then what's wrong?"

She looked around like a little girl lost on a field trip. "All of this, how can I ever compete?"

"Vonnie, it's not a competition. Harmony is gone. David wants to get to know you, his birth mother."

She shook her head. "But what do I have to offer him?"

"Look, he didn't follow Harmony's footsteps to become an actor. He's a paramedic. That should tell you something."

Before we could say more, David rounded the corner with a lovely silver serving dish filled with his breakfast enchiladas.

Vonnie looked a little more like herself. "That looks great, David. You'll have to give me your recipe."

Later when I was helping him with the coffee in his state-of-the-art kitchen, he asked me, "Is Vonnie okay?"

"She will be. This Harmony Harris thing has got her a bit intimidated."

David set the coffeepot down and took a step toward me.

"Donna, I have to tell you, you've really impressed me this weekend, the way you've looked after my mom."

I put my hand on my hip. "It's hard for me to hear you call her that. In many ways, Vonnie is my mom. We've adopted one another."

David looked amused, but he leaned back against a counter and crossed his arms. "Your mom?"

"You've grown up with Harmony. Why do you need Vonnie?"

"Vonnie is my roots. Harmony just played at motherhood. Actually, it was more of a photo op with her."

That caught my attention. "Really?"

"Yeah, all the stars were adopting in those days, so as not to ruin their figures. Really, I was raised by a professional nanny, not to

171

mention the groundskeeper, a good man who spent a lot of time talking to me. Other than that, it was pretty lonely around here."

I studied him. "For real?"

"'Fraid so. I'm a lot like you, I guess. I've never really had a mom either. And to see that fine woman out there, to see her character and her quality, it makes me wonder. What did I miss? And then I know—I missed Vonnie. I missed my mother."

"She's a great lady. You have no idea."

"Maybe not. But I'd like to find out. And I hope there's room in your heart for me to share her with you."

I turned away and picked up the sugar bowl. "I don't come with the Vonnie package, you know."

"Well, I—"

"I'm not available."

"Are you seeing someone?"

"That's none of your business," I said, turning back to the patio. "I'll consider sharing Vonnie, but I'm off limits. I'm just not interested."

The rest of our visit, through Maria's rosary and our Sunday morning good-bye, I kept my distance from David. I wouldn't get involved with him. I couldn't. I just didn't deserve a wonderful man like him.

When David dropped Vonnie and me off at LAX, he pulled our luggage from the trunk of his car, then gave Vonnie a hug. "I can't tell you how much I enjoyed getting to know you and the Jewel family."

"Are you still planning to move to Summit View?" she asked.

He reached for her hands and held them but directed his comments to me. "Wild horses nor feisty chicks couldn't keep me away." He winked in my direction. "Besides, I love a challenge."

Vonnie turned my way and said with a chuckle, "Well, son, if you've set your cap for Donna, you've got more than a challenge in store for you."

He turned back to her and gave her a kiss on the cheek. "Well, you're a woman of prayer. Put in a word for me."

I hit David in the arm with my balled fist. "All the prayer in the world won't help you when it comes to me, I'm afraid. I'm never getting married."

David raised his eyebrows at my involuntary revelation, then suddenly wrapped his arms around me, sliding his rough cheek next to mine. He whispered in my ear, "Never say never, Donna."

When he let go, I felt my cheeks burning from the intimacy of his embrace. And so help me if that man didn't notice with a look of smug satisfaction.

I pulled out the handle of my rolling luggage and turned to help Vonnie with hers. "So long, David."

Vonnie followed me dutifully into the airport, waving good-bye. "I'll call you," she said.

An hour after takeoff, our seat companion, an elderly gentleman, fell into a coma-like nap. Vonnie turned to me. "You okay?"

"I guess. This weekend was a little more than I bargained for."

"Me too," Vonnie said. She patted my hand. "But still, Donna, I'm worried about you."

"About me? What for?"

She made sure our neighbor wasn't awake. "Did you know you talk in your sleep?"

My heart almost stopped. "What did I say?"

"Last night. You kept talking about your baby. That got me to thinking. Remember the time you were in high school and you and a very nervous Wade Gage came up to the office where I worked?"

"Doc Billings? Yeah, I guess I remember."

"I was worried then. You didn't give me much to go on in the patient interview before you saw the doctor, alone. And with Wade pacing in the waiting room, I had my suspicions. Suspicions I could never confirm."

"We were just kids then."

"I know, but the thing is, I checked your chart after you left. The doctor hadn't written a thing down. Believe me, that was odd. I should have pressed you then, but I thought you'd come to me. When you didn't appear pregnant, as I had thought you might, I didn't know what to think."

173

I hung my head and stared at my fingernails.

"Donna, this thing with Wade—what's troubling the two of you? I wish you'd tell me."

Her blue eyes pleaded with mine. I felt the color drain from my face. *She knows, after all this time, she knows.* I almost laughed aloud at myself. Apparently I was the only one still in denial.

I shrugged. "I don't even remember, Vonnie. I probably had a cold." I chuckled. "Or maybe my first period or a yeast infection even."

Vonnie squeezed my hand. "Well, Donna, when you're ready to tell me the truth, I'll be waiting."

23

Another Notch in the Belt

Clay couldn't be more proud. By the first Saturday of December, he was down seven pounds and in need of either a shopping trip or another notch in his belt.

He wondered how long it would take before anyone noticed. Most specifically one special deputy from the sheriff's department.

As was his habit each weekday, he left his apartment early in the morning, walked down to the end of Main Street, then turned back toward the café. Eleana met him when he entered the café later than usual. "Where've you been?" she asked, smiling.

Clay was breathless. "Walking," he said, taking his seat.

Eleana was right behind him. "Hey, have you lost weight?"

"You can tell?" he asked, sitting up a bit straighter than he typically did.

"I sure can."

Clay grinned, then looked past the waitress as Wade Gage walked in.

"Clay," he greeted.

"Wade," Clay returned as his old friend took a seat opposite him. Wade looked up at Eleana and said, "I'll have a cup of coffee and the daily breakfast special."

"Coming right up," she said. "And you, Clay?"

"Ah . . . coffee . . . and something high in protein."

Wade guffawed. "Don't tell me you're on that diet."

Clay glowered at him. "I am. Do you want to make something of it?"

Wade chuckled again. "So, tell me, Clay. Who's Aunt Ellen?"

Clay shrugged.

Eleana arrived back at the table with their cups of coffee. "Here you go, Clay," she said. "And you too, Wade."

The two men watched her walk away.

"I believe," Wade said, "that someone has a crush on you."

"Don't be ridiculous," Clay said. "She's young enough to be my . . . younger sister."

Wade took a sip of the hot coffee before returning to the topic at hand. "Whoever Aunt Ellen is, she's got Donna all riled up." He chuckled again as he picked up the creamer on the table and added cream to his drink. "A little stronger than I like it."

Lizzie

Chinese-Style Beef, Broccoli,
and Rice
Ingredients:
1 1/4 lb. boneless top sirloin
Steak, trimmed of fat
1/2 tsp. Ground ginger
1 tsp. Sugar
3 TB. Soy Sauce
2 tsp. Corn Starch
1 TB. Vegetable Oil

24

Boiling Over

It was a strange group that met the first Saturday in December. And strange seems to be the only way I know to describe it.

I was the first to arrive at Evangeline's. As I entered her home I could smell coffee. It seemed almost symbolic. It brewed pretty much like the trouble in our lives, percolating to the point of overflowing. As soon as I entered, Evie took the casserole dish from my gloved hands, and I bent over to pull my snow boots from my feet.

"This smells good," Evie commented.

"It's a beef, broccoli, and rice dish I read about in a magazine."

"As long as it's not turkey," she said with a "humph" as she made her way into the kitchen.

I giggled as I placed my boots on the mat at the side of the door. "I think we got a good four or five fresh inches of snow last night," I called after her.

"Weatherman said five," she called back. "He's predicting more later this afternoon."

When she returned, I was hanging my coat on the coat tree in the foyer. "How was your Thanksgiving?"

"It was . . . different."

"How so?" I asked. We walked together into the living room, where Evie had instrumental Christmas music playing and apple-and-cinnamon-scented candles burning about the room. I noticed she'd already put up her tree—an old artificial one decorated with the same ornaments her mother had placed on the family tree, plus a few newer ones—and that her china nativity set graced the mantel of the fireplace, where a roaring fire blazed warmth into the room.

"Everything's starting to look like Christmas in here, Evie. Very nice."

"Thank you. Sit down, Lizzie. We may have a bit of a wait on the others this morning, what with the snow and all."

I sat down where I always sat, on the sofa, and Evie took her place in a fine antique chair. "So, what do you mean by 'different'?"

Evie shrugged. "Just different."

I grinned at her. "Did you and Vernon spend it together?"

She looked down at her hands and picked at her short nails for a moment before answering. "No, we did not." Then she looked back to me. "And that's really all I want to say about that."

I brought my hand up to my heart. "Oh no . . . oh, Evie. Did you two have a fight?"

"You could call it that. But, like I said, I don't want to talk about it."

She craned her neck to look out the front window. "There's Lisa Leann." She heaved herself out of the chair. "Wouldn't you know, nothing keeps her from the group."

"Evie . . ." I mildly scolded. I watched through the window as Lisa Leann scurried from her car to the front door.

"Goodness gracious alive," she exclaimed, entering the house. "Isn't it pretty out there?"

"First snow in December always is," Evie answered her. "But after a while, you'll grow to hate it when it turns into gray mush."

"Oh, I don't think I could ever hate it," she said. "To me, this is God at his finest."

"You can put your boots by the door," Evie said.

"Now, Evangeline, here's my new recipe for a bride's cake. I can't wait for you ladies to tell me what you think . . . although I

179

know you're going to love it." Lisa Leann's voice grew stronger as she entered the living room. "Lizzie, good morning." She reached over and hugged me.

"Well, good morning to you too, Lisa Leann. How was your Thanksgiving?"

Lisa Leann stood in front of the fire. "It could not have been better. The kids came, of course. My Mandy is just so precious with her little tummy bulging out. She's staying for a couple of extra weeks so I can have a little baby shower for her. Since Mandy's been training the teacher who will take her place in January, the school agreed to give the new teacher a trial run so Mandy and I could have this time together. So, y'all are invited to the shower, which will be sometime next week."

"That's nice that she can stay a while."

"Yes, well, the doctor said after this month no more traveling, so she and Ray talked about it and thought now was the best time. Then, Henry and I will go to her and Ray's for Christmas."

"It's a shame she couldn't join us this morning."

Lisa Leann pouted. "Oh, I know. We were planning for her to come, but she said she's just overly tired today."

Evie joined us. "The others might be a bit late," she said to Lisa Leann. "I see the snow didn't frighten you any."

Lisa Leann shook her red curls. "Goodness, no. Henry put some good tires on my car and said, 'You go, girl.' So, I went." She grinned. "Evangeline, how was your Thanksgiving? Did you and Vernon make up for all those lost holidays?" She giggled as she looked at me with a wink. I tried to shake my head discreetly, but Evie caught me.

"Don't worry about it, Lizzie," she said, then turned to Lisa Leann. "No, we did not, and no, I do not wish to talk about it."

"Oh," Lisa Leann said quietly. "Well, then . . . Lizzie?"

I nodded. "It was good. Harried but good. Tim's home, and I'd so hoped he and Samantha would have reunited, but it doesn't seem like that's to be right now." I looked from one of the ladies to the other. "Not right now. Not yet."

"What's new with Tim?" Evie asked.

"He's started working at the same resort as Michelle. Likes it."

"Oh, dear. Sounds like he's really settling in then," Lisa Leann commented.

I nodded. It was all I could do. If I tried to say anything more, my tears would start up again, and I was afraid that this time I might not be able to stop. According to Michelle, Tim was getting along famously at work. He'd made great contacts, was already hobnobbing with the brass and flirting his way to disaster with the women on staff. The fear of my son finding a "rebound" romance was very real for me . . . something I'd been praying about in my quiet time with God but was not yet ready to share with anyone else. Not even to ask for additional prayer.

"There's Vonnie," Lisa Leann said. "That little darlin'. She's been through it, hasn't she? I, for one, can't wait to hear about her trip to L.A."

"You haven't talked to her since she returned?" I asked.

"Of course, I've talked to her. But I figure today we'll get the lowdown. The good stuff with all the juices."

Evie made a wry face as she walked toward the front door. I watched from the sofa as Vonnie's plump body hurried from the car to the warmth of the house. "What about you?" Lisa Leann asked. "Have you had a chance to really talk to Vonnie or Donna?"

I shook my head. "No, not really. Only briefly to make certain they'd returned safe and sound."

Lisa Leann raised her chin as Vonnie entered the foyer. I turned enough to watch Von place a covered dish in Evie's hand as Evie greeted her with a "Come in out of the snow, Vonnie."

Vonnie said hello to everyone as she slipped out of her outerwear.

"Psst," Lisa Leann hissed at me from across the room.

I looked at her.

"What's going on with Evie and Vernon?" she whispered.

I shrugged. "She doesn't want to talk about it."

"Who doesn't want to talk about what?" Vonnie asked, entering the room and speaking just a little too loudly.

"Shhh," Lisa Leann admonished, then whispered, "Evangeline."

"What about her?" Vonnie sat next to me.

"Apparently she and Vernon broke up."

Vonnie's face fell. "Oh no. Bless her heart." She looked in the direction of the kitchen. "Poor thing. She's waited so long for this." Vonnie looked back at me. "What happened?"

I shrugged. "She doesn't want to talk about it."

"That won't last for long," Lisa Leann said. "Not as long as I'm in the house."

I patted Vonnie on the knee. "How was your trip?"

Vonnie's face seemed to register both excitement and anguish. "It was good to see Maria before she died. Good to bring David to her . . . to let her know that Joe's son survived. But it was bittersweet."

Evie returned to the living room. "Talking about your trip?"

Vonnie nodded. "Having Donna there was a godsend. I don't think I could have done it without her."

I sensed more than saw a stiffening from Evie, but I chose not to comment on it, or even to look her way.

"Donna's not here yet, I take it," Vonnie continued.

"No." Evie's answer was curt.

"Tell us how you really feel," Lisa Leann said, then shifted gears—thank the good Lord—as she tilted her head and said, "Uh-oh. My favorite Christmas carol in the whole wide world."

We listened to a moving version of Bach's "Jesu, Joy of Man's Desiring" played from the stereo system.

"Isn't that lovely," Vonnie said. For a moment we all just sort of bobbed our heads to the notes as Lisa Leann hummed and waved her arms about as though she were the director of a small symphony.

When the song ended, Lisa Leann said, "That was beautiful. Just beautiful."

The mood in the room had shifted, that is, until Lisa Leann said, "Speaking of Donna. Did anyone else get a visitor?"

Vonnie prickled. "What do you mean?"

"Some man came to my shop right before Thanksgiving . . . oh, I know. It was while the two of you were in California. Yeah, that's when it was. Anyway," she added with a wave of her hand, "he was asking all sorts of questions about Donna. Nice-looking fella. Said he was here from the State Department . . . that they were thinking about giving Donna some sort of award for bravery. Asked a lot of questions."

"An award?" Evie asked. "For what?"

"I have no idea, but I did notice that he had a copy of the newspaper article about the bear in his folder."

"You're kidding," I said. That article, which had come out only a month or so ago, told the story of one of our potluck meetings, held at Vonnie's, in which a wild bear had made an unexpected appearance. Evie's comment to a reporter about Donna's lack of heroism had stirred more than a little tension between the two women. Tension that was already tight as a wound rubber band. "That article was hardly complimentary to Donna."

"I wonder what this is about," Vonnie said. "No one better be messing with my Donna." She shot a quick glance toward Evie, who responded with, "What did I do?"

"Ladies," I said. Then, "There's Goldie."

Minutes later we were all saying hello to a new version of Goldie we were not yet accustomed to seeing. Her hair was chic and her clothes stylish. She'd even applied a little makeup, much to Lisa Leann's delight. "Look at her, just look at her," Lisa Leann gushed. "Isn't she gorgeous?"

"I'd hardly say I'm gorgeous," Goldie said, sitting beside Vonnie on the other end of the sofa. "But I do feel pretty."

"Does this mean things are getting better between you and Jack?"

Goldie's expression fell. "Not Jack, no. Me. This is about me. In fact, life is about me right now, and I can't tell you how wonderful it is."

"So, what is new with you and Jack?" Evie asked, once again sitting in her chair.

Goldie's shoulders drooped in the same manner as her face had a moment before. "Oh, my gosh . . . he and Olivia browbeat me into having a family Thanksgiving. Worst Thanksgiving of my life. You could have cut the air with a knife. Jack trying to hug me . . . Jack trying to kiss me . . . Jack trying to pull me into the bedroom." She rolled her eyes. "It was a nightmare."

Lisa Leann piped in. "I can't imagine a husband trying to pull his wife into the bedroom as being a nightmare," she said with a wink.

"Well, it was. He kept going on and on about how nice I looked and how we could work everything out; he's just sure of it. I told him, 'That only makes one of us, Jack. I'm not so sure.'" She pointed to her chest with her index finger as she shook her head a bit. "Anyway, I've got to move out of Olivia and Tony's. There's no two ways about it. So, if any of you ladies knows of a room for rent, a small apartment . . ."

"Why?" Vonnie asked. "I thought this was the perfect situation for now."

"Short-term," Goldie answered. "Now I need my privacy. I need to be away from Olivia's constant . . . harassment."

"Harassment?" Evie balked. "What's she harassing you about?"

Goldie pinked. "It doesn't matter." She straightened. "But speaking of changes in life, since when did you start going out with Bob Burnett?"

Every head in the room jerked toward Evangeline. "What?" we all asked in unison.

"Since when?" I asked.

"This meeting just keeps getting better and better," Lisa Leann added.

"I don't believe my ears," Vonnie said. "Not in all my life would I have thought the two of you . . . what about Vernon?"

"She doesn't want to talk about Vernon," Lisa Leann said, shaking her head in caution.

"Doesn't want to talk about him?" Vonnie practically squealed. "Evangeline Benson, you spill it right now!"

Evie stood. "Well, I can see I've been the subject of gossip already."

I looked at my knees and spoke quietly, "Lord, we need help here. This is not going well at all."

I'd no sooner whispered my prayer than Donna's Bronco slid to a stop in front of the house. "Perfect timing," I whispered, though I was speaking in jest. Her arrival was sure to be the icing on the cake. After all, if Vernon and Evie had broken up, no one but no one would be happier than Donna.

Instead, her entrance brought another level to the conversation. "Lisa Leann, we gotta talk." Her cheeks appeared to be flushed by something other than the cold air, which had rushed in with her.

Lisa Leann's bright blue eyes widened. "What did I do?"

Donna held up a copy of the *Gold Rush News*. "Are you or are you not Aunt Ellen?"

Lisa Leann beamed. "Whatever are you talking about?"

"You mean that new column in the paper?" Evie said. "That 'Ask Aunt Ellen' or whatever it's called?"

"Ask who?" Vonnie asked.

"Oh, I read that; it's cute," Goldie said.

"It's cute because you weren't the brunt of the letters," Donna said, waving the paper about.

"For your information," Lisa Leann said, "it's 'Aunt Ellen Explains Everything,' not"—she turned to Evie—"'Ask Aunt Ellen.'"

"Whatever it is, it's caused havoc in my life. Not to mention Vonnie's," Donna said.

"Me?" Vonnie slid up a bit to the edge of the sofa. "What about me?"

Donna shoved the paper toward Vonnie, nearly cutting off my nose in the process. "Be careful with that thing," I said, drawing back.

Vonnie took the paper and read for a moment, then looked up at Lisa Leann. "Lisa Leann, how could you?" she said quietly.

"Am I in the dark about something?" Evie asked.

"You usually are," Donna retorted.

"Donna," Vonnie said. "Stop it, now."

"Will somebody please tell me what's going on?" Goldie said, standing.

"I'll tell you what's going on," Donna answered, marching about the room, then pointing toward Lisa Leann. "This woman right here—this woman who calls herself our friend, no less—has printed some bogus advice column for the lovelorn. I cannot begin to tell you how many men have been calling me, asking me out on a date.

185

For the last time: I am not interested!" Donna actually managed to stomp a little jig.

"What does this have to do with you and Vonnie?" I asked.

Vonnie looked at Lisa Leann. "The letters from Joe. How did you find out?"

Donna grimaced. "I'm afraid I might have said something, Vonnie. I'm sorry."

"That's okay, dear." She smiled weakly. "Fred's been awful quiet since the last *News* came out. I think I now know why." She stood. "I'd best get home and try to work on some damage control." She looked at Evie. "I'm sorry, Evie. I can't stay." She walked over and patted Evie on the arm. "But we should talk later, okay? Friend to friend?"

Evie only nodded.

"You can't stay for prayer?" I asked. "Even for a minute?" I couldn't believe how badly our Potluck meeting was going. Couldn't believe it at all. Evangeline's breakup with Vernon was only slightly less a catastrophe than her dating Bob Burnett. Goldie was obviously not moving forward in her reconciliation attempts with Jack. Donna was peeved with Lisa Leann—not that I much blamed her—which meant she was now at odds with not one but two members of our six-member group. Vonnie, who had endured more in the past few months than many women experience in a lifetime, was hurting once again.

And me? I had a son who needed to go home to his wife and his children, a son who was more than a little too happy to be back in the house of his childhood.

Like I said, for the Potluck Club, trouble had most definitely been brewing.

I drove home in silence, having turned off even the evangelical teaching tapes I typically enjoy. There was too much to think about—to pray about—seeing as the Potluck ended in disaster.

Lisa Leann had thrown up her hands and said, "Well, I can't seem to do anything right around here, so I may as well just leave." Then she left in a huff.

Goldie had glanced at her watch, muttered something like, "Maybe I have enough time . . . if I hurry . . ." and slipped out as well. Donna then turned on Evangeline, I suppose waiting for the majority of us to leave what had begun to feel like a crime scene.

"And as for you, Miss Benson. I hope you're happy. My father is crying in his soup every night. Have you no compassion? I mean, come on. I thought you were at least fond of the man."

Evie turned blazing eyes on Donna. "Fond of the man? I love your father. At least I did. Not anymore. I can't love a man I can't trust."

"Can't trust? Lady, if you can't trust my father, you can't trust anyone." She shook her head a bit before adding, "What amazes me is that you think you can trust Bob Burnett."

Evie placed her hands on her hips. "My relationship with Bob Burnett is, quite frankly, none of your business, Donna Vesey. So, I'll thank you to keep your little nose out of it."

"As long as my father's feelings are at stake, this is most assuredly my business. Daddy's an absolute mess. I don't remember the last time I've seen him like this."

Evie began to pace around the room, blowing out candles and turning off the stereo while I pushed myself as far back into the sofa as possible. Inwardly I prayed that maybe, just maybe, it would swallow me whole and I'd end up in some other small town . . . . like Wonderland.

"You know," Evie said, stopping in her tracks, "I would have thought you'd be pleased that your father and I aren't dating anymore. After all, you've hardly been my biggest fan."

Donna crossed her arms and cocked her hip out. I found it hard not to smile. Donna Vesey is a cute girl anyway, but rile her up and she's just downright adorable, especially in jeans and a sweatshirt. For a fleeting moment I wondered why a girl like her had never married, never found that perfect someone. Of course, way back when Donna and my older children were in school, she'd been the sweetheart of Wade Gage, but like most high school romances, theirs had faded as they got older. Then it struck me that Wade had never married either. How odd.

"I'll tell you what, Evangeline," Donna now said. "I would be happy about the breakup. I would. And quite frankly, I don't care if you date Bob Burnett and the entire deacon board from Grace. But when I see my father hurting . . . over someone like you . . ." She ran her fingers through her blond curls. "I gotta go. I gotta get out of here. I've probably got a mountain of emails asking me out and at least a half dozen phone calls from lovesick puppies to listen to." She pointed her finger toward the fireplace, where Lisa Leann had been standing. "So help me, if that woman so much as goes one mile over the speed limit, I'm gonna write her a ticket so big she'll have to sell her bridal boutique to pay it off."

That left just Evangeline and me. It seemed it took her a good minute to even realize I was in the room. "Want to eat something?" she asked, moving ever so slowly to her chair. When she'd sat, she said, "We've got a tableful of food in there, since no one took anything home." Evie's voice was weak and defeated.

"Oh, Evangeline," I said. "It's going to be all right. We all go through these times."

"You know, I'd do anything in the world for that girl, but she just wouldn't let me." Tears began to course down her cheeks; she didn't bother to brush them away. "Never has, and I guess she never will."

"Evie," I said softly, "have you ever noticed how much she looks like her mother?"

"Oh, believe me, yes."

"Do you think that's a bit of a deterrent for you? I think that if I were in your shoes, it would be difficult for me."

"No, I don't think so . . . well, maybe. I don't know. Sometimes I think that because she looks so much like her mother she finds it difficult to like me. That, because of the resemblance, she owes it to Doreen, somehow, to stand against me, seeing as Doreen and I were such enemies for so long."

I crossed one leg over the other. "I wonder whatever happened to Doreen."

Evie shrugged. "She and the old choir director probably ran off to California, where Doreen tried her hand at being an actress. She would have failed, of course, and eventually she would have left him too." She snorted in a very unladylike way. "She's probably been married four or five times by now. Maybe even had a few more kids, though doubtful from the same father. Poor Donna doesn't even know her own siblings."

"Evie," I said with a chuckle. "You can be so funny."

"You know it's true. There was never a more unstable woman than Doreen Vesey."

I didn't respond for a moment. Instead I looked down at my fingertips, studied my nails that badly needed a manicure. When I looked back to Evie, I noticed the tears were really beginning to pour. I slipped off the sofa and dropped to my knees before her, extending my arms to hold her in a friend's embrace. When I did, she leaned into them. "Oh, Lizzie. Lizzie. I loved him so much."

"What happened, Evangeline?" I asked, pulling back.

"He's still in love with Doreen, that's what."

"What makes you say that?"

"I saw him . . . saw him looking . . . pining . . . over her photograph. One he's no doubt had for years. In my heart I just know what he was doing."

"What's that?"

"Comparing me to her. I can never be as pretty as she was . . . never sing like she did . . . never . . . I don't know . . . kiss like she did."

I felt myself blush. "Well, I don't know about that," I said, "seeing as I've never kissed either one of you." I smiled, and she giggled. "Evie, tell me about you and Bob Burnett."

"There's nothing. He's just . . . he's a nice enough man, Lizzie. We have a pretty good time. But . . ."

"He's not Vernon?"

"No. He's not Vernon." The tears began again. "Still, I can't fault him for trying. I could do a lot worse—like live alone the rest of my life."

"I think we need to pray." I fell back on the soles of my feet, clutching my hands in my lap. "What do you say?"

"I agree."

And we did. We prayed for the individual needs of the group and then for the group itself, Evie reminding God that this was his Potluck Club, not hers. It was the first time I'd ever heard such as that coming from her mouth, but I thought it appropriate. We also prayed for Tim and Samantha, asking God to move and move quickly. Though, I added, I trusted his timing.

He'd never been wrong before, and I was sure he wasn't about to let me down now.

When I arrived home I had my casserole dish and Lisa Leann's cake in hand. Samuel met me at the door.

"What in the world is that?" he asked, taking the cake from me. "You ladies weren't hungry enough today?"

I followed him into the kitchen. "We ladies didn't eat today."

He glanced at me over his shoulder. "Uh-oh. What happened?" He placed the cake on the counter, then reached for the casserole.

I sighed, handed him the uneaten dish, and said, "I'll make a winter's salad, and we'll have dinner off of this."

"Sounds good. But what happened at the meeting?"

I paused, taking time to consider how to answer his question. I then let out a laugh, then another and another until I was in an all-out giggle. I laughed so hard tears rolled down my cheeks. When I finally was able to compose myself, I sighed deeply and said, "Goodness, I needed that."

Samuel stood dumbfounded. "So, that's it? You aren't going to tell me?"

"Honey, it would be impossible to explain," I said, walking over to him and wrapping my arms around his neck. I pressed myself up against him and kissed him. "But I'd like to thank you."

"For?" he asked with a glint in his eye.

"For . . . just . . . being . . . normal." I gave him a quick kiss between each word.

It was his turn to chuckle. "I do my best."

It was then that I heard music coming from the downstairs bedroom our son inhabited. "Tim's here, I take it?"

"Mmm. And, by the way, there will just be two of us for dinner tonight."

I drew back, my arms resting on my husband's shoulders. "What do you mean?"

"Michelle has a date, some new fellow from work named Adam."

"But what about Tim?"

Samuel pulled my arms from his shoulders. "You're not going to like this."

"Tell me."

"He has a date too."

"What?" I threw up my hands. "Has the whole world gone mad?"

"Lizzie, lower your voice."

I took several deliberate steps toward the downstairs. "I will not. And I will not stand by and let this happen." I turned and looked at Samuel. "Did you say anything to him? Did you?"

Samuel nodded. "I told him I couldn't approve of this, of course. But he's a grown man, Lizzie, and he has to make his own mistakes. We can't press down too heavily, or he'll only push back all the more."

I shook my head. "I have landed in the twilight zone. I asked for Wonderland, and I got the twilight zone."

I sprinted down the stairs and the short hallway to Tim's bedroom door, which was closed. I knocked loudly enough to wake both the living and the dead. When Tim answered the door, I saw that he was wrapped in a towel from the waist down and that his hair was spiked from a recent shower. "Mom," he said, stepping back into the room.

I pointed my index finger at him as I entered. "We need to talk. We can either do it here and now with you half dressed or we can do it upstairs at the kitchen table after you've had a chance to dress."

He extended his arms. "Say what you've got to say."

191

"Tim Prattle, I didn't raise you to do such as this."

"Such as what?" My son actually had the audacity to look confused.

I heard Samuel come up behind me, and I turned enough to see him leaning into the door frame. "Don't play coy, son," he said.

"Listen, you two. It's not like you think. It's just dinner with a nice girl from work. What's the harm in that?"

"You are a married man!" I stomped my foot, reminding myself of Donna earlier in the day. "What part of the wedding vows confused you?" I nodded my head back toward his father. "I'm sure your father can go over them again with you if need be."

"Mom, I know I'm married. I'm not sleeping with the girl, I'm just taking her to dinner."

"Do not speak disrespectfully to me, Tim Prattle."

"I'm sorry, Mom. But, seriously, I'm just taking her to dinner."

"Just taking her to dinner," I repeated. "Where?"

Tim shrugged. "I thought we'd try the Whale's Tail over in Breckenridge."

"Son—" I heard Samuel say.

"The Whale's Tail? You'll spend at least a hundred dollars there," I reminded him.

"If I'm lucky," he muttered, drawing the towel tighter at the ends.

I turned to Samuel. "Do something," I pleaded.

"What do you want me to do?" he asked.

My eyes widened. "Men. Oh, my gosh. Men." I looked at Tim again. "Tell me this. What if you found out that Samantha was having dinner with some other man at the Whale's Tail? How would you feel?"

Tim paused before he answered. "Look, Mom. This is really between Samantha and me. Now, I'd love to stay and chat, but it's starting to get a little chilly in here—and I don't just mean the temperature. So . . ." He gestured toward the door.

"Come on, Lizzie," Samuel said. "The boy's going to do what he's going to do."

Tim took a step forward. "I'm a man, Dad. Not a boy."

"Do tell," Samuel said, then shook his head and walked away.

I sighed. "I think your father said it just perfectly." I lowered my eyes. "I'm disappointed in you, Tim. I really am. And I've never been disappointed in you before."

"Really? Not even when I was in college and got Samantha pregnant?"

I shook my head. "Not even then. I was scared for you, yes. And sorry things happened out of their timing . . . but God takes all things that were meant for evil and turns them into good. This time . . . this time I'm disappointed. You have a wife and two precious children. Don't throw it away." I pressed my lips together, then left the room and climbed the steps to see Samuel sitting at the kitchen table, eating a piece of Lisa Leann's cake.

"This is pretty good," he said.

I shook my head at the wonder of it all. One of these days, I'm sure, I'll understand men and how they can shift from disaster to delectable in so short a time. But right then I was about as perplexed as they come.

I walked over to the counter, where the cut-into cake sat exposed. "I'm going to take the majority of this back to Lisa Leann."

"Why didn't she take her own cake home?" he asked with a mouthful.

I reached for the cake knife and said, "She just didn't." I sliced off a hunk—enough for Samuel and me—then placed it on a plate and wrapped it in aluminum foil. I recovered Lisa Leann's plate and picked it up. "I'll be back in a bit."

When I arrived at Lisa Leann's, I gripped the plate and walked toward the door, being careful not to slip in the snow that had turned icy. She opened the door with a look of genuine surprise. "I saw you drive up," she said. "What do you have there?"

"I'm bringing you back your cake." I smiled. "What's left of it, anyway. Samuel took a slice before I left, and I cut enough for our dinner tonight. I hope you don't mind."

Lisa Leann stepped back and offered me entry into her home. "I don't mind. I hope y'all like it. So I guess the meeting fell apart after I left, huh?"

I smiled grimly. "It did. But it'll be okay." I extended the plate to her, and she took it. I looked around. "I know I've said this before, Lisa Leann, but you have a lovely home," I said, though I was as taken aback by it as I had been the first time I'd entered it for Leigh's baby shower. Who would have pegged Lisa Leann's luxury condo to have wall-to-wall white carpeting and Victorian antiques upholstered in pink velvet? The chandelier in front of the beveled glass entryway was a nice touch, even impressive, but it was all a bit much for my simple tastes.

"Come on in and let me introduce you to Mandy," Lisa Leann said. "She's resting on the sofa, watching *Notting Hill*. I just love that movie, don't you?"

I nodded, following her into the family room; over the mantel was a lovely oil painting of Lisa Leann draped in pink velvet and pearls. I was temporarily distracted. "The movie. It was good, yes."

Mandy herself was a sort of pregnant china doll with porcelain skin, strawberry hair, and sparkling brown eyes. She started to sit up until I said, "Don't get up. You rest. I know how important it is when you're this far along." I turned back to Lisa Leann. "I'll be going now."

We walked together to the front door. "Lisa Leann, I don't know a lot about the Aunt Ellen thing, but—"

"It's something Clay thought up," she said. "It's just a local thing. You can see that by reading the introduction to it in last week's paper."

"I'm sorry to say that with the holidays, I just didn't get around to reading it."

Lisa Leann shook her head. "I wasn't trying to hurt anyone, Lizzie. I was just trying to get the ball rolling . . . to get people to start writing in their own questions."

"And have they?"

She beamed. "You bet they have. Why, I've got a doozy coming up in the next paper."

"Sounds like you had a doozy in last week's too." I paused. "I'll see you in church tomorrow."

I left Lisa Leann's and headed back home, my heart heavy and my soul weary. *Oh, Lord,* I thought. *Church tomorrow . . . I wonder what disaster awaits me there?*

25

Potluck Day

Clay decided to add evening walks to his morning routine, as he'd done that first night, thereby speeding the whole weight-loss process along. The route up and down Main Street, however, was becoming a bit of a bore. To shake things up a bit, he walked toward the Summit View Mountain range in the east, then turned right on Fifth Street. It was a bit hilly, but Clay determined he could stand the extra strain on his muscles.

The cold air invigorated him. He took in deep breaths and blew out puffs of white-gray vapor from between his chapping lips. He'd worn a knit cap on his head, and he pulled it down farther over his ears. Burying his hands in the pockets of his jacket, he shivered a bit. Tomorrow, he vowed, he'd dress even more warmly.

When he finally reached the top of Fifth, he was on Tumbleweed and was forced to make a decision to go either right or left. If he went right, he'd be closer to home. If he turned left, he'd head into more of the residential areas. It was safer walking.

Energized by what he'd done so far, he turned left, then right again onto Pitkin.

Pitkin was where Lisa Leann lived. He opened his reporter's eyes a bit wider when he saw Lizzie Prattle's car in the driveway.

Today was Saturday, he remembered. Potluck day.

He cocked a brow. What might have transpired, he wondered, to bring Lizzie Prattle to the home of Lisa Leann Lambert?

Lisa Leann

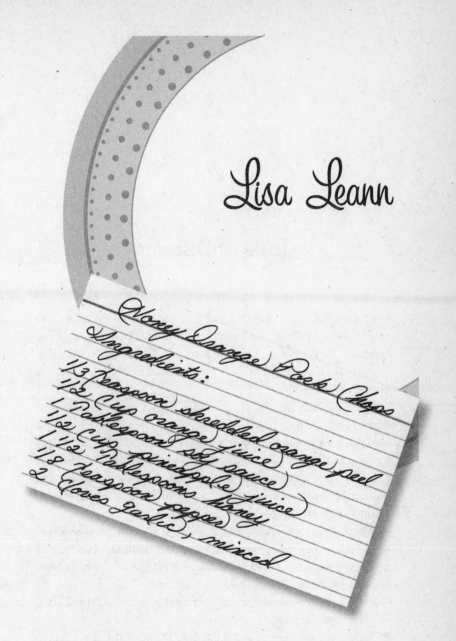

Honey Orange Pork Chops

Ingredients:

1/3 teaspoon shredded orange peel
1/2 Cup orange juice
1 Tablespoon soy sauce
1/2 Cup pineapple juice
1 1/2 Tablespoons honey
1/8 teaspoon pepper
2 Cloves garlic, minced

26

Taste of Disaster

Even though Lizzie's visit took some of the edge off my anger, the more I thought about the Potluck Club incident, the more I felt betrayed. I stomped around my kitchen, slamming drawers and cabinets as I prepared to make Mandy's favorite dish, honey orange pork chops.

I paused, rubbing my temples as a slight headache started to expand its territory. I needed to calm down. The last time I was this mad was back home in Houston when Darla Miller left my recipes out of the church choir cookbook on purpose, the little darlin'. Of course, as it was my recipes the ladies of the church had wanted in their personal cookbook collections, the fund-raiser was a bust. Though nobody can blame me for that one.

Those same ugly feelings I'd dealt with back in Texas revisited me the moment Donna Vesey barged into the Potluck Club, waving my wonderful advice column and hollering like her house was on fire and I was the one who had set it ablaze.

So, a few men asked her out. Was that a crime? I'd think she'd welcome the attention.

A thought struck me, and I giggled. If only I could get her to supply me with a list of names of those desperate enough to call her for a date. That list of lonely hearts would be a great start toward getting my dating service going.

I have to say, though, I felt bad about Vonnie. Of course, I wanted her to recognize the solution to her problem, but I'd never intended that she recognize herself. That's why I took care to disguise the situation. However, I don't think she would have known my advice was especially for her if Donna hadn't spilled the beans. And what was so wrong with my advice in the first place? If Vonnie was willing to give up those letters that inflicted so much pain in her marriage, Fred's feelings of betrayal would be resolved almost instantly. I shook my head. I guess there was more to her feelings about her dead husband than I'd first suspected. *That must be the problem. Vonnie's in love with a ghost. Poor girl.*

Vonnie aside, I had a good mind to give up on those Potluck ladies, and I would have too, that is, if Lizzie hadn't been such a dear to return what was left of my cake. Still, despite her advice, I wasn't ready to talk to Donna or Vonnie. I mean, I was as hurt as anyone in this. I was the dissed author. Did they know what it felt like to have your words slammed? So why did I get labeled as the bad guy?

I looked up to see Mandy rubbing her tummy. Though she was twenty-three years old, she looked like a pregnant schoolgirl. Her smooth skin glowed and her strawberry blond hair perched in a high ponytail on top of her head. Just precious.

"Did I wake you?" I asked. "I saw you'd fallen asleep during your movie."

"Oh no, the herd of wild elephants stomping through your kitchen woke me up."

I poured myself a cup of coffee and sat down at the kitchen table, and Mandy joined me with a glass of milk. "I'm sorry, darlin'; I didn't realize I was being so loud. I'm so used to being the only one around this place."

My daughter looked around the condo with an appraising eye. "This place certainly suits you. It's very elegant. Though I can't imagine where you're going to put your seven themed Christmas trees this year."

I took a sip of my coffee. "I'm hoping to squeeze in two. One angel tree in the front hallway, and then another full of dancing snowmen in the living room, and maybe I could get a drummer boy tree in the corner of the master bedroom. Though it might block Henry's closet."

Mandy smiled and rubbed her tummy again.

"Are you okay?"

"Oh yeah, the baby's kicking a little, I think. So, who are you so mad at?"

"No one."

"Mom, it's not me and Ray, is it?"

"You two? Oh no. Honestly, it's just my new column got a bad review."

Mandy picked up a copy of the edition, which was still lying on the table. "Your new Aunt Ellen advice column? How could anyone complain about that? You did a great job, Mom."

"That's what I thought, but apparently one of my so-called friends got a little bent out of shape when her life began to imitate my art."

"Well, that's not your fault."

"I know." I stood up and went to the refrigerator and pulled out my pitcher of orange juice. It was half empty.

"I just made this," I complained.

"Sorry, Mom, I had a couple of glasses while you were out."

"That's okay. I only need half a cup for the sauce."

"You're making honey orange pork chops tonight?"

"You bet."

"With your whipped mashed potatoes with garlic?"

"Of course. Should be ready by the time your father and Ray return from the ski slopes—in the next hour or so."

"What can I do to help?"

I pointed to a sack of potatoes and handed her a potato peeler. She stood up and moved to my side.

"Mom, now that I have to cook for Ray, I hardly remember cooking with you. Was I just too busy with cheerleading and my studies?"

I nodded, then glanced at her progress and gasped. "You've got peels all over everything. That's a job to do over the sink."

She studied me for a moment then moved her operation. "I remember now."

That caught my attention, and I stopped stirring my sauce. "You remember what?"

"The kitchen was always your domain. I could never do anything right."

I turned, wide eyed, and put my hand on my hip. "Amanda Ann, you know that's not true."

"That's how I remember it."

Before I could say more, a voice called from the study. "Mommm."

Mandy smiled. "You go see what Nelson wants, I'll be fine in here—alone in your kitchen. That is, if you trust me."

Her mischievous grin made me laugh, and I winked. I turned off my burner. "Just don't burn the place down, okay?"

She nodded solemnly, teasing me back. "I'll do my best, Mom."

I wiped my hands on my apron and scurried to see what my tall, handsome nineteen-year-old son wanted.

I found him draped over a web page he had pulled up on my computer. He looked almost preppy in his ivory sweater and jeans, that is, except for the way his auburn hair hung over his brown eyes. I'd have to coax him into a haircut before he returned to the University of Texas, where he was a business major minoring in the party life.

"What do you think?" Nelson asked.

I read the web address. "TheWeddingHelps.com?"

"Your new website."

I gasped. "Mine?"

I pulled up an antique straight-back chair I kept in the corner of the office and sat next to Nelson. Sure enough, there on the screen was the name I'd just painted in gold letters on my shop window: Lisa Leann's High Country Weddings.

"Why, Nelson, this is wonderful!"

"I'm going to need some more copy to put here and there, as well as a description of all the services you offer."

"Including my dating service?"

"You bet," he said. "I'm going to work on that software next. But be thinking of what else you'd like to include."

"Like my column?"

"Great idea. I'll work that up now."

I looked at my son as a warm feeling of pride began to grow. "How'd you know how to create all this?"

"Just finished a business web design class," he said.

I rubbed the top of his head. "You smarty."

Suddenly there was a scream from the kitchen, followed by a loud thud.

"Mandy?"

No answer.

I rushed to the kitchen door, but even before I rounded the corner, I could see potatoes rolling past the kitchen tile and onto the carpet.

"Mandy?"

And then I found her. My beautiful and very pregnant daughter lying in the middle of the floor, surrounded by potatoes and an upside-down pot. Water was everywhere.

I was running so fast, my slick tennis shoes slipped when they hit the tile, and I performed a ballet of sorts. Trying to keep from falling on my child, I ended up grabbing the double sink as if it were a handle and holding myself upright.

"Mandy!"

"I'm okay, Mom."

"What are you doing on the floor?" I asked as I bent down to lend her a hand.

Nelson appeared in the doorway. "What happened here?" he asked.

"Help me get her up," I commanded. "But watch your step." Together, we got Mandy to her feet, where she doubled over in pain.

"Mandy, what is it?"

"Help me to the couch," she said. "I'll be okay."

I wasn't so sure. "What happened?" I demanded as she tried to catch her breath.

She looked up, tears in her big brown eyes. "I was trying to take the pan of potatoes to the stove when I had a contraction that doubled me over. That's when I dropped the pot then slipped on one of the potatoes that rolled under my feet."

"A contraction? Are you still having them?"

"I'm afraid so. They're pretty strong too."

I looked up at her brother. "Nelson, get Mandy to the car. I'm going to make a quick phone call."

I dialed Vonnie's number. "Hey, Von, it's Lisa Leann."

Vonnie sounded relieved to hear from me. "Lizzie said you might be calling."

"She did, but—"

"I know you didn't mean any harm, but what you did hurt me. I'm not one to complain, but I wanted you to know I forgive you."

"Forgive me?" I was truly flustered. "Vonnie, I'm having a medical emergency here with my daughter, Mandy. She's just collapsed with contractions, and she's only seven months pregnant. Could you meet me at the hospital in Frisco? I could really use your support right now."

There was a brief silence on the other end of the line. "I'll be right there," she said. "Is there anything else I can do?"

"Pray!"

Less than half an hour later, Nelson was helping me walk Mandy into the tiny lobby of the high-country ER when Vonnie rushed to my side. She was dressed in faded navy sweats and looked as if she'd been crying. Disheveled or not, she took charge of the situation. She pointed to me. "You fill out the paperwork." She then pointed at Mandy. "I'll access Mandy."

Numbly, I obeyed. But first, I turned to Nelson and handed him my cell. "Do you think you could call Dad on his cell phone and tell him and Ray where we are?"

"Sure. Is Mandy going to be okay?"

"I don't know, but don't tell them that. Just tell them not to panic." I rolled my eyes. All I needed was for the men to break their necks, speeding down the icy roads.

After I filled in the paperwork, I sat next to Mandy and Vonnie. I brushed Mandy's bangs from her sweaty forehead. "How you doing?"

She leaned her head onto my shoulder. "I'm scared, Mom. I don't want to lose this baby."

I patted her hand and looked up at Vonnie, hoping she could tell me something. She motioned for me to follow her into the glassed hallway that led to the exit. "What do you think?" I asked.

"She's having contractions, and that can't be good. But maybe the doctors can put her on some meds that will help relieve them."

I nodded, glad for a bit of hope. I thanked Vonnie for her encouragement then rejoined Mandy. A few minutes later, a green-clad nurse called us to come through the double doors. "Sweetie, can you walk?" she asked my daughter. Mandy shook her head, and nurse Sandy, according to her plastic name tag, disappeared, then came back out with a wheelchair. "Here you go."

As if we were all on parade, Vonnie and I followed Mandy as Nurse Sandy wheeled her into an exam room. We left Nelson alone in the waiting room, looking a little green around the gills. He said, "I think I'll wait here for Dad and Ray."

When the men arrived, Ray came on back to hold Mandy's hand. "It's going to be okay," he kept whispering to her. She'd nod, but I could tell she didn't believe him. "It's too soon," she repeated, wiping away a stray tear.

She was right about that. *Oh Lord,* I prayed, *please keep my grandchild safe. Please!*

Four hours later, the doctors got the contractions under control. It was skinny Dr. Rollins who finally gave us a report. His green scrubs had a bit of blood splatter, probably from the victim of the car accident in the exam room next to ours. With only the curtains separating us, I already knew that the nine-year-old boy had broken his leg and had to have five stitches in his shoulder.

The doctor patted Mandy's arm. "You gave us a scare, young lady. Thought we were going to have to call in the Flight for Life to get you to a Denver hospital. But luckily you responded well to the meds."

I dared to breathe. "That's good news?"

The doctor nodded, his white surgical mask dangling from his neck like a bandana. He scribbled something on her chart. "Yes, it is," he agreed. "But young lady, you are going to have to promise me something."

She attempted a bit of humor. "Anything, Doc, as long as it's not my firstborn."

The doctor smiled. "I'm putting you on complete bed rest."

"That won't be so easy back home. I'm a schoolteacher. I've got to be on my feet eight hours a day."

"You are now a schoolteacher on leave. I'll write a note to your principal. Where do you teach?"

"At Wildwood Elementary, near Houston."

The doctor put the notepad down. "You're from out of state? Texas? Well, that presents a problem. Did you fly here?"

Mandy nodded. "Our flight home is Monday week."

"Not for you. What you've experienced is very serious. If you decide to travel, by air or by car, you'll risk your baby's life. You don't want to do that, do you?"

"No, but—"

I spoke up. "Mandy's my daughter. She can stay with her dad and me at the condo."

The doctor looked relieved. "Mandy, you'd better accept your mother's invitation."

Mandy looked up at Ray. "But Ray, he'll have to go home, back to work. I don't want to be here without my husband."

"Don't worry," I said. "I'll call Ray to fly back when it's time for the baby to come. This will only be temporary."

I turned to Vonnie, who had quietly been watching my family drama unfold.

She took Mandy's hand. "It will be all right, dear." She gave me a hard look then looked back at my daughter. "I'll be praying for you."

I would have made a batch of my world-famous cinnamon rolls to take to church to serve as a peace offering for the girls; that is, if Mandy and my family hadn't just spent the entire evening at the ER. When we got home, all I could do was fret over my daughter until Ray said, "That's enough, Mother Lambert; I can take care of my wife from here."

I couldn't help but smile. Not only because his gesture toward his wife was so sweet, but also because soon he would be on a plane headed back to Houston and I would have my very pregnant daughter all to myself. And barring any more emergencies, I couldn't be more blessed to be in this situation. Not only would I be there for the birth of my new grandchild, I would be in charge of the whole caboodle.

So, this Sunday morning, I woke up with a song in my heart and hurried to bake my lovely French toast casserole for my family.

I had a beautifully set table—my ivory china plates with the gold edging, placed with perfect linen napkins. A lovely crystal bowl with silk pink roses gave the table the perfect touch of color. My casserole was in one of my favorite dishes, an ivory enameled porcelain pan decorated with pink rosebuds.

Of course, as we gathered around the table, we all missed Mandy. She was still in her cozy bed in one of our two guest bedrooms. But who could blame the poor darlin'? After the events of yesterday, she certainly needed to catch up on her rest.

After Henry's prayer, the men dug in. How I love to watch men enjoy good food. Of course, I had warmed the maple syrup, and that was the perfect topper to my dish.

I didn't eat as much as they did. How could I? Even so, I knew Jane Fonda and I would be dancing to the beat later this afternoon, to make sure all that bread didn't stick to my hips.

After breakfast, Henry, Nelson, and I headed for church. We left the recovering Mandy and her adoring husband back at the condo. Honestly, they really were cute together. There they sat, cuddled on my pink velvet sofa; she was all sniffles, talking about their impending separation, while he held her close. How dear. It made my heart swell with love for them both.

I was glad we were making this trip to our quaint little Grace Church this morning. The building itself was a charming clapboard structure that had been around since the mid-1800s, when this area had been a busy gold rush town. The structure would almost be too small if the powers that be hadn't seen fit to add on an educational unit for Sunday school and other events.

How I enjoyed the drive. The morning was beautiful. The sky was blue, but there was just enough moisture in the air to create a frozen mist, which sparkled as if a crystal snow dome had been stirred to rain down glitter.

I loved the way the fresh snow glistened on the adorable antique shops, including my bridal boutique. It was all like a fairyland.

As we pulled in the parking lot, I saw Evie and Goldie walking toward the church. I waved, but they didn't. Maybe they hadn't seen me, but I'm guessing they were giving me the cold shoulder.

It was time for a little damage control.

After bustling around the church hallways for a few minutes, I saw my prey stepping outside his office just before the Sunday school hour. Pastor Kevin Moore, recent widower and best prospect for my dating service. This was my opportunity to quell any forthcoming rumors about me.

The pastor really was a handsome man. Though I think the shock of grief had grayed him a little more around the temples. Still, it only made him look even more distinguished.

I gave him my best smile. "Pastor, I was wondering if I could have a word with you."

"Mrs. Lambert. How are you this morning?"

"Please, call me Lisa Leann. Pastor, I've been praying for you since Jan died. How are you doing?"

His eyes moistened. "Honestly, it's been tough. It's no secret that Jan was the love of my life."

"Well, I'm happy to tell you I may be the solution to that."

He raised his eyebrows, but before he could comment I rushed on. "But first, I wanted to stop to ask you to pray for the dear ladies of the Potluck Club."

His eyes brightened. "How are Evangeline and her gang?" he asked.

I shook my head somberly. "Not very well, Pastor. In fact, that's why the ladies need your prayers. Everything is falling apart. Even my own daughter, Mandy, who's seven months pregnant, spent the evening in the ER with early contractions and is now on complete bed rest. Then, there's Evangeline, who is going through a terrible breakup with Sheriff Vesey."

"Oh?"

"Yes, and Lizzie's son has recently left his wife and has moved home to stay, not to mention poor Goldie—who needs prayer after she left her cheating husband. She's up to something too, I think. Then of course, you probably don't know about Vonnie. How her secret past has come back to haunt her? Though if you have time, I'd be happy to fill you in on the details. And then there's Donna—"

"My goodness, Lisa Leann, that's probably more information than I needed to know. But I promise you, I will pray."

"Oh, good. That's a burden off my shoulders. I've carried this all by myself. That's one of the reasons I came to you. Not only am I the answer to your problems, as I said, I think you are the answer to mine."

I smiled and batted my eyes, and the pastor shifted, darting his eyes around those passing by in the hallway. Why was he suddenly so nervous?

Just then Miss Evangeline Benson stood in front of us. "Pastor," she said, totally ignoring me, "I needed to ask you about the Christmas Tea. I know that was Jan's special project. But has anyone else been tapped to host it this year?"

My ears pricked up at that. "A Christmas tea? I'd love to help!"

Evangeline shot me a warning glance then turned back to the pastor. He replied, "That's a good question, Evangeline. Do you think the ladies of the Potluck, Lisa Leann included, would like to take a shot at it?"

I spoke for us all when I said, "Of course we would. Just this instant, while you were talking, I got the whole event planned and organized in my head. In fact, I'm hosting a baby shower for my daughter next Saturday; the ladies and I will talk about it then."

The pastor smiled at us both. "Perfect. I'll leave you two to the details. And if you would pardon me, I'm teaching the junior boys today, so I've got to scoot."

With that, he slipped into the crowd and out of sight.

Evangeline turned to me. "Just what do you think you were doing?"

"Just asking for prayer for my dear Mandy. You know she spent last night in the ER."

Her frosty gaze melted just a bit. "What happened?"

"Oh, it was just terrible. She's seven months pregnant, you know, and she fell in the kitchen. She was having severe contractions. Now the doctor's put her on complete bed rest. She can't even leave for home, and she's going to have to take a leave of absence from her teaching job."

Evie's eyes softened all the more. "Oh, my goodness."

"She'll be in my good care, so all is not lost."

"But what was that bit I overheard you tell Pastor?"

I crossed my arms uneasily. "Which bit was that?"

"How he's the answer to your problems and you're the answer to his? Do you know how that sounded?"

"Yes! I'm going to get him a date."

"With you?"

I gave her a sideways look. "Don't be silly. I'm married. I'm talking about my new dating service. Hey, and since Vernon didn't work out for you, and if Bob has the same fate, which seems likely in my opinion, we should talk. I'm sure I could find a good match for you."

Evie began to back away. "Ah, no. No thanks. I'm late for class, Lisa Leann. I'll have to catch you later, especially now that the pastor has assigned the two of us to work on the Christmas Tea."

She turned just in time to run smack into Bob Burnett. Luckily, he had only just walked up, missing my offer to help Evie find another beau. Whew!

But come to think of it, I'd have to slip around and make my dating service offer to him as well. Still, I couldn't see what Evie saw in the man. I knew he was a Grace deacon, but I'd heard he had never married, which of course makes you wonder. Not only that, Bob certainly wasn't much to look at. He was skinny as a stick, and with his bald head and arching eyebrows, he looked like he belonged in a comic strip. Though, to be honest, it was my understanding he had a lot of property holdings in the area. And with the price of real estate around here, the man had to be a millionaire, maybe even several times over. Okay, I could see why Evie might be interested. In some regards, Bob had a lot more to offer than that handsome sheriff. I grinned. Sheriff Vesey was yet another candidate for my matchmaking skills.

This was a proud moment for me. Look at all that I had accomplished since I had arrived from Texas only a few short months ago. I was giving the Potluck Club a new chance to regroup—starting at my house with an invitation to Mandy's baby shower. Then I would offer them a wonderful project, a Christmas Tea, no less. That could bring the girls together. Plus, I would have my precious daughter all to myself. Besides, preparing for a tea would give her something to do too. There would be so many little details and projects she could help with, right from her bed—like cutting out doodads to be glued on name tags and the like. It would be important to make her feel productive and keep her away from the blues.

I turned to head to the adult Sunday school class I'd joined with Henry and found myself staring at the sweetest sight. Standing in front of me were two young lovebirds. I'd never noticed them together before. "Allen and Becky from the singles class?" I asked. "I didn't know you two were dating. How long have you been together?"

Becky blushed, and Allen beamed. "Just since last week," Allen admitted.

Becky added coyly, "I never thought he would ask me out, and then when he did, we just clicked."

I had to ask. "So, what prompted you to call Becky, Allen?"

Becky giggled and answered for him. "It was that new column in the *Gold Rush News*, 'Aunt Ellen Explains It.'"

"Explains Everything," I corrected.

210

"Yes, that's it. Did you read the letter signed 'Fraidy Cat,' the one about the man who never acted on his attraction to his friend? Well, when Allen read that, he knew it was somehow written just for him. He went immediately to the telephone and dialed me up and asked me for a date." She giggled again. "Of course, I said yes."

I opened my red Brighton purse and pulled out one of my brand-new business cards and handed it to Becky. "I know this may be a bit premature, but if you decide to tie the knot, call me up. I'll give you two a very special discount."

Becky read the card and batted her eyes. "Well, you never know," she said.

"By the way," I added. "Isn't your singles group short on teachers? Maybe Henry and I could step in."

Allen said, "That would be an answer to prayer."

27

Will the Next Mrs. Pastor Kevin
Please Stand Up?

Clay enjoyed being at Higher Grounds on Sunday afternoons.

Well, technically, he arrived early morning for breakfast, returned home for a while, then came back a little before noon. A few minutes after noon meant losing his seat to some of the churchgoing crowd.

Clay especially enjoyed the hour or so when the Grace crowd came in. They would have just come out of church, but for the most part they could be easily persuaded to talk about one another.

Of course, these days, everything was fixed on Pastor Kevin's loss.

And, for a few of the single ladies—the opportunity to become the new Mrs. Pastor Kevin. That new development alone was like a toy box for Clay's sense of humor.

The women were like vultures.

But, for Clay, they were like the gravy on Sal's mashed potatoes, which he, according to his diet, could no longer eat.

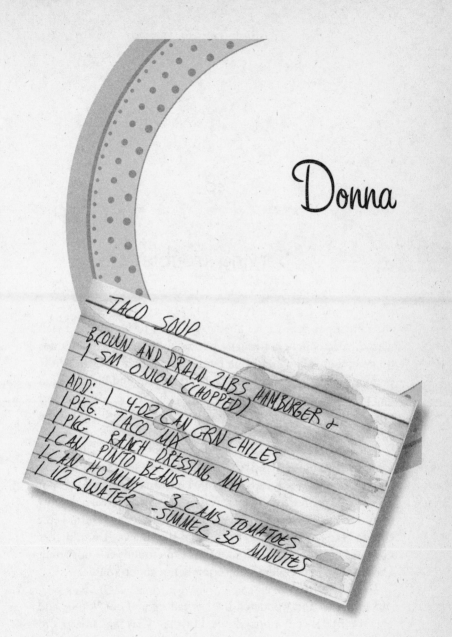

Donna

TACO SOUP

BROWN AND DRAIN 2 LBS. HAMBURGER &
1 SM ONION (CHOPPED)
ADD: 1 4-OZ CAN GRN CHILES
1 PKG. TACO MIX
1 PKG RANCH DRESSING MIX
1 CAN PINTO BEANS
1 CAN HOMINY
1 1/2 C WATER   3 CANS TOMATOES
-SIMMER 30 MINUTES

28

Serving Trouble

After my trip to balmy L.A., I had to wonder why I punished myself with these late-night hours in such frigid weather. And tonight was no exception. The Gold Mine Bank's digital sign proclaimed the evening chill to have already fallen to 20 degrees, and Weather.com had predicted the night's low at 8 degrees Fahrenheit. Brrrrr. As I was on duty, I'd have to somehow stay defrosted until 2:00 in the morning when I could finally curl up in the warmth of my bed.

I slowed my Bronco to drive by the Higher Grounds Café, trying to see if Clay's blue jeep was parked outside. All was clear. I realized I'd been holding my breath as I pulled into an empty parking spot just outside the restaurant. Clay was someone I had to avoid. How I had successfully maneuvered around him since my return, I just couldn't explain. Well, yes, I could. I'd stayed away from Higher Grounds because I couldn't face Clay's questions yet—not about David, not about Goldie, and certainly not about Vonnie.

I'd really missed my visits.

I grimaced and wondered if Clay had figured out Vonnie and David's little secret. I hoped not, but then Clay was smart, and reading people was his game. If he suspected the truth, any response on my face would confirm it.

I was one who didn't want to be read, not by Clay, or any man, for that matter.

I pushed open the café door and heard the bell jingle above my head. The place was hopping tonight. Must be Sal's new menu. She'd been working to spruce up the place, and it appeared to be paying off. The pine tables were varnished to a shine, and her new bakery case was full of delectable offerings like white chocolate macadamia cookies, homemade cinnamon bread, and cherry cobbler. In fact, it was the baked goods that lured me to take the risk of coming in.

Earlier this afternoon, hoping to avoid Higher Grounds, I'd packed my lunch, filling my jumbo thermos with taco soup hot off the stove top.

Later, as I had driven through the dark streets of Summit View, the lights of the restaurant had beckoned me. Feeling a little hungry, I realized I needed some hot coffee and a slice of fresh corn bread to go with my soup. So here I was, risking everything for a piece of bread and a cup of joe.

"Hey, Donna."

I looked up, surprised to see Wade Gage standing at the cash register with Pastor Moore. The pastor nodded in my direction, and I nodded back. "Kind of cold to be on the beat tonight, isn't it?" he said.

Wade patted me on the back. "Don't worry about Donna; she's pretty tough, aren't you, babe?"

Babe? I decided to ignore the remark and go straight to satisfying my curiosity. "So, are you two having dinner together?"

The two men looked at each other before the pastor answered. "Well, yes, as a matter of fact. I've been having dinner here more often since Jan died, and Wade and I have struck up a friendship."

My radar went up. "Really. So the two of you have dinner here on a regular basis?"

Wade nodded. "Yeah, you could say that."

"I would think that would interfere with your, uh, lifestyle, Wade. Aren't you running late for the tavern?"

Wade folded his arms over his grease-stained denim work shirt. He gave me a half smile. "The pastor here is talking to me about turning over a new leaf. What he's saying is making a lot of sense."

My eyebrows shot up. *Wade's getting religion? Wonders will never cease.*

Sally rang up Pastor Moore's bill, and he momentarily turned his back to us.

"Is this 'new leaf' business why you want to talk?" I asked my former beau.

"Partly." He took his hat off and held it behind his back. "But Donna, you know good and well that we have unfinished business between the two of us."

This time, I crossed my arms. "I don't think we have any unfinished business, Wade. Our past is said and done."

The pastor turned around. "Trust me, Donna, I don't think Wade is trying to make a move on you as it might appear."

Wade added, "Right, I only want to tell you something."

I felt my temperature rise. "So, tell me."

The two men looked at each other, then the pastor spoke up. "This wouldn't be the time or place. How about I see you both in my office, let's say 1:00 tomorrow?"

I started to say no. I mean, these two men had ganged up on me, and that was reason enough to tell them to take a hike. But something stopped me. Possibly it was the look in Wade's eyes—pure pain. He said, "I'm sorry we put you on the spot. But I kept the promise I made to you at the bank. Now it's your turn to keep your promise to me."

I think my mouth was still open when the bell jingled over the front door. I turned to see—oh no—Clay Whitefield looking almost gleeful.

I turned back to the men. "Okay. I know I'm going to regret this, but okay."

Clay walked up. "Doing a little street evangelism to the local sinners, Pastor?"

Pastor Moore chuckled. "It's been a while since I've seen you at church, Clay. So anytime you want to talk . . ."

Clay rolled his eyes good-naturedly. "Very good, Pastor. You've managed to corner another backslider."

Wade and Pastor Moore said their good-byes and walked out into the bitter cold. The frigid air that blew in reminded me of what I was in for tonight. Clay continued to stand behind me as if he, too, were waiting in line.

"How was your trip, Donna?"

"Not so great."

Clay looked absolutely relieved by this news. "Sorry to hear that."

Larry the cook took his place behind the counter to take my order. "Why, if it isn't the Ticket Master."

"Ha-ha. Just give me a large coffee and a big hunk of your corn bread, to go."

Larry grinned at me. He really wasn't a bad guy, but he always looked a little, well, greasy, with his dirty apron and slicked-back hair and hairnet. "Coming up," he said.

When he came back with my order, instead of ringing it up, he leaned on one elbow and stared me down. "Donna, I've been thinking about you lately."

Uh-oh.

Clay moved closer so he could watch this obvious come-on. I tried not to grimace. It appeared Larry was another fan of Lisa Leann's "Fraidy Cat" column. With that realization, I tried to keep my cool. "Really."

"Yeah, I was asking myself why a cute girl such as yourself was still unattached, and I decided it was because she hasn't met the right man."

I nodded. "That's a fair bet."

"Your search is over." He smiled at me, showing the large gap between his teeth. "Here I am. I know you like my cooking. Let's say you and I go out. Though, no speeding tickets. Okay?"

"Flattered by your offer, Larry. But I don't think so."

Larry stood straight and began to ring up my order. "Why not? We wouldn't even have to get personal to get close, if you know what I mean."

As I paid, I said, "I do know what you mean, and just wipe that idea out of your brain. Because that's not going to happen. No way, no how."

Larry frowned and handed me my order. I turned so fast I ran smack into Clay, who was standing a little too close.

"Excuse me," I said.

He grinned foolishly as he looked down at the top of my head. "Donna, I have more to tell you about the stranger who was looking for you the other day."

I had to hand it to him. Clay was good; he knew just what to say to keep me from bolting. "What do you know?" I demanded, gripping my brown sack of corn bread.

"Well, Pastor Moore told me this morning that this same man went to see him, told him you were up for a community service award. Wanted to know if you were a good little churchgoer."

"What?"

"Let's sit down at the table in the corner and try to figure this out."

Like a lost puppy, I obediently followed. As I sat, I said, "This is all so weird. What do you make of it?"

"Before I tell you what I think, I want to know—are you and David Harris an item?"

"Not really," I said. "We're friends."

"You went to L.A. to be with David, as a friend?"

I shook my head and looked away. "It's complicated. But we're friends, okay?"

"Well, I know Goldie didn't travel with you."

"Did I ever say she did?"

"No, but I still think you're protecting someone. Vonnie?"

"You think pure-as-the-driven-snow Vonnie is David's mother. What have you been smoking?"

Clay just stared at me and blinked. He was trying the read the truth from my best poker face, so I quickly changed the subject to the question at hand. "So, what do you think is going on with this stranger?"

"Well, Donna, quite frankly, I hate to tell you, but I don't think you're up for an award."

I snorted a laugh. "Well, that's obvious, isn't it?"

He shifted uneasily. "I think you're under investigation."

"Me? What did I do?"

"That's a good question. I doubt you're on the take. And as far as I know, your only enemies in Summit County are a few speedsters, right? I read the sheriff's blotter daily. There's not really anything linking you to any major accidents or wrongful deaths. Correct?"

My heart literally stopped. "Oh no."

"What is it? You're as white as a sheet."

"I gotta go. I gotta call my dad." I got up from the table in a fog.

He stood with me. "You don't think this has anything to do with that baby drowning up above Boulder, do you?"

I turned and stared at him. "You know about that?"

"I'm a journalist. It's my habit to read all the papers in the vicinity. You think I wouldn't read an article about you?"

I sat down again, hard. My cup of coffee sloshed beneath the protective lid. "Yeah, I guess you would have. I guess that means you've known my secret all this time. Why didn't you say anything?"

"You held on to it so tightly, I thought it would hurt you if I exposed it. Though it would have made a great front-page story. But I know you, and I know this baby's death couldn't be easy for you. I just didn't want to make it any harder." Clay kept standing but smiled down at me with a warmth I'd never seen in him before. "It was really a brave thing you did, going back into that flooded river to try to rescue that woman's child. I never told you, but I think you're a hero."

I stood again. "I gotta go." I rushed to the door and pulled it open, just as a blast of icy wind hit me dead in the face. Before I could recover, a man stepped next to me. "Pardon me, Deputy. You dropped this." I turned and stared at the stranger. Dressed in a brown overcoat, dress pants, and shoes, he seemed a bit out of place for this mountain town where everyone else was bundled in bright parkas and knit caps. He handed me an envelope. Blindly,

I took it, and he smiled. "Thanks, Deputy, you've just been served a civil lawsuit suing for monetary damages in the death of infant Bailey Ann Long. Good luck."

Before I could react, the stranger disappeared into the shadows.

"No," I whispered.

I was trying to breathe when a hand suddenly rested on my shoulder. It was Clay. I turned to him.

"He must have seen your Bronco parked outside and known you were here," he said. "I'm so sorry."

I stared up at Clay, trembling with either shock or the cold or both. I didn't know. Neither did I know what to say or what to do. Clay did. He swallowed me into his arms, holding me tight as I wept into his chest.

The dam had finally broken, releasing a flood of emotion I didn't even know one person could contain. Standing on the sidewalk outside the restaurant, Clay gently stroked my hair as I sobbed in his arms. I did nothing to resist. "Donna," he finally whispered in my ear. "How have you carried this all by yourself?"

I cried harder, and he pulled me to his jeep. "Get in," he instructed. "It's cold out here. Besides, we can't let all of Summit View see you like this."

I shook my head. "I'm on duty. I've got to get back to work."

"But I don't think you're in any shape to drive. Can I take you to your dad's?"

I wiped my eyes on the sleeve of my leather jacket. "I'm okay. I'm just going to sit in my Bronco for a while."

"Then I'll sit with you. I'll be your ride-along."

That's when I looked at him. I was startled to see how his eyes glistened with fire. I'd always thought of him as chubby, but had he been losing weight? I hadn't noticed till that very moment. And there was something else. It was . . . he looked so earnest . . . so . . . so in love?

My head was spinning. "No. No, I'm on duty. I'm okay. I need to be alone."

Reluctantly, Clay let me go, and I climbed into my Bronco and powered it up before pulling into traffic without looking back. It was 8:45, and I needed a place to hide, to think. I drove into the back of the bank's parking lot and let the truck idle.

I picked up my cell phone and dialed. "Dad?"

My father's deep voice resonated with concern. "Donna, you sound upset. Are you okay?"

I took a deep breath. "Not really."

The cell phone crackled as he asked, "Where are you?"

"At the bank."

"Was there a robbery? Are you hurt?"

I sobbed softly before answering. "No, no, but something's happened—the thing we were afraid of."

"You're not making sense. Stay put; I'm coming over there."

A few minutes later, Dad's Bronco pulled up next to mine, and my father climbed into the cab of my truck. He handed me his hanky and said, "Girl, tell me what's wrong."

I blew my nose before answering. "I got served."

"What?"

I handed him the papers. He hit the overhead light then read them in silence.

"Donna, you can beat this. No jury in the world is going to blame you for what happened on the river that night. You risked your life to save that child."

"But a baby's dead, and it's all my fault."

Daddy looked at me, then lifted my chin with his hand. "The baby's death is not your fault. It was a freak accident, an act of nature."

My eyes couldn't meet his. "Or God is punishing me."

He snorted. "I know I haven't been to church in years. But I don't believe that. I can't say I understand the mind of God or why these things happen. But you've suffered enough. It's time for you to face this thing so you can let go of it. Maybe this bogus lawsuit will help you put it all behind you."

"I've already tried to do that. But it's swallowed me whole. I don't think I can take any more."

221

"But why not? You're stronger than that."

I studied my dad in the yellowed light of the cab. Shadows deepened over his brow, and his blue eyes crinkled with worry. I dared to look into his eyes as I spoke in a hushed whisper. "I think you know."

His eyebrows arched. "Know what?"

"Maybe I didn't kill Bailey Ann, but you know that I killed my own baby. You were there. You drove me to the clinic. You waited for me in the waiting room. And now I just can't seem to separate one baby's death from the other."

Dad put his arm around me, and I leaned my head on his shoulder. "Oh, Donna. You were my little girl, and it was just too early for you and Wade to start a family. What were you, all of eighteen? You had plans, goals. I couldn't let your pregnancy take that away from you. And truthfully, after your mama left in such a scandal, I couldn't bear the thought of going through another one. I didn't want to see you start a family that way."

My breath caught on a sob. "But did you ever stop to think of the consequences?"

He pulled back and leaned his head back into the seat. "No. I'm afraid I didn't. As far as I knew, your baby was, what, just ten weeks along? It was only a clump of cells at that stage."

"I've tried to believe that. Lord knows. But in my heart, I knew the truth. I killed my baby, and now I'm paying for it with the death of Bailey Ann. At least, it was her death that made me realize what I'd done."

Dad sat quietly, but when he finally spoke, I turned to see him wiping tears from his eyes. "Donna, I'm sorry. I was wrong."

I nodded. "We both were."

We sat together for a long time, quietly breathing as pain engulfed us. Finally Dad gave me a hug. "You stay on duty. I'll call you in the morning, unless you'd like me to relieve you now," he said.

"No, you go on home. I'll be okay."

How I managed to outlast my shift, I'll never know. I was glad it was a slow night. Too cold for any pranksters to be out, and as it was Sunday, the weekend tourists had left for Denver. That gave me plenty of time to think in that frigid parking lot. I was glad I had the hot soup and coffee to keep me from turning into an icicle.

Later, when I got home, I collapsed into bed, drifting into a rare, dreamless sleep. I pulled about five hours of sleep and took a hot shower as my coffee brewed. Later, I sat drinking my joe as I looked out the kitchen window. The morning was beautiful. A cloud was lifting from the mountain behind my house, leaving ice crystals glistening on the pine trees. The phone rang. It was Clay.

"Donna, how are you?"

"Not so good. And yourself?"

"I'm worried about you."

"Don't, Clay. I'm not worth it."

There was a pause on the end of the line. "What are you saying?"

"Don't get attached to me, Clay. I don't have anything to give anyone. Even someone who has been a friend to me, like you."

"Donna, I don't believe that, and I'm not giving up. Why don't you meet me down at the café?"

"No, I can't."

"Then let me drop by."

"No, I'm sorry." Then with nothing more to say, I bid Clay goodbye, and I went back to the window. The cloud had completely evaporated, leaving a bright blue sky to contrast against the white landscape. The beauty helped my soul relax, if only a little. That's when it hit me. To my amazement I realized that Clay Whitefield, my enemy, was a real friend. Maybe my only one, unless you counted Vonnie and a few of the Potluckers.

I pulled into the church parking lot at 12:30, hoping to catch Wade before he went into the church. I was hoping to find out why we had to talk to the pastor together.

When he pulled his blue pickup into the lot at a quarter till, I got out and met him. He looked sheepish, though as handsome as ever. He was wearing khaki pants and a nice black cable-knit sweater with a white pointed collar. Gone was his ever-present Rockies baseball cap, and it looked as if he'd actually trimmed his golden locks and bothered to shave. This was a side to Wade I didn't know. Though, it was an improvement.

"What's all this about?" I asked him.

Wade looked around uneasily. "I'd rather not talk about it out here."

"Well, I don't want to talk to the pastor if I don't know what I'm facing."

Wade squinted his blue eyes. "Are you okay, Donna? Your face is swollen. Have you been crying?"

I shrugged. "Just tell me why I'm here or I'm leaving."

"It's about closure, Donna. You and me. We both need it."

"Wade, our relationship is long over."

"Is it? In one afternoon, fourteen years ago, I lost my family."

I stared at him. "We were never a family."

"You carried my baby. You'd agreed to be my wife."

I heard a car pull into the parking lot, but I didn't bother to look up.

"And?"

"And I lost you both. One trip down the mountain, to 16th and Vine in Denver, and it was over."

I heard a car door slam, but I stared at the ground. "You told the pastor?" I looked up at him. "Wade, I go to church here."

"I didn't mean to embarrass you."

"Embarrass me? You had no right. By telling Pastor Moore, you've taken the only thing I had left in my miserable life."

Wade reached for my hand. I looked up and once again saw his pain. "What did I take from you?" he asked.

"My pride." I pulled my hand away, and with tears blurring my vision, I ran back to the Bronco.

"Donna!" I heard a familiar voice call.

I turned my head to see Vonnie standing by my truck. I swung open the cab door and leaped inside. Between sobs, I managed to stammer, "I can't talk, Vonnie, I've got to run."

Wade walked up and stood next to this dear woman I'd always thought of as my mom. I looked back at them in the rearview mir-

224

ror as I peeled out of the driveway. Was Wade going to tell her too? But then, she already knew, didn't she?

My Bronco fishtailed on the road, but I didn't care. I didn't know where I was going—I thought maybe I should consider driving off the nearest cliff. Besides, what difference would it make if I lived or died? Though in most ways, it seemed I was already dead. I died the same night God ripped Bailey Ann from my arms.

29

Friendship with Attitude
Takes a Holiday

Clay wasn't sure what Donna had been thinking when he'd wrapped her in his arms, but he was keenly aware of his own thoughts and feelings. He suspected—though he couldn't be sure—that Donna had noticed his weight loss too. The very thought of it made him want to add another mile to his exercise routine.

But there was something else he'd noted. Maybe it was his sharp reporter's skills kicking in, or maybe it was something else, like his love and devotion to the little nut.

He was worried, truly concerned, and that was a new emotion for him. Not that he hadn't ever had a troubled thought for another human being; he'd been very anxious about his mother's well-being after his father died and still sent money from his paycheck to both her and his beloved grandmother so they could enjoy a few of life's "little pleasures." But his relationship with Donna had always been one of ribbing and teasing. Jest. Friendship with attitude.

When she'd fallen into his arms, he'd felt a sense of protection toward her. Something bold and warriorlike. It came to him, then, that Donna Vesey was a woman holding on to more than one secret. The floodgates of tears had been about more than just a baby drowning.

What more, he could only imagine.

Evangeline

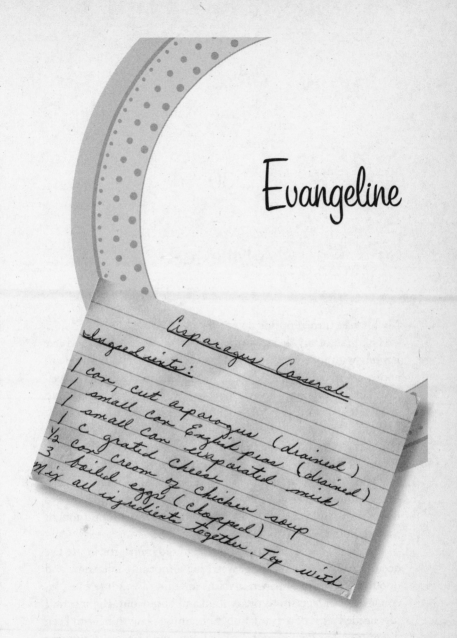

Asparagus Casserole

Ingredients:

1 can, cut asparagus (drained)
1 small can English peas (drained)
1 small can evaporated milk
1 C grated cheese
½ can cream of chicken soup
3 boiled eggs (chopped)
Mix all ingredients together. Top with

30

A Little Tart

My life had turned upside down.

The man of my dreams—the man I wanted to marry and live happily with for the rest of my life—was, once again, in love with another woman. My Potluck Club was going to blazes in a basket. Another meeting like this past one, and we might as well close up shop. If it hadn't been for Lizzie staying and praying with me, I think I would have just curled into a small ball in the middle of my bed, pulled the covers over my head, and never come back out.

But, of course, I had to come out. I had to go to church the following day, which only added another complication to my life. Lisa Leann's meddling led to Pastor Kevin pairing us together to direct the Christmas Tea. Well, if that little gal from Texas thought she was going to run the Tea . . .

I sat in the family room of my parents' old home, the house I've occupied my whole life long, watching a morning talk show and doodling on a pad of paper. It wasn't anything I was interested in. As a matter of fact, it was pretty loud and obnoxious. Right now, I just needed a bit of a distraction. Something—anything—to keep my mind off of Vernon, my Potluck Club, and Lisa Leann running (or ruining) the Christmas Tea.

The Christmas Tea made me think about Jan, and I made a note on the paper that we should somehow honor her at this year's event. How, I wasn't quite sure. I made another note: call Vonnie, Lizzie, and Goldie. Get opinions on honoring Jan.

I glanced up at the television, peering over the rim of my reading glasses. The host of the show, Jason Sanders, was speaking into his microphone, staring into the camera. "We're talking to women today who were dumped by their lifelong mates, and we're offering them hope and help for the future."

The camera swung over to a woman with thick blond hair and full cheeks. Her makeup was clearly locked in the eighties, as was her choice in fashion and accessories. I chuckled a bit, amazed that I would even be aware of such. Maybe knowing Lisa Leann for the past few months hadn't been such a bad experience after all. What that woman knows about makeup and fashion could fill a glossy three-hundred-page magazine. "I don't like to use the word *dumped*," the woman was saying. "It's demeaning. It says I wasn't worthy of this man. Well, the fact of the matter is, Jason, he wasn't worthy of me."

The audience erupted in applause.

"Preach it, sister," I said.

"Jason, may I say something?" a voice rang out over the ovation. The camera now rested on a slender woman with short, groomed hair and caramel skin. She wore a blue suit, and even my untrained eye could see it was expensive.

The name "Dr. Toni Mason" was printed at the bottom of the screen.

"Yes, Dr. Mason," the host confirmed her request.

"Women of today who have been left after years of love and loyalty must reach deep within themselves and see their inner worth. That's why the audience clapped for what Naomi just said. It's important that women see their own worth because they are valuable not only as human beings but as human beings capable of being loved and being able to give love."

I made a face. What in the world did that woman just say, and why did it take a degree in psychology to say it? Shoot, I could have said that and probably done it even better. What did she know, anyway, about loving someone since she was twelve years old only to have to give him away not once but three times to a woman like Doreen Roberts?

As if on cue, the cordless phone perched on the nearby end table rang. I pulled off my reading glasses and reached for it. "Hello," I said.

"Don't hang up."

I sighed. "Vernon. Why do you keep doing this? Why do you keep calling me . . . hounding me? Don't you think I see you driving by my house at all hours of the day and night? You know what I'm going to have to do, don't you? I'm going to have to get that caller ID service for my phone. Or move. That's what I'm going to have to do. I'm going to be forced to move, and it'll be all your fault."

Vernon remained quiet during my tirade. "Are you done?" he asked. "Because if you'll just talk to me, listen to me, I'll be glad to let you carry on from now until noon, so you just rant and rave all you want, Evie-girl."

"Don't call me that. I told you before, do not call me that."

"Come on, Evangeline," he practically whined. "Can't you just listen to what I have to say?"

"No."

"Why not? Give me one good reason why not."

"Because I am a human being who deserves to love and be loved." I nodded my chin in appreciation for what I'd just learned from Talk TV.

"What? What the tarnation does that mean?"

I pursed my lips. "I should have known you wouldn't understand simple psychology."

I listened to what sounded like traffic on the other end of the line. "Where are you, Vernon Vesey?"

"I'm sitting outside in your driveway. I want to come in . . . to talk to you."

I looked down at myself. I hadn't taken my shower, hadn't gotten out of my old pajamas and the ratty robe I wore when I wanted and needed comfort. My mouth held the lingering stench of morning breath and strong coffee, and my hair hadn't seen a comb or brush since earlier the day before. "I don't hardly think so," I said, rising from my chair and darting through the house toward the front windows whose blinds were, blessedly, closed.

"What do you want me to do? Do you want me to get up on the front porch and bang on the door? Do you want me to stand out in the middle of the yard and sing love songs? Evangeline, you've got to listen to me on this."

I pried open two slats of the front window blinds and peered out. There he was, sitting in one of the county Broncos, looking so handsome in his uniform I could have eaten him with a spoon.

"I see you, Evangeline."

I jumped back. "Well, so what if you did?" Inwardly, I chided myself for having admired him, even for an instant. "And, for your information, I don't have to do anything I don't want to do, Vernon Vesey. Now I'll thank you kindly to leave my property, or I'll . . . I'll . . ."

"What? Call the law? It's sitting here, right here, in your driveway."

I crossed the room and sat in a chair. "Vernon, say your piece from the car. I'm listening."

"I want to come in."

"Not now," I answered. "I'm not exactly presentable for company."

"Look, Evie. I'm tired—real tired; I had a long night last night, and I've still got something important to handle today. Something very important. And, after that, I promise you, I'll tell you what you want to know. Deal? I'll come pick you up at 7:00, we'll have dinner, and we'll talk. I know we can get this thing rectified if you'll just listen."

I didn't answer right away. I wasn't sure what to do. It wasn't that I had any plans—in fact, it was one of the first nights I didn't have plans to go out with Bob since our first date at Apple's. I wanted so badly to hear what Vernon had to say—to believe what he had to say—because I loved him so strongly. But, the problem was, I wasn't sure if I could believe him, no matter what he had to say, no matter how he tried to defend his actions from a couple of weeks ago.

And, darn it all, Bob Burnett was actually starting to grow on me. "If you can't marry the one you love," Mama used to say, "at least marry the one who loves you." From all indications, Bob Burnett was in love with me. He'd pampered me with dinners and flowers delivered from florists for no apparent reason except to say that he was thinking of me. He'd even surprised me during one date with a bottle of perfume. A real expensive one too. If I said yes to Vernon's request, would I betray what I was building with Bob?

"Evie?"

"What? Oh. Sorry. I was thinking."

I heard him chuckle. "Well, that's better than a downright no."

"I'll meet you at Higher Grounds at 5:00. Not Apple's at 7:00."

"But—"

"No, Vernon. I'll hear what you have to say, but on my own terms. Besides, I already have dinner plans." That was sort of a lie. My plans were to eat the last of Goldie's asparagus casserole she'd brought with her on Saturday.

I listened for a moment to the rhythm of his breathing before he answered. "Have it your way. I'll see you at 5:00."

I pushed the "end call" button on my phone, then took it back into the family room to replace it in its cradle. A quick glance at the television showed the studio audience of the talk show to be in an all-out war, each individual screaming and yelling at the others who were vying for the chance to share their opinion.

I picked up the remote and clicked off the TV. The television hummed to silence. As I laid the remote back on the coffee table, I pondered the similarities of the talk show's audience to the war within my own heart.

As the day dragged on, I found myself a little more excited about meeting Vernon at the café than I'd anticipated. I spent extra time in my bath, primping over my hair and dabbing a little extra eye cream onto the fine lines that my niece, Leigh, had said gave me character.

What does a twentysomething know about crow's feet and character? I wondered, leaning over the vanity and studying my face. My shoulders drooped. I'd read an article recently about some Botox alternative. I made a quick decision to look into it further.

A glance into my closet revealed that I had nothing new to wear—at least nothing new to Vernon. He'd seen me in all my new clothes, and I wanted to impress him. This afternoon would mean either the new start of our relationship or the absolute end of it. One way or the other, I needed a new outfit. He'd be pleased at what he was getting back or he'd kick himself all the way home at what he was losing.

I slipped into an old pair of navy blue slacks and an outdated sweater, pulled on a pair of thick socks, and then pulled on my snow boots. I studied the face of my watch as I hooked it around my wrist. If I didn't dawdle, I could drive up to Main Street Fashions, pick out something perfect for the meeting, be home in time for a little extra attention to myself, and make it to the café before 5:00.

Minutes later I was rolling my car down snow-plowed streets, turning onto a side street parking space, and darting into the small boutique.

"Evangeline," Lindy Follett greeted me from behind the counter, where displays of cashmere scarves were draped through brass towel rings. "What brings you in here on such a cold afternoon?"

I lingered over the scarves as I pulled my gloves from my hands, then lightly touched a chartreuse one trimmed with little beads tied into the fringes. "Pretty," I said, then looked up. "I'm just looking for a little something new. Nothing important."

Lindy lifted her multicolored reading glasses from the bridge of her nose and pushed them on top of her head, where they nestled in her curly, shoulder-length gray hair. "If you like that scarf, I have a sweater and pantsuit that goes with it very nicely." She walked from around the counter and led me to the clothes rack. Removing the set from the bar, she asked, "What do you think?"

"I like that. Not too fancy, not too informal."

"It's sharp," she said, extending it to me with a wink. "And a little more up-to-date than what you've got on. Why don't you try it on and see?"

I took the clothes and started toward the curtained-off dressing room. As I was stepping into the slacks I heard Lindy call from the other side, "Do you mind if I ask you a question, Evangeline?"

"Not at all," I answered, pulling the slacks over my hips and zipping them at the side.

"I've seen you sitting with Bob Burnett the past two Sundays at Grace. Are you two dating?"

I looked at myself in the mirror before me, half dressed in my bra and a sharp pair of lined gray wool slacks. My face turned crimson in spite of the fact I was basically alone. It felt as though my private life were exposed for the world to see. "I guess you could say that," I said.

"I was just surprised to see the two of you sitting together," she continued as I slipped the sweater from its hanger and pulled it over my head. "I thought you and the sheriff were dating and—"

I jerked the curtain back and stepped out. "What do you think?" I asked her, eager to change the subject.

"Oh, Evangeline. Well, honey, that's the color for you; that much is for sure. If you're trying to impress the new man in your life, this ought to do it."

What I was trying to do was impress the old man in my life. Not that Lindy Follett needed to know that, of course. "I'll take it," I said, turning to look at myself in the outside mirror. I had to admit, I did look sharp.

Lindy held the scarf in her hand and draped it over my shoulder. "You can wear it like this, or—"

"I'll take the scarf too," I said. "Let me get dressed, and I'll bring these to the counter." I looked down at my watch. "I have somewhere I have to be in a couple of hours, so . . ."

Lindy nodded. "I see. Okay."

I paid for my purchases—even adding a new pair of earrings to the ensemble—and headed back home. As soon as I turned on the car, my "low fuel" indicator light came on. I checked my watch again. If I hurried, I could drive down to the Pump 'N Go just outside the city limits where the gas was a few cents cheaper than in town and still make it home with plenty of time to spare.

I'm not real big on going to the Pump 'N Go except that the gas is less expensive. The problem I have is that it's in a less desirable part of town, an area where the tavern is and a few of Bob's white-trash trailer rentals. It's not that I think I'm better than anybody else, I'm just not comfortable outside of my element. But to save a few dollars—and with the price of gasoline these days—I was willing to risk my reputation.

I pulled up to one of the gas pump islands, popped the lever for my gas cap, and began the process of pumping gasoline into my car, careful not to get any on my hands. I looked around, checking things out, wanting to stay alert lest any of the lowlifes around here should try to abduct me or steal my car. That's when I noticed the sheriff's Bronco parked at the side of the tavern. I strained to see the license plate but couldn't. If it read Summit 2, it was Donna. But if it read Summit 1, it was Vernon.

My money was on Donna, but I knew it could be her father. But if Vernon said he had something very important to do today, what was he doing in the tavern now? Drinking? Had it come to that? Had my breaking up with him led to alcoholism? Or perhaps the arms of one of the floozies who worked there? I could certainly see it happening, Vernon not being a fully religious man. Maybe, I pondered, God had led me here on purpose . . . to find out the truth about the man who professed to love me so much.

The pump lever I was squeezing in my hand snapped off and spilled gasoline over the side of my car. "Oh, for heaven's sake," I said. I replaced the handle, then reached for the squeegee so I could wipe off the spillage, careful the entire time to keep my eyes on the tavern, lest Donna or Vernon came out.

They didn't.

What happened next is the kind of thing you only see in movies. I turned the key in the ignition of my car and drove right next to the Bronco, which by now I could see read Summit 1.

Vernon was in there. Vernon was in there, and I was about to find out why. Or, with whom.

I'd never been in the tavern before, not even in my younger years, but I pulled open the door like I'd been doing it all my life, then stood in the doorway gaping. Even in the middle of the afternoon it was filled with people, though certainly not my kind of people. Smoke permeated the room. Music—loud and raunchy from the sound of it—blasted from overhead. It took me a minute to focus my eyes in the dimly lit room, but when I did, I immediately spotted the sheriff sitting at a back table, deep in conversation with a woman who sported bleached blond hair worn dirty and long and tied back in a tight ponytail. She was smoking a cigarette, dragging on it so hard I was shocked she didn't choke to death right there.

Whatever the two of them were talking about, it seemed almost violent in nature. The crimson in Vernon's face was visible even from where I stood. I took a step forward, and almost as if on cue, Vernon turned to face me. The red in his face drained out, replaced by ashen gray. "Evie," I saw him mouth, though I couldn't hear a thing over the cacophony of the music and patron conversation.

The woman sitting across from him snapped her neck to face me then. I squinted my eyes, aware of Vernon standing, though it seemed to be in slow motion. Somehow my feet found their purpose, and I crossed the room, keeping my eyes on the blonde, who smiled wickedly as she drew on her cigarette once more. As I moved closer, I saw that she was wearing the tavern's work shirt, a long-sleeved black polo with an imprinted frothy glass of beer, and a name tag that read "Dee Dee."

"Evangeline, what are you doing here?" I heard Vernon saying, though I didn't bother to turn to look at him. I was more focused on the woman who smirked as she looked up at me.

Dee Dee McGurk, Bob had called her. Donna had described her as "washed up," but I saw something else . . . something more. Something that looked like my past sitting right smack in the middle of my present, ripping apart my future.

"Evie," she said, speaking at last. She eyed me up and down as I stood before them in my old clothes. "I see some things haven't changed about you." Her voice was hard and raspy; her face lined with years of hard living. But her eyes . . . I knew those eyes. Tired and haggard as they were, they couldn't fool me. These were the eyes of my enemy.

"Doreen Roberts," I said. "I see some things haven't changed about you either."

I looked at Vernon, who wore a pair of dress pants, a long-sleeved cotton shirt and tie, and a leather jacket that shone in the overhead light. He smelled of aftershave. "Don't even bother," I ordered. "There's absolutely nothing you can say to me now."

I don't remember what happened next. I don't know how I got to my car or even how I managed to drive out of the parking lot. Somehow, I found myself at Bob's bungalow office, located near Donna's home. I walked in on rubbery legs, looking through eyes that were blurred with both rage and confusion.

Bob was sitting at his desk, smoking a thick cigar, poring over what appeared to be a local tourist magazine. When he saw me, he stood. "Evangeline," he said. "Honey, what's wrong?"

I crossed the room as he came around to meet me. When we were practically nose to nose, I said, "I have a question for you, Bob Burnett, and I want an answer right now. Yes or no. No thinking about it. No pondering it."

"What is it, Evangeline? You look ill. Do you need to sit down? A cup of tea, maybe?"

"I don't need a cup of tea, Bob Burnett. I need an answer."

He smiled, showing nearly every one of his crooked teeth. His thick brow arched over his deep-set eyes as he said, "Well, then, I guess I need a question."

I placed my hands on my hips and squared my shoulders. Taking a deep breath, I then exhaled and said, "Yes or no. Do you want to marry me or not?"

"Marry you?" Bob took a step back. "Evie, have you been drinking?"

My face fell, and my shoulders drooped. I turned to leave, too humiliated to remain. Before I made it to the door, he caught me and spun me around. "Wait up, there. You caught me off guard, is all. Question is, do you want to marry me?"

I felt my stomach lurch as my heart turned inside out. "Would I have asked if I didn't?"

He jutted his neck forward a bit. "Isn't this supposed to be the man's job? The asking?"

I started for the door again, and again he stopped me. "All right, Evangeline. Yeah, I want to marry you. If you're game to marry an old man like me, then I guess I'm game to marry an old—"

"Watch it, Bob," I warned, then forced myself to smile.

I stood motionless as he put his hand on my waist and pulled me to him. "You know, I've never even kissed you, Evie. Never even held you tight."

I leaned my head back enough to say what I had to say. "Well, then. I guess now's as good a start as any for the first time."

As he pressed his lips against mine, a wild thought skipped through my mind. *Two can play this game, Vernon Vesey. And one of us might even win. You'll see.*

31

Two-Finger Tango

Clay Whitefield nearly bounced up and down in the chair positioned at the center of the desk in his apartment. He typed as fast as his two index fingers would allow. Behind the laptop, Woodward and Bernstein wrestled with each other like two sumo wrestlers, spewing wood shavings and pushing them into small hills along the cage's edge.

Clay barely noticed. He was Clay Whitefield, ace reporter, and he'd seen it all.

Earlier that day he'd received a call from his editor, asking him to drive over to the Pump 'N Go. There'd been a run of young people pumping and going and not paying. The owner thought it might be some kind of game implemented by some of the high schoolers. Clay was sent as an investigative reporter.

When he'd seen Evangeline Benson driving her car into the parking lot of the tavern, he quickly postponed the interview and followed her. By the time he'd made it inside, she was standing in front of a table near the back, where the sheriff and the new barmaid in town had apparently been sitting.

Clay slid along the wall so as to go unnoticed, inching his way close enough to hear what needed to be heard and stopping at the far corner of the bar.

He let out a sigh when he'd heard the name Doreen Roberts, then closed his eyes against the pain he knew Donna would feel when she found out the truth about Dee Dee McGurk.

As soon as Evie had stormed out, Clay dropped like a bowl of pudding into the nearest chair he could find. The bartender, an older man with a paunch just slightly bigger than his own, leaned over the bar. "Whatcha need?" he asked.

Clay jerked his head toward him, then cut his eyes back over at the sheriff and his ex-wife—Donna's mother.

"Bud," he said, then remembered his diet. "Make it a light," he added, then sunk as low as he could, praying he'd go unseen.

Goldie

Lazy Beef Stew

2 medium onions
4 celery sticks, chopped
5 white potatoes, peeled and diced
6 carrots, peeled and diced
1 green bell pepper, chopped
2½ pounds beef round steak, cut into 1½ inch cubes
1 envelope mushroom gravy mix (over)

32

Attempt to Defrost

I awoke Tuesday morning feeling a sense of dread. I knew why. I hadn't had quiet time with God in quite a while, not like I had when I was married to Jack and living at home.

I instantly corrected myself. *I am still married to Jack. I am still his wife. He is still my husband.*

I rolled over on my back and looked up at the ceiling in Olivia's tiny guest bedroom, where I'd stayed since I'd had the nerve to leave her father after his latest affair. It was such a tiny little room, nothing like the bedroom I'd shared with Jack.

One thing Jack had always done was give me carte blanche when it came to decorating our house. The loveliness of our home was something I had to admit I missed. The one place in the world I could call my own. That and my time alone with God early in the morning.

Why had I let it go? What was stopping me from pushing myself up in bed, fluffing the pillows behind my back, opening my Bible, and spending time in prayer?

I didn't even have to search for the answer. In the quiet moments of my day I heard my heart clearly stating what my mind did not wish to hear. Or, maybe it was the other way around. Didn't matter;

bottom line was that my feelings for Van had gone further than they should.

Chris had called me into his office just before Thanksgiving to have a "chat."

"I'm not your father, Goldie, and as your employer I hardly have any right to tell you what to do . . . how to live your life. But if you aren't careful, you could easily jeopardize your divorce settlement." He dipped his head a bit and studied me with his eyes. "That is, if you still want a divorce."

"That's the plan," I confirmed. "I don't see me going back to Jack."

Chris cleared his throat and leaned his elbows on his desk. "What role does Van play in this?"

I didn't answer, in truth because I didn't have an answer I thought he'd like to hear.

"I see," he said. "Listen, Goldie . . . and again, I'm not your father. But, I am a friend of Van Lauer. He's a nice man. A fine attorney and a good father to his son. But he's not marriage material, if that's what you're thinking."

I blushed. "No . . . I . . . no, I'm not thinking that."

Chris grimaced. "Uh-huh."

"But if he's such a nice guy, why do you think . . ."

"It's not what I think. It's what I know. I've known Van since we were in college. Since Mercedes died he's dated more women than I can count." He raised a palm to me. "Now, I don't mean this in a hurtful manner, but there's nothing in this . . . situation that would make me think this time is any different."

I'd wanted to die as I sat before a man I have such respect for. That evening, during another outing with Van, I drew up enough courage to broach the subject. "Van, I suppose you know that Chris is very concerned about our relationship . . . my divorce . . ."

We had driven to Lake Dillon's dam and reservoir to watch the sun make its daily descent behind the rise of a stretch of mountains and hills. We huddled against the chill in the air on a green wrought-iron observation bench just a few steps from a small monument and information plaque.

"How do you feel about that, Goldie?"

"Well, I don't know. I . . . I think of you as a good friend, Van. We haven't done anything I'm ashamed of." I blushed appropriately. "There's been nothing physical. Nothing physical at all."

"I have too much respect for you for that," he said. "I'm not saying that if you weren't still married I wouldn't have been kissing you." He winked sideways at me.

I blushed again, felt the heat from my body rising enough to melt the thin layer of icy snow along the banks of the lake that, in a month or so, would be completely covered in nature's thick white blanket. "Van," I said coyly.

He laughed. "I do have a good time teasing with you, Goldie." He sobered. "Okay, let me just say this: Chris has known me for a long time. Seen me through some dark days, and he's known me to date some young and foxy women." He turned to look at me. "Those aren't the kind of women I could ever ask to be a mother to my son, and I just couldn't imagine anyone ever doing the job Mercedes would have done. But, my son is grown now, and it's time for me to start doing some things for myself." He reached up and brushed a loose curl from my cheek, and a tingle ran through me. "For now, I'm content to be your friend. If you and Jack work things out, well, that's fine. If not, I'm thinking I'll still be here."

I furrowed my brow. "But your practice is in—"

"I don't live that far away, Goldie. I'll be here another couple of weeks or so. Let's just take it day by day, shall we?"

I agreed that we should. Of course, that conversation had taken place the day before Thanksgiving when Jack had joined the family at Olivia and Tony's—the day he had nearly worn me out with his attempts at renewing, if nothing else, our physical relationship. It was also before the disastrous Potluck Club meeting I'd managed to duck out of so I could dash up to Breckenridge with Van for a day of fun, and it was also before going to the movies with him the night before.

I heard Olivia padding through the house, down the hallway. Little Brook's gleeful voice echoed, causing me to stretch skyward and hoist myself out of bed. From the living room, the sound of

K-Love wafted its good morning through the household. "I Choose You" by Point of Grace was playing. I hummed along as I tied my robe's sash around my waist and slipped into my bedroom slippers, then opened the bedroom door and headed toward the kitchen.

As soon as my grandson saw me, he ran into my arms. "Good morning, my little love," I said, holding him close, squeezing him for all he was worth. I looked over his tiny shoulder to his mother—my only child—who was preparing the morning coffee. "Hello, my big love," I said to her.

She merely stared at me. I put Brook down as I said, "You want to watch some cartoons?"

"Yes! Cartoons, cartoons, cartoons!"

I reached for the remote control and turned on the television, then helped Brook settle in so I could go into the kitchen and make his breakfast, as was now my habit. I heard Tony shuffle into the kitchen.

"Good morning, Tony," I said.

"Good morning, Mom," he said.

Olivia sighed.

I reached for a cereal bowl and a box of Cream of Wheat. "Olivia, I thought I'd make lazy beef stew for dinner tonight. I can come home during my lunch hour and prepare it, if you don't mind going to the grocery store this morning to get the ingredients."

"Okay," she said.

"I'll take an earlier lunch so it'll have plenty of time to simmer."

"I love that stew," Tony said, pouring a cup of coffee for himself. "Corn bread too?"

I smiled in appreciation. "Corn bread too."

Olivia turned to me and put her fist on her hip. "So, does that mean you're not going out again tonight?"

"Olivia," Tony said. "We talked about this."

Olivia turned on her husband. "This is between my mother and me, Tony."

He shook his head and walked toward the living room. "I gotta get ready to go."

I finished preparing Brook's cereal in silence, then set it on the table. "Brook, come here, baby."

Brook rose obediently, and I helped him into his booster seat. I turned back to Olivia. "I'll go get ready myself."

She jutted her chin forward. "I think you should know that I've invited Dad to have dinner with us tonight."

"What?"

"He called last night while you were . . . out."

I crossed the room to where she stood. "Did he ask for me?"

"Of course he did, Mom. He's your husband."

"I know who he is."

"Do you?" She set her coffee cup on the counter, reached for a nearby dishcloth, and began to wipe an already clean countertop.

I grabbed her arm, stopping her in her chore. "Yes, Olivia. I do." I paused. "Where did you tell him I was?"

"I didn't. I don't have the heart to hurt him."

I nodded. "I understand."

"Do you?" she repeated.

"More than you know. I'm going to get ready for work. I'll see you during lunch—if you're here. If not, I'll see you tonight. For dinner. With your father."

"Your husband."

I shook my head at her, then walked out of the room and toward the bedroom I knew I'd soon be leaving.

During my coffee break that morning I scanned the weekly newspaper for rental apartments in the area. Most of them were way out of my price range, but a few were worth seeing. One was a condo on 6th near Main Street, which meant during the nice weather, I could walk to work. I called the number listed and made an appointment with the owner to swing by after work later in the day. "The carpet is kinda worn," she said to me, "but otherwise it's clean."

"Sort of like me," I said with a laugh, but she didn't laugh with me. I guess she didn't get the simile.

"No pets," she said.

"I have none."

"No parties."

"At my age?"

"Didn't know if it was for your college kid or something."

"No. It's for me. Just me. And I promise not to party." I laughed a little but basically got nothing in return. "I'll see you a bit after 5:00," I said. "That's when I get off work, but I'm less than a block away."

"I'll be there," she said.

I called Van on my cell phone after I'd gone home and prepared the stew for tonight's dinner. When he answered, he sounded winded. "I'm riding the stationary bike I rented for while I'm here," he said when I asked if he were having a heart attack or something.

"Well, don't stop," I said, wondering what it must be like to have enough money to take a month's vacation for just lazing around, skiing, dining out—whatever you wanted to do—without having to think or worry about the finances. Me, I was wondering how I'd come up with the first and last month's rent the landlord of the condo was sure to require. "I just wanted to tell you that I may have found a place to live."

"Really?" he puffed.

"Yeah. I'm going to go look at it after work today. It's a condo about a block from work, which will be good because I can walk when the weather's nice."

"You want me to go look at it with you? Check over the contract?"

A contract? I hadn't thought about that. "Sure. Sure, you can go with me if you'd like."

"Dinner afterward?"

"Ah . . . no. Not tonight. Jack's coming over to Olivia's for dinner, and I guess I should be there."

Van didn't answer right away, but I thought I heard the whirring from the bike slowing down. "I see."

"It's something I have to do, Van. It doesn't mean anything." I pulled into my usual parking place at work.

"It should, Goldie. The man is your husband. I guess I needed to be reminded of that." He cleared his throat. "Where should I meet you after work?"

"Ah . . . why not just be in the parking lot," I said, looking around and slipping the car's gearshift into park.

"Sounds good. We'll walk there."

I smiled both inwardly and outwardly. "Okay, then. I'll see you at 5:00."

I could hardly wait for 5:00. Every few minutes I would glance up from my desk to the wall clock hanging over the waiting area love seat near the door. It seemed that time was ticking away at a slower pace than usual.

But 5:00 finally came. I practically stumbled over my own two feet as I darted down the hall to the employee break room, where my coat hung waiting for me on the coat tree. I flung my arms into the sleeves, ducked my head into Chris's office to say good-bye, then dashed down the stairs to the card shop, out the door, and into the parking lot. Van stood next to my car, leaning against the driver's door with his legs crossed at the ankles.

"There you are," he said. "Right on time."

"Thank you for meeting me," I said, tying a silk scarf around my neck. "We just have to walk that way a bit." I pointed toward Main Street and 6th.

"Then, let's do it," he said, pushing himself from his resting place.

I looked up at him as we walked. "Thank you again, Van. I never even thought about contracts. I suppose I could show them to Chris, but since you offered . . ."

Van came to a stop on the sidewalk in front of the card shop, reached out his hand a bit to stop me from stepping out into traffic. We looked both ways. A few cars were heading our way, but we had a clearing. We took deliberate steps as we crossed the road, then stepped up from the curb and onto the sidewalk on the other side.

"What's the rent?" he asked me. When I told him, he grimaced. "That's steep. It's none of my business, but can you afford it?"

I shrugged. "Not really. I can't really afford anything around here, and it's the cheapest thing listed. Besides, I don't see myself staying at Olivia's much longer." I looked at the buildings to our right, reading the numbers on their faces. I pointed. "Here it is," I said. The condo was one of a four-unit building, painted a dull gray and sitting on the far right corner.

A front door opened. A stocky woman with short, unbrushed brown hair stood before us. "Goldie Dippel?" she said.

"That's me," I answered.

"I take it this is Mr. Dippel? I thought you said you'd be a sole renter."

Van approached the woman with an outstretched hand. "Van Lauer. I'm a friend of Goldie's."

The woman looked down at Van's hand as though she'd never shaken one before, but she took it and said, "Lu Redford. Come on in."

For the next fifteen minutes we were escorted from one tiny room to another. Lu had been correct when she said the carpet was worn but equally as correct about it being clean. The kitchen appliances were a bit outdated but scrubbed spotless. And there was a view of the Summit Mountains from the upstairs bedroom that was absolutely breathtaking. I could just imagine myself waking every morning with them as my vista.

When we'd made a complete tour and were back in the kitchen, Lu said, "First and last month's rent up front," then she quoted the rent again for good measure. She must have seen the grimace on my face because she then added, "Unless you want to work out a deal."

"A deal? What kind of a deal?" Van asked.

"My husband and I are wanting to move to Colorado Springs, where our children are living. I can hardly take care of these four units from over there, and none of the other tenants are interested. They're not here but on the weekends anyway, so you'd pretty much have the whole thing to yourself except two days a week and maybe on holidays. If you're interested in managing the building, I'd be willing to decrease your rent by one half."

"And the deposit?" I asked.

She shrugged. "I'm ready to get out of Summit View . . . so, if you say yes, we'll say half of that too."

My heart soared. Was God shining down on me? Or, was the devil opening a door? The very thought made me take a breath, but before I could argue with myself, Van said, "Do you have a contract I can look at?"

"I do," Lu said, crossing the room to the counter where a brief-case rested.

"Mr. Lauer is an attorney," I said.

Lu looked back at me. "Is that right? Well, Mr. Lauer, I think you'll find this is standard." She brought the contract to Van, who studied it for a few minutes. "It includes everything except what we just talked about, the new financial arrangements. I can have an addendum written up concerning our agreement in the morning."

"Looks good, Goldie. You'll just have to make a decision."

I glanced down at my watch. It was nearing 6:00. Olivia had told me during my lunch break that her father would be arriving at 6:30. The very thought of the tension I'd be experiencing during the course of the evening was almost debilitating. "Where do I sign?" I asked.

When I arrived at Olivia and Tony's I saw that Jack's car was already in the driveway. I frowned. It was just like him to be early when I needed him to be late. Goodness knows the man had always been late when I needed him to be on time.

I entered the house through the front door to find him sitting on the sofa in the living room, Brook snuggled up to him as he read to our grandson from a little Rainbow book. A cup of coffee rested in front of him on the coffee table. When he looked up to see me standing there—looking flustered, I'm sure—he jumped up, nearly throwing Brook off the sofa. "Goldie," he said. "It's good to see you."

"Nana," Brook called out, reaching for me. I took him in my arms, hoping to avoid any type of physical contact with Jack.

I was unsuccessful. He walked over to me and gave me a cautious peck on the cheek, and I caught a whiff of his favorite cologne.

"Hello, Jack." I put Brook down. "Let Nana hang up her coat," I said to my favorite little boy. "And then I'll finish dinner."

Olivia entered the room from the hallway, beaming at the sight of the two of us. "I've got it all done, Mom." She looked at her father. "Dad, doesn't Mom look wonderful with her new haircut and the way she's wearing her makeup?"

I gave her a disapproving look, then glanced over at Jack, who seemed to be quite taken with me. "Like I told her on Thanksgiving, she's a sight for sore eyes."

I rolled my eyes. "I'll be right back," I said, then walked into my bedroom to hang up my coat and deposit my purse. Olivia was right on my heels. When I looked back at her, she said, "Mrs. Prattle called."

"Lizzie?"

"She said it was important."

"Oh? Then I should call her right now," I said, reaching for the phone on my bedside table.

"Mom," Olivia nearly hissed.

"What?" I asked, already dialing Lizzie's number.

"Don't be too long."

"I won't."

"And be nice to Dad," she whispered, closing the door behind her.

I sighed as Lizzie answered. "Lizzie? It's Goldie. Olivia said you called."

"My friend, we have to talk."

I sat on the bed. "What's wrong?"

"I was driving down Main Street today . . ."

"Okay." I was truly confused as to where this was going.

"About 5:00 or so."

"And?"

"I saw you, Goldie. Is that the friend of Chris you were telling me about a few weeks ago?"

I blanched. "Yes, but—"

251

"Goldie, when I saw the two of you crossing the street, an awful feeling went all over me. I'm your friend, and I want you to know I prayed all the way home before I called. I just see this relationship as being a disaster in the making. You are still married, Goldie."

"I know that, Lizzie, but my relationship with Van is nothing more than a friendship."

Lizzie was quiet before she said, "You want to try that again?"

I moistened my lips. "Nothing has happened. Nothing. I haven't even been kissed by him or had him hold my hand or anything. We're just friends, and I don't see anything wrong with that."

"All right, Goldie. Let me ask you this: if he ever did kiss you— or hold your hand—how would you feel?"

I couldn't answer her. Well, I could, but neither one of us would like the answer, and we both knew it. "Lizzie," I finally said. "Jack is here for dinner, so I have to go."

"Oh? I'm glad to hear that. I really am. I love you, Goldie. And I'm not going to say that Jack Dippel didn't deserve you leaving him when you did. But he seems to be trying, and I think you owe it to your marriage to keep trying."

"I love you too, Lizzie. I'll think about what you've said. I will."

I replaced the phone's receiver, then checked myself in the mirror before joining the rest of my family in the living room. When I did, I saw that Tony had come home. He and Jack were sitting down, talking about whatever fathers-in-law and sons-in-law talk about. Once again, Jack stood.

I lifted my hand to stop him. "Don't get up," I said.

Olivia came in from the kitchen. "Mom, why don't you sit down by Dad?" she asked. "Dinner will be ready to serve in a few minutes."

"Are you sure you don't need me to help?" I asked.

"No," she answered firmly. "I've got it."

"But, the bread—"

"Mom. I've got it." Her eyes widened, a sign telling me to hush up and sit down.

I nodded, defeated, then sat next to my husband. As much as I hated to admit it, he looked quite handsome. He'd dressed for dinner—he wasn't wearing the sweats I'd grown accustomed to over the years of our marriage. He was groomed right down to his socks and shoes.

He turned to me and cleared his throat. "So . . . uh, Goldie. How was . . . uh . . . work today?"

"I don't think you've ever asked me that question before, Jack," I said.

Olivia laughed nervously from across the room. "Mom's a modern woman now, huh, Dad?"

"I suppose so," he said. "Yeah."

"Well," I interrupted. "Maybe more than you know."

"What does that mean?" Olivia asked.

I opened my mouth to tell them about my new condo, then stopped. My daughter looked so genuinely happy to see both her mother and father sitting side by side, I just didn't have the nerve to burst her bubble. "Oh, nothing."

Minutes later we sat around the dining table for dinner. Olivia had strategically placed her father and me so that we sat together. It was uncomfortable at first, but by the time we'd said the blessing, I was beginning to relax. After the meal, Jack suggested that we—he and I—give Brook his bath and get him ready for bed.

"What do you say, Nana?" he asked.

I swallowed. "Sure."

While I sat on the side of the tub bathing Brook with the sleeves of my sweater pushed up to my elbows, Jack knelt on the floor and made faces at our grandson. Brook, in return, giggled and splashed until I was soaked. At one point, Jack reached behind him, pulled a towel from the rack, and began to pat my arms dry. I quickly took the towel from him. "I've got it, thank you," I said.

Jack blushed. He actually blushed as though he'd never touched me before in his life. The tension was both unbearable and, at the same time, sweet.

When it was time for him to go home, Jack asked if I would mind walking with him to his car. He had something he wanted to give me. "I hope it's not jewelry," I said.

A look of pain crossed his face. "No. It's not jewelry."

"Go on, Mom," Olivia coaxed from the rocker where she was rocking Brook to sleep.

I relented, following Jack out the front door and down the steps to his car. He opened the back driver's side door and retrieved a package beautifully wrapped and finished off with a bright bow. "I didn't want to give this to you in the house with the kids watching," he said.

I took the package, my lips pressed together. From down the block, a dog began to bark, and I looked over my shoulder.

"It's just a dog," Jack said. "Open it, Goldie."

I looked upward. The dome of darkness overhead was bright with dancing stars, almost as if God were smiling down on us. "Oh, Jack," I said, looking into his eyes. "What is it?"

"Open it," he said again.

I did. Inside, wrapped in protective tissue, was a photograph taken on our wedding day, newly matted and framed in white and gold leaf. I pulled it out of the box and attempted to study it in the light of the street lamp. It brought back a flood of memories I wasn't sure I was ready to dwell upon. Two young people with the whole world ahead of them. So many dreams. So many hurts and wasted moments they had yet to experience.

"There's something else," Jack said, pulling an envelope from his pocket.

It was a card. A beautiful card in which Jack had written a message of love and promise—and faithfulness—to me. I swallowed so hard, I'm sure he heard me. Tears began to slip down my cheeks, and I inhaled deeply to keep from breaking down altogether. This was all too much . . . too much for one day.

"I'm willing to give you your time," he said in a voice so soft I almost missed the words. "But I want you to at least know that I do love you, Goldie."

"I know," I whispered.

"And I've been seeing Pastor Kevin. He says I have an addiction." I looked up at him as he finished what he had to say. "But he says I can be cured. He says that with God all things are possible."

I nodded, swallowing again. "Jack . . . I don't know what to say."

Jack touched my nose with the tip of his finger. "Say nothing, Goldie Brook Dippel. Let's just take this one day at a time."

One day at a time. Nearly the same words Van had said to me at Lake Dillon.

Oh, Lord, I prayed from deep within my heart. *I guess it's time you and I started really talking again.*

33

Faded Photographs

Years before, when Clay had moved into the small second-story flat he called home, he'd shoved all his worldly goods into a few boxes, stacked the boxes into the walk-in closet located near his bed, and pretty much let them sit there to rot.

That evening, however, when he'd returned from a trip to the outlet stores in Dillon, where he'd bought "skinnier" clothes, he emptied the closet racks of all the old duds and replaced them with the new. That was when he spotted the old boxes. Like everything else in his life, he decided, it was time to plow through and get rid of the old.

The first box he removed was filled with his old college papers. He found a king-sized trash bag and began stuffing it with the past assignments, but kept a few of those he'd been most proud of—including his report on the effects of *Pretty Woman* on young girls who found the movie believable—returning them to the box.

Several hours later, he was plopping the last box onto his bed and peeling away the cracked tape. He peered inside. It was filled with photographs, some black and white and some in color turned to an orangish hue. There were stacks of them, taken by his mother and father, his grandparents, friends and relatives, and the Davy

Crockett School Pictures Company. He picked up the box and carried it over to his La-Z-Boy, determined to look at each one, though maybe not all of them tonight.

It took only a minute or two before he realized there were a great number of photographs with Donna's image. He began to form a stack on the end table next to him. When it had grown to the point of toppling onto the floor, a new and decidedly brilliant idea came to him, and he smiled.

He knew exactly what was to be at the top of his to-do list for tomorrow.

If he was careful, he could win Donna's future with the past.

Vonnie

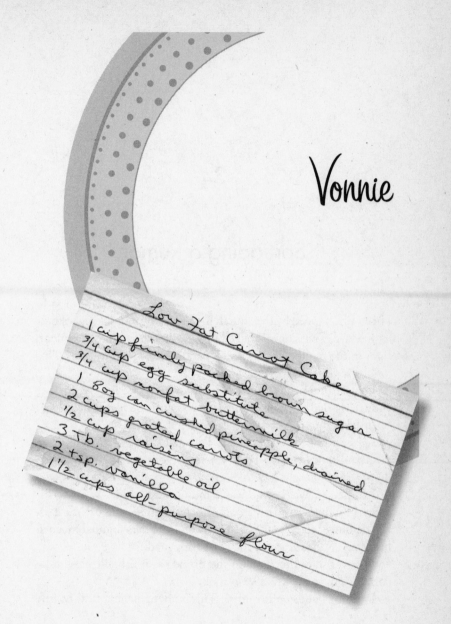

Low Fat Carrot Cake

1 cup firmly packed brown sugar
3/4 cup egg substitute
3/4 cup nonfat buttermilk
1 8oz can crushed pineapple, drained
2 cups grated carrots
1/2 cup raisins
3 Tb. vegetable oil
2 tsp. vanilla
1 1/2 cups all-purpose flour

34

Spreading a Rumor

I had only stopped by the church to change my Sunday school bulletin board. That's how I walked into Wade and Donna's argument, right in the middle of the church parking lot. Good heavens! This looked serious.

Donna practically knocked me down as she lunged for her Bronco. I tried to call to her, but it was as if she hadn't heard me. She peeled into the street, never looking back.

As she'd bolted for her truck, I'd caught the expression on her face, and it scared me. I'd never seen Donna looking so . . . so desperate.

I turned to Wade, who was standing next to me. What was it about him that was so different? His clothes? His haircut? Yes. This was definitely a new look. Then I saw his shoulders slump. I touched his arm. "Wade, dear, tell me what happened."

His eyes stayed focused on the Bronco as it fishtailed around a corner. "I'm sorry, Mrs. Westbrook, I can't."

I put my hands on my hips. "This is about ancient history, isn't it?"

He looked at his shoes.

"It's about two high school kids in Dr. Billings's office."

His eyes shifted to mine, and he nodded. "Then you know."

"It's taken me a while to figure out what happened. But I do know. Donna aborted your baby."

He looked at the ground again, this time his eyes glistening. He bit his lip. "Yeah. The quick solution that neither one of us ever got over."

Pastor Moore came out of the front door, sliding his arms into his suede jacket before zipping it up. "What's all the commotion out here? I thought I heard shouting."

Wade turned to him. "Donna bolted when I told her what our meeting was about."

"Oh no," the pastor said. His face fell. "I'm sorry, Wade. I know how much this meeting meant to you."

I interrupted. "Fellows, I'm really worried. I've never seen Donna this upset. I feel like the Holy Spirit is impressing on me that we need to pray for her, now. I'm sensing she's in danger, maybe even from herself."

Together, the three of us joined hands and began to seek God, right where we stood. Wade started us off. "God, I know I've just been introduced to you, just met you, thanks to Pastor Moore. Maybe I don't have any right to ask, especially considering how I've thrown my life away. But God, please help Donna. You know the burden she's been carrying. It's too much for her. Please, God, lift it. Give her peace."

I patted Wade's shoulder and added a prayer of my own. "Father, if the enemy is speaking thoughts of suicide to our Donna, still his voice in Jesus's name. Keep her safe. Help us to reach out to her and her to us."

The pastor added, "Father God, turn what appears to be a hopeless situation into good as only you can. We trust you. In Jesus's name."

When I looked up, Wade turned to me, his eyes downcast. "I'm so sorry, Vonnie. If anything happens to that girl, I don't think I could live with it. I believe I love her as much as I did when I fathered our child."

261

"I believe you," I said, giving him a quick hug. "Can I borrow your cell phone?"

He unclipped it from his belt and handed it to me. I stared at it and blinked. "How do I use this thing?"

He punched in Donna's number for me, then hit "send" and handed me the phone set. I put it to my ear. It rang once, twice, three times. I turned to the men and said, "Pray she'll pick up." They nodded and bowed their heads. Four times it rang, then finally, "Wade, I *hate* you!" an angry Donna screeched into the receiver.

"Donna, dear, it's Vonnie."

I listened to dead silence that turned into muffled sobs. "Vonnie, I . . . I can't live with this. I've got my gun. I . . . I don't want you to think you failed me, but I—"

"Donna, now you listen to me. I know you're hurting. All I'm asking is a chance to talk to you. You at least owe me that. I want you to come by the house. I'll meet you there in five minutes. No arguing."

She hesitated but answered in a small voice, "Okay, Vonnie, but only because I love you." She hung up, and I handed the phone back to Wade. "Donna's meeting me at the house."

"Let me go with you," Wade said.

"No, Wade. I need to talk to her alone. I'll call you later."

As I climbed back into my car, I called over my shoulder, "Stay here and pray. I'm afraid this is a matter of life and death."

Donna's Bronco was already idling in my driveway when I pulled up. I walked to her window, and she lowered it. I could see her service revolver lying in the front seat. She said, "I'm here; so what do you want?"

I shivered in the cold as the wind began to pick up, rushing through the swaying pines in my front yard. "Let's go inside, dear. This is a bit too chilly for me."

Reluctantly, she turned off her engine and followed me up the steps and in through the front door. Little Chucky was absolutely delighted to see her, jumping in complete circles and barking with joy. Donna looked down at him and blinked as if she'd never seen the dog before.

"Come join me in the kitchen. I want a cup of tea."

She followed, and when I pointed to a kitchen chair, she sat down. Chucky jumped into her lap and snuggled in. Usually she didn't allow that when she was in uniform. Instead of shooing him away, she looked down as if she was surprised my dog enjoyed her company. She slowly stroked his white curly head and whispered, "Chucky."

I bustled around the kitchen, putting the kettle on the stove, cutting thick slices of carrot cake, Donna's favorite, and readying the teacups.

I put the cake in front of her; Chucky lifted his head onto the table and licked the edges of the dessert. "Bad boy," I scolded.

Donna broke off a piece of the cake and fed it to him. "It's okay."

I sat down across from her, waiting for the water in the kettle to boil, and took a deep breath. "We've got a lot in common."

"What do you mean?"

"We've both kept secrets about our babies."

"I hardly think our situations are similar. You didn't kill your baby."

The teakettle started to whistle, and I jumped up to take it off the burner.

"True, but carrying that secret hurt me, hurt my marriage, and hurt my relationship with you. Did I ever tell you how much I regret keeping that secret from you and Fred?"

I poured the hot water into rosy china cups. Donna said, "I seem to remember how painful it was for you when I finally guessed you even had a secret."

"Yeah, it was much like what you're going through right now. But you know, when I finally allowed that secret to come into the light, something wonderful happened to me."

"Besides being reunited with David?"

"Yes. I was also reunited with my life. What I've come to realize is my secret kept me from deeper relationships, even with my husband as well as my friends, and"—I smiled as I handed her a cup of cinnamon tea—"my daughter."

She cocked her head as the tea steamed in front of her. "I can see that."

"Listen, Donna, the same thing can happen for you now that your secret is in the light. I know it's painful, but this secret of yours can draw us closer. That barrier of secrecy we once shared won't come between us anymore. I'm not saying you need to tell everyone. Especially avoid sharing with people like Lisa Leann. But I think, in your case, you have a few people who need to know."

"But you . . . they . . . will think less of me."

I stood and walked to her side. I leaned down and opened my arms to hug her. "No, Donna, I think more of you. You've survived a difficult thing. Now it's time to finally talk about it with someone who loves you as much as I do."

Slowly, Donna lifted her arms and embraced me. I whispered into her ear, "Donna, I love you like a daughter. Don't you dare leave me."

Donna buried her head into my shoulder. "Mom, I love you too."

Later, after we finished our cake, I gave our teacups a warm-up, and we withdrew to the living room to recline in the La-Z-Boys.

That's when Donna began to pour out her heart. It seems she and young Wade had been in love. They'd never intended to have sex, but gradually their relationship became more physical. With her dad at work in the afternoons and no mom in the house, she and Wade had spent their time together in her bedroom after school. Then, when she suspected she was pregnant, her world fell apart.

"Telling Daddy was the hardest thing. He didn't yell at me. He did something worse; he cried. Then he made a phone call to Dr. Billings. You remember the day Wade and I came in? It was for a pregnancy test, to prove what I already knew.

"After the 'positive' report confirmed it, Daddy was determined there would be no more scandal in the family. He drove me down to see the abortionist. But I don't think he had any idea how this decision would stifle my entire life with guilt and regret."

"Is that why you decided never to marry?"

Donna took a sip of her tea. "Yeah. I didn't deserve happiness, and I didn't want it, not after what I'd done."

"But Donna, you do deserve happiness and love. God will forgive—"

I heard the low rumble of Fred's truck as it pulled into the driveway. I looked at my watch. How had it gotten so late? "Oh, dear."

Donna stood. "I'd better go. I lost track of the time too, and I'm supposed to be at work in a few minutes."

I put my cup and saucer down and rose from my chair. "Are you going to be okay?"

She nodded and leaned over to scratch a sleepy Chucky behind his ear as he stood and stretched. "Yeah." She hugged me. "Thanks, Vonnie."

"Before you go, I'd like to invite you to have dinner with Fred and me this week. When's your day off?"

"Thursday. Let's make it Thursday night."

"Okay, promise me you'll be safe out there, especially with loaded guns."

She turned at the door with a little smile. "I will, Mom. I promise."

Donna stopped to chat with Fred on the front porch, and I quickly dialed Wade. "I'll call you later, but I wanted you to know that Donna's going to be okay."

He breathed his response, "Oh, thank God."

"Gotta run." I hung up and looked out the window again, in time to see Donna drive off. I hadn't prepared anything for dinner. Hmm. I did have a pound of hamburger thawed. I'd ask Fred to fire up our backyard grill. Sure, it wasn't picnic weather, but we grilled all year long.

Fred walked in, shuffling through our mail and wiping his feet on the blue braided rug in front of the door. He was dressed in his oily blue overalls with his name embroidered in red across his breast pocket. I could see that they would need to be thrown in the wash as soon as possible. "Hi, Fred. How was your day?"

He gave me a nod like I was an acquaintance on the street. "What did Donna want?" he asked me.

"You know how I've prayed for that girl, prayed she would come to me and tell me what we've known all these years about the baby. Well, it's happened."

Fred turned and looked at me. "You're kidding me. She finally told you?"

I pretended to mop sweat off my forehead. "Whew. Yeah, it was pretty heavy. I'll tell you about it over dinner tonight. Would you mind firing up the grill for me?"

Fred took two steps toward me. "You're giving in?"

"What?"

"You're going to let me burn those letters from Joe?"

I took a deep breath. "I was thinking more about barbequing some hamburgers."

"But the column in the paper said . . ."

"Fred, I know all about that silly column, and I know you shouldn't believe everything you read."

"Vonnie, why can't you give those letters up?"

I took a step toward Fred. "I've been asking myself the same question, and I think I've come to an understanding and a solution."

Fred moved closer. "What's that?"

"Fred, you have to understand that I love you. Joe is gone; he's been out of my life for decades. And I'll admit, when you and I were first married, I thought a lot about the man I'd lost. But then I had you." I took another step. "I grew to love you as much as a woman can love a man." I felt the tip of my nose burn. That always happens when I get emotional. "But here's the problem. Those letters are all that's left of a man's life. I can't destroy them, but neither is it right for me to keep them, especially when they hurt you.

"So this morning I bundled them up, took them to the post office, and sent them to my son. They're his heritage. Those letters will help him know how loved and wanted he was."

Fred reached for me and drew me into his arms. "My Vonnie, you've come back to me."

I hugged his neck. "Fred, I never left."

Before Fred could tug me into our bedroom, there was a knock at the door. "Yoo-hoo, Vonnie!"

Oh my goodness, it sounded like Lisa Leann. I went to the door as Fred tagged along behind me. I opened it a crack, and there she was, holding a lovely platter of cinnamon rolls. Once again, she looked as if she had stepped off a fashion runway, dressed in a short mink jacket and black velvet pants. Her hair stayed in place in spite of the stiff breeze.

"A peace offering," she said. "I'm sorry about the other day and what I did. My Mandy's been talking to me about how I need to respect other people's privacy. She says I messed up. So will you forgive me?"

"Of course."

"But, also, I wanted to bring these over to thank you for helping me with Mandy at the ER. I don't know what I would have done without your help."

A humbled Lisa Leann was a sight to see. "Thank you, this is so thoughtful."

She smiled. "Before I go, well, I know I shouldn't say anything. But I just can't resist."

Oh dear. "Resist what?"

"Well, what I want to know and what I'm hoping you'll share with me is what is going on between Clay and Donna."

I was so surprised by the question, I could only shake my head. "Clay and Donna?"

"Yes. I was at the shop late last night, and there the two of them were, locked in a passionate embrace. I think they were necking right on the street."

Fred stepped forward. "I would appreciate it, Mrs. Lambert, if you wouldn't talk about our daughter like that."

"Your daughter?"

"Donna is our daughter of the heart," I said. "But Fred's right, Lisa. You are speaking out of turn. And your words hurt people. If you want to know what's going on between Clay and Donna, you should ask them, instead of spreading it all over town."

"Well! I was not spreading it, I was trying to confirm it."

"Same difference," Fred said. "Thanks for the sweet rolls and have a good night."

Fred shut the door right in her face, and I couldn't help but giggle. "Why, Fred, you're so forceful. Did I ever tell you how much I like forceful men?"

Fred took the tray of sweet rolls and put it on the coffee table, then took my hand, pulling me toward the bedroom. "Is that so?" he asked. I nodded as he shut the door behind us.

Bang! What a crash. We opened the bedroom door and looked out. There was Chucky, standing in the middle of the carpet, gobbling sweet rolls as fast as he could.

35

The Price of a Memory

The morning after he emptied the old boxes in his closet, Clay made several trips up and down the stairwell leading to his room, lugging dilapidated cardboard and large bags of what represented the first thirty-some years of his life. With one load deposited at the large green Dumpster behind the building, he headed back for another until everything was gone except what little bit he wanted to hold on to.

That and the old photographs, which now lay in two piles in front of his La-Z-Boy. One he mentally labeled "My Life in General" and the other "My Life and Donna's."

When he'd finished his task, he took his morning walk, arching his back a little more than he had when he'd first started. Several of the locals had begun to accustom themselves to seeing him out on the streets and took to saying things like "You're looking good there, Clay."

After his breakfast at the café, he sprinted down Main Street, just in time for Alpine Card Shop to open its doors. There was a new girl working the cash register, but Clay didn't have time for introductions right then. He went directly to a glass shelf lined with sample photo albums and scanned them with his eyes until he found the one perfect for his idea. He carefully lifted it from the shelf and took it to the front, where the new girl, Britney, stood smiling behind the counter.

"Would you like to purchase this?" she asked.

"Yes, I would."

She took the album from his hands, checked the stock number on its back, and said, "I'll be right back."

Clay leaned against the counter as Britney went to the storeroom for his purchase. He heard a creaking from overhead, then remembered that Goldie would be at work already. Britney reappeared, carrying a large but thin blue box with her. "This is a beautiful photo album," she said. "The material on the front looks like lapis. That's why it's called 'Lapis.'"

Clay merely nodded. He didn't care what it was called. All he knew was that it was pretty and that Donna would like it.

"The artisans use traditional bookbinding techniques. That's why it's a little more expensive than most."

"Artisans?" Clay asked.

"Mmm-hmm."

He snickered as he pulled his wallet out of his back pocket. "I don't think I ever thought of it that way."

"Thought of what, what way?"

"Those machines that put all these books together."

Britney laid the box on the counter and reached for the credit card Clay now held out to her. "Oh no. These are handmade."

Clay smiled at her. "I see."

Britney finished the transaction and said, "That'll be $102.65."

Clay swallowed hard. "Say that again?"

Lizzie

Smothered Pork Chops

Ingredients
6 thick pork chops
16 oz can stewed tomatoes
   with basil
1 large onion, sliced
1 green pepper, sliced
2 tbs. Margarine
1 can mushrooms
1-2 garlic cloves

36

Serving Second Chances

I had pretty much decided the world was coming to an end. In a matter of a little more than a few months, Jan had died, leaving a painful gap in my heart; my son had moved home and actually had the audacity to go out on a date; and word on the street was that Evangeline Benson and Bob Burnett were engaged. (I'd nearly died when Lisa Leann phoned me to report what she knew, then added, "Well, she won't have to change her monogram, will she?")

If all that weren't enough, I feared my friend Goldie was falling for a man to whom she was not married. Did anyone take their marriage vows seriously anymore?

If ever I needed Jan Moore, it was now.

I hadn't realized how special and important she was in my life until she was gone. In spite of not being a formal member of the Potluck Club, she was one who, when I asked for prayer, I knew would pray. Not just a one-sentence offering, either. Jan spent time alone in the presence of God for those she called her friends.

If she were here right now, I could call her and ask her to pray with me . . . or ask her what she would do in a similar situation.

She isn't, but God is, a familiar voice spoke to my heart.

"Oh, Father," I prayed from the middle of my bed, where I'd been curled up like a baby, drinking up the silence of my home. "Tell me what to do."

I waited for a few moments, listening as hard as I could to what God might say. When a half hour passed and still I had nothing but the ache inside my heart, I rose from the bed and walked down the staircase, which was wrapped in the holiday garland I'd put up the weekend before, to the family room Michelle had decorated with Christmastime china dolls.

Michelle and Adam, a new beau she had yet to introduce to us, were going out after work, so she wasn't home. Samuel had a late afternoon meeting at the bank, and Tim hadn't come home yet. The house—quiet and nearly abandoned—was all mine.

I sat in my favorite chair and flipped on the television with the remote. A classic movie was playing on AMC; I curled my feet up under me and settled in to see if I'd ever seen it before.

I had: *Girl on a Mission*, which ironically starred Harmony Harris. In the movie, Harmony plays Zina Nolen, a secretary who is paid by her boss's wife to flirt with her husband while the wife is away on a Christmas vacation in the Caribbean. The wife wants to know if "when the cat's away the mouse will play." When Zina appears to be taking her "mission" too seriously, the boss's mother calls her daughter-in-law and says, "My dear, if you have half a brain in your head, you'll wipe off that suntan oil and get home immediately."

My eyes brightened and my mouth formed an *O*.

Why didn't I think of that?

I popped up from the chair, praising God all the way to the front window of the living room. "Thank you, thank you, thank you. Who says you don't use the media to reach your children?"

I leaned around the Christmas tree and peered out the window and down the street. No sight of Tim's car.

Perfect.

Minutes later, I was once again curled on my bed—though this time upright. I dialed the number of my daughter-in-law.

"Hello," she answered.

"Samantha?" I said brightly.

"Mom?"

"My dear, if you have half a brain in your head, you'll wipe off that suntan oil and get home immediately."

"Excuse me?"

I shook my head in amusement. "That's a line from an old movie."

"Oh."

"I have a question for you . . . ready?"

"I suppose."

"Do you want Tim back?"

"I do . . . but not the way things have been. I'm sorry, but it's true."

I crossed my legs. "Samantha, nothing will change if you remain thousands of miles apart. I want you to pack up the kids and get yourself out here. They're out of school when?"

"Friday."

"I suggest you make a sacrifice and take them out early. It won't kill them, and in the long run it'll be for the best."

Samantha paused before chuckling. "I can't believe I'm hearing you of all people say that."

"Well?"

Again, she paused. "Okay. I'll do it. Should I call him and let him know?"

"No. I'll take it from here." I swung my legs over the side of the bed. "Call me on my cell phone and leave a message as to your flight, okay? Don't call the house." I felt deliciously wicked. "And whatever it costs for the tickets, I'll reimburse you."

"Wow. Okay, then," she said with another laugh. "Uh . . . Mom?"

"Hmm?"

"Is there any particular reason you've felt the sudden need to get us up there?"

It was my turn to pause. A gold-beaded reindeer standing on my dresser caught my attention, and I said, "It's Christmas. Christmas is for families, and families should be together."

I hung up, then looked up at the ceiling and gave God an imaginary high five just as I heard the front door open and close.

"Mom? Dad?" Tim called up.

"Right here," I called back, then met him at the foot of the stairs.

He eyed me suspiciously. "What are you up to?"

"What do you mean?" I asked, brushing past him. I could smell the smothered pork chops I'd left simmering on the stove since I'd arrived home from work. They were no doubt perfect for eating.

Tim was on my heels. "I know that face. What's going on?"

I removed the frying pan from the stove top and set it on a trivet. "Nothing. I was just watching a cute little movie on AMC."

From where we stood he could easily see into the family room. He looked from there to the stairs I'd just come down. "But you were upstairs."

I fluttered my hands about and said, "Oh, for heaven's sake, Tim. Do you have to know everything about your mother? Now, go get ready for dinner. It's just the two of us." I looked down at my watch. "Unless your father makes it home fairly soon."

My son complied. I watched him head downstairs then blew a pent-up breath out of my lungs. "Lizzie," I said aloud, "that was close."

A quick check of my cell phone inbox the following morning revealed that Samantha would be flying in at around 2:30 in the afternoon. The school wouldn't like it, but I would have to sneak out early so I could pick her up.

I called Samuel shortly before he headed out for lunch.

"I have to go to the airport after work," I began my confession.

"The airport? Someone from the Board of Education flying in?"

"Um, no." I sat in the chair at my desk.

"Well, what then?"

I closed my eyes to the scolding I was sure to get when he heard what I'd done. "I invited Samantha and the kids to join us for the remainder of the holidays." Samuel was so quiet he frightened me. "Samuel?"

"Lizzie, didn't we agree not to interfere?"

I crossed my legs and opened my eyes. "No. No, we did not. You may have decided that you wouldn't get involved, but I didn't."

More silence. Then, "Does Tim know?"

"No."

I heard him sigh, though it sounded more like a growl.

"All right, then. Dinner should be interesting tonight."

I brightened. "I was thinking we could all go to Apple's. Sam and his family and Sis and hers too."

Silence.

"Samuel?"

"Won't that be a little awkward? For Tim, if not for both Tim and Samantha?"

I nodded as though he could see me. "I thought about that, and here's what I'm thinking. If we go out as a family, Tim may be more at ease . . . can see what he's missing . . . and they won't be pressured to have an emotional, heartfelt discussion about their future. And, Samuel, they do have a future."

I heard him take a deep breath and exhale before saying, "Sounds good. I'll see you this evening."

I grimaced as I disconnected the call, though I couldn't have been more pleased with the way things were going so far. I reached for my cell phone and dialed Tim's new office number.

"Tim Prattle," he said efficiently.

"Tim? It's Mom."

"Hey, there."

"Just wanted you to know that we're having a family outing tonight at Apple's. Would you let Michelle know? Maybe she'll even bring this new guy we keep hearing about."

"He's a nice guy. You'll like him."

"I'm sure he is. What about dinner? Sound good to you?"

"Sure. Sounds fine. What about Sam and Sis?"

"I'll call them." A sudden thought struck me, and my stomach knotted up. "Tim?"

"Yeah."

"Please don't bring anyone I wouldn't approve of."

"I wouldn't do a thing like that," he said.

Well, I would have never guessed you'd leave your wife and children either, but you have.

"Besides, I told you it was nothing."

"Does that mean you're thinking about your marriage again?"

"Mom, I always think about my marriage. I miss my wife and the kids so much I hurt. I just . . . something is just not right, and it has to get fixed."

"And you think you can do it apart?"

"Right now, I don't know any other way."

I grinned in spite of myself. "Well, son. I believe God will provide that way. I really do."

"I know you do, Mom. Uh . . . I have to get back to work. I'll meet you at the house."

I disconnected the line, stood, and danced around my chair. "It's beginning to look a lot like Christmas," I sang. "Everywhere you go . . ."

Summit View's Main Street was ablaze with Christmas lights and garland wrapped around the old Victorian lampposts and lining the storefront windows. There was a Christmas tree laden with large bulbs of bright colors on each block. Frost was in the air, the snow had begun to fall, and my heart was warm as I drove my daughter-in-law and grandchildren to the house after their flight had come in a little later than it had originally been scheduled to arrive.

Because the days had grown short, darkness had already descended and the street was lit up, causing the children to giggle as they sang Christmas carols from the backseat of the car. From deep within, my soul continued in its own song. *Thank you, Lord. Thank you, Lord. Thank you.*

"Does Tim know?" Samantha asked as we drew closer to the house.

"No," I said. "But he does know we're going to Apple's for dinner as a family."

"Oh."

"We're gonna see Daddy!" Brent squealed from the backseat as he informed his sister of their upcoming reunion.

"I hope we haven't made a mistake," Samantha said, low enough that the children couldn't hear her.

"We haven't," I said, pulling into the driveway.

"Look, kids," Samantha said from beside me. "Look at MeMa's nativity in the front yard."

The kids jumped out of the car as soon as we were parked in the driveway. "Let's get you unpacked and settled before the others show up," I said as I looked at the digital clock on my dashboard. "We've only got a few minutes, though. So, we'll have to hurry."

She nodded. "That'd be nice," she said, grabbing for an overnight bag at her feet.

A few minutes later, with the kids watching television in the family room, Samantha and I stood in the darkness of the living room, breathing in rhythm, watching for the headlights of Tim's car to come driving down the street. When they finally appeared, Samantha said, "Let me go out to meet him alone, okay, Mom?"

"Certainly," I said. In the end, that was for the best. My stomach flip-flopped as I imagined the range of emotions Tim might experience at seeing his wife here.

I watched as she slipped out the front door and stood on the porch. I looked back to the car, where my son was stepping out slowly. For a moment, Tim and Samantha only stared at each other, then Samantha descended the steps and ran to her husband, who opened his arms wide. When they embraced, I bent my knees and leaped for joy.

"Yes!" I said.

I squeezed my fisted hands against my chest. "It's a start, Lord," I said. "It's a start."

37

I'll Take "Early Church History" for 100

Clay wondered if the locals over at Higher Grounds or Apple's would wonder what had happened to their most frequent customer. He'd hardly appeared at all since he'd purchased the photo album the day before.

Sure, he'd gone to work, and certainly, he'd had lunch at Higher Grounds the day before. But, for the most part, he'd stayed shut up in his room, working diligently on the photo album.

First, he'd had to get the photos in some sort of chronological order. Then he had to separate the pictures viewed side to side versus the ones viewed up and down. He didn't want Donna spinning the book around like a top as she relived the years they'd already spent together.

Clay frowned. He was beginning to feel like a stalker, and of course he wasn't. He was just a nice guy, a friend, a man who felt shaken to the core by a wisp of a girl.

When he came upon a copy of the photo taken of their Sunday school class—the one Vonnie Westbrook had taught—he stared at it in wonder. *When did I stop going to church?* he asked himself.

The quick answer: when he'd gone off to college.

Why hadn't he gone back after his return?

He didn't have the answer to that one. Maybe because he wasn't so sure about the whole religion thing anymore. Wasn't it Josephus who said, "Everyone ought to worship God according to his own inclinations, and not to be constrained by force"? Seemed to Clay he remembered something along those lines.

He slid the photograph carefully into the sleeve.

The problem was that he hadn't actually worshipped God according to any inclination. Not even privately.

Then again, he surmised, Donna had done a pretty good job of worshipping publicly, yet he was sure that was about as deep as it went.

From where he sat, they made a pretty good pair.

Lisa Leann

Fruit Cake Cookies

1 1/2 Cups sugar
3 well beaten eggs
1 tsp. soda dissolved in 1/3 cup
  hot water
1 tsp. Cinnamon
1/2 tsp. nutmeg
1 large box raisins
1 lb. pecans (chopped)
1 cup (coconut)

38

Chewing on the Facts

Two nights ago, it had been my own Mandy who had tried to comfort me when Fred Westbrook slammed the door in my face, just after I handed him an entire platter of fresh cinnamon rolls. "You would think my rolls would've counted for something," I said as we sat down at the kitchen table with fruitcake cookies and a cup of coffee.

It really was too close to dinnertime to bring out the sweets, but my feelings had been hurt. I needed a cookie.

Mandy, who was still in her red and black maternity pj's with the words "Bad Hair Day" printed across the front, took a bite and thought for a moment. She said, "I'm sorry my suggestion of a peace offering turned out so badly."

I flopped my chin into my hands. "I'm always so underappreciated. I just can't understand it."

Mandy had patted my arm. "Fitting into a new community is tough, Mom. But don't give up. You'll get your breakthrough."

Thursday morning I picked up my pink and silver watering can and watered the ivy in my kitchen window, thinking about the wise words my daughter had shared with me.

She was right. All I needed was a breakthrough.

However, with all the fighting among the members of the Potluck, I was even wondering if the girls would rally in time for Mandy's baby shower on Saturday. It would be such a shame if the cold shoulder I was getting was turned against my precious daughter.

To tell you the truth, I was worried about her. As she and Ray had originally planned, Ray had left for Houston on Monday, since he had to get back to work. Mandy hadn't planned to follow him home until the following Monday, giving me time to host a baby shower for her and time for us to shop the outlets in Dillon. But I'm afraid Mandy wasn't taking the forced separation with Ray well, at least judging from the dark circles under her eyes.

When I tried to talk to her about it, she pushed me away. "You just don't understand how I feel, Mom."

I did. Of course I did. It was just that I wanted her to see the good in her situation. Even before Ray left, Mandy's situation had inspired me to replace my original column with brand-new words of inspiration. Clay had been more than gracious to help slip it into the *Gold Rush News* in time for this week's edition. He had dropped by the shop on Sunday night to pick it up, seen Donna's Bronco, and hightailed it across the street.

I had to trust God that this little column of mine would help Mandy see her situation wasn't nearly as bad as it seemed.

Speaking of bad situations, if only I could come up with an idea to get me back in everyone's good graces back at the Potluck.

I refilled my watering can and walked over to my ferns by the sliding glass door overlooking my snow-covered patio. They weren't as vibrant as they had been in Houston's muggy air, but they helped remind me of home.

Now, think, I told myself. *When I've been at odds with my girlfriends in the past, it helped to bring out not only the cinnamon rolls but juicy news that my friends could share with their friends.* It had been my experience that folks were always glad to hear from people "in the know." So the question was, what could I come up with now? Evie's engagement? Donna and Clay's hug? Those tidbits would both do nicely.

Earlier today, after I had decorated the foyer Christmas tree till it danced with snowmen, I had tried my idea with a quick phone call to Lizzie before she left for work. "Just imagine that," I'd said. "Evie's engaged to Bob Burnett."

"I really can't fathom that," Lizzie had replied, dumbstruck. "How do you know this is true?"

"Bob Burnett dropped by my shop and told me himself."

"I've got to call Evie to see what's going on," Lizzie said before hanging up.

I'd put the phone back in its cradle, pleased that this piece of news had opened a door between Lizzie and myself. I was proud of myself too, because I'd kept the juiciest bits of the story to myself. I didn't want Lizzie, who was so prim and proper, to accuse me of gossip.

The parts I'd left out? Well, when Bob had dropped by my boutique to sample some of my pecan cookies, he'd said, "Looks like Evie and I will be in need of your services in the coming weeks."

That got my attention. "Did you propose?"

"I did, just after she proposed to me."

My eyebrows made for my hairline. "You don't say?"

"After she popped the question, it was only fair that I ask her in return. The gentlemanly thing to do."

"I agree wholeheartedly," I said with a smile. "Just how did she pop the question?"

Bob leaned back with a warm smile and a faraway look in his eyes. "She said, 'I don't need a cup of tea, Bob Burnett. I need an answer. Yes or no. Do you want to marry me or not?'"

"She didn't!"

He nodded. "She sure did."

"And what did you say?"

"Yeah, I want to marry you. If you're game to marry an old man like me, then I guess I'm game to marry an old, ah . . ."

My hand went flat against my breast. "Then it must be love, if you called her an 'old' . . . and she still said yes."

"You bet. It was the kiss that followed that was the best part of the deal. She was all steamed up and ready to pucker."

Despite Bob's gaiety over the whole affair, I sensed something was wrong. So in fairness to Evie, I decided to ask her about it myself. Confirmation was what I needed. I simply couldn't share the rest before I had confirmation. Besides, who would believe it?

It was already Thursday, and I had a lot to do to get ready for Saturday. I put my watering can in the sink, then picked up the new copy of the *Gold Rush News*. I opened it to my column and left it on the table. I couldn't wait till Mandy read it. After all, she was the inspiration.

That deed done, I decided it was more than high time to call Miss Evie, to not only remind her of the baby shower but also to start on our plans for the Christmas Tea as well as to check my facts.

I dialed her number. Her voice sounded a bit glum. "Evie, it's Lisa Leann. Just wanted to remind you of Mandy's baby shower Saturday morning at 10:00, at my house."

"Oh, I think I'm busy."

I heard Mandy walk into the kitchen behind me. I turned and smiled at her as she helped herself to another glass of milk and an apple. She was dressed in a blue pair of pj's covered with the phrase "Cat's Meow."

I pointed at the *Gold Rush News* on the table and mouthed, "Read it."

She reached for it, and I turned my back.

"Going to Denver to pick out an engagement ring?" I now asked Evie.

"How do you know about my engagement?"

"Everybody knows. Bob Burnett's telling everyone he sees. He especially likes to describe that hot kiss that sealed the deal."

I couldn't see Evie's face over the phone, but it was as if I could hear her blush. "What's wrong, Evie?"

"Nothing."

"You don't seem like an excited bride-to-be. Is everything okay?"

"Yes."

"Well, I hate to see you break up with the sheriff. Some of the gang at Higher Grounds said something about you coming in the tavern to see him, then making a fuss about a barmaid, just before you dropped by Burnett's office. Is that story true? I didn't believe it, and I didn't pass the story along, either."

The silence on the other end of the line was all the confirmation I needed. So, it was true.

"Well, Evie, about that kiss between you and Bob. Let me tell you what my mama always said: 'Never let a fool kiss you or a kiss fool you.' Evie, it's not that I want to talk you out of using my wedding services. But I consider you a friend. And if I were you, I'd take my mama's advice to heart."

When I was met by more silence, I finally said, "Well, we're going to miss you Saturday. The girls and I have it all worked out to plan the Christmas Tea after the shower."

Suddenly, Evie found her voice. "Ah. On second thought, I think I can make it after all. Though, I do have a request."

"Anything, Evie."

I could hear the angst in her voice as she said, "Let's make this shower a do-over for our last Potluck meeting. It should serve a dual purpose, agreed?"

"Why, Evie, I like the way you think. I don't know what we ladies are going to do if we don't get a little more prayer support into our lives. Trouble seems to be brewing at every turn."

Evie sighed. "I find it difficult to believe that I agree with you, but in this incidence, I do."

There was another long silence, then Evie said, "On another matter, don't forget, you're not in charge of the Christmas Tea, not by a long shot."

"But the pastor said—"

"Pastor Kevin said that we are both in charge."

"Right. Oh, and before you say good-bye. Now mind you, this may not be any of my business, and I probably shouldn't say anything. But this does concern one of our girls."

"Who?"

"Our own Donna Vesey. Now, I don't mean to be starting any rumors, but is it true that she and Clay Whitefield are an item?"

"Donna and Clay? Don't be ridiculous."

"Well, then can you explain why they were necking just across the street from my bridal boutique last Sunday night? I was there late, putting another coat of varnish on my new cabinet. I haven't mentioned this to the other girls, but I thought it would be safe to ask you."

"You mean they were kissing?"

"Hugging is more like it. Intimate like."

"I can't help you. I'm just not into gossip, especially when it concerns Donna or any member of her family."

"Mom?" Mandy called from above the newspaper article.

I held up one finger to signal I was almost done. Then I said to Evie, "I understand. Well, got to go, my Mandy needs me." I hung up the receiver and turned around.

"What is it, darlin'?"

I pulled up a chair and sat down across from her. I was surprised to see her lower lip trembling. "What's wrong? Are you feeling okay?"

"Mom, your Aunt Ellen column, it's unbelievable."

I smiled proudly. "Thank you. I believe it's some of my best work to date." I picked it up and began to read it aloud to her.

Dear Aunt Ellen,
    While I was skiing, I fell and broke my leg in three places. Now because of the doctor's orders, I'm stuck here with my parents, 2,000 miles away from my home. As my husband had to go back to work, I'm very homesick. What should I do?

Signed,
Broken Up

I smiled up at my daughter, whose face had turned an interesting shade of gray. I continued to read.

Dear Broken Up,
    What a lucky young lady you are. You have a family who loves you, and a mom and dad who have dropped their lives to take care of you. That is your silver lining in your ordeal. While you heal, concentrate on how blessed you are to spend time with your mother.

She won't be around forever, and you'll want to cherish every moment you have together.

So, put on a smile and change your attitude. It will serve you well to create memories to last a lifetime.

Yours,
Aunt Ellen

I looked up, beaming. "Great advice, as usual, if I must say so—and I simply must."

"Mom, 'Broken Up' is me! You wrote a letter about me and published it in the community's newspaper. How could you?"

"No, no. That letter's not about you."

"Mother, is this what you did to your friends at the Potluck? Did you write thinly disguised letters about their personal lives so you could give them advice?"

"I wouldn't use the terminology 'thinly disguised,' but I suppose my comments were meant to help one or two of them."

"Could this be why Fred Westbrook slammed the door in your face?"

"Well, I don't know."

"And Mom, I heard what you said to Evie about Donna. You were gossiping."

"Well, I—"

She stood up and put her hands on her hips, or at the place where, before her pregnancy, her hips used to be. "Shame on you."

I looked up at her. "What I said was harmless, both about Donna and in print to 'Broken Up.'"

"Your words were not harmless. You hurt Donna by what you said to Evie, and you hurt me by putting my problems into print. Don't you think people will know you were writing a letter to me? Of course they will."

"But my advice, it was good, don't you think?"

"That's not the issue; you exposed me with words you can't take back. As Grandma says, 'You can't unring a bell.'" She crossed her arms, allowing them to rest on her swollen belly. "Mom, you've got to break your bad habit of gossip. It's hurt you your entire life."

This time I stood up, ready to protect myself from Mandy, who was turning into a drama queen. I waved my arms for emphasis. "I don't gossip. I check out the facts, go to the sources. I only repeat what I learn when it's newsworthy. It's what the TV networks do."

"Well, here's some news. You're flat wrong. The trouble with you and gossip, Mother, is that you enjoy telling people about other's faults and troubles. When you find pleasure in talking about the pain of others, something is wrong. It's time for you to learn how to hold your tongue."

Before I could protest, Mandy pushed her chair back and waddled out of the room. I think she was actually crying.

I picked up the article and looked at it again. I had really hurt her. The thought stunned me. I had hurt my own daughter.

I sat back down at the table. Had I hurt others this same way?

I felt my face grow hot. *Oh no.*

It was as if I could hear a bell ringing, but this time it was ringing for me, reminding me of all the words I had spoken, words that I couldn't take back.

Lisa Leann, I admonished silently, *you have some fences to mend, girl.*

39

Good Old-Fashioned Snail Mail

Clay decided not to drive to the newsroom but rather to walk. After all, he was now up to a couple of miles every morning and at least one in the evening. According to the odometer in his jeep, the large and modern building housing *Gold Rush News* was just a little over a mile away. He could walk there and back and have his two miles in.

Of course, he couldn't walk to work and stay. He'd need his jeep for runs. He could, however, do the little things like check his mail—the old-fashioned kind that comes in envelopes and bears stamps of dead famous people or pretty flowers or holiday cheer. According to a call he'd received on his cell phone from the office secretary, there was quite a stack piling up.

"You haven't graced us with your presence in a couple of days, Clay. I think you'll be surprised at all the snail mail you've got on your desk."

"Snail mail? What's that about?"

"You know, the kind that comes via the U.S. Post Office? Not email but snail mail."

Clay sighed. "I know what snail mail is, Edie. What I'm asking is why I suddenly have so much of it."

"Oh. Well. It's not you, per se. It's actually addressed to Aunt Ellen."

"Then why is it sitting on my desk?"

"Because the boss said this is your little project, you can deal with the backwash."

Clay nodded. "Oh, yeah. All right. I'll be down there in about twenty minutes."

Clay could hear the rumbling of a nosy woman leaning in for the kill on the other end of the line. "Say, Clay . . . tell me something. Just who is this Aunt Ellen anyway? Anyone I know?"

Clay chuckled. "Good try, Edie. But, you see, it's like this: if I tell you, I have to kill you. Then I'd get arrested, and they'd take me down to the county jail and, well, to be honest with you, I just don't look that good in orange jumpsuits."

With that, Clay ended the call, and with a "see ya later" to Bernstein and Woodward, he pulled on his jacket, walked out the door, bounded down the steps, and began his sprint toward the office.

To do so, he had to walk past "Aunt Ellen's" bridal boutique. It was dark. Unoccupied, but at the same time, open and inviting.

Much like its owner.

Evangeline

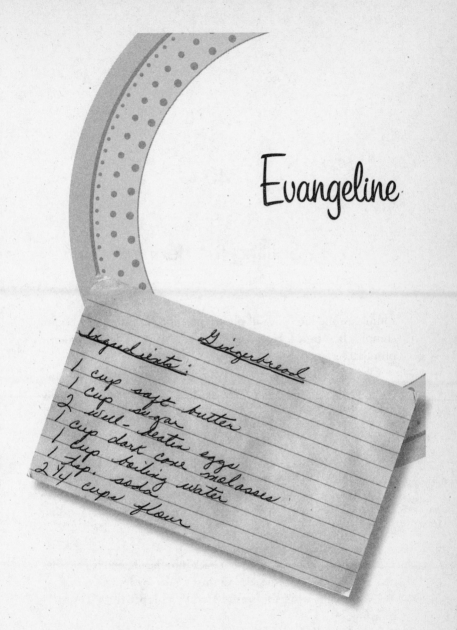

Gingerbread

Ingredients:

1 cup soft butter
1 cup sugar
2 well-beaten eggs
1 cup dark corn molasses
1 cup boiling water
1 tsp. soda
2½ cups flour

40

Spilling the Beans

I hung up the kitchen wall phone after the call from Lisa Leann, completely stunned. How could Bob have told everyone about the proposal . . . the kiss?

Okay, he hadn't told everyone. But he'd told Lisa Leann, and that was just as good as telling everyone to my way of thinking. I vacillated between calling him or driving to his office. One way or the other, we were going to talk about this; I just wasn't sure about when.

I went into the living room and sat in my favorite chair, picked up the Bible I'd left sitting on its arm, and began to read again. Word of God or not, I couldn't seem to focus on the text. All I could see was Bob standing in the middle of Lisa Leann's shop, talking about our most private moments.

How could he?

I put the Bible down and went back into the kitchen to call Vonnie. She answered on the second ring, a new joy in her voice.

"Von? That you? You sound awfully chipper for a Thursday morning."

Vonnie giggled. "Let's just say things are good between me and Fred again."

I pinked an old maid's blush. "I wouldn't know about such things," I said.

"But you will soon enough," Vonnie reminded me. Vonnie was the only person I'd told about the engagement—so far. Obviously, I couldn't account for how many people Bob had told.

I sighed. "Yeah, I suppose I will."

"What's wrong?"

I walked over to the kitchen table, pulling the telephone cord with me, then sat in one of the hard chairs. "I just got a call from Lisa Leann."

"Uh-oh."

"Why do you say that?" I asked, leaning my elbows on the table. With my free hand I curled my hair around my index finger.

"She came over the other night."

"To your house?"

"Mmm. Wanted to say some hurtful things about our Donna."

"She said some things to me too."

"About Donna? What things?"

"About her and Clay Whitefield." I stood, walked over to the shelf where I keep Mama's old cookbooks, and pulled one from its place. I needed to think about supper tonight, though I didn't feel like eating. I'd hardly been hungry since the afternoon I proposed to Bob Burnett. If this kept up, by our first anniversary, I'd be little more than a skeleton.

"Same here. Of course, you know if we keep talking about Lisa Leann we're just as guilty of gossip as she is."

I looked up and glanced out the window to the skies that had turned ashen gray, ripe and ready for another snowfall. "I suppose so," I admitted.

"Well, then, Evie. Why'd you call this morning?"

"Lisa Leann is having a baby shower for her daughter on Saturday."

"I know. I don't know if I can make it. I'm still a little prickly on the subject of Lisa Leann Lambert."

"Vonnie," I said, crossing back over to the table and carrying the recipe book, "yes, you can. We really must. Lisa Leann wants to discuss the Christmas Tea, and I'm thinking that we need to have some PLC prayer time as well. We owe this to our group . . . we owe this to Jan, if nothing else."

Vonnie didn't answer right away but finally said, "I agree."

"Good. Then will you help me? Will you call a few of the others? Encourage them to go? We should show the love of Jesus to Lisa Leann—whether she deserves it or not."

Vonnie said she would, taking two of the names: Donna, whom I still couldn't face, and Goldie, who had been busy moving into a condo and who put a buzz in motion when she sat with Jack in church on Sunday. "I'll call Lizzie," I said. "She called earlier and left a message for me while I was taking my bath."

With a "sounds good," Vonnie and I ended our call, and I placed another, this time to Lizzie's workplace. While I waited for her to come to the phone, I opened the recipe book and pointed. Whatever my finger settled on would be dinner.

"This is Lizzie Prattle," I heard her say as I peered at the recipe at my fingertip. Gingerbread. Oh well. I certainly wasn't in the mood to challenge my fate these days. Gingerbread, perhaps with a tall glass of ice-cold milk, would have to do. At least the milk had some nutritional value.

"Lizzie? You called?"

"Evangeline, what's this about you and Bob Burnett?"

My shoulders sagged. "Who told you? Bob? Did Bob tell you too?"

"No. Lisa Leann called about—"

"Lisa Leann," I said with a roll of my eyes. "That woman . . ."

"I know. Let's not go there right now. The point is, are you really engaged to Bob Burnett?"

I tried to smile. "I am."

"Evie—"

"You don't have to say anything, Lizzie. I'm not even sure how I feel about the whole thing."

"What about Vernon?"

"Vernon. Vernon Vesey is a snake," I said, then remembered what Bob had said the afternoon of our first date. *"I'd say the snake has just crawled in, and Eve's got a decision to make. You gonna eat from the tree or not, milady?"*

"Why do you say that?"

I sighed, something I seemed to be doing a lot of lately. "I'm going to tell you this, Lizzie, but I'd appreciate it if you keep it to yourself. I haven't even told Vonnie."

"Vonnie doesn't know about the engagement?"

"Oh, she knows about that, yes. But she doesn't know about Doreen Vesey coming back to town and Vernon practically fawning all over her." I took a breath. "Again."

"Doreen Vesey? Are you sure?"

"Positive. I saw them together at the tavern."

"You were at the tavern?"

I began to pace about the kitchen. "It's a long story, but I'm sure God led me there. The point is, Lizzie, I saw them. Saw them together. At a table, in the darkest, most private part of the room."

"Did you talk to her? To Doreen?"

"Oh, yeah. And she is just as snide as ever, I'll have you know. She looks like a dried-up old prune, but she hasn't lost her sass."

Lizzie was quiet for a moment. "Well, my word. Does Donna know that her mother is back in Summit View?"

I paused. "I don't have any idea."

Lizzie was quiet again. "Evie, tell me everything you saw."

"In the tavern? I walked in—Lizzie, have you ever been in that place? It's a den of iniquity, I'll tell you that much. If Sodom and Gomorrah were even half as bad—"

"Evie, get to the point."

I stopped my pacing. "They were sitting in the back, at a table."

"What were they doing? Holding hands? Talking?"

"No, they weren't holding hands. Doreen was smoking like an old chimney. I wonder when she picked up that nasty habit. And, if you ask me, she's doing more than smoking cigarettes. I'll bet she's an alcoholic from the looks of things."

"Evie!"

"Sorry. That woman just riles me up."

"Well, get off the rabbit trails, my friend. Were they talking or just—I don't know—sharing a drink?"

I had to think, to take myself back to that moment when life as I knew it had ended. "They were . . . they were . . . arguing."

"Arguing?"

I found my chair and sat in it. "Oh, dear. Oh, Lizzie. They were arguing. Why didn't I realize that sooner?"

"Evie, have you spoken to Vernon since then?"

"No. He and I were supposed to get together later that afternoon, but then . . . And he hasn't bothered to call me or come by. For a while there, he was driving by several times a day. Oh, Lizzie. I've blown it. I've blown it big time."

Lizzie suggested that we pray and that I make a phone call to Vernon, asking if we could talk. "Then," she said, "you'll either have closure or a decision to make."

"You mean, between Bob and Vernon?"

"Yes. I'm afraid so."

"Oh, Lizzie. When did life get so complicated?"

Lizzie laughed a little laugh and then said, "Let's pray, Evie. Let's pray right now before you go off and do anything else we'll need to pray to get you out of."

Vernon agreed to come by, though I practically had to beg him to. "Just say what you have to say," he kept repeating to me on the phone. He sounded like a rejected puppy.

"Vernon, please. Please, I'm begging you."

He finally relented and said he'd see me in a half hour.

I dressed in the new outfit I'd bought at Lindy's but had yet to wear. When he arrived—looking handsome in his uniform but laden with a look of hurt and confusion—I ushered him into the living room and asked him to have a seat on the sofa. He held his uniform cap in his hands and slid his fingers around the brim as he did so. I chose to sit next to him, a decision that, I could tell, made him uncomfortable.

I folded my hands in my lap, leaned over a bit, resting my elbows on my thighs. "When did she come back?" I asked, getting right to the point.

He shrugged and looked me in the eye. "I'm not sure. A few weeks ago—two days before you saw me with her picture—I got a call out to the tavern. She managed to dart into the ladies room as soon as she saw me so I wouldn't get a good look at her, I suppose." He shook his head. "She looks awful, doesn't she?"

I wanted to rant and rave that she deserved to look awful, considering what she'd done to me over the years, not to mention what she'd done to him and his daughter. But instead I said, "She does. She's obviously been through some rough times."

"I went home that afternoon, trying to figure out why the barmaid had made such a hasty retreat when I entered. There was something about the eyes . . ."

"I thought the same thing."

"You did?"

"Yes. Otherwise, I don't think I would have recognized her."

He pursed his lips. "Donna's seen her, but she doesn't recognize her. Apparently, no one else does either. But . . ." He took a deep breath.

"But?"

"I was married to the woman. I know her—knew her intimately."

I prickled.

"I'm sorry. We're both adults here, Evie. Doreen's the mother of my daughter. We've been intimate."

"It's just not a mental picture I need right now."

"Sorry." He looked down at the cap in his hands and began to curl it into something resembling a taco. I watched him intently, wishing I could reach out to him in a more physical way; that I could take him in my arms and hold him until all the ugly in life melted away.

But I couldn't. At that moment, I was an engaged woman, and I needed to stay focused on my purpose for our meeting. Closure, Lizzie called it.

"So, Donna doesn't know?"

"No. After that day, when you saw me with the photo, I began to do some investigating before I just headed out there and made accusations." His blue eyes shot up to mine and held them for a moment before going on. I could read them clearly. "As you accused me," they seemed to say. I deserved that look, so I let it slide by saying nothing in return. "She's been married six times, Evie. Six times."

"My Lord have mercy."

"She had three more children, all of whom were taken away from her either by the state or by their fathers. She wasn't even married to the father of two of them."

"Reminds me of the woman at the well."

"Who?"

"I'll tell you later," I said. I wanted to hear the rest of Doreen's story. "Keep going."

"She's worked as a barmaid across the country. Got arrested more than once for prostitution."

I gasped. "Oh, Vernon." In spite of my resolution to the contrary, I reached for his hand. He took mine in his and squeezed. "How horrible for you. For Donna."

"That's why we were arguing when you came into the tavern. I finally walked in when she wouldn't expect it. She wants Donna to see her as more than just Dee Dee McGurk. But I said no. This isn't the kind of thing we can just spring on Donna. Especially now."

My brow furrowed. "Why now?"

He shook his head. "I can't go into that right now. Donna's having a difficult time and I'd . . . I'd appreciate your prayers, quite frankly."

I smiled, scooting a tad closer to him. "Prayers? Why, Vernon Vesey, I didn't think you were a praying man."

He squeezed my hand again, then winked at me. "You might be surprised." He inched closer too. "Forgive me?"

My heart began to race, and my head went fuzzy. "Of course, I do," I answered, looking down.

He ducked his head as though he were going to kiss me. "Evie," he whispered. "My Evie-girl."

"Vernon," I whispered back. "I . . . I can't."

"Can't?" He drew back. "Can't what? Kiss the man you love? The man you're going to marry?"

"Marry?"

"You are, you know. I'm not wasting any more time. Not taking any more chances. I'd already bought you a ring."

"You did?" My eyes widened.

"I was going to give it to you for Christmas. But, then—Doreen."

My head dropped. "Oh, Vernon." I began to cry. "Oh, what have I done?"

With the fingertips of his free hand he lifted my chin. "What are you talking about, Evie-girl?"

I pulled my hand free of his and pushed myself back. "I'm already engaged," I said, then bit my bottom lip.

His brow furrowed. "To whom?"

I made a wry face. "Bob Burnett."

41

If a Picture Paints a Thousand Words

It seemed to Clay that he was working every free minute on the photo album for Donna. He wasn't complaining, of course. As far as he was concerned it was a true labor of love and friendship. He hoped she'd feel the same way when she saw it. He hoped she'd appreciate the amount of time and effort he'd put into the project. He wondered if she could possibly know how much money he'd laid down for the album alone.

The more time he spent on it, the more value he placed on its craftsmanship. It was, indeed, a work of art. Even an old boy reared in the high country could see that. Each time he worked on it—slipping in photographs and writing captions with the new Bic Pilot he'd bought over at Wal-Mart—he'd finish by closing the book and running his hand over the material. Even the binding was special.

Like Donna.

This time, when he'd put in more time than he should have allowed, he took the album back to a safe place on the bottom shelf of the closet, then turned to shut the door. Minute rays of sunlight escaping heavy snow clouds were peering through the blinds, and he paused to open them wider, to allow as much light as possible to fill the small places of his domain.

That's when he saw it. A tiny snapshot, lodged between a leg of the old chrome and Formica TV stand and the Brady Bunch shag carpet underneath. He bent over and retrieved it, turning it toward the window for better viewing.

It was taken at Donna's fifth birthday party. Clay knew that much because there were five distinguishable candles standing proudly on a large round cake with white icing. Donna stood at the center of the far side of an outside picnic table, beaming as her little friends sang "Happy Birthday" to her. It didn't take an investigative journalist to know that this was what they were doing. Every mouth but Donna's was wide open, paying tribute.

Clay was among the throng. He was wearing the Indian headdress his mother had not been able to coax him to remove that year. Other than for baths and bedtime, of course. That was the year he'd come to understand his heritage, or at least half of it. Not once, however, had he taken to carrying around a sack of Irish potatoes.

Clay smiled at the memory. The innocence. The joys of childhood. He remembered how each child there had received a copy of the photo with a thank-you card from Donna a few weeks later. Then his vision rested on what lay in the shadows. The photograph had been taken with the sun directly behind its photographer; the form of her shadow—arms raised and camera to her face—stretched over the children. Next to hers, the shadow of a man who had to be Sheriff Vesey.

Donna's mother and father, clearly marked as doting parents.

No one—not a single one of them—knew the sadness that was so close to follow. The betrayal. The abandonment. And the worn-out old woman working as a barmaid over at the tavern.

Not to mention the young woman who didn't know her mother had come home.

Goldie

Sour Cream Coffee Cake

2 sticks butter
2 eggs
1/4 ts salt
2 cups sifted cake flour

2 cups sugar
1 ts Baking powder
1 cup sour cream

Topping:
3/4 cup chopped nuts
2 TB Brown sugar

1 ts cinnamon

(over)

42

Tasting a Possibility

I was sitting at the desk in my office, pondering whether or not to go to Jack's house to pick up a few more things for my condo—even little things like the pan I make my sour cream coffee cake in. What I should have been doing was organizing a stack of affidavits for an upcoming trial for Chris.

In the past week I'd moved furniture—remarkably, with Jack's help—from one of our guest rooms and into the bedroom of my new place, along with the family room love seat and a small television for my den. Jack had even given me a small spending account at Everything's Daisy, one of the cutesy shops along Main Street.

"When you come home," he'd said one morning as we were standing in the middle of the shop, "you can just bring all this with you and knock yourself out redecorating."

We were looking at framed prints of rabbits on wooded, snow-covered trails I was considering buying for the condo. "Don't get too assured of that, Jack. I'm not promising anything."

He reached for my hand, clasping it in his. I flinched at first, then allowed my hand to relax. "Will you do something for me?" he asked.

I looked around. The owner of the shop, Reggie Tyre, a woman with silvery hair and a smooth complexion, was standing behind a bar-style counter, staring at us. When she caught my eye, she returned to her work. "It depends," I said in a hushed voice.

"Will you go to counseling with me? I'm meeting with Pastor Kevin again on Thursday evening at 5:00."

"I work until 5:00," I reminded him. "You know that."

He shrugged. "So you'll be a few minutes late. I'll wait for you."

I picked up a porcelain bunny and studied it for a moment. "I like this. I think I'll take it home for the den. I don't really have much of anything in there for decoration."

"Goldie," Jack said a bit more forcefully than I would have preferred. I looked again at Reggie, who frowned at us.

"Jack, shhh."

"Isn't this what you always wanted?" he asked, turning his back on Reggie. "What more do you want me to do?"

I put the bunny down and crossed my arms. "I want you to lower your voice, Jack." I moved toward the door with the intention of leaving. Jack followed me onto the sidewalk outside, where holiday tourists were strolling, taking in the magnificence of the Colorado mountains surrounding our town while sipping take-out coffee from Higher Grounds and stopping to look in storefront windows at the overpriced items within.

I turned toward 6th, and Jack jogged a bit to catch up. When he did, he grabbed my arm. I jerked it out of his grip. "Jack, stop it," I demanded, then raised a hand in hopes of ending our minor dispute. "Okay, I'll go with you to the counseling session." When Jack smiled, I added, "Once. Then I'll decide from there."

Jack nodded in triumph. "Fair enough," he said, then walked me back to my condo, where, after a peck on the lips at the front door, he left me to spend time alone in my new home.

Vonnie was not the only Potluck member to call me at the office on Thursday, though the second call was hardly for me.

"Goldie," Donna's voice said from the other end of the line. "I . . . uh . . . This is Donna Vesey."

I had, of course, recognized her voice. Donna has one of those voices that's unmistakable. "Hi, Donna. I already know about the meeting on Saturday."

"The what?"

"The Potluck meeting slash baby shower."

"Oh, yeah. That. Well, that's not why I'm calling."

"It's not?"

"Uh . . . no. I need to . . . uh . . . I need to set up a meeting with Mr. Lowe. A consultation, I guess you'd call it."

"Donna, is something wrong?"

"No, no. Nothing's wrong. I just need some advice. It's nothing major. I'd say an hour ought to do it."

I opened the computer program with Chris's schedule and, after scanning it, said, "I have something next Wednesday."

"Wednesday?"

"Two o'clock."

"Ah . . . okay. Perfect."

I typed her name in as she asked, "So, how's it going with you and the coach? I saw Olivia the other day at Higher Grounds, and she mentioned things might be looking up for the two of you."

I rolled my eyes. "Olivia's declaration is a bit premature, but we'll see. God only knows what the future holds, and we can't go around predicting, now can we?"

"I guess not."

"We're seeing Pastor Kevin tonight, so if you want to pray about that, you can."

"You're kidding," she said. "You're counseling with Pastor Kevin?"

"Mmm."

"Aren't you a little nervous about airing your dirty laundry to someone you know so well? And who knows you?"

"I'm sure Pastor Kevin is a good counselor, Donna. He's God's servant, and he's someone I know we can trust." I took a breath. "Jack has been meeting with him for a while, and I'm going to see how it goes tonight."

"I see. Well, then, Goldie. Allow me to wish you good luck."

I thanked her, then hung up and went back to work, glancing occasionally at the clock. Not too many days ago I'd been anticipating the 5:00 hour—waiting to see Van—but now I almost dreaded it. What if Pastor Kevin insisted I go back to Jack? What if he said I was wrong to live in the condo? What if he asked me if I'd had any feelings for any other man since I'd left Jack?

Nah, I scolded myself. *Why would he think that?* It was just a rush of guilt, though I still argued with myself that I'd done nothing to feel guilty about.

When it was five till, I went ahead and began shutting everything down. I retrieved my coat from the break room, then stuck my head in Chris's office to say good night. He looked at his watch. "You in a hurry to get to that new condo of yours?" he asked, teasing. "Keep this up, and I'll have to reevaluate your raise."

I smiled at him. "No. You might be interested to know that I'm meeting Jack and Pastor Kevin in a few minutes for a counseling session."

Chris's brow shot upward. "Really? Does this mean you aren't seeing Van anymore?"

I folded my arms and stood upright. "Chris, I swear to you, we're just friends."

He nodded. "Well, keep me posted." Then he pointed a finger at me in jest. "But if you and Jack work this out, let me just make it clear that I'm not willing to give up my new secretary."

I smiled all the more broadly. "Don't worry about that. No matter what, I won't ever be a house frau again. I know that's fine for some women, but I've discovered it's not okay for me. After all, Olivia is grown and gone, and, like Jack, I need a purpose too."

"All right, Goldie. I'll see you in the morning."

I drove a little slower than I needed to, taking in the sights of downtown in all its holiday splendor. When I pulled into the church's parking lot I saw that Jack's car was already there, parked next to Pastor's. I frowned, then sighed. "Well, Lord," I spoke aloud. "Let's see what's in store for this afternoon."

Pastor Kevin and Jack were already in the pastoral office, but they'd left the door open so they'd be sure to see me when I entered,

I suppose. Jack jumped up from his chair opposite Kevin's desk and escorted me to the empty chair next to his.

"Hello, Goldie," Kevin greeted me.

"Pastor." I crossed my legs and clutched my purse in my lap.

"Thank you for meeting with us," he continued. "As I'm sure Jack has told you, we've been meeting for a few weeks."

Jack shifted a bit in his chair. "I couldn't bring myself to come right away," he informed me, almost too eagerly. "I thought you were the one with the problem, Goldie, but now I know better." Jack seemed to be almost gleeful at the new revelation about himself.

Pastor continued. "You understand that Jack has a disease, Goldie."

"A disease," I repeated, perhaps a bit flat.

"That's right, Goldie," Jack interjected. "I've got a disease."

I kept my eyes on Pastor Kevin. "Is this . . . excuse . . . supposed to absolve Jack?"

"No, of course—"

"Make me feel better about the bum deal I got?"

"Goldie," Pastor Kevin said, "of course not. This has been a learned behavior from Jack's father and, I suspect, his father before him. But sex—forbidden sex—acts on the brain like a drug." Pastor cleared his throat a bit, and I suspected the subject was a bit uncomfortable for him to speak of in front of us. "I think it's important for you to understand what Jack's been dealing with."

I straightened. "What Jack has been dealing with?" I asked. "What about what I've been dealing with? Do you have any idea how many years I've been living with his infidelity? How many years I've heard the whispers and the giggles behind my back?" I shifted in my seat, uncrossed my legs, and then crossed them again. "What he's been through?"

Jack looked at Pastor Kevin—who nodded at him—then turned to face me. "I was wrong, Goldie."

I flustered a laugh. "Yes, well. What's new, Jack?"

Pastor Kevin leaned his forearms against the top of his immaculate desk. "Goldie, it's important that you be open to hear what your husband is saying. Now, I'm not trying to make something small out of this, but sin—in God's eyes—is sin. Jack's asked God to forgive him, and I have to believe that God has. Now, Jack has to ask you and eventually Olivia too."

Jack reached over and touched my arm with his fingertips. An odd mixture of repulsion and attraction shot through me so fast that I shivered. "Goldie, I'm sorry. I'm sorry for every single time I was unfaithful to you . . . to our vows. And, I promise you, if you'll just give me a chance to heal personally, I believe our marriage can be healed too."

I looked from Jack to Pastor and back to Jack again. "I'm not moving back to the house. Not yet. So don't even think about asking me to."

Jack smiled at me. "I'm not asking you to."

"But . . ." Pastor said, as though he were helping Jack to remember his lines in a play.

Jack nodded once. "But I would like to ask you to do something with me."

I narrowed my eyes at him. "You mean, besides coming to counseling?"

Jack looked at Pastor one more time, then looked back at me. He coughed out a laugh, then wrung his hands together. He was like a schoolboy asking a girl out to the prom.

"Jack?" I asked. "What else do you want me to do?"

"Ah . . . Pastor Kevin has a cabin up on Summit Ridge, and he's agreed to let us go up there for a weekend alone to regroup . . . to try to see where we are in all this."

"I don't think so," I said, stopping him with a raise of my hand. I looked at the pastor. "I appreciate it. I do. And I remember how fondly Jan spoke of your time up there alone, but I'm not ready to leave my new condo for a weekend . . . or—to be perfectly honest—to be alone with you."

Jack's face flushed. "What's so bad about being alone with me?" he asked.

"Jack," Pastor Kevin said. "I believe what Goldie is referring to is the conjugal side of your marriage."

Jack's face went from flushed to crimson.

Pastor Kevin continued, this time speaking to me. "If it makes you feel any better, Goldie, there are two bedrooms in the cabin, and they're at opposite ends of the house."

"Oh." I looked down at my hands, studied the single band around my left ring finger. Alone with Jack for two days. Alone in a remote cabin with a crackling fire and banks of evergreens reaching their snowy branches toward the blue sky. Alone with the man I'd promised to love forever. "Oh," I repeated.

Before I knew what was happening, Jack slid out of his chair and down on his knees before me. "Please, Goldie. Please give me another chance. Two days and two nights at Summit Ridge." He held up his right hand. "I swear to you, you don't even have to talk to me if you don't want to."

I burst out laughing. Jack and Kevin looked at each other, then began laughing with me until I stood. "Get up, Jack Dippel." I shook my head at him. "When are we talking about here? What time frame are you looking at?"

Pastor stood with Jack and said, "The cabin is pretty much booked up during the holidays, but the couple staying there this week is leaving Saturday evening."

I blinked at him. "Meaning?"

"If you can take a couple of days off from work, it's yours Sunday through Tuesday of this coming week."

Jack sat up a bit. "I've already cleared the time with the school and—I hope you don't get mad—I spoke with Chris about your getting a coupla days—"

My head jerked as my mouth fell open.

Before I could say anything, Jack said, "He's all for it, Goldie."

"He is?"

Jack smiled triumphantly. "Said our marriage is more important than any work that needed to be done around there."

I nodded, then edged my way around my husband and walked toward the door. Once there, I turned and looked at the two men who stood looking back at me, puzzled. "All right," I said. "I'll do it. I'll go."

Jack exhaled so hard I thought the air would blow me over. "But," I said, "no monkey business, Jack. Separate bedrooms."

"Whatever you say, Goldie," he said, taking a step toward me.

"And," I added with a smile, "maybe even separate dining tables . . . but we'll take that as it comes."

Jack returned the smile as Pastor Kevin looked down at his watch. "Boys and girls," he said, "I've got another appointment I must scoot out to." He looked at Jack. "Jack, I'll see you again next Thursday."

Jack nodded. "I'll be here, Pastor." He looked at me one last time. "This hasn't been easy, but I know it's going to be worth it."

"Well, we'll see what God allows," I said, pulling an old quote from my father.

"Yes," Jack answered, "I believe we will."

43

Advice from a Couple a' Rats

Clay vacillated between keeping the photograph and throwing it in the trash. At no time did he do to it, however, what Doreen had done to her daughter, though he wanted to. More than anything he wanted to lay it flat in the palm of his hand and crush it like an autumn leaf left on the ground too long.

He finally chose to lay it on the table next to Woodward and Bernstein. "So, what do you think, boys? What should I do with this? Open an old wound in hopes that Donna will fall into my arms again or . . ."

The thought of Donna wrapped in his embrace hadn't come to him consciously. When it slipped out of his mouth, he was pleasantly surprised by both the thought and the memory. He picked up the photograph again and grinned.

The gerbils scurried about the cage as though a storm were brewing, blowing up the waters of Lake Dillon.

Clay picked up his cell phone to place a call to Donna's home number, something he'd been doing a lot of lately, though she hadn't returned any of the calls.

Just as quickly, he put the phone back in its cradle.

He'd let this rest for a while.

He could, he decided, call her about something else . . .

Donna

ONE POT SPAGHETTI

1 LL GRD BEEF
1 Tbs. INSTANT MINCED ONION
8 OZ CAN TOMATO SAUCE
15 OZ CAN OR JAR SPAGHETTI SAUCE
(WITH MUSHROOMS)
1 1/2 tsp SALT
1 tsp SUGAR
2 CUPS WATER   1 7 OZ PKG SPAGHETTI
3 Tbs. PARMESAN CHEESE (OPTIONAL)

44

Sweet Peace

I'm so glad for a day off, I thought, luxuriating over a second cup of coffee. Last night's shift had been icy cold, down to two degrees with snow showers. Not much action though, except a tourist hitting a deer out on the highway to Breckenridge. Luckily no one was hurt, but the rental car was totaled.

I thought I'd never finish my paperwork. But even as I turned it in, I knew my report would provoke a call from Clay.

I thought of Clay and blushed. Had we really shared an embrace right on Main Street? I wasn't sure how I felt about that. Though at the time I felt comforted and safe.

But how did Clay feel? I knew the answer to that. I'd seen the look in his eyes, and it had made me feel . . . heady, warm, confused. A feeling that still lingered.

Once again I'd avoided the Higher Grounds. He was surely there, waiting for me, and I wasn't sure what I'd say. "Thanks for the hug, pal." Or "Hey, sexy." Or . . . good grief.

So I stayed home and let his messages build up on my answering machine.

"Donna, are you home?" *(BEEP)*

"Donna, I'm worried about you." *(BEEP)*

"Donna, I've got something to show you when you think you've got a minute." *(BEEP)*

"Donna, want to meet me for lunch? Call me." *(BEEP)*

So far, I hadn't responded, but I would have to talk to him sooner or later, especially now that a tourist had hit a deer. With the lack of real news around this place, Clay might run the story on the front page. He would want a quote from me.

It was almost noon when I looked out my kitchen window at Mount Paul. The weather could change in an instant, and today was no exception. The sun was shining bright, but the high winds that swept over the mountain's fresh powder created what appeared to be a snow squall surrounding my cabin.

The phone rang, and the caller ID said "Westbrook."

"Hello?"

Vonnie's chipper voice asked, "Did I wake you?"

"No, no, I've been up for a whole half hour."

"Oh, good, I just wanted to remind you about dinner tonight. I'm making your favorite, one-pot spaghetti."

"With a loaf of garlic bread?"

"And my apple pie for dessert."

"What time?"

"Five, and bring your coat, gloves, and snow boots. Fred and I want to take you out on a drive to show you something."

"What?"

Vonnie sounded a little nervous. "You'll just have to trust us, dear."

When we hung up, I wondered if I should head down to the Higher Grounds for a bowl of chili, or if I should just make a baloney sandwich here at the house. Before I could decide, the phone rang again.

It was Clay, and this time I decided to pick up. "Hi, Clay."

He sounded relieved. "Heard about the run-in with the tourist and the deer last night."

"Yeah," I said. "Not much else to report except for what the man who was driving said, and I quote, 'I didn't know the Colorado

Mountains had deer thingies. Someone should have warned us. The deer should at least be kept penned up at night.'"

Clay laughed. "Great line. I'll use it in my story." He paused for a moment. "Today's your day off, right? Want to hang out tonight?"

"You mean like a date?"

"Just dinner. I'm worried about you."

I put my coffee cup in the sink and rinsed it out. "I can't. Going over to Vonnie's."

"Vonnie's a great cook," Clay said. "Do you think they could set a place for one more?"

I was tempted to invite him but quickly changed my mind. Knowing Clay, he'd get Vonnie to spill the beans about David Harris, which could be his true intent in the first place. I frowned. "Ah, this is more of a . . . they've got a . . . thing they want to show me. This probably wouldn't be a good time."

"A thing? What kind of thing?"

"I don't know. I was told to wear snow boots."

"December nights aren't warm enough for a barbecue in the backyard."

"I know." I opened the refrigerator.

"I could come along and protect you from bears. I know how you run when you see one. It was in the paper."

"Ha-ha, very funny. Not tonight, Clay, though . . ."

"Another time?"

"Maybe."

"How about meeting me for lunch?"

"Just ate," I said, slapping a piece of baloney on wheat bread.

"Okay, well. Keep me posted about the Westbrooks' backyard mystery. Hope it's not a body. Wait, maybe they found that missing gold from that 1864 stagecoach robbery. We still get a few treasure hunters stopping by the paper, interviewing the staff for clues, as if we'd tell them if we knew where to look. But wouldn't it make a great headline? 'Westbrooks Unearth Riches in Their Own Backyard!'"

"I'll call you if that's the case. Talk to you later," I said.

"Okay, but before you go, did you get my message about wanting to show you something?"

"Oh, yeah. I did. What's up?"

"Uh-uh. You'll have to wait and see. My turn to say good-bye. Good-bye."

I hung up and took a bite of my sandwich and chewed slowly as I thought about Clay Whitefield and, well, my feelings for him. What were they exactly? Who knew? My so-called feelings were as muddled as my thoughts.

That night at dinner, I stowed my boots, gloves, and coat at the Westbrooks' coatrack by their front door.

"So what's the big mystery?" I asked. Fred and Vonnie exchanged secretive glances. I stopped in my tracks. "It's not something bad, is it?"

Fred surprised me when he quoted what his wife had said earlier. He swiped at a few gray hairs that had strayed from covering his bald spot. "Donna, you're just going to have to trust us."

I should have left right then. But Fred and Vonnie, well, they were a hard pair not to trust.

The table was beautifully set with Vonnie's favorite blue and yellow pottery. When Fred bowed his head to say the prayer, I should have realized I was getting yet another clue.

"Dear Lord, thank you for our food and the hands that prepared it. Thank you for my wife, Vonnie, whom I love with all my heart."

I peeked and saw Vonnie smile and give Fred a light shove of her elbow into his ribs. He smiled too but kept his eyes shut. I closed my eyes again and listened as he continued. This time, his voice softened, sounding teary even. "And Lord, please be with our Donna. Let her know how much we love her and that we . . ."

I peeked again and saw Vonnie pat Fred's arm, as if in warning.

". . . love her. In Jesus's name, amen."

When I looked up, I could have sworn Vonnie was wiping at a tear. I shifted uncomfortably, then turned my attention to the big pot of spaghetti on the table. I put my napkin in my lap, and Vonnie handed me her big spaghetti-serving fork, which I twirled through the dish, heaping a lovely serving onto my plate.

I smiled and looked up. "Looks good."

Fred was already munching on a piece of garlic bread, studying me. "Thank you," Vonnie said a little too cheerfully.

Still, despite their strange behavior, I tried to relax. *Whatever is going on here, how bad could it be?*

After the meal, Vonnie said, "We'll have pie later, after we get back from . . ."

"From where?" I asked.

"It's a surprise," Fred said.

"Okay. Then let me help you with the dishes," I said, stacking the dirty plates and silverware and carrying them to the kitchen sink.

"Let them soak for a while. We've got to get going."

A few minutes later, the three of us were bundling up. "I'll drive," Fred said. "But let's go in Vonnie's Taurus."

"Okay," I agreed, seeing as I didn't know where we were headed anyway.

After we got in the car and pulled out of the driveway, I had a sinking feeling. What if they were setting me up to meet with Wade and the pastor? What would I do? I wouldn't be able to peel out of the church driveway again, not without my Bronco.

I sighed in relief when we passed the church. But frowned again when we pulled into the All Saints Cemetery driveway. Well, Clay had warned me about bodies, but this? What was this?

We drove to a remote area that was lit by a spotlight. I was surprised to see Daddy's truck. Uh-oh. It wasn't the only vehicle there. There was a gray car I didn't recognize. Wait, Pastor Moore's? Yes, I thought so.

From the backseat, I said, "Fred, this is creeping me out. You have to tell me what this is."

Fred pulled to a stop and turned to face me. "This is an intervention." His voice suddenly cracked, and he couldn't go on.

"Like you think I'm an alcoholic, so you're taking me to a graveyard?"

Vonnie turned, leaning her elbow over the front seat. "No, dear, we know you're not an alcoholic. But this is an invention nevertheless. You know, you really scared me the other day, threatening to take your life like that. Fred and I talked late into the night, and we both agreed. You've never had closure with the loss of your baby. And according to Wade, he needs it too."

"What?"

There was a tap on my window, and I saw my dad's face as he leaned down. He was wrapped in his heavy dress coat over his uniform. "Open the door," he said. "It's cold out here."

I complied, and he slid into the backseat with me, where he rubbed his hands together. "What's going on?" I asked.

"We've gathered here to say good-bye to your baby, Donna. Wade's here too. He needs to do this as much as you do."

He reached for my hand, but I hesitated. "I don't think I can do this."

My dad clasped his hand over mine. "Yes, you can. I'm with you, Donna. I need to do this too. If anything, do it for me. I lost my grandbaby, and it's really starting to hit me. I need closure too."

I slid out of the backseat and walked with my dad over a rise to where Pastor Kevin and Wade waited. We stood around a small, hand-carved wooden marker, which simply read, "Baby Gage."

I looked up at Wade and tried to say something, but words wouldn't come. Wade walked over and put his arm around me. "I'm sorry to surprise you like this, Donna. But we're all worried about you. Pastor Kevin thinks this will help."

I turned and looked at Pastor Kevin; he was bundled against the cold in a navy blue parka over dark ski pants. He wore a wool cap over his dark hair. His eyes were closed in prayer. He finally looked up and said, "Family and friends, we're gathered here today to say a long-awaited good-bye to the baby of Wade William Gage and Donna Renee Vesey."

Somewhere deep inside of me, I felt grief bubbling to the surface as my shoulders began to quiver. The pastor continued. "We are not here to pass blame. For we know the holy Father forgives, but it's we who are left behind who haven't been able to forget. This good-bye service has been deemed to be a time of closure. And it's a time of new beginnings." He paused, then looked at the faces of those gathered. "Who would like to say a few words?"

I was surprised when my dad walked to the little marker. He looked down at it and said, "Dear grandbaby, I'm so sorry. It's all my fault, me and my foolish pride. I talked your mother into, well . . . and I drove her to the clinic. I didn't realize what I was doing. And now, how I miss you. I know you're safe in the arms of Jesus, but please know how sorry I am to have ended your life."

I began to tremble harder. Wade gave me a squeeze as my dad wiped his eyes with his hanky, then walked back to where we were standing. Vonnie took his place.

"Dear baby, your parents have never stopped loving you. When one day we each cross over to the other side, we will at last hold you in our arms. But until then, know we miss you terribly."

I was surprised when Wade pulled his arm away and made the journey to the marker himself. He looked so somber, so mature, unlike the drunk I sometimes had to drive home from the tavern.

"Dear baby," he said. "I'm your father. And I've named you Jamie. Jamie Lee Gage. Your mother and I were going to get married. You would have had my name.

"Jamie, your mother and I were so young and so in love. Your conception may have been an accident, but your life, however brief, was a miracle.

"I've missed you so much. Until now, I've been stuck in the past. But the pastor tells me that you are with the heavenly Father, and that gives me such peace. It's time for me to move on with my life. But I want you to know you will be in my heart forever. Until we meet again, with Jesus."

The pastor looked at Fred, and Fred shook his head. Then Pastor Kevin looked at me. "Donna, do you have anything you want to say?"

How had it gotten so cold? I looked around the tiny circle of those who loved me and saw the hope in their eyes. Vonnie leaned over and gave me a hug. "Go on, now," she said. "Speak your piece. It's time."

I nodded and took shaky steps to the marker. I didn't know what to say. I took a deep breath. "I'm sorry. I'm sorry, Jamie. I'm so sorry."

That's when the shaking returned, robbing me of my ability to stand. I sank to my knees. "I'm so, so sorry."

Behind me, I could hear someone take a step toward me, but Pastor Kevin said, "Let her be. Let her get it all out."

I cried until there were no tears left. When my shoulders quit shaking, Wade knelt down and wrapped me in his arms as I leaned into him. Finally, he gave me his hand and helped me stand. We took our places in the circle.

The pastor looked directly at me. "God forgives you, Donna. A mistake was made here. It cost you your baby's life."

I nodded.

"Donna," the pastor continued, "leave your broken heart at this marker tonight, and know how much your heavenly Father loves you." He turned to the circle. "Let's pray. Dear Lord, please close this chapter in the lives of this family. Heal their broken hearts and give them peace."

I leaned into Wade and wept. Peace? I'd never known peace. I wasn't even sure how to get it, but it sounded so wonderful.

Later, back at the house, I sat on the sofa with Wade while Vonnie cut the pie. Wade said, "I'm sorry, Donna, this was the only way I thought I could get closure. And I knew you needed it too. So the pastor and Vonnie helped me organize this memorial to our baby. Are you okay with that?"

I nodded and stared at my hands, which I had clasped in my lap. My dad came over and hugged me. "We all love you, Donna."

I looked up at him. "I know."

When Dad walked back into the kitchen, Wade said, "That goes for me too, Donna. Loving you, I mean. I've never stopped. I know I don't have the right to ask. But if there's a chance for us, then . . . do you think there's a chance?"

"I have too many emotions to answer you tonight, Wade. But I'll think on it."

He smiled and gave my shoulders a squeeze. "Don't think too long. I'm ready to make up for my lost life." He hesitated for a moment, then looked me in the eye. "I know about that baby in Boulder."

My eyes snapped to his. "You do?"

"Yeah, I saw the original story about it in the Boulder *Camera*. Clay showed it to me down at the café. Then, again today, while I was painting at the hotel, the paper spread on the floor was from the *Camera* too. It said, 'Boulder County Sheriff's Department Named in Lawsuit.' It was about the baby you tried to save. The story named you in the suit as well."

I nodded. "I've been in contact with the Boulder County Sheriff's Department, and I've scheduled a meeting with Chris Lowe. I don't know where all this is going yet."

"Wherever it goes, I want to be by your side," Wade said. "If you'll let me."

I looked up at him. Why did he have to look so much like Brad Pitt? He smiled, and his cheeks dimpled. "Okay?" he said.

"I can't promise anything tonight," I said. "But we'll see."

"That's all I can ask. But I'll be praying for you."

"I appreciate that."

Together, we sat side by side, thinking about the past and wondering about the future. I felt too numb to know if I'd found peace, but I did know one thing. My family loved me, and tonight, even though I didn't know if I could love myself, their love made it possible for me to hope that I could.

45

Guess Who's Coming to Dinner

Clay was slipping. It took him a few hours before he realized what Donna had said about going over to the Westbrooks'. Even if he wasn't invited, it surely didn't mean he couldn't follow her there—unnoticed, of course—if for no other reason than to find out what the big mystery was about. It was practically his job, wasn't it?

He looked down at his Timex. It was nearly 6:00. Donna would probably be heading over to the Westbrooks' any minute. He reached for his down jacket, thrown hastily over the back of his chair, but didn't bother to put it on. Instead, he took the stairs two at a time with it looped over his arm. It wasn't until he reached the frigid outdoors that he put it on, then jumped into his jeep, turned it toward Donna's bungalow, and drove as fast as the speed limit would allow.

Her Bronco was already out of the driveway. Clay checked his watch: 6:14. He'd probably just missed her. Or maybe she and the Westbrooks were already sitting down to dinner.

He pulled into Donna's driveway, using it for a turnaround.

Minutes later, he was pulling into the Westbrooks' neighborhood. As he came around the turn toward their home, he slowed his jeep, then rolled it to a stop in the middle of the road.

Not a car in sight.

His shoulders sagged. Something was up. Hadn't Donna said something about snow boots? If they'd gone on one of those sleigh ride dinners so popular with the tourists, he was really out in the cold. Without another clue to follow, he might as well go home.

Evangeline

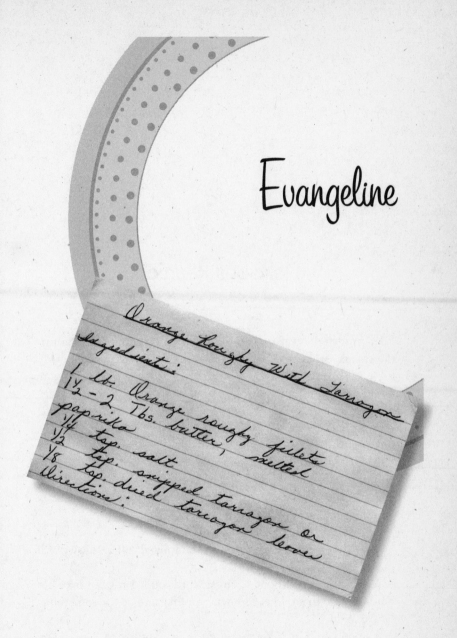

Orange Roughy With Tarragon

Ingredients:

1 lb. Orange roughy fillets
1½ - 2 Tbs. butter, melted
paprika
¼ tsp. salt
½ tsp. snipped tarragon or
⅛ tsp. dried tarragon leaves

Directions:

46

Delicious Reunion

I determined to break up with Bob. The whole thing—the dating, the engagement—was foolishness to begin with. As anyone who knows me can attest, I am a private person—as private a person as anyone in Summit View can be. The fact that Bob had gone directly to Lisa Leann without ever discussing it with me was more than I could live with. The shame and humiliation were nearly unbearable.

Lisa Leann Lambert, of all people.

Then, yesterday, when I was forced to tell Vernon that I was engaged, and to Bob Burnett of all people, and to see the expression on his face. Oh my, it was awful. Just awful.

"Why?" he said. "Just tell me why?"

I put my face in my hands and stammered out an answer. "I don't know. I just don't . . ."

Vernon stood without saying a word; pulled his cap over his head. "I have to go. I have somewhere I have to be . . . something I have to do."

I stood with him. "Vernon, don't leave. Not like this. I . . . I'm sorry. I acted in haste, and I . . ." I took a step toward him. "You asked for a chance to explain, and now I'm asking for the same thing."

He laughed, though I could tell he was not amused. "I'm not sure you can explain this one, Evie-girl."

Then he turned and walked out the door, leaving me alone to collapse on the sofa and cry until there were no tears left. When I was finally spent, I stood, wiped my eyes, and walked into the kitchen to make a phone call.

"Burnett Realty," sang the voice on the other end. "This is Bob."

"It's Evie."

"Hello, my wife-to-be."

Ugh. "Bob, I . . . I need to talk to you about some things."

"Wedding plans, no doubt. Now, here's what I'm thinking. Lisa Leann Lambert has that new boutique in town, and it would be wise, I think, to let her take care of the whole shebang. What do they call that? A wedding person . . . whatchamacallit . . ."

I took a deep breath. "Wedding coordinator."

"That's it. Now then, I went in there the other day and checked things out. Flowers, music, the food, the gown. She can do it all. What do you think? . . . Evie? What do you think?"

"Yes. Lisa Leann Lambert. Well, now. Before I can really talk about that, I need to talk to you about some other . . . things."

"Well, sure, sugarfoot. I'm thinking dinner tomorrow night. We'll start the weekend out with a bang."

I took another deep breath. "What about tonight? Or this afternoon?"

"Nah. No can do, Evangeline. I've got a Chamber of Commerce meeting tonight. Tomorrow night though. I'll pick you up at 7:00."

I couldn't wait until the following night. "Bob-I'm-ending-our-engagement!" I said so fast it sounded like a one-word sentence.

There was a palpable silence from the other end. "I see," he finally said.

"I'm sorry. I really am. I . . . I should never have come to your office like that." I drew myself upright. "And you had no right to go to Lisa Leann Lambert and tell her of our engagement . . . of how I asked you first. I don't appreciate that, Bob Burnett."

"So now it's my fault?" he stormed.

"Yes! No! Bob, it's just not right." I sobered. "It's just not right."

"It's Vernon, isn't it?"

I didn't answer.

"I knew it. You're not really over him. Well, let me tell you something, Miss Benson. There are more fish in the sea than you. Maybe even better fish."

"I'm sure there are, but—"

"Take that Dee Dee McGurk, for example."

"Dee Dee McGurk?" I laughed out loud.

"Don't be so uppity. You don't know her. You don't know anything about her."

I smiled in spite of myself. "And I suppose you do?"

"I know she's new in town. Could probably use a friend or two. Don't think I won't go after her, Evie. Don't think I can't get on with my life in spite of you."

I didn't answer for a moment.

Dee Dee McGurk.

Doreen Roberts, out to gain another of my beaus. So be it. "Bob, let's not argue. We were . . . friends before this thing happened with us. We should remain friends."

"Yeah, whatever," he said, then hung up on me.

It took me several hours to get up the nerve, but I finally called Vernon to ask him to have dinner with me on Friday night. Sure, I could have said tonight—meaning Thursday evening—but I didn't want to sound too desperate.

"You don't have a date with your fiancé?" he asked.

"No date," I answered. "And no fiancé."

"What does that mean?"

"There is no engagement, Vernon. I can't marry Bob Burnett. Not when I love you like I do. So . . . tomorrow evening? I'll make orange roughy."

Another pause. "With tarragon?"

My heart began to soar. "Yes."

"What time?"

"Six?"

"I'll see you then."

Vernon arrived at ten till six, carrying a small bouquet of flowers and making apologies as he entered the front door. "I'm early, I know."

I gave him my best smile. "That's okay."

He took a moment to eye me. "You look wonderful this evening."

Earlier in the day I'd dipped deeper into my bank account and had gone back to Lindy's store and bought yet another becoming outfit for my dinner date with Vernon. Lindy took a moment to ask about Bob, and I delighted in telling her that I was no longer engaged to him but would be having dinner with Vernon later in the evening. She looked as happy for me as I was for myself.

"Thank you," I now said to Vernon. "You also look nice."

Vernon stared down at himself. He wore dark pants and a long-sleeved shirt with a complementary sweater. "Thank you." He extended the bouquet. "These are for you."

I took them, pursing my lips as I contemplated how lovely they were, even in contrast to the large arrangements I'd received over the past weeks from Bob. "They're perfect," I said. "I'll go put them in water."

Vernon followed me into the kitchen, where I found a vase and filled it.

"The roughy smells delicious," he said.

I dropped the flowers into the vase, leaning my hip against the counter as I did so. Smiling, I said, "Are we going to just compliment each other all night? I look wonderful, you look nice, the flowers are perfect, and the food smells delicious . . ."

Vernon laughed. "I guess so."

I handed him the vase. "Put these on the dining table, will you?" He took the vase from my hands. "Would you like something to drink before we eat?"

"I wouldn't mind some water," he answered. "My throat's a little dry."

"Water it is, then," I answered, then turned to open a cabinet to get a glass.

Vernon reentered the room, and I gave him his water, then watched him drink it. I don't remember ever in my whole life feeling this nervous around him, but I surely was. "So, how's Donna?"

He nodded. "She's good. Better now, I think."

"Better? Was she sick?"

Vernon shook his head. "I can't really talk about it. But . . . she's better." He eyed me for a moment before going on. "Can we go into the living room? I want to talk to you about something."

"Sure," I said and allowed him to escort me there. When we had sat on the sofa, he set the glass of water on the coffee table and then cracked his knuckles a few times before continuing.

"Evie . . . I've been thinking . . ."

"Yes?"

"About a couple of things, actually."

"Yes."

"Pastor Kevin Moore, for one."

"Pastor Kevin Moore?" I studied Vernon's eyes. Something inside them was different, but I didn't know exactly what it was. "What about Pastor Moore?"

"He's a nice guy, isn't he?"

"He's a very nice guy. Why do you ask?"

"I was thinking . . . and just thinking, mind you . . . that maybe . . . maybe I'd like to go back to . . . to church again."

"Are you serious?" I scooted toward him. "Oh, Vernon, that's wonderful."

"Evie, I don't want you to think I lost my religion when Doreen took off like she did. I was just . . ."

"Humiliated?"

"Yeah."

"Embarrassed?"

"Yeah."

"Shamed? Mortified? Disgraced?"

Vernon pinked. "Okay, that's enough, Evie-girl. I think I've got the point you're trying to make."

"Mmm. I remember feeling the same way when we were twelve."

Vernon leaned against the back of the sofa. "Oh no. Not that again."

I scooted even closer to him. "Okay, not that again. You were saying?"

Vernon pushed himself upright. "I'm thinking about going back. Once you stop going, you know, it's just so hard to get going back. But Pastor Kevin . . . well, I saw him for a bit last evening and . . . he's just a very kind man, I think, and I'd like to hear him preach." He paused for effect. "That is, if . . ."

"If?"

"You'll promise to sit with me."

I beamed. "I think I can arrange that."

"And you'll hold my hand," he said, taking mine in his.

I blushed, but only a bit. "I think I can arrange that too."

"And you'll wear this," he said, turning his hand over with mine and revealing a diamond ring slipped onto his pinky.

"Oh, Vernon," I breathed. "It's . . . it's . . . just . . ."

"Wonderful? Nice? Perfect?" he asked with a wink, then slid the ring off his finger and onto mine.

I looked at it for a moment, allowing the light from the table lamp to catch its prisms and send rainbows into my heart. Sighing, I slid my arms around Vernon's broad shoulders and leaned in for a kiss.

It was the kiss of a lifetime.

When we finally broke, I said, "Delicious."

47

I'll Have What He's Having

Clay was sitting in his usual place at the café on Saturday morning when he saw Donna's Bronco bob into the parking lot next door. He pulled his shoulders back a bit, heard the bones in his spine crack, then glanced down at the seat of the chair beside him. The photo album, completed, wrapped, and tied off with a big blue bow, was there—on the chance she'd come in for one of Sally's breakfast specials.

As for Clay, he was having poached eggs and bacon. Hold the toast and no thank you on the muffin. A protein dieter's delight.

He drew his eyes toward the window again, just in time to see her mop of blond curls sticking out of a thick wool cap. She had a matching scarf wrapped around her neck and her regulation black leather jacket.

She was beautiful.

He kept his eyes focused on his half-eaten breakfast, listening for the sound of the door opening, then closing. He shot a look that way. She spotted him and smiled.

"Care if I join you?"

Clay felt as if someone had knocked the breath out of him.

"Be my guest, Deputy."

Donna peeled off her jacket. She was wearing black jeans and a red sweater that fit like a second skin. "Hey, Sal," she called over her shoulder, smiling in a way Clay had not seen her smile in a very long time. "I'll have what he's having." She pointed to him, and he beamed up at her. "And you can put it on his tab too."

"That a girl," Sal called back.

Donna sat across from him.

"Cute," Clay said. "What do you think I'm made of? Money?"

Donna folded her arms on the table, leaned in, and asked, "What do you pay for that rattrap you got across the street?"

"'Bout half your rent. Why?"

"And, let's say you make a pretty decent salary."

Clay leaned over, mimicking her. "Let's say I do."

"Then, to my way of thinking, you're way ahead of me in the money game."

Sal appeared just then, dropping a mug in front of Donna, who now leaned back a bit. Sal poured a hot cup of coffee from about two feet up. Not a single drop missed its mark. "More for you, Clay?" she asked him.

"Thanks," Clay answered and pushed his mug toward her.

Sally refilled it, then walked away without a word.

Donna locked eyes with his and held them for a few moments before he asked, "So, where'd you eat last night?"

She took a sip of her coffee. "I told you. Vonnie's."

Clay noted a fleeting twitch as she said the words. "Oh."

"What, you don't believe me?"

"Thought I might surprise you last night, and I drove out that way," Clay answered, dropping his fork onto his plate. He was no longer hungry.

"Well, you're the one who would have been surprised," she mumbled, but Clay understood each word.

"Oh, yeah? In what way?"

Donna's eyes widened. "You're not going to pull out your notebook?" she asked.

Clay shook his head. "Not this time."

Sally returned to the table with her order. "Thanks, Sal," Donna said, picking up her fork.

"No problem."

Clay waited until Sal had left before he pulled the wrapped photo album from the chair. "This is for you," he said. "You don't have to open it now. You can eat first."

She dropped her fork. "What is it?"

Clay shrugged. "Eat. There's plenty of time for this."

Donna beamed. "No. A present for me? Is it my birthday?"

"Wouldn't you know?"

"I'm teasing you."

"Oh." Clay's chin jerked a bit. Behind Donna's back, beyond the window, Wade Gage's blue truck slid by. *Keep going,* Clay willed it. *Keep on going.* He saw Wade's head whip around, and Clay frowned. He'd spotted them.

"What's wrong?" Donna asked him.

"Gage will be walking in any minute."

He thought he saw both a smile and a wince cross her face simultaneously, but she said nothing. Instead, she tore into the paper, exposing the photo album. "A photo album?"

"Open it," he said, looking at her, then cutting his eyes over at the front door. Wade had yet to walk in. Maybe, Clay hoped, he wouldn't find a parking place.

Donna pulled back the front cover and hunched over his handiwork. "Oh, Clay. Where'd you get these?"

"My mother took most of them. Later ones—the ones in the back—those were taken by me with my Canon and the ones before that with one of those 110 cameras."

Donna looked up. "I remember. You had a blue one with funky green stripes."

Clay paused. "Yeah, I guess it was. How strange you would remember that and I wouldn't."

Donna tilted her head like a little girl in wonder. "How about that?"

Clay cut his eyes over at the front door again. Still no Wade. He jerked when he felt Donna's hand touch his.

"Clay," she said, her voice barely above a whisper. "Stop worrying about whether or not Wade is going to walk in. This is our time, okay?"

Clay visibly relaxed. "Mean it, Deputy?"

She nodded. "I mean it."

"What if he wants to sit with us?" Clay narrowed his eyes at her and playfully cocked a brow.

Donna looked back at the album, flipped another page. "I'll tell him to go away for now," she said.

Clay took another sip of his coffee. For now, she'd said. Not forever, but for now.

For Clay Whitefield, it was good enough.

Lisa Leann

Red Velvet Punch

Ingredients:

2 qt. Cranberry juice
6 oz. orange juice concentrate
2 cups grape juice
2 1/4 cup lemon juice
3 cups pineapple juice
1 qt. ginger ale, chilled

48

Party Platter

It was an absolute answer to prayer to see the Potluckers arriving in my driveway before climbing the stairs to my front door. I hadn't been totally convinced they would come, and had actually worked behind the scenes to enlist some assurance.

Though I made the punch, Lizzie was bringing the mints for the shower, while Goldie was in charge of the nuts. Plus, I had pulled Donna into my confidence concerning one of the shower games.

Each woman climbed my carefully shoveled and salted front steps with their potluck dish, a baby shower gift, and whatever item I had requested, while Mandy sat like a pregnant queen on my pink sofa. "Now, you're on bed rest," I'd scolded her before the guests arrived. "You're not allowed to move a muscle. I'll take care of everything."

And I had.

The house was decked to the nines with my Christmas decorations, including my Christmas trees and my pink velvet stockings on the mantel. My early arrivals, Vonnie and Donna, were already admiring the tree in the living room, which was decorated with doves and pink hearts. "Nice look for a baby shower," I'd explained. "I'll change it later to little drummer boys for Christmas."

I heard a car pull up and ran to hold the door open for Evangeline Benson. "My, don't you look pretty in your new outfit," I said as I took her baby shower gift and placed it beneath the tree with all the others. I pointed to the kitchen. "Just put your little ole casserole in there, with the other dishes," I said, following behind her, hoping to speak to her in private.

I cornered her by the fridge with my back to the door. "Darlin', I'm so sorry to hear of your breakup with Bob. How are you holding up?" I asked.

"Lisa Leann, can you tell me how it is you already know about that?"

"Oh, Bob came by and told me. He'd already put a deposit on my services and wanted a refund. Too bad you're no longer engaged."

Evie held out her diamond-sparkled hand. "You are behind the times, Lisa Leann. I am engaged."

I put my hand to my breast; it was a lovely little diamond. "Bob is a lucky man," I cooed.

"I'm not engaged to Bob, I'm engaged to Vernon."

"What!" screeched a voice from behind me.

I turned to see that the voice belonged to the sheriff's only daughter. Her face was absolutely white with shock, in contrast to her black sweats. I couldn't help but think she needed to go shopping for some new duds. Maybe she'd let me take her.

"Oh my," I said. "Donna, you didn't know?"

Donna shook her head, and Evie said, "I know he called you."

Donna narrowed her eyes. "He didn't leave such news in a message. We were getting together for dinner tonight. I suppose he was going to try to break it to me then." Donna looked none too happy. She crossed her arms and leaned one hip against the doorjamb. "I can't believe this."

Evie took some hesitant steps toward her. "Donna, I'm sorry. But I do love your father." She hung her head. "Look, I know we haven't been close over the years." She extended her hand and said, "What say we bury the hatchet and try to act civilized toward each other?"

341

Donna blinked. "If you can change your actions toward me, Evie, it will go a long way in changing my mind about you."

Evie nodded. "Well, I think that's as good a start as any."

I clapped my hands with glee. "This is a beautiful moment, girls. God is going to do something big here today. I first felt it in my quiet time this morning. Now, if you'd excuse me, I hear the doorbell."

When I opened the door to Lizzie and a tall, beautiful woman with long dark hair, I said, "Well, hello!"

Lizzie, wearing a black velvet pantsuit, smiled. "Lisa Leann, I'd like for you to meet my daughter-in-law, Samantha."

I was thrilled. "This must be Tim's wife. Why, darlin', no one told me what a beauty you are. I bet Lizzie's son is crazy about you."

Lizzie frowned and tried to signal me to silence, but Samantha loved my words as she practically giggled. "Thank you, Mrs. Lambert."

Goldie slipped in as we were talking, just as a winter gust made the snowmen on my foyer Christmas tree do a jig. I shut the door quickly behind her.

"Welcome, Goldie, I'm so glad you could make it."

She looked good. She was still wearing her makeup, just like I had taught her. Good girl.

A few minutes later, after everyone was seated around my beautiful daughter, I made sure they all had a crystal cup full of my red velvet punch. "I'm serving only nuts and mints for now," I explained as I passed out the napkins and crystal plates. "We don't want to ruin our lunch."

Soon, the partygoers were oohing and ahhing over the gifts swathed in pink, yellow, and aqua wrapping paper printed with bunnies and baby rattles.

Some of the presents were charming, like the wee embroidered baby pillow with a smiling sun, from Lizzie. Then there was the sturdy car seat from Vonnie and Donna. Donna had smiled at Mandy. "We knew you'd need this for the airplane trip home."

Once the gifts were unwrapped, it was time for the shower games. I said to the room, "Donna has been taking careful notes of everything Miss Mandy has said while she opened your gifts. Actually, I have it on good authority that these were the same words spoken to her husband the night they conceived the baby. Donna, please tell all."

Donna actually grinned and imitated Mandy's Texas drawl. "'Oh, my!' 'This is great.' 'What fun!'"

Mandy held up her hand, her face as scarlet as her red velvet maternity dress. "That's enough, y'all. You're embarrassing me."

We all laughed and clapped for Donna's performance. That's when I took a hard look at Donna. There was something different about her. Yes, her curls were growing out, but her face looked softer, gentler, and my goodness, she was actually blushing. Must be love, I decided, thinking of Clay.

"All right, everybody," I said. "Before we go into the dining room for lunch, I thought we'd take prayer requests and pray now. Plus, I've prepared a few remarks. Later, we'll go over our ideas for the Christmas Tea."

"That's my department," Evie said.

I nodded. "Right; our department."

I reached for my Bible. "In the last few days, a couple of things have come to my attention. I've actually heard from some of you that our precious Potluck Club could soon become a thing of the past. Now, I know our last meeting ended in disaster. And I know that I played a part in that. So, first off, I want to offer my apologies."

Everyone in the room looked at one another, then back at me.

"I apologize for, well, what my Mandy has made me see is gossip."

I reached for a tissue and patted my eyes, hoping my mascara didn't run like Tammy Faye's. "Y'all, I'm really sorry. And I could understand if you want me to remove myself from the group. So, I'm offering my resignation. I mean, I don't want to leave, but I'd rather go than see this wonderful group fall apart on account of me."

It was sweet Vonnie Westbrook who spoke first. "Lisa Leann, some of the things you said and did hurt me. But I forgive you, and I am inviting you to stay. What do you say, girls?"

One by one, the members of the Potluck Club nodded their heads and smiled. Evie said, "Well, I do believe, Lisa Leann, that you are putting all of us to shame." She looked around the room at the rest of the girls. "And I admit that you are not the only one who has, well, misbehaved. I, for one, also offer my apologies to the group, and especially to a young woman who will soon be my stepdaughter."

"Evie, you're engaged to Sheriff Vesey?" Vonnie practically shouted.

Evie nodded. "Yes, but before we turn to that subject, there's something I want to do." To my amazement, Evie crossed the room and gave a surprised Donna a hug.

Donna accepted it. "I haven't always been kind to you, either, Evie. So, I guess I'm sorry too."

This was just getting better and better. Hurray for me and my party!

After everyone settled back down, I cleared my throat. "Apologies accepted by all, which leads me to a word from Hebrews 10:24–25." I put on my reading glasses and started to read. "'Let us consider how we may spur one another on toward love and good deeds. Let us not give up meeting together, as some are in the habit of doing, but let us encourage one another—and all the more as you see the Day approaching.'"

"Amen," Lizzie said when I closed my Bible. "Great choice for today's meeting."

I smiled. "Let's go right to prayer time," I offered. "My prayer request is . . ." I reached over and gave my daughter a hug. "My Mandy. Pray for her precious baby to come into this world safe and sound, in the right season."

Mandy spoke up. "And for me. I love my mama, but I'm really missing my husband, Ray."

The group nodded their heads in understanding, and several wrote the request down in their prayer notebooks.

Lizzie spoke next. "I want to ask you to pray for Michelle. She's dating a man I've never met—he's new in town—a man named Adam Peterson."

Goldie spoke up. "Oh, I've met his sister, works at the card shop. Nice girl. Seems to be from a nice family."

Lizzie looked relieved, then wrinkled her brow. "That's good to hear . . . You all know how we worry a little extra about Michelle. I've got a request for my daughter-in-love as well," she said as she gave Samantha a squeeze. "It's unspoken."

Samantha interrupted. "You can tell them, Mom." She turned to the group. "I don't think it's a secret here, anyway. Please pray for my marriage. The kids and I have come up from Louisiana to reclaim my husband, Tim. So, please do pray."

"Got it," Vonnie said, writing it down, pushing her gray curls out of her eyes. She looked up, her eyes shining above her turquoise sweater. "And I have a praise report. Fred has accepted the fact that I was secretly married before. He's even had a couple of conversations with my son, David, on the telephone. It's a miracle."

"Wonderful!" Goldie said.

"How about you, Goldie?" I asked.

Goldie looked absolutely sheepish. "Now nobody get excited. But I've agreed to spend a weekend in Summit Ridge with Jack next month." When everyone got excited about the possibilities, Goldie held up her hand and said, "However, we will still have separate bedrooms."

Lizzie turned to her. "Then the other prayer concern I've had?"

"It's much ado about nothing," Goldie said.

I looked at the glances exchanged between the two women. Hmmm, I'm wondering if there was another man in the picture. I decided to keep the idea to myself. "Let me know when you want to book my services to help you renew your wedding vows."

Goldie looked uncomfortable, and I turned to Donna. "How about you?" I asked, wondering if she'd share about her intimate moment with Clay. I'd wanted to say something, to ask, but I looked at my daughter, and she shook her head no. That girl can read my mind.

Donna sounded hesitant. "A lot is going on in my life right now, including a lawsuit."

345

Evie looked stunned. "You're suing someone or someone is suing you?"

"I got hit with a lawsuit for a failed attempt to rescue a baby from a flash flood."

"Oh, Donna," Evie said. "I'm so sorry to hear this. This didn't happen around here, did it?"

"No, in Boulder. Just before I returned to Summit View."

Vonnie spoke up. "Our girl is a hero, if you ask me. She doesn't deserve this. She risked her life to save that baby."

Donna turned to Vonnie. "You knew about this?"

"Clay showed me the story in the Boulder *Camera* when it first happened." She patted Donna on the leg and turned to her. "Why do you think I've been so worried about you?"

"Well, I didn't know about it," Evie said, giving Vonnie a look that said, "Why keep the secret from me?"

Vonnie said, "You know now, and the girl is asking for your prayers."

After all had checked in, we each individually said a prayer for one another. I ended our session with, "Dear Lord, I want to thank you for this group of wonderful women. Thank you for forgiving us when some of us, me especially, did not act in love toward one another. Knit us together and bless our food. Thanks for joining us here today, and of course, you're invited to lunch." Everyone laughed, and I said, "To the kitchen, girls. Grab a plate off the dining table and fill it up."

As everyone began the bustle of serving their plates in the kitchen, the doorbell rang. Donna and I walked to the window and looked out. "Oh my," Donna said. "Vonnie, come quick. Fred is here, and there's someone with him."

"Who, dear?"

"You're just going to have to check this out for yourself."

Vonnie scurried to the door and opened it. "Fred! David! What are you doing here?"

It was David who answered. "I flew in from L.A. to surprise you. Fred here helped me plan it. When you overnighted those letters from my dad, I knew I had to come."

Vonnie hugged her son, then turned to her husband. "You little dickens. And I suppose you want to join us ladies for lunch?"

"Bring 'em on in, there's room for everyone," I said, scurrying to the door. "Why, Vonnie, you never told me how handsome your son is."

That's when David saw Donna. Uh-oh. Looks like she had another stringer on the line. He bounded across the room and wrapped her in his arms in front of God and everybody. Why, I didn't need to gossip about this, not at all, because everyone saw it.

Donna hugged him back. They did make a cute couple, both of them dressed in black. But I had to ask, at least myself, what about Clay?

Just as I was about to close the door, I called Donna back over. "I don't want to alarm you or anything, darlin'. But that Clay fellow, he's sitting in his jeep, watching what's going on over here." Before Donna could react, Vonnie, who had overheard what I said, swooped back to the door and opened it wide. David came and stood by her side to see what the commotion was all about. Vonnie called out, "Clay Whitefield, you get yourself up these steps." She beamed up at David as Fred came to the door and stood beside her.

Clay didn't miss a beat. In an instant, he was bounding up my front steps, dressed in a gray wool parka and what appeared to be new jeans. He looked remarkably thinner than he had a month or so ago. Vonnie stood proudly. "Hello, Clay." She turned to David. "I want to introduce you to my son, David Harris."

Clay reached out and shook David's hand. He looked from David to Vonnie then back to David. "It's a real pleasure to finally get a chance to know who you are."

David slapped him on the back. "Well, come in, Whitefield, the party's just starting."

David was more correct than he knew. Judging from the Potluck prayer requests, Donna's varied love interests and pending lawsuit, not to mention Goldie's troubled marriage and Evie's impending wedding, and . . . well, I could just go on and on. But all that to say, truer words were never spoken.

The Potluck Club Recipes

Easy Meatballs in a Crock-Pot

½ pound hamburger
½ cup rice
½ cup finely chopped onions
½ cup finely chopped green peppers
1 egg
1 teaspoon salt
¼ teaspoon pepper
1 10-ounce can of tomato soup

Knead together all ingredients except tomato soup. Shape hamburger mixture into roughly 20–24 meatballs about 1½ inches around. Place meatballs in Crock-Pot and pour soup and canned tomatoes with juice over them. Cover Crock-Pot and cook meatballs on low for 7–8 hours, or on high for 4 hours.

Serves 6–8.

Donna's Cook's Notes
I can throw this dish together before my shift and come home to a nice hot meal. I freeze my leftovers for meatball sandwiches. I just plop the frozen meatballs and a few spoonfuls of canned spaghetti sauce on my open sandwich, top with cheese, and place the whole spread in the microwave. It's the perfect quick fix to end a night shift.

Grilled Hamburgers

> 1 pound hamburger (go for the Angus beef if you can . . .)
> 1 pound ground sausage
> 1½ cups mushrooms, finely chopped
> ½ cup onions, finely chopped
> ¼ cup barbecue sauce
> ¼ cup ketchup/mustard mixture
> salt and pepper

Mix well, then form into patties. Grill to your preference.

Lizzie's Cook's Notes
I learned the secret of really good hamburgers years ago when Samuel and I lived in a little neighborhood of couples just like us: newly married and just making ends meet. Typically on Saturday evenings, when the weather was warm, we'd have block party cookouts. That's where I learned the secret (double secret—the Angus and the sausage) of the best grilled burgers!

Upside-Down Hamburger Casserole

2½ cups macaroni
½ cup diced onions
3 tablespoons margarine
1 pound ground beef
1 8-ounce can tomato sauce
1 teaspoon salt
dash of pepper
3 ounces of grated cheese (a heaping ¾ cup)
3 eggs (beaten)
¾ cup milk

Cook macaroni and drain, set aside. In sauce pan, sauté onions in margarine then add ground beef. When hamburger is well browned, stir in tomato sauce, salt, and pepper. Simmer for several minutes then spread in greased 2-quart casserole. Next, mix cheese and macaroni together before spreading over top of casserole. Pack firmly.

In separate bowl, mix eggs and milk then pour over dish. Bake at 350 degrees for an hour and a half or until golden brown. Let cool for 15 minutes before serving.

Serves 6–8.

Vonnie's Cook's Notes
Fred loves this simple recipe. It's very filling and goes great with my apple pie. Though, these days we both have to dish up smaller servings, that is, unless we want to head down to Wal-Mart for a new, expanded wardrobe, if you know what I mean.

Chicken and Poppy Seed Casserole

2 small chickens
2 cans cream of chicken soup
1 8-ounce carton sour cream
½ can water
1 stack of Ritz crackers
1 teaspoon poppy seeds
1 stick melted margarine

Boil chicken until tender (about a half hour). Tear the meat from the bones, place in mixing bowl. Add soup, sour cream, and water. Crush crackers and mix with poppy seeds. Spread over chicken mixture. Melt margarine and pour over. Bake 350 degrees for 30–45 minutes. Will look bubbly when done.

Goldie's Cook's Notes
This recipe was one my mother-in-law gave me when I was a young bride and was, as yet, unskilled in the kitchen. The beauty of this dish is that even though it is very easy to prepare, it is absolutely delicious and remains a favorite of my family (and the Potluckers) to this day!

Chocolate Meringue Kisses

> 3 large egg whites (room temperature)
> ¼ tablespoon cream of tartar
> pinch of salt
> 12 tablespoons sugar
> ½ cup cocoa
> 2 tablespoons vanilla
> 1 cup chopped walnuts or Rice Krispies cereal

Stir egg whites with cream of tartar and set. Beat till soft peaks form. Gradually add sugar and salt, sprinkling about 2 tablespoons at a time. Beat till firm peaks form.

Fold in cocoa and vanilla, then nuts or cereal. Drop by teaspoonfuls onto baking sheet lined with brown paper. Bake at 275 degrees, about 45 minutes until set and dried. Store in airtight can.

Yields 35–40 cookies.

Lisa Leann's Cook's Notes
This recipe was handed down by my grandmother. However, the Rice Krispies is my contribution to this wonderful recipe. This is a great one to serve for the holidays, or even at a wedding reception. In fact, I made them for Mandy's wedding, just two years ago. It's hard to believe she's about to make me a grandmother.

Mama's German Chocolate Cake

    1 4-ounce package Baker's German's Sweet Chocolate
    ½ cup water
    2 cups plain flour
    1 teaspoon baking soda
    ¼ teaspoon salt
    1 cup butter, softened
    2 cups sugar
    4 egg yolks
    1 teaspoon vanilla
    1 cup buttermilk
    4 egg whites

With a double boiler, melt the water and chocolate. Mix flour, baking soda, and salt. Set mixture aside.

Beat butter and sugar in large bowl on medium speed until light and fluffy. Add egg yolks, one at a time, beating well. Stir in chocolate mixture and vanilla. Add flour mixture alternately with buttermilk, beating after each addition until smooth.

In another large bowl, beat egg whites until stiff peaks form and then gently stir them into batter. At this point, you can make 3 regular-size layers or you can pour smaller amounts into 4 pans for a taller cake.

Now for the frosting . . .

FROSTING
    1 can (12 ounce) evaporated milk
    1½ cups sugar
    ¾ cup margarine
    4 slightly beaten egg yolks
    1½ teaspoons vanilla
    1 package coconut (14 ounces)
    1½ cups pecans

Mix everything except coconut and pecans in a large saucepan and cook over medium heat until thick and golden brown. Add coconut and pecans and cool to room temperature and spreading consistency. I always make my layers thin and double the icing (yum-yum). Be sure to stick toothpicks in to secure the layers, because if you don't, they'll slide to one side. (You don't want to know how I found this to be true . . .)

Evangeline's Cook's Notes
My mother made the best German chocolate cake. When I was in college I wrote her a letter asking for the recipe. . . . I missed her and her cake and actually thought if I did a little baking, I wouldn't be quite so homesick. It's the one thing over the years I've cooked (or baked) without complaining about being in the kitchen. I can still remember Mama's words, written in the return letter, which went like this:

> My dearest daughter,
> This recipe that I've used for years is fairly common, but I've made a few variations.
> I love you!
> Mama

Reuben Sandwiches

⅛ cup mayo
¼ tablespoon chili sauce
4 pieces of rye bread (if you want to make two sandwiches)
⅛ pound of sliced Swiss cheese
⅛ pound of sliced cooked corned beef
¼ can (about 4 ounces) sauerkraut, drained (freeze the rest
    in a plastic bag for later)

Mix mayo and chili sauce, then spread onto four slices of bread. Then, layer Swiss cheese, corned beef, and sauerkraut on two slices of the bread. Top layers with the two remaining slices. Heat for 1 to 2 minutes in microwave to melt cheese.

Makes two sandwiches.

Donna's Cook's Notes
I may not be much of a cook, but nevertheless my specialty is probably gourmet sandwiches. It's probably because the Higher Grounds Café closes at 9:00 p.m., and often my shift doesn't end till 3:00 or later. The only place open for a very late supper is the brown paper bag that I keep in the front seat of my cab. So, I have the Gold Rush Deli slice the Swiss cheese and corned beef for me, and the result is one of my favorite midnight meals. I prefer the sandwich warm, but it's also good cold with a thermos of hot coffee.

Apple's Restaurant Eggplant Parmesan

>
> 1 small eggplant
> 1 large egg (beaten)
> ¼ cup all-purpose flour
> 2 tablespoons cooking oil
> ⅓ cup grated Parmesan cheese
> 1 cup spaghetti sauce
> 1 cup shredded mozzarella cheese

Peel eggplant and cut into ½-inch slices (going crosswise). Dip eggplant into egg, then into flour, making sure to cover both sides well. Pour cooking oil in a large skillet and let it get nice and hot, then cook half of the eggplant in the skillet at a time for about 5 minutes (maybe a little less, it just depends) until golden. If necessary, flip the eggplant. Let drain on paper towels.

Place eggplant slices, single layer, in a 12-by-7½-by-2-inch baking dish. Sprinkle with Parmesan cheese, top with sauce and mozzarella. Bake at 400 for 10–12 minutes or till hot.

Evangeline's Cook's Notes
Seeing as I have known David and Mica Apple since they were children (and obviously before they were married), I have managed to snag their recipe for serving to the Potluck Club. Their closely guarded secret, they told me, is that they use "off the shelf" spaghetti sauce, such as Ragu, Prego, etc. Now, that's my kind of cooking . . .

Stuffed Peppers

2 large green peppers
¼ teaspoon salt (for sprinkling)
¾ pound ground beef
⅓ cup chopped onion
1 7½-ounce can of cut-up tomatoes (undrained)
⅓ cup long grain rice (uncooked)
1 tablespoon Worcestershire sauce
½ teaspoon dried oregano, crushed
½ cup water
¼ teaspoon salt
¼ teaspoon pepper
½ cup shredded American cheese

Cut peppers in half, removing stem ends, seeds, and membranes. Put peppers in boiling water for three minutes, remove, and then sprinkle insides with salt. Place upside down on paper towels to drain.

In a skillet, cook meat and onion until browned and tender. Drain fat, stir in tomatoes, rice, Worcestershire, oregano, water, salt, and pepper. Bring to boil, reduce heat. Cover and simmer for 15–18 minutes or until rice is tender. Stir in ¼ cup of cheese. Fill peppers with meat mixture. Place in baking dish with any remaining meat mixture.

Bake at 375 for fifteen minutes. Remove and sprinkle with remaining cheese. Let stand for 2 minutes before serving.

Goldie's Cook's Notes
My mother-in-law was a great cook, and with a houseful of boys, it was imperative that she be able to cook food that was both filling and quick to prepare. Stuffed peppers was one of the first recipes she handed down to me. It remains a favorite in our family . . . busted as it is.

Chocolate-Topped Prayer Bars

FIRST LAYER
½ cup butter
4 tablespoons cocoa
1 slightly beaten egg
2 teaspoons vanilla
½ cup powdered sugar
½ cup coconut
½ cup chopped nuts
2 cups crushed graham crackers

SECOND LAYER
¼ cup butter or margarine
1 teaspoon vanilla
2 tablespoons cream
2 teaspoons dry vanilla pudding mix
2 cups sifted powdered sugar
1 large milk chocolate bar

First layer: melt shortening over low heat in large saucepan. Stir in cocoa. When blended, add vanilla and beaten egg. Mix well. Add powdered sugar, coconut, chopped nuts, and crushed graham crackers. Crush mixture into 9-by-13 pan.

Second layer: in saucepan, melt butter. With heat on medium, add vanilla, cream, and pudding mix. Cook for one minute. Add powdered sugar and stir. Spread over bottom layer. Melt chocolate bar over hot water (double boiler) or low heat and spread on top.

Vonnie's Cook's Notes
My mother used to make these for Fred because he was her prayers-come-true for me. I've always served these when prayer was the only answer to a difficult problem.

Breakfast Enchiladas

> 2 cups shredded cheddar cheese
> ¼ pound chopped ham
> ⅓ cup sliced green onions
> ⅓ cup chopped red bell pepper
> 8 corn tortillas
> 4 eggs
> 1½ cups milk
> ¼ cup salsa
> 1 tablespoon flour
> sliced ripe olives

In a small bowl, combine cheese, ham, onions, and bell pepper. Place cheese mixture into open tortillas. Next, roll tortillas closed and place seam side down in greased 11-by-7 baking dish. In medium bowl, beat together eggs, milk, salsa, and flour. Pour mixture over tortillas and refrigerate overnight.

The next morning, cover with foil and bake at 350 degrees for 45 minutes or until firm. Remove foil and sprinkle with cheese and olives.

Serves 8.

Donna's Cook's Notes
Who knew David Harris could cook. This is one of my favorite souvenirs from our trip to California.

Chinese-Style Beef, Broccoli, and Rice

> 1¼ pounds boneless top sirloin steak, trimmed of fat
> ½ teaspoon ground ginger
> 1 teaspoon sugar
> 3 tablespoons soy sauce
> 2 teaspoons cornstarch
> 1 tablespoon vegetable oil
> 1 cup water
> ¾ cup quick-cooking long-grain rice
> 1 pound fresh or frozen broccoli cut in 1-inch pieces

Cut steak diagonally into thin slices. In a medium bowl mix together next four ingredients. Add meat strips and toss to mix well. Let stand 5 to 10 minutes. Then, in a 10-inch skillet, heat oil over high heat until hot. Add meat mixture. Cook, stirring over high heat, until meat loses its redness (5 minutes). Remove to a plate.

Add last three ingredients to skillet and heat to boiling. Reduce heat to medium-low, cover, and simmer five minutes or until broccoli is tender. Return meat to skillet and heat to boiling, stirring often. Simmer, stirring for one minute.

Lizzie's Cook's Notes
This takes a little time in the preparation, but it's well worth it!

Honey Orange Pork Chops

⅓ teaspoon shredded orange peel
½ cup orange juice
½ cup pineapple juice
1 tablespoon soy sauce
1½ tablespoons honey
⅛ teaspoon pepper
2 cloves of garlic, minced
4 pork chops (approximately 1½ pounds)
1 tablespoon cornstarch

Cut away fat from chops. In a shallow baking dish, combine shredded peel, orange juice, pineapple juice, soy sauce, honey, pepper, and garlic. Pour over both sides of meat.

Place meat on the unheated rack of a broiler pan, 4 to 5 inches from the heat. Broil 6 to 7 minutes on each side, until meat is no longer pink in the middle.

Pour remaining sauce and pork chop drippings into saucepan. Stir in cornstarch, then cook and stir till thick and bubbly. Cook another 2 minutes, then rebaste chops with sauce.

Serves 4.

Lisa Leann's Cook's Notes
Not all great dishes have to be complicated, and this dish is a case in point. I always make it when the kids come home. Usually I like to marinate the chops for 6 to 24 hours, but if I'm in a hurry, I'll skip that step but spoon the drippings onto the meat when I turn it over.

Taco Soup

2 pounds hamburger meat
1 small onion, chopped
1 4-ounce can green chilies
1 package taco mix
1 package ranch dressing mix
1 can pinto beans
1 can kidney beans
1 can hominy
3 cans tomatoes
1½ cups water

Brown hamburger with onion. Drain grease. Add remaining ingredients. Simmer for 30 minutes.

Serves 6–8.

Donna's Cook's Notes
This is my kind of soup—brown a little hamburger and onion, then open a few cans and dump the whole mess into a pot. When I have to work the night shift, I pour this steaming hot into my jumbo thermos. It's great for cold nights on a lonely beat.

Asparagus Casserole

1 can cut asparagus (drained)
1 small can English peas (drained)
1 small can evaporated milk
1 cup grated cheese
½ can cream of chicken soup
3 boiled eggs (chopped)
crushed potato chips

Mix all ingredients together. Top with enough crushed potato chips to cover. Bake at 350 for half an hour. Serves 4.

Evangeline's Cook's Notes
Not everyone is an asparagus fan, but if you are, this is a recipe you won't want to throw away!

Lazy Beef Stew

2 medium onions
4 celery sticks, chopped
5 white potatoes, peeled and diced
6 carrots, peeled and diced
1 green bell pepper, chopped
2½ pounds beef round steak cut into 1½ -inch cubes
1 envelope mushroom gravy mix
½ cup dry white wine
1 6-ounce can tomato paste
½ teaspoon salt
½ teaspoon pepper
1 16-ounce package frozen French-style green beans,
     thawed

Begin by turning the setting of your Crock-Pot to "high." Throw in all ingredients except green beans. Cover, reduce heat to low, and cook 7 to 8 hours or until meat and veggies are tender. In the last half hour of cooking time, add green beans.

Goldie's Cook's Notes
Lazy beef stew is a recipe I clipped out of a newspaper just after I married Jack, back in the days before he began running around on me. It was a favorite of ours when the weather turned cold and the days grew short. I remember when Olivia was a little thing; as soon as a little chill fell into the air, she'd ask for it. The best thing about it is that it takes only 20 minutes to prepare and then cooks all day.

Low-fat Carrot Cake

1 cup firmly packed brown
    sugar
¾ cup egg substitute
¾ cup nonfat buttermilk
1 8-ounce can crushed
    pineapple, drained
2 cups grated carrots
½ cup raisins

3 tablespoons vegetable oil
2 teaspoons vanilla
1½ cups all-purpose flour
½ cup white flour
2 teaspoons baking soda
2 teaspoons ground
    cinnamon
¼ teaspoon salt

Combine brown sugar, egg substitute, buttermilk, pineapple, carrots, raisins, vegetable oil, and vanilla in large bowl. Next, combine flours and baking soda, cinnamon, and salt. Pour batter into 9-by-13 pan coated with vegetable cooking spray. Bake at 350 degrees for 30 minutes or until done. (Test with toothpick.) Cool in pan. Once cool, spread with frosting. Cover and chill.

ORANGE CREAM CHEESE FROSTING
½ cup low-fat cottage cheese
1 8-ounce package reduced-fat cream cheese, softened
1 teaspoon vanilla
1 teaspoon grated orange rind
1 cup sifted powdered sugar

Process cottage cheese in blender till smooth. Add cream cheese, vanilla, and orange rind and blend. Next add powdered sugar and blend till smooth.

Vonnie's Cook's Notes
With my Fred's cholesterol on the rise, I've been looking for ways to make old favorites a little more diet friendly. Besides, carrot cake is a comfort food, and right now, I can think of several people who need to be comforted, starting with a big slice for me.

Smothered Pork Chops

> cooking oil
> 6 thick pork chops
> 16-ounce can stewed tomatoes with basil
> 1 large onion, sliced
> 1 green pepper, sliced
> 2 tablespoons margarine
> 1 can mushrooms
> 1–2 garlic cloves, minced
> 1 cup cooking sherry

Coat bottom of frying pan with oil. Brown chops on both sides. Remove from pan. Melt butter and sauté onion, pepper, and garlic for five minutes. Add tomatoes, mushrooms, and sherry. Place pork chops on top and simmer for forty minutes. Spoon vegetables over chops and serve over rice.

Lizzie's Cook's Notes
It doesn't get any easier than this.

Fruitcake Cookies

    1½ cups sugar
    1 cup butter, softened
    3 well-beaten eggs
    1 teaspoon soda dissolved in ⅓ cup hot water
    1 teaspoon cinnamon
    ½ teaspoon nutmeg
    1 large box raisins
    1 pound pecans, chopped
    1 cup coconut
    3 cups flour
    1 teaspoon ground cloves
    ½ teaspoon salt
    1 box diced dates
    1–2 slices candied pineapple chunks
    ½ cup candied cherries, chopped

Cream sugar and butter, then add the beaten eggs and dissolved soda. In separate, large bowl, add dry ingredients, a few at a time, and mix well. Batter will be stiff. Drop dough by spoonfuls onto a nonstick cookie sheet. Bake at 350 degrees for 8–10 minutes or until golden brown. Cool on wire rack.

Lisa Leann's Cook's Notes
When it's beginning to look a lot like Christmas, at least around the Lambert household, it's time to decorate my Christmas trees and start my Christmas baking. These fruitcake cookies top my list for Christmas cookie fun. Some folks might add a splash of bourbon, but as I'm a good Baptist, I don't.

Gingerbread

  1 cup soft butter
  1 cup sugar
  2 well-beaten eggs
  2¼ cups flour
  1 teaspoon cloves
  1 teaspoon cinnamon
  2 teaspoons ginger
  1 cup dark cane molasses
  1 cup boiling water
  1 teaspoon soda

Cream butter and sugar. Add eggs. Sift flour and spices together. Add to butter mixture. Alternate with molasses. Dissolve soda in boiling water and add to mixture (which will be thin). Pour into greased 9-by-13 or Bundt pan. Bake at 375 for 20 minutes or until done. Cool. Dust with powdered sugar or whipped cream and cherries.

Evangeline's Cook's Notes
Mama used to make this at Christmastime. There's not a year gone by since her death that I have not baked it, filling the house with warmth and love, floating on the scent of ginger.

Sour Cream Coffee Cake

> 2 sticks butter
> 2 cups sugar
> 2 eggs
> ½ teaspoon vanilla
> 1 cup sour cream
> 2 cups sifted cake flour
> ¼ teaspoon salt
> 1 teaspoon baking powder
>
> TOPPING
> powdered sugar
> ¾ cup chopped nuts
> 2 tablespoons brown sugar
> 1 teaspoon cinnamon

Cream together butter, sugar, and eggs. Fold in sour cream and vanilla carefully. Add sifted dry ingredients. Spoon ½ batter into greased and floured 10-inch angel food cake pan. Cover with half the topping. (To make topping, mix the nuts, brown sugar, and cinnamon.) Then repeat both. Bake at 350 for 55–60 minutes. Cool. Sprinkle top of cake with powdered sugar. Top cake with the rest of the topping. Bake another 30–35 minutes.

Goldie's Cook's Notes
One of my favorite things to bake for a party or just to nibble on at home is sour cream coffee cake. The scent of cinnamon and vanilla wafting through the house just cries out "home, sweet home."

One-Pot Spaghetti

1 pound ground beef
1 tablespoon instant minced onion
8-ounce can tomato sauce
15-ounce can or jar spaghetti sauce (with mushrooms)
1½ teaspoons salt
1 teaspoon sugar
2 cups water
7-ounce package spaghetti
3 tablespoons grated Parmesan cheese (optional)

Brown ground beef in Dutch oven over medium high heat until brown. Remove fat. Stir in minced onion, tomato sauce, and spaghetti sauce. Add salt, sugar, water, and spaghetti (uncooked). Heat to boiling over medium high heat, stirring occasionally to prevent sticking. Cover and simmer over low heat about 15 minutes or until the spaghetti is tender. Remove from heat and stir. Sprinkle with grated Parmesan cheese before serving.

Serves 6.

Donna's Cook's Notes
Vonnie has made this dish for me since I was a little girl. I often stayed over with Vonnie and Fred when my daddy had the evening shift. Sometimes I would stand on a chair and help Vonnie stir in the ingredients. It always brings back warm and happy memories.

Orange Roughy with Tarragon

    1 pound orange roughy fillets
    ¼ teaspoon salt
    1½ to 2 tablespoons butter, melted
    ½ teaspoon snipped tarragon or ⅛ teaspoon dried tarragon
        leaves
    paprika

Place orange roughy fillets on greased rack in boiler pan; sprinkle with salt. Drizzle with butter; sprinkle with tarragon. Set oven to broil. Broil with tops about 4 inches from heat until fish flakes very easily with fork and is opaque in center, 5–6 minutes. Sprinkle with paprika. Serves 4.

Evangeline's Cook's Notes
Everyone in Summit View knows I hate to cook. Okay, that may be a bit of an exaggeration, so let me rephrase that. Everyone in the Potluck Club knows I hate to cook. So, for me, the simpler the better. That's why, if I have to cook, I go for quick and simple. Like this recipe.

Red Velvet Punch

2 quarts cranberry juice
6 ounces orange juice concentrate
2 cups grape juice
2¾ cups lemon juice
3 cups pineapple juice
1 quart ginger ale, chilled

Mix together. Makes 12 cups of punch.

Lisa Leann's Cook's Notes
This quick and easy punch serves me well at weddings, baby showers, and even church potlucks. I make it several times a year. Come to think of it, I made it for Mandy's wedding as well.

Acknowledgments

The authors send a special, love-filled *thank-you* to our wonderful editors, Jeanette Thomason and Kristin Kornoelje. Without your help and encouragement and especially your wisdom and prayers, we would not have been able to pull this off!

Thank you! Thank you! And thank you to our exceptional recipe artists: Connie Salmen, Barb McCauley, Betty Purvis, and Gayle Scheff. Write on, ladies!

Also a special thanks to the women of AWSA (Advanced Writers and Speakers Association). We've appreciated your love and prayers as we wrote our second Potluck book. You ladies rock, and it's a privilege to be a part of your lives.

Linda writes: A special thanks to my family, Paul, Jimmy, and Laura, for your patience, love, and support. I am so blessed by having you all in my life.

Another shout-out to the women in ministry who subscribe to the Right to the Heart of Women electronic magazine. You've not only become readers, you've become friends. I so appreciate the work you do in your church and communities.

And again, a big thanks to my dear friend Eva. We've laughed, cried, and prayed our way through this manuscript. You are a true friend.

Eva writes: Thank you to my husband, who releases me into the cold tundra of Colorado every year for the writing escapades Linda and I manage to get ourselves into. Thank you to my dear family and friends (especially my Bible study group!) who have prayed me through some tough times this year. You da best!

And, of course, thank you to my coauthor and friend, Linda "E.S." There were days (and nights) I could not have gotten through this year without your love, encouragement, prayers, and snoring. (Okay, heavy breathing . . .)

About the Authors

Linda Evans Shepherd has turned the "pits" of her life into stepping stones following a violent car crash that left her then-infant daughter in a yearlong coma and permanently disabled (see LindaAndLaura. com).

Linda is the president of Right to the Heart Ministries and is also an international speaker (see ShepPro.com), radio host of the nationally syndicated Right to the Heart radio, occasional television host of Daystar's Denver Celebration, the founder and leader of Advanced Writers and Speakers Association (see AWSAWomen. com), and the publisher of Right to the Heart of Women ezine (see RightToTheHeartOfWomen.com), which goes to more than ten thousand women leaders of the church.

She's been married twenty-six years to Paul and has two teenagers, Laura and Jimmy.

Linda has written more than eighteen books, including *Intimate Moments with God* (coauthored with Eva Marie Everson), *Tangled Heart: A Mystery Devotional*, *Grief Relief*, and *Right to the Heart of Prayer*.

Award-winning author and speaker **Eva Marie Everson** is a Southern girl who's not that crazy about being in the kitchen unless she's being called to eat some of her mama's or daddy's cooking. She is married to a wonderful man, Dennis, and is a mother and grandmother to the most precious children in the world.

Eva's writing career and ministry began in 1999 when a friend asked her what she'd want to do for the Lord, if she could do anything. "Write and speak," she said. And so it began.

Since that time, she has written, co-written, contributed to, and edited and compiled a number of works, including *Sex, Lies, and the Media* and *Sex, Lies, and High School* (co-written with her daughter, Jessica). She is a Right to the Heart board member and a member of a number of other organizations, and is a mentor with Christian Writers Guild.

A graduate of Andersonville Theological Seminary, she speaks nationally, drawing others to the heart of God. In 2002, she was one of six journalists chosen to visit Israel. She was forever changed.

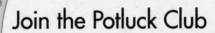

Join the Potluck Club

To read more about the authors or to find additional recipes, visit www.PotLuckClub.com

A Sneak Peek

at the Next Adventure of the Potluck Club

Some days you'd just as soon wish away. Turn back the hands of time. Jump into bed, pull the covers over your head, and pretend they never happened. Such was this day.

It's not that I haven't had bad days before. The good Lord knows I've had some pretty bad ones. You can't be married to an unfaithful man for nearly thirty years and come away unscathed.

But this one . . . this one was the worst of all. This one was such a slap in the face; I thought I'd never recover. What had started out as a cold and crisp December morning touched with a hint of promise, followed by an evening of dining and laughter with one of my best girlfriends, had turned into a night filled with despair.

Despair and anger. Fury.

Remorse.

Oh, why did I ever say I'd go away for a weekend with my estranged husband, Lord? What in the world was I thinking?

"Charlene Hopefield is out of your life," Lizzie had said.

But she wasn't. Isn't. Not by a long shot.

Lizzie hadn't been gone five minutes when my doorbell rang. I'd already stepped into the small bath adjoining my bedroom and begun to scrub my face when I heard the gentle chime. Grabbing a hand towel, I patted my face dry as I moved toward the front of the condo, calling out, "I'm coming."

When I got to the front door, I switched on the porch light and peeked out the peephole. The hair on the back of my neck stood straight on end. It was Charlene Hopefield. *No store to walk out of or street to cross,* I thought as I drew back.

"What do you want?" I called through the closed door. I peeked through the hole again.

She wrapped her arms around herself as though she were freezing to death. "Goldie, I need to talk to you. Please. It's very important."

I stared at her for a long moment. What in the world did that woman think she had to say that would be of any interest to me?

"My name—as far as you're concerned—is Mrs. Dippel."

I watched her roll her eyes. Even in the dim overhead porch light, her disdain for me was evident. "Whatever. I need to speak with you. It's important. I'm being nice here. Nice enough to come to you instead of going over to Jack's and talking to him."

I flipped the lock and jerked the door open. "You stay away from my husband," I said.

She just stared at me. "May I come in or not?"

I stepped aside. "May as well." I looked down at her snow-covered boots. "But wipe your feet; I don't need your slushy mess on my carpet."

Charlene pounded her feet on the front mat for a few moments, then looked back up at me. "Will that do?" she asked, arching an eyebrow.

Cocky little thing.

"I guess."

She stepped over my threshold, pulling her long dark wool coat from her somewhat pudgy body. She held it toward me, as though she actually expected me to take it, then threw it across the chair behind her. "Is that coffee I smell?" she asked. "Decaf? Because I can't have regular."

"It's stale," I answered, crossing my arms over my middle. "What do you want, Charlene?"

She turned toward the sofa and extended her arm a bit. "May I?" she asked.

I arched my brow. "May you what?"

"Sit? I'm exhausted," she said, sitting in spite of the fact I hadn't invited her to do so. "Not to mention I've been waiting across the street for your friend to leave. My gosh, what do you people have to talk about so long? My back end was going numb from sitting in my car that whole time." She paused. "Please sit, Goldie."

I coughed out a snicker. "I beg your pardon? I'll decide when or if I sit down. This is *my* home."

She nodded, looking around. "So it is. It's . . . nice. Certainly not the home you left, but it's . . . nice."

On that note, I sat in the nearest chair, one I'd picked up cheap at a thrift store down on Dyer Street. "You know nothing about my home."

She slid herself back on the sofa like a plump goddess, crossing one leg over the other. "Oh, Goldie, Goldie, Goldie." She laughed, sounding more like a cat than a woman. "Silly, silly Goldie."

I flushed red with a mixture of anger and embarrassment. If Jack had brought that woman into my home, he could take her and Summit Ridge and all the years we had between us and choke on them as far as I was concerned.

"I hear you're going away for the weekend," she purred. When the question she clearly expected from me flashed in color on my face, she answered without my saying a word. "Oh, you know. One person tells one person, and that person tells another. Eventually, it got to me. Summit Ridge, I understand?" I raised my chin before she went on. "Quaint. Not anywhere I'd want to be—least not with Jack—but for the two of you . . . well, I suppose it could be . . . quaint. Anyway," she said, stretching and draping her arms around her knees, "that's not why I'm here. I'm here because we have a bit of a problem."

"I can't imagine what," I said. "You are no longer a part of my husband's life and therefore no longer a part of mine." My heart began to pound as though it knew that life as I'd known it not ten minutes earlier was about to change forever.